BRON, THE GIRL WITH THE GOLDEN ANKLE

The Story of Bron
Part III

Iris Lloyd

Pen Press

First published in Great Britain by Pen Press
an Imprint of Indepenpress Publishing Ltd
25 Eastern Place
Brighton
BN2 1GJ

ISBN13: 978-1-906710-35-4

Printed and bound in the UK

A catalogue record of this book is available from
the British Library

Cover design by Jacqueline Abromeit
Photograph by Sarah Cook

Acknowledgements

My thanks to…

Brother-in-law, Jim, for putting me right on some of the sailing matters;

Howard Davies of Classis Britannica for emails full of useful information about naval affairs in Britain at the end of the Roman occupation;

Doug Watts, again;

The reader (name unknown) of the Romantic Novelists' Association who bullied me into tightening up the writing;

Cynthia Pocock and other friends and family for their encouragement.

Dedication

To my daughters, Julie and Meryl, who are somewhat bemused at seeing their mother in print and question where some of my knowledge comes from!

CONTENTS

The Story So Far…

Parts I and II are set on an archaeological site I help excavate at Beedon, north of Newbury, on top of the Berkshire downs; I have worked some of the discovered artefacts into the story.

Midsummer day AD 385 – as the sun rises over the pagan settlement of Byden, Bron is born, a member of the Atrebate tribe. The witch in the wood, Umbella, has warned her parents that this birth will unleash "sword, fire and total destruction" on the village.

    The event coincides with the sacrifice of a baby girl on the orders of Vortin, High Priest, in an attempt to persuade their sun god, Ashuba, to provide a consort for his son and heir. Vortin claims Bron as his daughter and decrees she must enter Temple life at the age of three, for nine years of training in preparation for this high priestly role.

    During that time, Vortin becomes obsessed by her. He burns down the family home and her father's pottery business to impoverish her parents so that they will be unable to buy her back at the age of twelve years. However, they succeed in doing so by presenting the Temple with an amber and pearl necklace of great value, saved from the fire.

    On the day Bron is due to leave, Vortin kidnaps her and hides her in a cellar beneath his house. He rapes her moments before she becomes an adult at twelve years of age, so breaking Temple law. She is rescued by her father and Pulcher, a dwarf who loves her.

    When it is discovered that Bron is pregnant, her mother takes her to Umbella for an abortion, which is unsuccessful. Vortin finds out, and to hide his duplicity, decrees she is to marry – anyone – until the baby is three years old, when mother and son will enter Temple life, she as his High Priestess.

    Her childhood friend, Soranus, is chosen by the family to be the bridegroom. Vortin sends wedding gifts, among them a gold torque for the baby, and returns the necklace.

Unexpectedly, the Roman ex-governor of Eboracum attends the marriage ceremony, and it is obvious to everyone that he is Bron's natural father. One-time slave master of Bron's mother, it is he who gave her the necklace on learning of her pregnancy.

Bron and Vortin's son is born but later, during a period of depression, she smothers him to save them both from the excesses of Temple life and to avoid splitting up her growing family. The baby's death appears natural. She is now free of Vortin, but he continues to stalk her.

Bron's husband, Soranus, fathers two children, Layla and Alon. However, she then falls in love with Aurelius Catus, a junior Roman army officer, and is not sure whether Soranus or he is the father of her next son, Darius.

Circumstances take her to the walled city of Calleva Atrebatum, from where she brings home a brothel baby, whom she names Gift.

Disillusioned by the evil authority of the Temple, the people of Byden finally take matters into their own hands, and after a trial, banish Vortin and his followers. They reject their sun god and begin to explore the new religion, Christianity, brought to them by a pilgrim, Asher.

However, Vortin returns with a rabble to sack and set fire to the village in an effort to abduct Bron. The villagers put up a valiant fight but are defeated and Asher is killed.

Thus, Umbella's prophecy of "sword, fire and total destruction" has been fulfilled.

Aurelius Catus is about to leave for the coast, his legion having been recalled to Rome, and in the midst of the battle, suggests taking Bron with him to safety. With sorrow, Soranus releases her from her marriage vows so that she is free to escape with their four children. Her widowed brother asks her to take his baby daughter, Lucilla, as well.

Veneta, Bron's friend and mentor, was once a priestess at the Temple but has embraced Christianity. She agrees to go with Bron, having been told that her own husband has died in the fighting. Only the reader knows that her husband is still alive, having sent false news of his death so that she would not refuse to escape to safety.

When one of Vortin's rabble intercepts the party of women and children hiding in the wood, Bron gives him the amber and pearl necklace as a bribe to let them escape. As arranged, they meet up with Aurelius Catus and flee the settlement, hidden in a carrier's cart.

Pulcher, the dwarf, is left mourning the departure of Bron. He vows that Byden will be rebuilt so that, when she returns as she has promised, there will be a home waiting for her.

Now read on...

SECTION I

AD 406

LEAVING BRITANNIA

Pollus harbour

CHAPTER 1

As Bron and Aurelius walked through the iron gates of Pollus harbour, her self-control, fragile at best, collapsed at the sight of the troop ship *Eagle* berthed further along the quay. Seagulls circled and squealed above its tall mast, their bodies silhouetted grey and white against the blue September sky.

"Aurelius," she whispered, her head bent low and her long hair muffling the words to all but him, "I can't bear it that you're leaving me…"

She knew, even as she spoke, that officers of the Imperial Roman army, junior or otherwise, allowed nothing to impede their duty, and certainly not love.

"Sweetheart, you'll come through, you always do."

He entwined his fingers through her girdle and pulled her towards him, his other arm encircling her with his cloak. Smiling, he gently nuzzled the lobe of her ear, sending shock waves of pleasure throughout her body.

"It won't be for long." He was trying to comfort her, as well as himself, she knew.

"We may never see each other again."

He tightened his grip. "Not the emperor nor the whole Roman empire will keep me from you forever, I swear it!"

The coarse repartee and blasphemies of the dockers around them jangled discordantly with his tender words of love.

Then hooves clattering on stone finally broke the spell, as civilians, dockworkers, military and naval personnel scattered from the path of a turma of cavalry. Aurelius drew her into the safety of a warehouse doorway.

The riders were led by a young decurion, and behind him, a signifer carried their spear-shaft standard.

Bron shaded her eyes against the rays of the sun reflected like arrows off the silver discs climbing the standard, and noticed that the commotion had brought a man to the rail of a small ship tied up opposite. He leaned over, above the name written in plain black lettering on the prow, *Juniper,* and she caught his gaze briefly before he shifted his eyes to watch the spectacle.

At a barked word of command, thirty-two men reined in their horses, in perfect formation, and at the next command, dismounted. Another command, and each began to unbuckle leather straps and remove harness and saddle. Their mounts were led away as the cavalrymen, their arms full, awkwardly climbed the gangplank of the *Eagle*, embarking in readiness for departure on the next day's tide.

"Which will be our ship, Aurelius?"

The young man removed his arm from around her.

"This one – the *Juniper* – if the captain will take you. I'm going on board now to ask him."

The vessel moved lazily on the slack water, squashing the basket-weave fenders between her planks and the quayside. Aurelius, about to cross to her, was impeded by the unsteady progress of a big man in a brown tunic that looked slept in, who was singing loudly and tunelessly as he tacked from side to side along the quay, sometimes teetering dangerously near the water's edge. Scavenging cats and dogs and the slippery surface outside the fish market added to his hazards. Bron wondered how it was possible to get so drunk so early in the day.

The man bowed unsteadily when he saw Aurelius, paying mock respect to the uniform. Then he staggered towards the *Juniper*, hauled himself up the gangplank, saluted the man at the rail with a sardonic flourish, and swayed past, presumably seeking his hammock. Bron hoped that this sailor wasn't an example of the rest of the crew.

Aurelius squeezed her hand in encouragement and she followed him across to the ship. The hobnail studs beneath his leather boots clattered noisily up the gangplank as he mounted, two ridges at a time, Bron following more carefully behind. The man left the rail and met them at the top. He looked older than her father and his bearing betrayed his authority.

"Captain Stokovius?"

The man nodded. "Theon Stokovius."

"Officer Aurelius Catus."

"State your business, sir."

"To arrange passage to Ostia. You sail at the end of the week, I believe."

"That's so. For how many?"

"A party of seven – two women, five children."

The captain raised his eyebrows. "The *Juniper* is an imperial naval ship, sir, not a nursery," he replied tartly.

Aurelius ignored the remark. "I'll pay their passage plus a sum to be agreed, for you personally, upon their safe arrival in Ostia. I sail with my Legion, the Third Victrix, on the *Eagle* tomorrow."

Stokovius seemed tempted to accept but looked at Aurelius in his expensive fringed cloak over immaculate scale armour and was honest enough to shake his head.

"She's an old ship. It's the broker's yard for her when we reach Ostia. Hardly fit for women and children – at least, not yours. There'll be families coming aboard, I've no doubt, but not officers' women."

"Who else is boarding?"

"Bound to be a few stragglers who miss sailing with you, convalescents from the military hospitals, veterans, camp followers –"

"How long to landfall?"

"Given good winds and no mishaps, I should think six months."

"And your first port of call?"

"Vectis – just across the water – but overnight only, no longer."

"I wish to get my – my family away as soon as possible. Will you take them or not?"

The captain hesitated again and fingered his thick beard. Like his hair, it was a mixture of grey and black.

Bron recognised that he resented the sharp interrogation. They had covered their tracks as best they could since fleeing Byden, but neither Aurelius nor she could guess how close Vortin was behind them. What they both knew, however, was that the High Priest's obsession for her would drive him to hunt her down till the day he died.

Eventually, the captain nodded. "For the right consideration, yes. Like my ship, I'm heading for retirement once we reach Ostia and, like you, I have a family to support."

Aurelius breathed a sigh of relief and urged, "Then let us agree a price."

While money was changing hands, Bron became conscious of the gentle movement of the ship and the slapping of waves against the dockside. A breeze cooled her cheek and she took a deep breath that was laced with dead fish and seaweed.

"*So,*" she thought, with some misgiving, "*this is to be our home for the next six months.*"

Her only consolation was that Aurelius would be waiting for her when she reached Ostia. From then on, their plans were vague. He refused to allow her to follow the legion, to become part of the entourage of camp followers. This left her with two choices: either to wait for him to complete his duties and return to Ostia, where Vortin might be searching for her, or travel on and eventually meet him in Rome.

Aurelius was looking squarely at the older man.

"Captain Stokovius," he said, "these are not camp followers. They are respectable women with their children, and I want them treated as such by you and your crew. Is that understood?"

"We're sailors, not barbarians," the captain growled. "They'll come to no harm, you have my word on it."

"Thank you. As promised, there'll be the amount we agreed waiting for you in Ostia when you deliver them safely. Ask at the port authority office."

The captain nodded and walked away, leaving Bron and Aurelius to descend the gangplank as noisily as they had come up it.

CHAPTER 2

It was the first time that Stokovius had visited Pollus, the largest natural harbour in the world. For both him and the *Juniper*, it would be their only visit, as this was their last tour of duty – the culmination of nearly thirty years' service for him, for his ship much longer.

Many seafarers were superstitious about last voyages and on this trip they would be sailing under the influence of two – ship and captain. He hoped fervently that there wouldn't be any trouble during the passage. Perhaps a visit to Noden's shrine in the prow would be a wise precaution.

Leaning over the rail, he shouted obscenities at a driver who had toppled a sack of flour while unloading it from his cart. The sack had split, spreading its dusty contents across the quay and into the water. Then he turned his attention to the steady stream of bare-chested porters, dirty tunics tied round their waists, as they struggled up the gangplank with packing cases, bundles and crates.

He was distracted again when he became aware of officer Catus and his young woman. Other legionaries taking leave of weeping women and children were standing on the quay in full view, but these two had screened themselves behind piles of crates containing the previous night's catch of fish.

She had her arms round him, her face buried against his chest. He was stroking her hair and talking to her, then tried to disengage himself, but obviously thought better of it and began kissing her with an almost brutal ferocity.

Fascinated, Stokovius watched. He guessed that the girl must be in her early twenties. Her dark blue tunic revealed a slim waist and buttocks round and taut beneath the young man's squeezing fingers. The captain was not too old to feel a pang of envy.

He was startled by an unexpected clatter behind him and turned to find a short-bladed knife lying on the deck a few feet away. Glancing up, he saw the bo'sun, sober this morning, looking down at him from high in the rigging.

"You could have killed me!" he shouted angrily.

"Sorry, Cap'n," boomed the man and came scrambling down the ratlines, hand over hand. He landed heavily on the deck and retrieved his knife.

"Be more careful in future!" growled Stokovius.

"Sorry," apologised the bo'sun again, "but I lost concentration." He jerked his head in the direction of the young couple. "Touching, ain't it?"

"Get back to your work!"

"Yes, Cap'n!"

The bo'sun began clambering upwards again and Stokovius turned back to the rail. He wasn't sure why he felt so irritated. The man had only been doing what he himself had been doing – watching. But watching by his bo'sun seemed more like voyeurism.

By now, the officer had taken the girl's arms away from his neck and was holding her hands firmly down by the sides of her thighs. Still talking to her, he released his hold and retrieved his helmet with its horse hair crest from the box on which he had placed it. Her head was bent low now as he turned away. She made no movement.

Stokovius waited. He knew that, if he were in the young soldier's place, he would return for one last kiss, and sure enough, Catus paused in his tracks, turned and came back. Placing his helmet under his arm and taking the girl's face in his hands, he looked at her intently for a few seconds, kissed her soundly on the lips, then strode away towards the *Eagle*.

She stood quite still until he had disappeared across its deck, then turned to leave but slipped on a nondescript patch of fish guts and fell heavily, reaching out to the crates for support. The captain could see that they were in danger of toppling over and burying her beneath their fishy contents.

Without thought, he descended the gangplank and crossed to where she was struggling to her feet.

"Don't be frightened," he reassured her gruffly. "I saw you go down, and this is no place to be kneeling on cold stone. You're welcome to recover on the *Juniper*."

Her lovely green and dark brown eyes flashed gratitude at him and he continued to speak soothingly to her as he effortlessly picked her up in his arms, carried her across to his ship and began to climb the gangplank.

"I've got a daughter your age. She's at home in Illyricum with my wife."

Mention of home started him wondering how much longer Avala would welcome him into her bed. It was eight years since he had seen her. She must have stopped bleeding by now and may have lost interest. He had heard other men talk about their women losing interest. His own passions had dulled a little, he knew, but had not dissipated.

The young woman in his arms moved and brought his mind back to the present. He could not imagine what had turned his thoughts towards Avala and bed at that moment. Gently he set her down on a pile of coiled ropes.

"I'll fetch you a drink."

He returned with a beaker of water and watched while she drank.

Females on board ship always created a problem one way or another. He had promised the officer that he would look after these women and children, but with this one, he might have his work cut out. Hopefully, she was as much in love with the young Roman as he appeared to be with her, and would keep herself to herself, at least when it came to the crew.

"What's your name? What may I call you?"

"Bron."

"Just Bron?"

"We've no need of two names where I come from," she explained.

"And where's that?"

"A village – north of here."

Stokovius looked at her again. She could converse with him in

Latin passably enough, and her features and skin colouring appeared Roman, but judging by her accent, she was British. He decided that he had asked enough questions, and there would be plenty of time to learn more during their long voyage.

"Do you want to see the *Eagle* sail? If you go astern, you won't be in our way, and no one will disturb you."

"I'd like that."

He helped her up, made sure she was steady on her feet, then left her.

For two hours she stood there, watching the *Eagle's* crew preparing to sail. Taking pity on her, Stokovius brought her some wine mixed with honey.

"The oculus on the *Eagle* is staring straight at me," she told him.

He looked across at the troop ship's large red and blue eye painted above the jutting ram in its bronze sheath.

"You've no cause to be afraid. Every oculus is there to search out and menace the enemy, the only eye on board that never sleeps, the most faithful member of the crew. The men take good heart from that."

It was strange how her plight unsettled him, taking into account all the farewells, his own and others', he had endured over the years.

He stood with her then while the *Eagle's* securing ropes were cast off the bollards and thirty or so men on shore with stout poles pushed the prow away from the quayside. Aided by the flow of the outgoing tide, the ship swung round to face the harbour entrance. Only crew were busy and there was no sign of Bron's officer.

They heard the rowing master begin beating out a rhythm below decks. Suddenly, both banks of oars on each side of the ship sprang to life, hesitated, then dipped forward as if gripped by one pair of hands, slipping into the green depths of the harbour waters.

They watched the ship glide away from the quay, responding to the thrust of the oars – enter, sweep, out, recover, enter, sweep, out, recover. Smoothly and swiftly, it negotiated the gap between the curved stone moles of the harbour and was embraced by the inland waters, setting a course towards the Channel. A square sail was already billowing in the light breeze when the ship passed the heads.

Stokovius left Bron to watch its further progress until ship and sail disappeared over the horizon.

When she was ready to leave, he insisted that a member of his crew should walk behind her to the inn where she was staying.

Once again he leaned on the rail of the *Juniper*, his eyes following her slow progress as she skirted the bustle of the dockside and passed through the iron gates, and contemplated with guilty pleasure her presence on board during his last voyage.

Section II

THE VOYAGE

CHAPTER 3

"All ashore that's going ashore!"

Just for an instant, Bron was overcome with such anxiety about the unknown journey ahead that she wanted to gather up her children and run with them back down the gangplank, back to all that was familiar, taking her chances on Vortin not finding her. After all, Pollus was a long way from home. Then she thought of Aurelius – even thinking about him made breathing difficult – who would be waiting for her in Ostia, her young Roman who had vowed constancy for the rest of his life, and her resolve to follow him returned.

She watched as the gangplank was raised and stowed on board, and knew her last opportunity to jump ship was lost.

"Single up the lines! Let go fore and aft!"

The ropes securing the ship to the dock were slipped and the men on the quay bent over their poles to push the prow of the *Juniper* away from the dockside. Slowly the ship began to move.

Alon was bending down at his mother's side to peer between the wooden stanchions supporting the *Juniper's* rail.

"We're moving, Veneta!" he yelled when she appeared from their cabin aft, little Lucilla toddling at her heels.

She smiled and ruffled his hair, cut short in preparation for the long voyage.

"Are the babies sleeping?" asked Bron.

Veneta nodded. "I was tempted to stretch out beside them. The cabin is more comfortable than I expected."

Bron said she thought it was the captain's. "They've rigged up a canvas contraption for him in the prow."

Layla said she felt sick.

"You can't, not yet," groaned Bron.

"Yes, I can!" she insisted.

"No you can't, Layla!" argued her brother.

A young sailor standing nearby smiled at them as he picked up a rope and offered Layla the end of it.

"Here, little lady, hold on to this and pull when I tell you."

Obediently, Layla caught hold.

"Ready?" She nodded. "Right then – one, two, three, pull!"

Layla pulled with all her strength, and went quite red in the face. Bron could not see to which cleat the rope was fastened, but it was obvious that her daughter thought she was helping to pull the ship out to sea.

"Don't leave go till your mother tells you," the sailor warned her.

"I won't," panted Layla.

He grinned at Bron and Veneta, pushing back several strands of dark hair that were falling over his eyes; they were radiating mischief above his unshaven cheeks and chin.

"Can I help, too?" Alon pleaded. He was gazing with fascination at three silver rings climbing up the young man's right ear, a fourth through his nose.

"Would you check the oars are working properly? Don't get in the way, though – and don't lean out too far and fall in!"

"I won't!" promised the boy as he ran to the rail on the other side of the ship.

"That's going to be a constant worry," Bron told the young man.

"If they do go overboard, there are plenty of us to go in after 'em," the sailor assured her, "and by the time we reach wherever it is you're disembarking –"

"Ostia."

"– they'll both be excellent swimmers, you'll see."

As he left her and crossed the deck, Bron looked at his muscular shoulders and arms and decided she could relax a little, at least about the children falling overboard.

It was not long before the ship slipped through the harbour entrance and was out into coastal waters.

Now, from far below their feet, they felt as well as heard the echoing *boom! boom!* of the rowing master's mallet pounding against a wooden block, setting the rhythm and therefore the speed at which the oarsmen were rowing.

"You can stop pulling, now," Bron told Layla. "Come and say goodbye to dear Britannia. We may not see her again for a long time."

"I miss Daddy," Layla said, waving to the receding coastline.

"We all miss Daddy," Bron admitted. "We'll see him again as soon as we can." She turned to her friend. "I just hope that what I'm doing is for the best."

"That old devil Vortin will hunt you down if you stay," Veneta reminded her.

Bron sighed. "We'll never be able to come home again, will we?"

"Yes we will, once we receive word that he's dead."

"But who's to send word? No one will know where we are."

"Soranus will come looking for you and the children."

"I'm not sure that he will, not after the way I've treated him, and not now he's freed me from my marriage vows. Anyway, if he does, what will happen to Aurelius and me?"

Veneta had no answer to give her.

The loop of rope round Veneta's wrist began to tug. The other end was tied to Lucilla, Bron's niece, and the toddler, bored with inactivity, was trying to escape.

"I'll take her for a walk round the deck," Veneta decided. "Perhaps we'll be able to talk to some of the other passengers."

They had watched them coming on board – smart young soldiers and marines; older men in uniforms that had seen better days; women and children. The male passengers had disappeared down a companionway amidships and those on stretchers had been lowered by ropes through a hatchway into the same hold. The women and children had been directed forward.

Bron was thoughtful. "We're going to be at sea a long time, and there are a lot of children on board. Veneta, how about starting a school?"

"School?"

"Don't pretend the thought hadn't already crossed your mind."

"Well, maybe," Veneta conceded. "It would certainly keep them occupied. Now, Lucilla and I will take that walk."

Bron and Layla watched as the crew hoisted sail under the direction of the bo'sun. Soon, the large square of strong, brown linen was flapping in the wind with its triangular topsail above.

The ship, in spite of its age, was skimming over the water, keeping up with the herring gulls that called and circled ahead of it. Sparkling eyes in the green waves flashed golden glints back at the sun, and Bron noticed an occasional white bonnet on the peaks.

"Offshore wind, medium to strong," said a gruff voice, and Captain Stokovius stood at her elbow. "If we could keep up this speed, we'd be in Ostia in no time at all. Everything all right for you?"

"Very comfortable," Bron enthused, "and we are so grateful to you for giving up your cabin – you have, haven't you?"

The captain waved aside her thanks.

"You can repay me by praying for a speedy and safe passage. There's a small shrine to Noden for'ard."

"Yes, I know, I saw it the day the *Eagle* sailed."

"The old lady hasn't let me down in all of fifteen years, but this is our last voyage together. It doesn't worry me, but some of the crew are nervous about last voyages."

"You'll miss her after all that time."

"No doubt, but I've had enough sailing, and my woman will be glad to get me home for good – at least, I hope she will!" He laughed. "I might even marry her, though we're probably grandparents by now, and there seems little point."

"How many children, Captain?"

"One for each home leave – five – plus the one I left inside her when I ran away to sea – too young to face the responsibility, I'm ashamed to say. Then there's the girl she conceived when she got fed up waiting for me to return. Can't blame her." His smile bore no resentment. "But I must get back to the job I'm paid to do. Just wanted to make sure you were all right."

"Oh, by the way, Captain, we won't need Noden's shrine. We're sort of Christians."

"What's a Christian?" asked Layla when he had left them.

"It's when you believe there's only one god, and his name is Jesus Christ. Veneta can tell you more about it than I can. She used to be a priestess in the Temple at home, but then she became a Christian and married Selvid – about the time you were born."

"Was he killed in the fighting, before we escaped?"

"Yes, he was, and that's why Veneta has come with us, but don't say anything to her, because it makes her unhappy."

"Am I a Christian?"

"You've been baptised, but you were also admitted into the Temple, so you're free to choose, I suppose."

"I'm hungry. When are we going to get some food? Where's the kitchen?"

Bron laughed and kissed the top of Layla's head.

"It's called a galley on board ship, and it's next to our cabin. Let's go and find the cook and ask him."

CHAPTER 4

"That sheep and vegetable stew was delicious," enthused Bron as she descended the steep companionway to return the dirty dishes to the galley, accidentally banging her head on a pan dangling from an iron hook. A terracotta stove was still giving out heat after bread making and the cook wiped the sweat from his forehead with a greasy cloth as he beamed his pleasure.

As fat as he was, she wondered how he found room to move around among the high stacks of cooking pots, storage jars and pitchers.

"Don't expect it every time," he warned. "It will be cold meals if the weather gets rough – can't risk a fire on board," and he pointed to the hearth, where a large copper cauldron was suspended above embers dying in the tiled firebox.

"You're going to be busy, with all these people to feed," Bron sympathised.

"One hundred and thirty," he told her, without concern, turning to the used bowls wobbling in piles, awaiting washing up.

When she arrived back on deck, Veneta told her that the captain had been to ask whether they had eaten well.

"We'll be docking again, during the afternoon," Veneta added, pointing towards the silhouette of an island on the horizon, "at Vectis."

Several hours later, the *Juniper* sailed into Brading Haven, a large inlet, and was berthed at a sheltered quayside. The harbour was of modest size, but busy, with several small ships and many fishing boats tied up to the jetties.

At once, loading and unloading began. Some of the passengers disembarked and wandered off towards the village, clearly visible along a roadway to the north. The downs above the harbour reminded Bron of Byden and homesickness became a lump that constricted the back of her throat.

She noticed the captain leaving the ship and climbing into a farm cart that was waiting for him, which trundled off in the direction of the village.

Alon was complaining that the flat pebbles and shells borrowed from Lucilla were making his game of 'five stones' too easy.

"They don't roll about like sheep's knucklebones," he said. "and I'm *bored.*"

"Why don't we go and find the twin boys we saw coming on board?" Veneta suggested. "You come along, too, Layla", and hand-in-hand the three of them went forward towards the women's quarters.

After they had disappeared down the companionway, Bron checked on the three babies asleep in the cabin, then returned to the deck and leant over the starboard gunwale. She could still see the farm cart in which the captain was being conveyed and watched as the horse turned left, entered a wood and was lost to sight.

"All right for some," remarked a voice at her side, and turning, she saw the young sailor.

"Who?" she asked.

"The old man," he replied. "He's off to Brading Villa. Got friends there."

"Is he allowed to abandon his ship?" asked Bron.

The sailor found that very funny and chuckled. "We're not abandoned. He's left us in charge of the bo'sun. He'll be back before the turn of the forenoon tide tomorrow. Can't blame him, sleeping ashore instead of cramped up on board."

"Because we have his cabin," remarked Bron, guiltily.

"I can't say it about many cap'ns I served under, but he's a good 'un – looks after his crew. He don't punish unless there's good reason, and we seldom lose a man at sea."

"How long have you served with him?" asked Bron.

"Eight years," he told her. "By the way, my name's Declan."

"And mine's Bron."

"Yes, I know, bo'sun found out – and your friend is Veneta. Not much the crew misses!"

She laughed. "So it seems."

"It's going to be hard work looking after the children for weeks on end – you don't know how hard," he told her. "Call me if you think I can help – when I'm off duty, of course. I got young brothers and sisters and know how to keep 'em occupied, some of the time, at least."

"Thanks, we will."

He smiled and left her.

It was not long before Veneta returned, chatting easily to a grey-haired, motherly woman enveloped in voluminous folds of tunic with a none-too-clean undershift drooping below it. They had watched her coming aboard, panting up the gangplank, stopping to draw breath, then stumbling heavily on to the deck. Her sons, identical twins, probably a year or so older than Bron's children, were now lagging behind with them, deep in conversation.

Veneta introduced the woman as Sythia and the boys as Tiegan and Joas.

"I'm the oldest," boasted Tiegan.

"Only by eight minutes," retorted Joas.

Joas was shorter than his brother, with a slightly heavier bone structure, his brown eyes were set further apart, and his black hair was thicker and a shade darker.

"Sythia's legionary also sailed on the *Eagle*," Veneta explained.

"So you and the boys are following him to Italia?" asked Bron.

The woman winked at her. "That's right, m'dear, but 'e don't know it yet. 'E thought 'e'd got away and 'is face'll be a picture when we show up!" She chuckled at the thought. "I sold everything to raise the passage money. The boys need their father, y'see."

"Do you know where he'll be stationed?"

"No, but I'll find 'im," Sythia replied resolutely. "Then, if 'e won't desert, I'll wash the army's smalls till I've raised enough money to buy 'im out!"

Bron had no doubt that she would.

Declan arrived with lengths of canvas and rigged up two

hammocks for the babies, slung between various deadeyes, and later Darius, Gift and Lucilla spent a contented couple of hours rocked from side to side by the lazy movement of the ship. When the two older children and the twins asked if they, too, could have hammocks, Declan promised he would do something about that during their long days at sea.

The time came for their evening meal and Sythia said she would take her boys back to the women's quarters. She looked enviously at the cabin that Bron and Veneta and the children occupied.

"It's so small downstairs," Layla told her mother.

"It *is* very cramped, m'dears," confirmed Sythia, and when no offer to make room for the three of them was forthcoming, added brightly, "Still, we won't be spending time there. We'll be up on deck as much as possible."

Their evening meal enjoyed and the children in bed, Bron and Veneta decided to spend the evening on deck. A group of men passengers who had not gone ashore were talking together at the prow, watching the red sun as it dropped towards the western horizon, promising a spectacular sunset. Many of the women had gathered round the mast, laughing and gossiping and introducing themselves to each other.

Their chatter paused abruptly at the sudden appearance of a boy at the top of the gangplank. He was followed by a young man. They were obviously brothers – neither very tall, of stocky build, and both with high, pale foreheads topped with hair the colour of dark, wild marigolds.

The women stared, one or two of the younger ones giggling, which so embarrassed the elder brother that he blushed bright red.

"Are any of you Bron?" he asked.

"Over here," called Bron, mystified.

He stepped past his younger brother and came towards her.

"We're from Brading Villa," he explained. "I'm Briard and this is my kid brother, Koch."

Bron shook the hand held out to her and smiled across at the boy hovering at the top of the gangplank.

"The captain's staying with us for the night. He said he had a Roman officer's family on board and my mother wondered whether you would be more comfortable sleeping at the villa. Koch and I have been sent to fetch you."

There was a surprised murmur from the women, and Bron looked at Veneta. Her friend was probably thinking the same – that this further favouritism would not endear them to the other women on board. It was going to be an unpleasant voyage if the women wouldn't speak to them. She decided to refuse politely.

"It's very kind of your mother, but my children are already in bed, asleep, and I can't leave them."

Koch stepped on to the deck. "Briard, while we're here, can I have a look round?"

"Not now."

The younger boy turned to Bron enthusiastically. "I want to join the Imperial Navy," he explained, "though Father says there isn't much of it left."

"He's right," interjected Briard. "Anyway, you're too young."

"I'm sixteen!" Koch retorted.

Veneta turned to Bron. "Why don't you go? I can cope and you'll be back before the children know you've gone."

"You go, m'dear," Sythia encouraged her. "I would, if I had the chance." She turned to Briard with a wide smile. "Don't suppose you'd take me instead?"

The young man blushed again and began stammering an apology.

"No, I thought not," she said and laughed at his discomfiture. "Only joking, boy. You go, Bron," she repeated.

Finally, Bron nodded. "I'll be ready in a few minutes," she said.

Still giggling, one of the girls said there was time to show the brothers the women's sleeping quarters. Briard looked round frantically, as if seeking a way of escape.

"Take no notice of them, m'dear," soothed Sythia.

The two lads moved away while Bron went to her cabin to gather together all she needed for the night ashore.

On returning to the open deck, she was surprised to be greeted by an earful of obscenities. Veneta came across and indicated the tall figure of the bo'sun at the foot of the mast. He was craning his neck to look upwards, his right hand resting on a belaying pin that was hanging from his belt.

Following his line of gaze, Bron saw Koch swaying in the canvas bucket in the crow's nest. Startled by the bo'sun's invective, he was reaching over, fumbling for the nearest handhold, then began descending the rigging.

Watching him, Bron was reminded of a large spider slithering across its web, he was so sure footed. She looked across to the bo'sun and was alarmed to notice his hand tightening its grip on the wooden pin. Briard was regarding his brother with great apprehension as he neared the deck, and the women had stopped their barracking and were silent.

Quickly, Bron moved across and placed herself and her woollen bundle between man and boy as Koch leapt to the deck, unaware of the possible descent of the heavy belaying pin across his shoulders.

"Thank you, bo'sun." She smiled at him brightly. "If it hadn't been for you, we might never have got him down."

The bo'sun hesitated and looked at her keenly as if he were trying to make up his mind whether she was making fun of him or not. Her smile was dazzling. He took his hand off the pin and picked up her bundle and gave it to her.

"Thank you. We're going ashore now."

Together, Bron and the two lads descended the gangplank. At the bottom, she turned and waved to Veneta and Sythia. Several of the women were draped over the rail, calling out ribald suggestions, amid much laughter, about how the three of them could while away the night hours. The bo'sun had disappeared.

As he helped Bron into the enclosed carriage that was waiting for them, Briard glared at his brother and apologised for his wayward behaviour.

"That bo'sun's a bully as well as a drunk," Bron said.

CHAPTER 5

Iron tyres on wooden wheels along the rough road made for an uncomfortable ride. Sitting on a bench between them, Bron was thrown first against one brother then the other, until she was embarrassed to apologise yet again and lapsed into silence. They were faring no better, each being caught between her and the low, wooden side of the carriage.

About twenty minutes later, they turned left and entered the wood, where the track, if it could be called that, was even more rutted. Bron hoped the villa wasn't too far away. The driver drew back the dark curtain that hung between himself and his passengers, presumably to give them more light.

She guessed that it had been peaceful among the trees until their arrival, but now, even if birds were singing, they could not be heard above the rattle and squeak of the carriage. A wild boar that was rummaging for acorns among the roots of a great oak looked up in alarm, then scurried off into the undergrowth, in its turn disturbing a fallow deer, which they saw bounding away through the trees.

When they emerged from the wood, the villa lay before them, the sunset-stained road leading straight to the main gates set in a high brick wall.

As the carriage approached, the large wooden gates were pulled wide open by invisible servants. They drove through into a courtyard, grassed in the centre. The horses followed the gravel path as it turned left then right, past a huge granary and other farm buildings, and right again, stopping before the front door of a large, two-storey, timber-framed house. A red-tiled roof rose above white-painted wattle and daub.

Briard untied the canvas at the back of the carriage and clambered out, then helped Bron down. Koch leapt out and landed beside her.

The front door swung open noiselessly, again by means of invisible hands, and Briard led the way into the entrance hall.

"My parents and the captain are waiting for you in the triclinium," he told her. "This way."

He led her across a mosaic of a god playing a lyre, surrounded by birds and animals, and crossed to a door facing them. Passing through another room, they entered the triclinium. She had time to gain an impression of walls painted with scenes of the countryside around the villa, before three people stood to greet her.

In the background hovered the captain, drink in hand, smiling and nodding. Coming towards her, hands outstretched, was a tall, elegant woman dressed in rich brown with a golden girdle slung loosely over her slim hips. Her fair hair was piled high in a sophisticated, intricate style.

"Good evening," her hostess said, a welcome in her blue eyes. "I'm Regina and this is my husband, Reginus Marcellus."

Bron smiled and shook hands with wife and husband. He was a broad-shouldered, tanned man with calloused fingers and hair the same colour as his sons.

"You've come alone?" Captain Stokovius asked, sounding surprised.

"The children were settled for the night, so Veneta offered to stay with them."

"Then you can relax," smiled Regina. "Come and sit down and eat."

She led Bron across another fine mosaic to a couch covered with a throw-over that matched the colours of floor and walls. Koch was despatched to the kitchen behind the house to ask for the prepared refreshments and more wine.

Comfortably reclining around the three-sided table, the guests were invited to select delicacies from expensive Samian pottery and black Vectis ware, a product of the island. Although she had eaten earlier, Bron had no hesitation in tackling goats' cheese, hard-boiled eggs, salads and imported olives, stoned and stuffed with anchovies, but looked apprehensively at the unfamiliar oysters, cockles and mussels. However, she found they appealed to her palate.

The servants filled and refilled their black beakers with white wine from the villa's own grapes, and the face of Reginus Marcellus lit up with pleasure when the captain, who had drunk copiously, grasped his beaker firmly, raised it high and congratulated their host on the fine vintage.

"It *is* difficult to achieve, in this climate," Reginus Marcellus nodded.

After the meal, Koch disappeared to his own room, and Briard left the triclinium with his father and the captain, discussing farming matters as they went.

Regina, obviously an experienced hostess, chatted to Bron with ease. During the conversation, she mentioned that the villa was often used for public business.

"Most legal matters are conducted here, as we have the largest room on the island," she explained. "It also contains my husband's library. He's a local councillor and very proud of his library – probably the best on the whole of the south coast. I'll show you."

She led Bron back to the entrance corridor, turned left and so into a large, rectangular room on the north side of the villa. Around the walls were tiers of shelves crammed with scrolls, kept in place by wooden bars. The scrolls were rolled and tied with red ribbon, some with wax seals dangling from them.

But it was the mosaics that claimed Bron's attention. They were standing on a square panel divided into sections by a twisted rope design, the smaller panels picturing mythical sea creatures, the four winds, a nymph and shepherd, vines, cereals and a plough.

"We never forget that our lives and livelihood depend on the land, the sea and the weather," Regina explained.

At the far end of the room stood a large armchair, used by the judges. Bron settled herself against its wooden back and laughed when her feet couldn't reach the floor. She stroked the worn gold silk padding and Regina sighed.

"I regret that it's much in use."

"Why's that?" asked Bron.

"The pirate raids along the south coast are increasing," Regina explained. "We're having to strengthen all the defences on the island – not that we have any here at the villa. It's a situation of great concern to my husband, and everyone else."

"But who are these pirates?" Bron wondered.

"If we knew that, we'd be well on the way to catching them. Any lawless pagan who can steal a ship can attract a band of men around him by promising rich pickings from our villas and farms. From reports we receive, some come from as far away as the Ibericum Mare."

"From where?"

"It's the sea in the centre of the empire, which is the same as saying the centre of the world. They wouldn't be attacking if Emperor Honorius wasn't recalling his legions back to Rome and leaving us quite defenceless."

At this point her husband came to find her.

"My dear, the captain has to be away early in the morning, and Briard and I also need an early start."

"Of course. Have you seen Koch?"

Reginus Marcellus shook his head. "Not since we finished our meal."

"Then he's probably in bed already. I'll not disturb him."

Bron followed her hostess to a small, comfortable bedroom at the back of the villa, and they wished each other good night.

However, she wasn't feeling tired and wandered out into the courtyard at the front. The sky was clear and bright and there was little need for the burning torches secured in brackets high above her head.

On reaching a semi-circular structure set into the wall, she discovered an ornamental pond dedicated to a water nymph. Several small, lit pottery oil lamps were hidden among the bulrushes and waterweeds or floated on the large lily pads. The effect was magical.

Sitting on the low wall that encircled it, she watched the goldfish as they flashed red, gold and black liveries round and under the delicate pink water lilies, in and out of the lamplight.

Footsteps approaching along the gravel path caused her to look up. She was surprised when Captain Stokovius emerged from the darkness.

"Bron," he greeted her. "I didn't startle you, did I?"

She shook her head.

"I'm just not used to sleeping in a bed that stays still," he joked.

They both laughed and he sat down, facing her across the pool. Bron asked how he had come to know Reginus Marcellus and learned it was through a chance meeting on the quayside many years ago.

"Our host and hostess are British," he told her, "but greatly influenced by Roman culture. That comes of living on this marine highway. Where's your village, Bron?"

"Byden, just south of the Ridgeway. I'm of the Atrebate tribe."

She described briefly her settlement and the lives of its inhabitants, then lapsed into silence. She felt too upset and guilty to confess that she had unwittingly caused the battle that had destroyed her village and killed so many of the people she had just been talking about. She might even have caused the death of her young husband, Soranus, who had stayed behind to fight. They hoped that, by fleeing to Italia, she would escape from Vortin but secretly she feared he would not be outwitted so easily and was still hot on her heels.

"Would you like to walk a little?" the captain finally asked, breaking into her thoughts, and she nodded. They crossed to the lawn, where the grass was cool around her sandaled feet.

"I was also born in a small settlement. Have you heard of Illyricum?"

Bron shook her head.

"It's a small country to the east of the Adriaticum Mare. My homeland is so beautiful that, when I think about it, it breaks my heart not to be there," Stokovius confided.

"But you will be there soon, after we reach Ostia," Bron said, looking across at him, then added sadly, with head bent, "but I don't know when we shall return to Byden – if we ever do."

She was aware that he was studying her face, and when she looked up, saw in his eyes an expression she could not quite fathom. She reminded herself that he was old enough to be her father.

"I have my woman and my family waiting for me," he said hurriedly, "and you have a handsome young husband impatient for you in Ostia."

Bron's face brightened at the thought of Aurelius.

"Yes, it's all going to be wonderful," she enthused, "but Captain, you are mistaken. Aurelius is not my husband."

"From what I have seen, he is so, though perhaps not in ceremony," the captain commented, and Bron did not enlighten him further. "But now it's time to return to our beds. I must be away before dawn, and you not long afterwards."

They walked to the front door, which was opened silently before they could knock, and went their separate ways.

Tomorrow, thought Bron, as she dozed off to sleep, *our long voyage begins, and who knows what awaits us?*

CHAPTER 6

When Bron entered the triclinium for breakfast, she discovered that the captain had already returned to the *Juniper* and had left a message that he would see her on board.

"My husband has sent some of our oysters to the ship, collected early this morning," Regina told her, "and a few of our Italian chickens."

"Oysters?" queried Bron, wrinkling her nose.

Regina laughed. "They'll keep fresh for a long time if they're not opened and are continually doused with sea water. The cook will know that," she assured her guest. "And the chickens will not only give you plenty of eggs, and fresh meat when they stop laying, but their entrails will warn of any dangers."

"But they're not sacred chickens," Bron objected.

"That's easily arranged," commented Regina mischievously. "If the captain says a few words of mumbo-jumbo over them, they'll provide predictions, though he said there isn't a gut-gazer on board."

"I hope there won't be any bad news to predict."

"I'm sure you'll all arrive in Ostia safe and sound," Regina comforted her. "You couldn't sail with a better man than Captain Stokovius."

"I believe you," Bron nodded.

After breakfast, Regina sent for the carriage.

"My husband and Briard were sorry to miss you," she said as Bron kissed her on both cheeks, "but they had to be out harvesting. I'm not sure where Koch is. I haven't seen him since last night. He should be helping, but is probably roaming the downs somewhere, checking his traps."

When Bron arrived back at the ship, all was bustle and preparation for their departure and it was not long before they were in the Channel again, sailing westward, with the coastline of Vectis receding behind them.

Joining a huddle of noisy children and women amidships, they found a small roped-off area where the captain had placed the wire coop containing the six chickens and rooster from Brading Villa. Bron looked down at the silver-bodied hens with their soft pink breasts and was surprised to see that they had five toes on each foot, instead of the usual four like chickens at home. Perhaps, after all, they were special.

One of the hens was squatting and squawking noisily, and when she walked away, she left a large, white-shelled egg behind her. Immediately, a well-built woman with lifeless yellow hair artificially curled, unlatched the wire door and scooped up the egg. The other women began to complain in angry voices that it didn't belong to her and should be taken to the cook or shared among the children.

"Don't be ridiculous!" The woman with the egg was scornful. "How can one egg be shared among all your brats?" At once a tussle broke out between several of them, and it was not long before the egg had fallen to the deck and smashed.

"Now no one gets the egg," commented Bron.

Veneta was trying to keep the children away from the rumpus. Sythia was also making sure her twins stayed in the background by gripping the necks of their tunics so tightly that they were squirming and wriggling to free themselves, more concerned about being strangled than watching what was going on.

A couple of the other chickens were also squatting and one of the mothers gave her son a long bone hairpin so that he could poke them to make them stand, in case they had also laid eggs. The unfortunate birds were clucking and squawking and jumping in the air. The cock was crowing loudly. All of them would have flown into the rigging if their wings had not been clipped.

Two of the crew came over, sent by the captain to enquire what the commotion was about, and hustled the women and children away. One of the young men threw a bucket of seawater over the deck, to wash away the remains of the broken egg, while the other reported back to the captain. It was not long before he sent for Bron and Veneta.

"This will just not do," he told them. "I and my crew cannot concentrate on sailing this ship if there are women and children squabbling and fighting on deck. Something will have to be done about them. We are in sheltered coastal waters at the moment, but when we get out to sea and the weather worsens, as it will, my crew will need all the deck space to manage the sails and work the ship, and can't be falling over passengers – though, hopefully, they'll all be sick in their hammocks."

Bron smiled.

"Please do what you can to calm them," he pleaded. "I knew there would be trouble with all these women on board. If they continue in this vein, I can't guarantee their safety. My men are not above throwing any troublemakers overboard. A troubled ship is a dangerous ship. The crew all know it." He ran his fingers distractedly through his hair. "Men I can handle, but women…"

"We'll try," Veneta promised.

"Did you mention something about a school?" he asked, hopefully.

There was more trouble during the morning when the cook complained that someone had been into his galley and stolen some food – bread baked during the night, cheese and apples, and probably fresh water.

The captain assembled passengers and crew on deck. No one owned up to stealing the provisions.

"This must stop!" he thundered. "The food on board is for the health and well-being of everyone, crew first and then the passengers. It is rationed to last until we take on fresh supplies. This pilfering will not be tolerated. Anyone found stealing from the galley will be chained to the mast and put ashore at the next port of call. Do I make myself clear?"

Bron was mystified that anyone should want to steal food when they were being fed so well by the cook.

It was a very quiet ship during the meal break, neither passengers nor crew saying much and, when they did, speaking in subdued voices. Only the captain's orders could be heard ringing round the deck. He was angry, and Bron felt sorry for him.

Some of the younger women, lounging against the gunwale and endeavouring to speak to any sailor who passed, grinned and nudged each other when they saw Bron and Veneta enter the captain's cabin and the entrance flap close behind them. The remark, "It didn't take 'em long!" could be heard from inside the cabin. Bron was indignant, but Veneta said philosophically, "They'll know why, soon enough."

There was very little furniture under the canvas, just a mattress, a small table and two chairs, with charts and instruments stacked on a wooden chest, not at all as ornate as the one left in their cabin, and spilling over on to the floor.

The captain listened attentively as they explained their ideas about the school. Bron was relieved to see his stern expression relax and the lines on his forehead clear. He gladly gave his blessing and they emerged into the sunshine on deck, well-pleased with their reception.

The girls were still there, chatting and gazing out to sea, looking as if they had not been trying to eavesdrop. Veneta asked them to gather all the women and children around the mast as they had some news to give them.

Bron stood with her own children and looked around at those who were assembling. They sat spread out where the deck was bare and warm, or on closed hatchways, or on the keels of two small, inverted rowing boats.

Veneta stood before them, composed and confident, appearing every inch a schoolteacher. The women looked impressed, Bron thought, as Veneta outlined her plans. Some of them appeared very doubtful about the whole project, but others were enthusiastic. Fabia, one of the single women – the one who had pilfered the egg – commented that at least it would keep the children out of her way for the best part of the day.

Bron suggested making use of everyone's skills and wondered

if some of the soldiers would be willing to teach the boys exercise and fighting techniques.

"You can include me in that class!" called out one of the girls on the edge of the crowd. "I'll wrestle with any of 'em!"

Bron ignored her.

When she and Veneta went back to report to the captain that most of the women were supportive, he was looking worried.

"The cook has been to see me again," he informed them. "More food has gone missing. I must get to the bottom of this, but can do nothing until morning. I will not hesitate to put everyone on starvation rations until the culprit owns up. Please ask the women to let me know if they see or hear anything unusual."

During the night, the ship sailed into more open water and the movement as it cut through the waves was less comfortable. But it was not that which awakened Bron at about three o'clock. She listened, but there was no sound. So what had disturbed her? It was not the bell for the fourth watch, because that was only now being rung.

Rising quietly so she would not waken Veneta and the children, she slipped a shawl round her shoulders and left the cabin. The moon was on the wane but still large enough to shed a gentle light across the open deck, and the stars were bright. She could see the Plough and the brilliant northern star that she hoped one night would guide her and her children home – though she wondered yet again where Aurelius fitted into that picture.

Shadows flitted across the deck, but they were only sailors changing watch. Above her billowed the great square sail, the triangular topsail above it, and below she could hear the even *plop* and *swish* as the oars rowed rhythmically through the water.

Shivering a little, she turned to go back to the cabin but stopped, mystified by a pale orange glow aft. The galley was next to their cabin. Its door and hatchway were closed but it was through the window that the light glowed and it was growing brighter by the second.

What was it? Could it be? Surely not! But there was no mistaking

34

the orange plumes of flame that began leaping towards the window, seeking a means of escape.

"Fire! Fire! Fire!" screamed Bron, running towards the cabin where her children lay asleep. She woke Veneta and together they scrambled out on to the deck, meeting all those scrambling up from below. Now other people's shouts were echoing her own.

"Fire! The gods help us! The galley's on fire!"

The whole vessel was in tumult. The rowers had stopped in confusion. The captain and his officers were shouting orders and relaying them across the decks. The crew, some naked from their hammocks, were racing up the ratlines and furling sails, to slow the ship so there would be as little wind as possible to fan the flames.

The sailors forcibly cleared a pathway through the frightened, disoriented passengers in their night attire and hustled them into action as buckets of sea water were hauled aboard and passed from hand to hand, to be discharged through the broken glass of the galley window and hatchway, now open.

If the fire should take hold, there was no escape for anyone except into the lifeboats, and there were only two of them. Everyone else, including the rowers who were only now appearing on deck, would be burned alive unless they jumped into the dark, green watery grave beneath them.

The screams, cries and shouts ceased and now there was no commotion, not even from the children, only an occasional grunt from one of the men and the steady, determined rhythm of full buckets swinging carefully along the line on their way to the galley and the swifter passage of empty utensils back to the sailors at the rail.

Several minutes of this unrelieved activity passed and it was of supreme relief when those nearest the galley pronounced that the fire had been extinguished.

No one spoke as the captain squelched along the pathway between them.

"Like Moses through the Red Sea!" Veneta whispered with a nervous giggle.

"Where's the cook?" the captain thundered. The cook and his

assistant came forward through the crowd, both looking extremely apprehensive. "Explain how this happened!"

The cook was nonplussed. "I swear, Cap'n, that the fire was out when I left the galley this evening."

"Then how –?"

"Can't say, Cap'n. It's a mystery."

The captain ordered them to follow him down the companionway of the galley. By now, dark grey smoke was billowing out on to the deck, bringing with it the smell of burning wood. As the three men entered the galley, those listening could hear much coughing and spluttering, a babble of confused voices and oaths that caused Bron and Veneta to put their hands over Layla's and Alon's ears. Then the group emerged, stumbling through the smoke – not three figures, but four.

"Bring some light!" ordered Captain Stokovius, and people obliged with oil lamps and torches.

Bron's eyes were watering, but not so much that she could not recognise the young man whom the captain was holding by the scruff of his very wet and dirty tunic.

"Koch!" she exclaimed in surprise.

Others had also recognised the young boy from Brading Villa, and all started talking at once, many shouting accusations at him, until the captain thundered "Quiet!" The jumble of voices subsided.

"I fancy we have caught the food thief," announced the cook with satisfaction.

"Koch!" accused the captain, "You could have burnt us all to death! What have you to say for yourself? Speak up, boy!"

Koch, looking thoroughly frightened and miserable, burst into tears. Bron felt very sorry for him, in his humiliation, but knew that what he had done could have had disastrous consequences for everyone, including all the children.

As Koch was still sobbing, the captain shouted at him, "You stowed away, that is obvious. Who smuggled you aboard?"

"No-no one," stammered the boy. "I c-came on b-board during the night, while the ship was docked."

"But someone has sheltered you?"

"I h-hid under one of the r-rowing boats, Captain," Koch explained.

The captain relaxed his grip a little. "And stole our food during the night?"

"Y-yes, sir."

"Then nearly set us all alight," persisted the captain.

"Yes, sir, I'm sorry, sir. I lit the fire in the galley – I was cooking a sea-bream – but then I spilt oil on the flames."

The cook spluttered his indignation.

"Go with Cook and make sure that the fire has been completely extinguished," the captain growled. "You will then clear up the mess you have caused, before he prepares breakfast. After breakfast, you will come to see me in my cabin. I will put you ashore at the first available opportunity, but in the meantime I must decide what to do with you, and how we can send a message to your mother. She will be out of her mind with worry."

"Sir, I think she will guess –"

"Quiet!" the captain ordered him. "Cook, I put him in your charge. When he's cleared up, find him a dry, clean nightshirt and let him sleep on the floor in the crew's quarters."

"Aye, aye, Cap'n," the cook answered, and ushered Koch down into the galley.

"The rest of you, back to your hammocks," ordered the captain, "and I know you will be patient in the morning if breakfast is late."

Bron, the children and Veneta returned to their cabin, picking their way across the dark, wet deck, avoiding the litter of buckets, ropes, scattered clothes and possessions. Everything in the cabin smelt of smoke, most of all the bedding, but it couldn't be helped.

She lingered over the five children as she tucked them up again on the mattresses, soothing them back to sleep with whispered words and gentle kisses and stroking damp hair away from flushed cheeks. She looked at her friend. Both were acutely aware that the night could have ended quite differently.

Kneeling down, Veneta uttered a simple prayer of thanks to her Christian god for their escape.

"Amen," added Layla's sleepy voice. "I wonder what other adventures we will have tomorrow."

CHAPTER 7

Everyone who could be there was on deck next morning, after the expected late breakfast, to see Koch enter the captain's cabin. He was now clean and tidy in a borrowed tunic, but still looked very abashed.

Mothers hushed their children, so that the conversation could be heard through the canvas walls. Most of the time it seemed one-sided, as Koch's replies were almost inaudible. Bron thought that the captain sounded calmer now but guessed he must be unhappy at having to discipline the son of his friends. She could also guess how distressed his mother, Regina, would be if she knew.

After about ten minutes, the entrance flap was pushed aside and the captain emerged, Koch following him.

"I'm sure you've all heard my decision," announced Stokovius. "I will put Koch ashore when we arrive at our next port of call, Magnus Portus, a week away. In the meantime, he will work his passage. I have made him pularius, responsible for the chickens, and he will also help the ship's carpenter, cook, bo'sun and anyone else who needs an extra hand. From now on, he is a member of the crew, under my command, and I do not want any passengers talking to him as if he were not." He looked sternly at the boy. "I hope to be able to attract the attention of a passing ship on its way to Britannia and ask its captain to take a message to your mother."

"Thank you, sir," mumbled Koch, his head bowed. That settled, and nothing else to be said, the crowd drifted away.

Later, all the children who had been promised to Veneta, except for one little girl who was sick, were brought to the school. She and Bron divided them into small groups.

Declan, off duty, perched on the upturned rowing boat on the starboard side, his long brown fingers demonstrating to a group of boys how to tie knots.

"It was too interesting to be a lesson," Alon enthused later.

Very reluctantly, the cook allowed some of the girls down into the galley to help him prepare meals for the rest of the day. Sythia was put in charge of this group as her twins were occupied, fishing with rod and line off the stern. In spite of the cook's misgivings, the girls were soon happily taking turns in pounding seeds, herbs, saffron, pine kernels, honey and oil in a mortar, preparing a sauce for roasted meat.

"Just watch how I do it, m'dears," Sythia told them happily and then, when the cook wisely took over their instruction, kept herself busy brushing up the flour and mopping up the oil her enthusiastic but clumsy interference had spilled on bench and floor.

Layla and a couple of other girls, with Veneta, were watching one of the crew mending a fishing net, and asked to be shown how it was done.

Bron had been requested by Veneta to judge the success of the whole experiment, ready to report back to the captain, so she was moving from group to group. She was also trying to interest some of the single women in attending lessons.

"School's not for the likes of us," said one of them, a pretty girl, who was sitting on a coil of rope. Her grey eyes were regarding Bron candidly. "We know what we're good at, and we'll stick to that. What help is lessons when you're pleasing your man?" Those around her nodded their agreement.

The girl was of medium height, with light brown hair that flowed free to her shoulders. A low neckline revealed the swell of plump breasts, and a knotted girdle emphasised a slim waist above slim hips. She was about twenty years old.

"Is that all you want from life?" Bron asked.

"What more is there?" asked the girl. It was she who had offered to show Briard and Koch the women's sleeping quarters, and had jokingly volunteered to take part in exercising with the military. "Anyway, it's all I got or is likely to get."

"What's your name?" asked Bron.

"Asandra." Then she asked insolently, "What's yours?"

Bron told her, though she believed the girl already knew it. Veneta had introduced herself and Bron to the women on several occasions, and she felt sure that Asandra had been present some of the time.

A sailor approached and Asandra deliberately raised one foot on to the top of the coil of rope, grinned at him and hitched her undershift up above her knee. One or two of the others giggled and did the same. Bron decided that, if she could interest this girl in the lessons, or anything else for that matter, the other young women would follow her lead.

As Bron left, the young sailor passed. "I'm busy," he told the girls, "but I'll be back later!"

The morning sped by and classes broke for the midday meal. Declan came to Bron to discuss swimming lessons when in port and suggested he could also show the boys how to manage a rowing boat, if the captain gave permission.

Bron agreed but asked, "Why only the boys?"

After the children had rested, she and Veneta organised activities on deck – a cat and mouse game in a circle, guessing games with one child wearing a blindfold, hunt the sea shells, memory games, and finally all marched behind Veneta round the ship and copied her movements, but only on Bron's instruction of, "The captain says, 'Do this!'"

Several of the mothers, who had been watching, asked to join in. Their antics were curtailed when the captain sent word that the noise was too distracting and would they please play something quieter.

"The captain says, 'Do this!'" Bron called out, and put a finger on her lips. The children obeyed, and Veneta quietly told them that the day's schooling was over and she and Bron would see them all again the following morning.

"Now all we have to do is repeat the performance every day for the next six months, but more quietly," teased Bron.

That evening, gathered round the mast, the women discussed the events of the day. It soon became obvious that some had taken the

41

opportunity, with the children and their mothers out of the way, to visit the crew's quarters, where the men passengers were also berthed.

"At least it means that nearly everyone on board is in favour of the school," Veneta said to Bron later, "even though it may be for very different reasons."

The ship was following the coastline of Gallia. They seemed to be making good progress in fairly peaceful sea conditions. So far, no one had complained of sickness, except the little girl, who had stayed below with her mother.

Veneta said she was worried about her.

CHAPTER 8

"No need to tell you that the wind's gathering strength," Declan remarked when he joined Bron at the ship's rail next day. "There's also a strong current flowing north and we're battling against it."

They watched as the sea spat froth and white spray from one angry wave to the next.

"The sea's always rough here and I think we're not seeing the worst yet."

"Where are we?" asked Bron. "Land has been out of sight since yesterday."

"The Bay of Burdigala – it's two hundred miles across."

"So we should be through during the night?"

"The cap'n hopes so."

"Declan," Bron said, "tell me why the colour of the sea has changed from green to this lovely deep blue."

"Because we've left the Channel for the Atlantic. It's very deep here – no one knows how deep, as we can't plumb the depths. You'll find the sea colour changes all the time."

"Why's that?"

"It reflects the sky," he explained, "and I also wonder whether the sea bed changes – you know, from sand to rocks. I don't see why there shouldn't be deserts and mountains and valleys below us, like on land." He smiled. "No one who has gone down there has ever come back to tell us."

Bron shuddered.

"Bron!" Veneta was approaching, a frown on her face.

"What is it? You don't look very well."

Veneta grabbed the rail. "I'm all right now I'm up here on deck. I don't think I've found my…" She turned to Declan. "What do you sailors call them?"

"Sea legs," he told her. "Don't worry – the *Juniper* may roll a lot, but she's as safe as Rome. Veneta, the cap'n said to tell you to watch out for whales and dolphins. We get a lot in the Bay. Have you ever seen a whale or dolphin?"

"Never. How will we know which is which?"

"There'll always be someone around to tell you, if you ask."

He nodded to them and left. Bron turned to her friend.

"What is it?"

"I'm still worried about the little girl who's sick."

"Why were you down there?"

"Layla and Alon wanted to play with the children, and I went with them."

"What's wrong with the little girl?" Bron asked. "Do you know her name?"

"Yes, it's Leeza. She's very hot, with a runny nose and dry cough, and her mother said she's been complaining of a sore throat. She's also got a rash – small red spots, though they're difficult to see, as any light hurts her eyes, so all the lamps have been extinguished."

"Where are Layla and Alon now?"

"On deck."

"Don't let them go down there again."

"Don't worry, I won't."

"What do you think it is?"

"Measles."

Bron was shocked. "Then we must bring all the children up on deck – let's tell them they're going to look for sea creatures this morning."

"I intended going back to Leeza and her mother."

"You'll feel better up here, let me go."

Veneta hesitated and Bron reassured her.

"I know you've had measles, but so have I – when I was living in the Temple, about four years old, remember? And you always told us that children who had it and survived never caught it again."

Veneta nodded. "I did notice that."

"What does worry me, though, is the health of our five." Bron looked at her friend anxiously.

"Very young babies don't often catch it, so Darius and Gift should be all right. I'm not sure about the other three. We'll just have to hope for the best. I can't promise anything."

Bron turned to go below. Veneta laid a hand on her arm.

"Take a look in the mother's mouth – see if she has any greyish spots."

Bron slowly climbed down the companionway into the forward hold, cautiously feeling her way on each rung of the ladder, helped only by natural light from the deck above.

"I can't see!" she called into the darkness on reaching the bottom. She wrinkled her nose, unsuccessfully trying to shift the stale odours of overheated bodies, unwashed clothes, urine and faeces and sickness, that made her want to retch. She felt even more grateful for their cabin on deck.

"Over here!"

She waited until her eyes accustomed themselves to the gloom, then carefully picked her way through a jumble of mattresses and discarded clothing, avoiding hammocks swinging freely as the ship rolled and lurched, guided by the sound of a child's barking cough.

In a far corner, a girl of about eight years lay on a pile of rags. A young woman reclined beside her, cradling her daughter's head in her lap, gently stroking the straggling, wet hair and wiping red eyes and face with a damp, smelly cloth.

"Thank you for coming," the woman whispered.

"I'm Bron."

"Yes, I know. My name's Zohira."

"Tell me about Leeza's sickness."

Zohira recited the symptoms already described by Veneta, concluding, "She's saying such strange things."

"That's the fever."

"What's causing it?" asked Zohira.

"Veneta thinks it's measles, but we can't be sure. How are *you* feeling?"

"Not very well, but it's so hot down here, and the ship *is* rolling a lot."

"Have you had measles?"

"I don't think so."

"Would you mind if I looked in your mouth?" Zohira shook her head. "But first I will need some light."

Immediately, an oil lamp flared a few feet away.

"Who's there?" Bron asked, surprised.

"Asandra."

"You should be on deck, safely out of the way!" Bron said, more sharply than she intended.

"It's all right, I got measles as a kid. I stayed 'cause I thought I might be of use, but if you rather I went…"

"No, no," interrupted Bron hastily. "I'll be glad of your help. Thanks. Would you bring the lamp over here?"

By its light, Bron peered into the mouth of Zohira and found the greyish spots she was looking for.

"I'm afraid you've caught it from your daughter, Zohira," Bron told her. "Leeza should be better by the time your rash appears, but you'll be passing it on to everyone who hasn't been infected by her."

"Can't they be put somewhere on their own?" Asandra asked.

"I think it's too late for that," Bron answered. "Have you done any nursing?"

"Some."

"It's the complications we're afraid of," Bron whispered. She had seen the mayhem that had followed severe outbreaks among the children in Byden Temple.

Aloud she said, "All we can do, Zohira, is keep you in darkness and cool Leeza down by fanning her all the time. I'll also ask cook if he has any medicines to relieve the coughing and reduce the fever."

"I'll stay with them," Asandra offered.

Zohira tearfully thanked them both.

Bron went to the galley to speak to the cook.

"Figs drive out measles," he told her.

"Something more gentle," she suggested. "Stinging nettle or honeysuckle for her cough, lemon balm or feverfew to cool the fever, fennel lotion to soothe her eyes?"

"I'll see what I can do," he promised.

Bron sought out Veneta at the ship's rail.

"The sea monsters have been wonderful!" The wind was bearing away much of what Veneta was shouting. "The children are so excited! Only a couple of them have been sea sick."

At that moment, a small female sperm whale breached, distinguishable, according to Veneta, by its large, square head. Bron watched as it lifted its dark blue-back body with white belly clear of the water, to the delighted cries of those at the rail.

"There's a pod of 'em," Sythia told her, repeating what one of the sailors had called down from the crow's nest. "Whoever would've guessed that fish could show such love for their babies? Almost human."

"And see the dolphins!" exclaimed Alon.

"They're pretending the ship is one of them," Layla told her, "and are showing us the way!"

Bron took Veneta aside.

"I must talk to you. Come into the cabin."

Once there, Veneta asked, "Do you agree it's measles?"

"Yes. I found the grey spots in Zohira's mouth. The chances are that everyone who sleeps in the women's hold has been infected, unless they've had it in the past. We may have a crisis on our hands."

Veneta considered the problem. "The only way we might contain it is to ask the captain if everyone who hasn't had the disease can sleep on deck. I think we're probably too late to make much difference, though."

"It will create chaos for the crew," Bron said, "and the weather and sea conditions will make sleeping nigh impossible. However, we've got to try."

"We'll ask for help from everyone who thinks they're immune, and co-operation from the women – no fraternisation – we don't want it spreading to the crew."

"Then the captain will have to give that order. He won't be very pleased. He's said all along that women on board cause trouble."

"Then I'll leave you to sweeten him."

"Why me?" asked Bron.

"Don't say you hadn't noticed –"

"Noticed what?"

"That he has a certain regard for you."

"Nonsense, he's got children older than me, and a wife," Bron remonstrated, but it didn't stop a flush spreading over her cheeks.

Veneta looked at her friend. "Then you *have* noticed," she commented. "Be careful, Bron. This will be a long voyage and you don't want any further complications in your life."

Bron went to find him and returned after ten minutes, her face sombre, and joined the crowd who were still at the starboard rail.

"You can guess his reaction," she said. "He wants to disembark anyone who threatens the health of his crew, no matter who they are, as soon as we dock in Magnus Portus."

"But that will likely spread the disease on the mainland."

"He's not concerned about that."

"Though, if anyone gets wind of the fact that there's illness on board, they probably won't let us disembark anyway," said Veneta prosaically.

"Any dead he will bury at sea," added Bron.

"Good gracious, I hope it won't come to that."

"But it could."

"I suppose so," conceded Veneta, "but I'll be Hell-bent to make sure that doesn't happen."

Bron smiled at her friend's comment. Veneta believed in this Christian place called Hell, and it was the nearest she ever came to blaspheming.

"Do you think the women will take notice of the captain's order and not sneak below?" Bron wondered.

"Perhaps if we asked Asandra to set an example of restraint, hopefully, the others will follow her lead."

"We can but ask." Bron sounded doubtful.

Veneta told the children that schooling was over for the day as they had learned much more from watching the sea creatures than ever she could have taught them.

Bron's four children and Lucilla were confined to the cabin as much as possible, but it wasn't easy to make them stay there.

With the captain's reluctant permission, canvas protection was being erected for the healthy passengers who would be sleeping on deck.

Below decks, the situation was difficult. Those whose health was suspect were taken to the women's quarters for nursing. Most of the sickness was caused by the movement of the sea, but there were a few children and mothers whose malaise, Veneta suspected, resulted from the infection. Some of the women complained about the sudden rush of male sore throats and confided they were embarrassed to have three men, all veterans, sleeping in their quarters.

Sythia was also suspicious. "Love us, are they all sickening?" she demanded.

"If not now, they soon will be," Bron commented wryly.

As Veneta guessed, once news of measles on board spread round Magnus Portus harbour, the captain was refused permission to land any passengers, so could not disembark Koch as he had intended. However, he was able to shout a message for Regina Marcellus to the captain of a merchant trader about to set sail for Britannia, who would be putting into Brading harbour.

Koch was delighted at being able to remain on board.

CHAPTER 9

As soon as money left in a bag at the bottom of the gangplank had been replaced by fresh supplies and water, the *Juniper* set sail about midday.

Having enlisted the help of willing mothers to organise games and activities for the children, Bron and Veneta returned below decks to find out how their patients were faring. Veneta made her rounds of the women, then the men, while Bron stayed with Leeza and her mother. Asandra was there and Bron sent the girl on deck to get some fresh air.

"It's so hot down here," Zohira complained, pulling her tunic away from her neck.

"It will become cooler once we're further out to sea," Bron comforted her. "How's Leeza?"

"She's no better."

Bron felt the child's forehead. It was hotter to the touch than before and the rash had spread down her face and neck.

"It's all over her body, now," said her mother.

"Are you giving her plenty to drink and the potions from the cook?"

Zohira nodded. "And I'm bathing her all over all the time."

"I'll bring some fresh water. How are *you* feeling?"

"I'm all right – at least, I will be when Leeza's better. Just a runny nose."

"Where's your man?" asked Bron.

"Aqintus? He sailed on the *Eagle*."

Fortunately, the wind was easing off and passengers who had been experiencing sea nausea and vomiting were feeling and looking much better. When Veneta returned, she said it was now easier to identify those with measles. She whispered to Bron that she was as suspicious as Sythia of most of the male coughs, though she had found the telltale grey spots in one mouth. These had appeared too soon to have been caused by the sickness on board, so the legionary must have brought the infection with him.

"It's going to get worse before it gets better," Veneta said dully.

In the meantime, Bron was becoming increasingly concerned about the unwelcome attentions of the bo'sun.

It was difficult not to notice him about the ship. He was probably a little older than the captain, a big man, with massive hands and stout fingers that were adept at wielding the belaying pins that hung from a leather belt round his ample waist – more often than not across the shoulders of a crew member who was not obeying his orders quickly enough. Bron had been upset on a couple of occasions to see the harshness of his discipline and had mentioned it to Declan.

"The crew need it sometimes," he said, and when she still looked unconvinced added, "On board ship, orders must be obeyed, above all else."

Often the man seemed to be wherever she was, so that she had to walk round him or dodge out of his way. If she saw him coming towards her, she would sometimes turn and head off in another direction. When she was taken unawares and found herself face to face with him, she was unnerved by the intense way he looked at her, his eyes ensnaring hers as if trying to sear them with messages she did not want to read. She was even more uncomfortable when his eyes slid down her body, resting where she had rather they were not resting.

Two days after leaving Magnus Portus, following a busy time spent with the children and the patients, she came out on deck and stood with her arms on the starboard rail, breathing deeply of the sea air and letting the wind cool her body.

She never ceased to be fascinated by the colour of the sea – this evening, the deep shade that the rainbow captures between blue and violet, with hardly a wave between the ship and the bright blue line gleaming along the horizon.

With a steady wind in the sails, the oars were not needed, so only the ship's hull was disturbing the surface of the sea, leaving a white froth alongside which then stretched way back beyond the stern. There, the cutting hull had brought to the surface a wake of aquamarine, lightly coloured at the sides among the froth but deeper and brighter in the centre, a confectionary that looked enticing enough to eat.

The sun in the west was laying slithers of gold, paths across the ocean, leading away to the horizon. Bron wondered, if she and the children climbed over the rail and began to walk one of the watery paths, whether it would lead them home, to all that was familiar and safe. Then she thought of the ravaged village she had left behind, and the fancy deserted her, to be replaced by the desire to be with Aurelius.

"A siliqua for them!" Bron jumped, and turning, found the bo'sun standing behind her. "Did I spook you?" he asked in thick, guttural tones. "Sorry 'bout that. You scare easy."

"I didn't hear you coming."

She turned her back on him, to avoid the stare of his dark grey eyes, and leaned on the rail again. He took the couple of steps necessary to close the gap between them and rested his right arm beside hers, so close that she could feel the coarse hairs scratching her skin. She moved her arm away.

"Wrapped in your thoughts, weren't you? If I gave you a siliqua, would you tell me what – or who – you were dreaming about?"

"They aren't worth a siliqua," Bron replied, wishing he would go away.

He turned to face her and dropped his right arm down at his side. She was not sure, but had the uncomfortable feeling that he was fingering the folds of her tunic. With his left elbow now resting on the rail, he propped his chin in his hand and regarded her profile closely. She tried not to react and continued staring out to sea.

After a moment, he asked, "Then you weren't thinking about your Roman officer?"

Bron caught her breath and could not control the blush that spread over her cheeks as she turned towards him.

"How did you know –?"

"I saw you, down on the dock, the day the *Eagle* sailed," he said.

"You were spying on us?" she asked angrily.

"I wasn't the only one. The old man was having a good look, too. Soon brought you on board, didn't he?"

His insolent laugh repulsed her but she forced herself to regard him levelly. "Your insinuations insult your captain and me. Haven't you work to do?" she asked icily.

"As a matter of fact, I have," he replied, moving away. Looking over his shoulder as he left, he added, "Enjoyed our chat, goddess. Must do it again some time."

Not if I see you first, thought Bron, *and what's all this about a goddess?*

Suddenly, the sea and western sun had lost their appeal, and Bron escaped to the cabin. She mentioned the incident to Veneta but her friend had so much on her mind that she seemed not to pay attention.

CHAPTER 10

At Calle, at the mouth of the River Durius, a gang of dockworkers armed with cudgels prevented the cook and Koch, who were first off the ship, from stepping ashore and they had to retreat back up the gangplank. Several of the traders already tied up at the quayside had been with the *Juniper* in Magnus Portus, and obviously, news of the illness had preceded their arrival.

As before, after shouted negotiations, money was exchanged for supplies. The ship anchored offshore overnight and set sail the following day.

Two more days passed and by now the passengers were well used to the routines of the school day.

Each morning brought new cases of measles among both children and adults, some showing early signs – colds, coughs and eyes sensitive to light – while others were feverish and breaking out in the rash. Bron was amused to observe that all three veterans who had moved into the women's quarters early on were now showing genuine signs of the illness.

Both she and Veneta were very worried about Leeza, who was making no progress at all.

"She is just as hot, when she should be almost better by now," Bron confided to Sythia. "She's covered from head to toe in the rash, and the spots are beginning to blend together so that she looks as if she's been slapped in the face, though Veneta says that's normal. What's worrying us is that her chest rattles so when she breathes, and she's so weak. We think the sickness may have turned inwards and is inflaming her lungs."

Sythia's twins were eavesdropping on the conversation.

"Is she going to die?" asked Tiegan, with interest.

"Mercy! That's not a question you should be asking!" chided his mother.

"I don't know," Bron answered truthfully.

She returned below decks, leaving Veneta and Sythia to organise the school.

Asandra had been on watch all night, doing what she could to cool faces and bodies and relieve parched throats, and Bron sent her away to get some rest.

Zohira looked skeletal and exhausted as she cradled her daughter, listening to the noise in Leeza's chest every time she breathed in or out.

"Let me hold her," Bron offered, sitting beside Zohira and taking Leeza's head into her lap. "You try to get some sleep. I'll wake you if I need you."

Zohira relinquished her daughter without protest and in seconds was fast asleep, leaning against the bulkhead, oblivious of the creaking and groaning of the ship's timbers.

After about twenty minutes sitting in one position, Bron moved to make herself more comfortable, and woke Leeza, who moaned slightly.

"It's all right, dear, I'm here," she told the child, who reached her arms out towards her mother. "Your mother's here, too, but she's having a little sleep."

"Bron, Bron –" It was the voice of Joas, urgent in the darkness.

"I'm here, Joas," Bron answered him. "You shouldn't be down here. What do you want?"

"To see Leeza."

"She's too sick. You really should go, Joas, or you'll catch the sickness, too."

"I've got something for her," he persisted.

"What is it?"

She was answered by a faint miaow, followed by another.

"Have you brought a cat down?" Bron asked him in surprise.

"It's a kitten. I borrowed it from one of the crew," he explained shyly. "It's for Leeza. It might make her feel better."

"Oh, Joas, that's such a kind thought. I'm sure it will. What colour is it?"

"Orange and black and white."

"Kitten?" repeated Leeza huskily, hardly awake.

"Yes, for you," and the boy knelt down on the rags that served as her bed and placed the little bundle of fur into her still-outstretched arms. The kitten miaowed again, Leeza murmured, "Hello, kitten," closed her arms round the tiny creature, and both settled down contentedly to sleep.

"Now you must go, Joas, or you'll be ill," Bron warned him.

He turned and clambered up the companionway, and she laid her head against the bulwark, thanking any god listening for the kindness of a little boy and asking that he should not be harmed because of his visit.

She was not sure how long she slept, but was woken by someone shaking her gently by the shoulder. Opening her eyes, she saw Asandra kneeling beside her, oil lamp in hand. The circle of light also revealed Veneta and two of the women who had volunteered as nurses.

"What is it?" Bron asked. "How long have I been asleep?"

"Long enough," said Asandra. Her grey eyes were bright in the lamplight.

Bron shifted her position. She was hot and uncomfortable and was suddenly aware of Leeza's weight in her arms. The kitten seemed to have escaped.

Veneta crouched at the other side of her. "Let me take the child from you," she offered, her voice husky.

"It's all right, I can manage." Bron was unwilling to give up the little girl until she could give her back to her mother.

"No, Bron, we'll take her."

The instruction was clear and suddenly Bron understood. She looked down at Leeza and tears filled her eyes.

"You can't take her away from her mother," she remonstrated.

"We have to," one of the women said, but kindly.

"You go with 'em, I'll stay here with Zohira," offered Asandra.

"Tell her I won't let them put Leeza over the side until she has seen her for the last time," Bron said.

"I'll break the news to her just as soon as she wakes," Asandra promised.

But Zohira never did wake up.

CHAPTER 11

Around the chicken coop, all was confusion. One of the children had opened the door and everyone was playing "hunt the chickens" with great enthusiasm, as if forced enjoyment would shut out yesterday's memory of two slight, wrapped, weighted bodies sliding from wooden planks over the side of the ship and down into the waves.

As fast as one chicken was cooped up, another would escape to a perch just out of everyone's reach, anywhere where there was a foothold, quite unwilling to be coaxed down and restricted by wire again. The cock's raucous fanfare of rebellion gave away his whereabouts and he was captured first.

After more than an hour, when his concubines were also safely contained, it was noticed that one was missing. On searching, its bloody remains were found behind a locker. Joas looked appalled.

"The kitten couldn't have done that," Bron comforted him.

"No, but its mother could," declared Declan and went to look for the ship's cat, returning with it under his arm. Her drooping furry stomach was circumstantial evidence of the feast she had lately enjoyed.

"I'll get the deck swabbed down," Declan said, allowing the cat to jump out of his arms and scamper off in a rush of orange, black and white. "Can't blame the cat. She's on board to hunt. She's a good ratter."

As they watched her go, there was a momentary lull in the conversation.

"There's going to be a fight."

The voice was clear and authoritative. Everyone turned to look at the boy who had spoken so strangely.

"What are you going on about, Tiegan?" his mother asked dismissively. "What fight?"

"I don't know. It's what I see in the guts of the chicken."

"Mercy, tell me something new! If I'd eaten a parson's nose every time you and your brother came to blows, I'd be fatter than the ship's cat."

"No, Mother, not children fighting."

Everyone gazed from his face to the remains of the bird, its uneaten innards trailing blood at their feet. Bron looked again at the boy. His manner was calm. Declan nodded to one of the crew to fetch the captain. A few moments later, Stokovius arrived, and the crowd opened to make way for him. He looked at the mess on the deck.

"Tell me, boy," he ordered.

"I see a fight – two grown-ups, two women," the boy stated with growing confidence.

The captain turned to Sythia. "He's your son?" She nodded. "What do you make of this?" he asked.

"I don't know, Captain. Love us, 'e's never said anything like it before."

"Then we shall see," said Stokovius. "Declan, have this cleaned up. Boy –"

"'Is name's Tiegan," Sythia protested.

"Tiegan, come to my cabin." He nodded at her. "You come, too."

The captain walked away, followed hurriedly by Sythia and her elder son, with Joas trailing along in the rear. They left behind a babble of speculation.

"A haruspice? So young?" was the general comment.

"What do you think?" Bron asked Veneta.

"I don't like it. All I can tell from this chicken's innards is that it's well and truly dead," Veneta whispered. Bron grinned.

When mother and son returned, there was a clamour for information.

"What did the captain say?"

"What do you think, Sythia?"

"Has Tiegan ever shown signs of prophecy before?"

Sythia took on the appearance of a plumped-up cushion as she found her son and herself the centre of attention. "No, never, m'dears, but that doesn't mean that he 'asn't the gift." She winked knowingly at her audience. "Only time will tell."

A sailor arrived with bucket and mop. The children were taken off by Veneta to their lessons, the crowd dispersed, and Bron found herself standing with Asandra. Bron had not taken to the girl initially, but could not help admiring the way she had used her natural nursing skills and had been so willing to help.

They were still in the vicinity of the wire coop, where the cock was again crowing his sovereignty. Koch was inspecting the remaining hens. He had been taking his duties of pularius seriously and had been very upset at the loss of one of the chickens to the ship's cat.

"Asandra, I haven't had a chance to thank you – for the way you – Leeza and Zohira…" Bron tailed off.

"But you helped me find things out about me I didn't know I got – like looking after sick people and such and not minding the filth."

She really is very pretty, Bron thought, *in spite of looking so grubby.* But it was no wonder, now that they were twelve days out and considering the work she had been doing. Surprisingly, she had also prevailed upon the other girls to keep away from the crew, to avoid spreading any infection, which Bron thought showed great strength of character.

"So you didn't know you were a natural nurse?" Her compliments brought a flush to the girl's cheeks.

Bron was amused to notice that she wasn't the only one who admired Asandra. Whenever the girl looked across at Koch and smiled, he blushed to the roots of his marigold-coloured hair, and quickly looked away. However, when she was not looking at him, his bright blue eyes followed her every movement. Adoration was written all over his face.

Well I never, thought Bron with amusement, *the boy's in love with her.* She wondered what his mother would say if she knew, guessing that Asandra was not at all the sort of girl she had in mind for her son.

Asandra appeared not to notice Koch's adoring glances, but perhaps she was just used to men looking at her like that and, anyway, he was probably much too young to be of any consequence to her. Bron hoped so, as she felt some responsibility towards him until he was delivered safely home.

The two young women sat on a locker.

"Are you really going to look for Leeza's father when we get to Ostia?"

Bron nodded. "What are *you* going to do when we reach Ostia, Asandra?"

"Same as I done before I left Britannia," Asandra replied tartly. "What do you think? Get a man trapped into settling down and drop dozens of children, and live happy ever after? Like you and your officer?"

"I'm sorry, I didn't mean to pry."

"Don't you know what me and the other girls do?"

"Not really," said Bron, feeling very uncomfortable, because she had a good idea.

"We follow the garrison around. Where they go, we go. They need us, we need them. That simple."

"You live in the garrison, among the soldiers?"

"'Course. Don't sound so surprised. We're well fed, and it's shelter over our heads – better than living on the streets."

"Do they look after you?"

"Not particularly. We look after ourselves. We're nobody's, you see. We belong to all of 'em, and none of 'em."

Bron stared at her, aghast.

"It's not so bad. Some are quite kind to us."

"And the others?"

Asandra shrugged. "We get used to it."

"Will you one day settle with one, for good?"

"Doubt it. One will never be enough. For a time maybe, but I'd get to wandering after a couple of years – crave new scenery, new faces, new – you know – I'd be off again."

"And children?"

"Sometimes, by accident, and then we have to do something about it. You can't drag children around from one posting to the next. Anyway, they'd have no life worth living and wouldn't be safe from some of the bastards. Children's for your sort, maybe, but not for us."

Bron's reply was interrupted by a wail from Gift, who was in the cabin. After a few seconds, there was an echoing wail from Darius, who seemed to be entering into competition.

Anticipating Bron's thoughts, Asandra continued, "Don't you feel sorry for *me*. I have it good. Not tied down like you are all day, every day." For a brief moment, Bron empathised with what Asandra was saying, then smiled resignedly and walked across to the cabin.

As she passed Koch, she looked at him. He would have heard every word. Bron wasn't sure how much he had understood, but he must have gleaned enough to know the sort of life that Asandra led.

CHAPTER 12

Next morning saw the *Juniper* sailing quietly between the green banks of the River Tagus and into the thriving port of Felicitas Julia, the western capital of the Roman empire. Because they had spent so little time at the previous port, she was ahead of the other vessels they had encountered, and her arrival went unannounced. Passengers and crew alike took advantage of the port authority's lack of knowledge of the sickness on board and disembarked without hindrance.

Bron and Veneta stood by the rail, eyes raised to the fort cresting the highest of the town's seven hills, debating whether to go ashore.

"I'm longing to tread firm ground again," Bron confided wistfully, "and I want to find out if the *Eagle* berthed here."

"Then go, and take Layla – she'll enjoy looking round the markets."

"Will you be able to cope with all the nursing?"

"Asandra's around, she'll help."

"There'll be children staying on board."

"I've already spoken to Declan. He's agreed to give them swimming and sailing lessons. They'll be safe enough – several of the crew have been bullied into lending a hand."

"I don't want to wander about on my own, though."

"Then take Koch. He's been so useful, I think everyone's forgotten he's supposed to be sent home, but he'll be glad to keep out of the captain's way, just in case."

This was the largest port they had entered since leaving Britannia. Bron asked Koch to make enquiries and he was able to report that the *Eagle* had anchored alongside a large quay some distance away, had stayed two days, and sailed the day before yesterday. A thought struck Bron.

"Koch," she said, "it may be there's a message for me."

"Who from?" asked Koch.

"A friend on the *Eagle*."

"Why would he leave you a message?"

"It's only a 'maybe'. We'll enquire at the port authority office."

The boy continued to look doubtful.

"If you were travelling half way round the world," she said mischievously, "and Asandra was following on behind, wouldn't you leave her a message as often as you could?"

She knew she had hit the target when he flushed bright red, and she laughed at his discomfiture. He grinned back at her.

Leading the way and holding Layla tightly by the hand, she wove a path among the amphorae, boxes and sacks, avoiding dirty puddles and dead fish and arriving at the door of a square stone building just inside the large iron dock gates. Koch knocked and was invited to enter.

A man who was sitting writing at a plain wooden table paused and looked up as they entered, regarding them without interest. The table was littered with scrolls and charts, inkwells, wooden writing tablets, styli and other paraphernalia of the civil servant.

"Yes?" he asked.

"I'm sorry to interrupt you," Bron apologised, "but I understand that the *Eagle* docked here?"

"The troop ship? Yes, that's right. She sailed two days ago."

"I wondered if anyone had left a message for me."

"Is your name Bron?"

She caught her breath and blushed and her heart jumped about beneath her attempted composure.

"Mummy, you're hurting my hand," Layla complained.

"Sorry," she apologised, loosening her grip.

"I have a message here from a Roman officer for such a person."

"Yes, I'm Bron"

"State the officer's name."

"Aurelius Catus."

The official nodded his satisfaction with her replies.

"Is it a written message?" she asked.

"No, he wouldn't write it down – too sensitive, he said. He gave it to one of his men."

"I don't understand."

"They left one of his legionaries behind. A sailor fell from the rigging and landed on top of this soldier. Everyone joked there were two breakages – landing on the legionary broke the youngster's fall and saved his life, but the soldier was sent sprawling and broke his hip. No joke though, he was – is – in great pain. Your officer left the message with him, hoping you'd call here and ask."

"Where is he?" asked Bron urgently.

"You'll find him in the mansio by the landgate."

He gave them directions and they left, Bron hurrying ahead and Koch following with Layla.

The cobbled streets were thronged with townsfolk and visitors. They passed through the fish, fruit and vegetable markets, the shops and warehouses of those whose livelihoods depended on the sea, and the large buildings of the shipping and port authorities. As they left the area and traversed the criss-cross of streets, they passed foul-smelling slaughterhouses and tanners' sheds, then a large assortment of shops and side-street brothels.

On another occasion, Bron would have spent time admiring the buildings in the city centre – the extensive forum, temples, public baths, and elegant private houses – but today her only thought was to find the legionary to whom Aurelius had entrusted his message.

The Landgate was visible as soon as they turned a corner, its two huge stone towers rising above archways, one for pedestrians and sedan chairs, and a wider and higher access for those on horseback or in covered wagons. The mansio stood stolidly to one side of the gateway, the city wall doubling as its side wall.

They entered the yard where ostlers were busy stabling tired horses and releasing fresh ones to travellers leaving the city. She enquired of a boy and was directed to a green wooden door that stood open in one corner, next to a wheelwright's workshop. Stepping over the threshold, they found themselves in a large room with stone floor strewn with straw, leather couches and chairs around the walls, and a wooden desk to one side. Bron approached the clerk behind it and asked if the young soldier was still there. The man nodded.

"Upstairs," he informed her, "second door on the right."

She was not quite sure what awaited her through the second door on the right so suggested to Koch that he took Layla to watch the horses being shod, then mounted the staircase.

At the top she found herself in a long, dim corridor that turned a corner at the far end, with doors on both sides. She approached the second on the right and knocked loudly. Faintly, a young man's voice invited her to enter.

Inside, she waited a moment by the open door, adjusting her eyes to the gloom.

"Come in," the voice said again with little interest. Then, as the eyes of the room's occupant must also have adjusted and seen her silhouette, he asked with more animation, "Who, in the name of Venus are *you*?" Before she could answer, he added, with sudden clarity, "You're Bron, aren't you?"

Bron closed the door and approached the low bed, appraising the slight form beneath the light linen cover. He had turned and raised his head slightly to look at her.

"No wonder officer Catus –" His head dropped back on to the pillow again.

Bron smiled at the compliment. "I'm sorry they had to leave you behind. Are you in much pain?"

"You could say that," he replied, without humour. "Come nearer – don't worry, I won't grab you. I'd like to, but I'm told I have to lie here on my back without moving for six weeks."

"I'm so sorry," said Bron again. "Is there anything I can do to help?"

"I could do with a drink."

There was a jug of water and a mug on the table by the bedside. She poured the water then sat beside him and cradled his head in the crutch of her arm, holding the mug to his lips while he drank deeply.

His straight yellow hair lay flat against his head and was plastered to his forehead with perspiration.

"Thanks. I wish it was wine, but I'm not allowed any. You smell good," he said as she replaced the mug on the table.

"I don't know why," she replied, and laughed. "All I can smell is fish and worse – it's so hard keeping clean on board ship, especially when – incidentally, have you had measles?"

"As a baby," he said.

"That's all right, then," and she told him about the sickness on the *Juniper*.

"Do you know much about nursing?" he asked her, and sounded hopeful.

"Not a lot but I help where I can," she replied.

"But with sickness, not broken bones?"

"I watched work being done on broken bones, when I was home, in my village. Why?"

"It's just that my leg is being tortured with Mars' javelins and I wondered if you could ease it. I wouldn't ask, but the physician isn't coming back till tomorrow and I don't think I can take much more – I'm sorry, I'm not supposed to complain, but –" He stopped, flushing with humiliation.

"It's all right," Bron soothed him. "I've heard that even Roman legionaries are human."

She was glad to see that he managed a smile.

"Haven't they left you anything to kill the pain?"

"There was a phial of poppy juice on the table, but someone stole it while I was asleep."

"Why? Is it expensive?"

"Not especially, but people use it to deaden other sorts of pain."

Bron nodded. "I have a friend downstairs, off the ship. I'll ask him to find a pharmacy and buy some more. I'll be right back."

"Promise?"

"Promise," Bron assured him.

It did not take her long to locate Koch and Layla where they were watching the farrier fashioning shoes for a carthorse and, having delivered her instructions and handed over some coins, she ran back to the room on the second floor. The young man smiled to see her return.

"You haven't told me your name," she said.

"It's Palladius. I know yours. Aurelius – Officer Catus – never stopped talking about you."

Bron felt her heart swelling with love.

"I'm glad you feel the same way about him," Palladius commented, watching the expression on her face. "He's a good man."

Gently, she pulled the thin coverlet away from his legs. The left one was bandaged over splints from his ankle, presumably up to his hip, though his tunic covered the upper part of his thighs. The leg was resting on a woollen pad inside a sturdy, hollowed-out tree branch. Seeing it, she was not sure that she had the courage to do anything that interfered with the dressing. Seeming to read her thoughts, he reassured her, "Whatever you do, I don't think you could make the pain any worse."

"I'd rather wait till the poppy juice arrives," she said, covering his legs again, and drew up a chair to sit beside him, taking his hand in hers. "I was told that Aurelius left a message for me."

"Yes, he did. I don't understand what it means, though I realise it's not good news. I would rather wait to tell you until after you'd rebandaged my leg, as it may cause your hands to shake, but I had better tell you now in case I pass out later."

Bron was puzzled but promised that, whatever the news, she would make sure her hands were steady when she touched his leg. "In any case, there can't be much he can tell me now that he couldn't tell me when he left Britannia."

"It's something that happened when we arrived here, after we'd berthed," he told her. "He saw someone he knew hanging around the dock."

Bron was mystified. "Someone?" she asked. "Who?"

"Aurelius was on deck, just watching all the activity, when he saw this person lurking in the shadows at the entrance to the fish market. The person didn't see Aurelius."

Her heart was thumping uncontrollably now, but with fear, as the young man's words at last began to make some sense.

She choked on the name. "Not Vortin?"

"I'm afraid so. Bron, go easy on my fingers."

She realised that she was digging her nails into his hand and quickly loosened her grip, and apologised.

"Vortin's here, in Felicitas?"

"He was, he met the *Eagle*, but he's left now. Aurelius wouldn't disembark but he sent a couple of men ashore. They bribed the clerk at the dock gates and were able to prevent this priest – Vortin – from getting a sight of the passenger list, though he tried. Eventually he took ship for Ostia and sailed the day before the *Eagle*." When Bron was silent, he added, "Aurelius said the priest was looking for you, and was only interested in the *Eagle* because he guessed that, if Aurelius was on board, you wouldn't be far away."

"He was right about that." Bron was puzzled. "Then why leave?"

"He wasn't sure that Aurelius was on board, and there are so many ships, military and otherwise, calling here, from all parts of Britannia, that I suppose he decided his best option was to go on to Ostia and wait there. And, of course, whatever ship you were on might not have called here, anyway."

"I hoped we had seen the last of him."

Palladius only just heard her frightened whisper and was curious. "This priest – who is he?"

While they waited for Koch to arrive with the poppy juice, and to take the young man's mind off his pain, Bron told him about the shadow that the High Priest had cast over her life since the moment she was born. She broke down in tears when she spoke of the son she had smothered, Vortin's child, and fingered the small leather pouch hanging from a thong around her neck. "We buried him by our door post and I always carry with me earth from his grave."

"So Vortin is following you to Italia?"

"It seems so," Bron replied. "Why can't he leave me alone? Is there no end to the misery he causes me?"

Before Palladius could say anything further, there was a tap at the door and Koch came into the room. Layla hovered in the doorway. Bron took the phial from Koch and would have sent them downstairs again, but Palladius said she would need another pair of hands to do what she had to do. Taking a chair into the corridor for Layla, she told her to wait quietly and not move no matter what she heard, then closed the door and returned to the bedside.

Palladius drank deeply. They waited a while for the opium to take effect, then Bron set to work, guided by his advice.

First, she and Koch together gently unwrapped the bandage, noting carefully how it had been wound, from groin to ankle, keeping in place a continuous strip of bandage on each side of the leg, which in turn kept two splints from slipping.

"Each time they rebandage, they extend my leg," Palladius told them between gritted teeth, anticipating the pain. "It will take two of you to do that."

"I'm afraid," said Bron. She looked at Koch. His face had turned sickly white.

"Go ahead, I'm used to it," Palladius assured them. "Just stretch it as straight as you can." When she still hesitated, he added, "The physician will be back to check it tomorrow, anyway."

With great trepidation, Bron sent Koch to stand behind the head of the bed, to hold Palladius under the armpits and keep him still, while she laid her hands on his leg.

"Koch, tell Palladius about what has been happening on board – about you stowing away, and the fire, and the lessons and the chickens escaping – everything."

While he did so, in a thin, strained voice that sounded more like a girl's than a hefty young farm lad's, Bron worked on hip and leg. She massaged the muscles as she had seen Veneta do many times when dealing with bone injuries, until Palladius was relaxed and sleepy. She knew it was pleasurable for him to feel the gentleness of her hands.

Then she mouthed a silent warning to Koch and, when Palladius least expected it, took hold of his ankle and pulled his leg straight towards her, praying that she was not causing him any harm. He would have leaped out of bed in agony if Koch had not been holding him in a vice-like grip.

"The worst is over now," she said, relief flooding her body and voice, and while Koch splashed cold water on their patient's face and neck, Bron deftly replaced splints and bandage.

When all was done, Bron asked Koch to take Layla downstairs again.

"How does it feel?" she asked Palladius, dreading his answer.

"It's good, much easier," she was pleased to hear. He told her what a treasure she was, and how astute his young officer had been to fall in love with her, and he could not thank her enough. "But the day may come when I can repay the good deed," he added.

Bron was preparing to leave when a sudden thought occurred to her.

"Do you know Aqintas?" she asked. "He was Zohira's husband – though they weren't married, of course – Leeza's father – the two we buried at sea."

Palladius thought for a while. "Yes, I do remember him. One of the quiet ones, never had much to say for himself."

"Veneta and I want to find him once we get to Italia, to tell him what happened to Leeza and her mother. But now we should be getting back to the ship. I'll make sure that your midday meal is being prepared."

She kissed him lightly on the forehead, pressed his hands firmly, and left.

CHAPTER 13

The fight began in the prow. It started low key, just a couple of women's voices slightly raised. Bron glanced forw'd and recognised the tall figure of Fabia, the egg stealer. Fists clenched, she was facing a much younger girl, who was not someone Bron knew well as she had never helped with the children's lessons but had preferred to spend most of her free time down in the men's quarters.

Attractive because of her youth, without being pretty, she was tossing her brown curls in defiance and describing the older Fabia in none-too-complimentary terms. The bo'sun's name was being flung from mouth to mouth across the closing gap between them. Bron was glad that her children were out of earshot.

The voices grew louder and more confrontational and a small crowd of women and children, with a sprinkling of crew, began to gather. No one was ready for what happened next. Fabia drew back her right fist and smashed it into the younger girl's face. Momentarily, there was a shocked silence, then the injured girl let out such a scream of pain as blood spurted from her nose, and she jumped upon her attacker.

Both fell to the deck, where they lay rolling over and over, sometimes one finding an advantage, sometimes the other. Teeth were used when close enough and, when not, nails and fists, knees and kicking feet. There was bright red blood everywhere.

The crowd moved back in a circle to make room for the two women as they sprawled over each other, some who were watching too horrified to make comment, others noisily urging on one or the other or both. Some of the men cheered when tunics were roughed up, revealing ample thighs and hips.

Bron noticed that the bo'sun had arrived at the edge of the crowd.

His eyes sought hers and he acknowledged her presence with a slight bow of the head before turning his attention to the fighting women. He seemed to be enjoying the spectacle but kept silent, and grinned in acknowledgement when a young sailor knowingly and playfully punched him on the arm.

It was not long before Captain Stokovius emerged from his makeshift cabin. Behind him trailed Tiegan and Joas, the twins, both holding ship's charts. The captain sent them back into the cabin.

He then motioned to several of his crew, who pushed their way through the onlookers and grappled with the two women, hauling them to their feet. The women were kicking the sailors' shins and struggling to free themselves from restricting arms and hands and, eventually, ropes. The captain ordered both to be tied to the mast, where they could kick each other to death, if they had a mind, or until both came to their senses and quietened down.

Then all eyes turned towards Tiegan, where he stood with his brother at the entrance to the captain's cabin. People began to whisper to each other. Sythia pushed forward from among the crowd and stood by her sons, her arms protectively around them.

One of the women said, "Sythia, your son was right. Tiegan was right – there *was* a fight."

"Yes, he saw it in the chicken's guts," confirmed another, nodding her head in agreement.

"Then we do have a haruspice on board, Captain," volunteered one of the crew.

"Maybe," agreed Stokovius cautiously. "We shall see. But I don't intend killing chickens just to predict the future. They're more use alive than dead. What do you say, boy?" and he turned towards Tiegan, whom his mother had pushed into the centre of the circle where, shortly before, the women had been rolling around.

"His name's Tiegan," she insisted.

"Well, Tiegan?" asked the captain.

The boy was obviously scared but looked round at all the faces gazing at him with such curiosity, and gained courage.

"I saw it plain, in the guts," he stated firmly. "I said it would be a fight between two women, didn't I?" No one could deny it.

"We'll see," reiterated the captain. "Now, everyone, back to what you were doing before we were treated to this spectacle. And you come to my cabin," he ordered the bo'sun.

The man took a detour so that he passed Bron. "Would *you* fight over me as ferociously, goddess?" he whispered to her, and laughed when she flushed with annoyance and turned from him. He reached out a hand to touch her but she was quicker than he was and had moved out of his way.

"That hateful man!" she complained to Veneta when he had gone.

"Hateful he may be, but I can't see that he can do you any harm as long as you keep your distance, especially with the captain around."

Asandra had joined them by now. "I heard the commotion from below decks," she said. "I seem to have missed all the fun."

"If you call two women rolling around deck 'fun'!" Bron replied vehemently. "It was humiliating!"

"Can't be the first time you seen women fighting over a man?" Asandra asked, amused.

"It certainly is!"

The girl sighed. "Such a sheltered life. Lucky you!"

"How is it below?" Veneta asked, changing the subject.

"The infection is winning, though they're all going to pull through, thanks be to Minerva. But Joas says he has a sore throat."

Bron remembered the boy's visit to Leeza, when he gave her the kitten. "Surely it's too soon to have been infected, but we must keep an eye on him."

The two women tied to the mast asked to be released as soon as it began to get dark and cold. The captain kept them there for another two hours, to further cool their tempers, before allowing the ropes to be loosened so that they could join their companions in the warmth of the hold. He told them he hoped they had learned their lesson and he would have no more trouble from them, otherwise they would be put ashore at the first convenient port.

On the turn of the tide late next morning, the *Juniper* left Felicitas Julia and once again sailed between the grassy, weedy banks of the River Tagus and out into the Atlantic Ocean.

CHAPTER 14

Neptune and Noden, powerful gods of sea and ship, were now smiling favourably upon the voyage. The weather stayed bright, with only an occasional rainstorm, and sufficient wind strength to give them a good run. The sea remained fairly calm but, in any case, the passengers had found their 'sea legs' and no one was being seasick any more.

Happily, the sore throat complained of by Joas developed into nothing worse than a heavy cold. The measles epidemic had caused no more deaths or serious complications and all the patients were recovering and moving back into their original accommodation, and no one was now sleeping on deck.

The *Juniper* sailed on towards the south, negotiated Sacrum Point at the southernmost tip of Lusitania, then headed east, docking at Portus Hannibalis and Hispalis before reaching the wealthy isthmus city of Gades.

The ports of call provided a welcome break. The adventurous children took every opportunity of jumping into the water in the harbours to take part in the games and races organised by the young sailors, who were very proud of the progress their pupils were making. Among the strong swimmers were Alon and Layla and one of the twins, Tiegan.

The more nervous among the children were lowered into the sea by basket, to be met by the young instructors, who dodged flailing arms and legs and encouraged them in slow but safe progress.

Joas discovered that his skills lay in seamanship and Declan allowed him to sail or row the small boats round the harbours. On one occasion he rowed through the harbour entrance, out of everyone's sight for half an hour, noticed only when he was seen returning.

In Gades harbour, however, there was no such opportunity. Large Lusitanian merchant vessels were unloading their cargoes for onward shipment to Rome, and any intervening space was filled with tiny bobbing boats that had brought in salt from the pans up river in the extensive marshes.

Their captains were shouting, cursing and swearing at their counterparts. All were jostling for anchorage and some had been quick enough to row in and berth at the jetties. Their crews were triumphant but in immediate danger of being crushed between tall sailing ships. Many vessels were anchored out in the bay, awaiting their opportunity to tie up alongside.

At each port, Bron had enquired whether the *Eagle* had berthed there and, if so, whether there was any communication for her from Aurelius. She was rewarded at Gades by a scribbled message incised on a strip of rolled-up lead, which was delivered to the ship by a market trader.

"Bron, darling," she read, *"I hope you are well. Did you receive my message through Palladius? Please don't worry. I will be waiting for you at Ostia to keep you safe. I love you to distraction. Always and ever yours, Aurelius."*

Bron had the urge to kiss the messenger, but gave him a coin instead, and hurried back to the cabin to place the strip of lead beneath her pillow and tell Veneta.

Most passengers went ashore at Gades. Bron, Veneta and the children wandered out of the port to the sandy shore, where they took off their sandals and paddled in the warm sea.

Wandering further across the sand, they chanced upon a temple dedicated to the god Cronus and sat down nearby to rest on the grass. Layla, Alon and little Lucilla amused themselves by collecting shells and pebbles and chasing each other round the rocky outcrops and up and down the steps of the temple. At sea, a fountain of water announced the presence of a whale.

Veneta sighed with contentment and lay back on the grass, hands clasped behind her head, eyes watching the flight of a heron on its way inland.

Bron, supervising the babies crawling about on a blanket, turned her attention to her friend. She thought that Veneta was looking much happier than at any time since boarding ship.

Hearing a shout, she looked up to see a figure approaching across the sand, and realised as he came nearer that it was Declan. He eased his long frame on to the grass beside them, his back to the sun, and indolently crossed his legs.

"Hope you don't mind my company."

"No lessons today?" asked Veneta, her eyes now closed.

"Nearly everyone's gone ashore, except Koch and Asandra. They're sitting close to each other on deck, engaged in a very serious conversation. The poor boy's in quite a state over that young woman."

"I hope she won't lead him on too far," murmured Veneta. "It will break his heart."

"Too far? She'll chew him up and spit him out before breakfast!" declared Declan.

Bron was occupied in preventing Gift from feeding Darius with sand. "Asandra's not as brittle as she likes to make out," she said, remembering the girl's considerable nursing skills and selflessness during the measles epidemic.

"It won't do any good to warn him," counselled Declan. "I know that I wouldn't have taken any notice at his age." He got up and joined the children at the edge of the waves, to show them how to skim pebbles.

"I think he followed you here," mumbled Veneta, her eyes still closed.

Bron was surprised. "Me? Of course not."

"Then why did he bother to come this way and spin pebbles with your children when the city must hold many more attractions for a young sailor?"

"We're friends," Bron protested, "nothing more. There's never been any suggestion of anything more. He's as friendly with you as he is with me."

"We'll wait and see, then," commented Veneta.

Bron stood up. "I'm going to explore the temple," she said. "Don't let the babies eat anything they shouldn't."

She mounted the wide flight of steps to the stone podium, passed tall pillars on each side, and entered the temple, illuminated only by daylight. It was cool in there and she spent some time studying the wall paintings and stone altar carved with a dedication to Cronus.

When she came out into the sunlight again, she was surprised to see Asandra sitting with Veneta and the babies, her arms clasped round her raised knees, chin resting on them, watching the group at the water's edge.

Koch was there, his pebbles bouncing in competition with Declan's and the children's.

"Ain't 'e a sight for sore eyes?" Asandra asked appreciatively.

"My dear, I wanted to speak to you about Koch –" began Veneta, sitting up, but the girl interrupted her.

"I wasn't meaning Koch," she said, and laughed.

"Oh." Veneta looked up at Bron, standing behind Asandra. Bron raised her eyebrows and shrugged.

"Even at your advanced age, Veneta," teased Asandra, "you can't say you 'adn't noticed those raunchy arms and shoulders." She sighed contentedly and added, almost under her breath, "And backside."

"Declan? Well, yes. But it isn't Declan I'm concerned about."

"Koch is a baby," Asandra replied dismissively, but added with enthusiasm, "though I'm teaching him how to kiss like a grown man. 'You've got a tongue in yer 'ead, 'aven't you?' I asked him. 'Then use it!' He's learning fast – I must be a good teacher – but it's only calf love he's feeling."

"Don't dismiss it," said Bron, remembering how she had fallen in love with Aurelius when she was only twelve years old. "It can wound just as deeply, and perhaps one never does fully recover from first love."

"Goodness, we *are* getting serious," commented Asandra.

Bron echoed Veneta's concern. "We just don't want him hurt."

"Oh, it's too late for that," replied the girl.

They were at that moment interrupted by loud shouting and laughing from the group on the foreshore and saw that a little white puppy with large black spots had joined the fun on the beach and was running into the water after every skimmed pebble, shaking his coat dry over the children. Several times he waited till they were about to grab him, then wagged his stubby tail and set off again.

During one of his assaults, he raced up the beach and invaded the area of the blanket, tipped up the babies where they were contentedly munching flowers, stole a toy, a misshapen rag doll, then set off towards the temple with it in his mouth, Asandra in pursuit. He scampered up the steps and disappeared inside, Asandra following. Moments later, she reappeared with him and the doll clutched tightly in her arms.

The children were delighted with their new playmate.

"We'll call him Cronus," Layla announced, "like the god."

When it was time to leave, Koch looked at Asandra appealingly but she said there was no point in going any further as there was nothing more to see, and besides, she wanted to look round the markets. So they all turned to walk back the way they had come.

Alon pleaded to take Cronus back to the ship but his mother replied firmly that he didn't belong to them and probably had a home nearby.

Everyone except Alon and Layla then forgot about the puppy but his presence following along behind became noticeable when he started sniffing and snuffling at the carcase of a long-dead rodent. Several times he was told to go away, to go home, but he persisted in pattering after them. When Bron turned round yet again, she noticed that Alon had his hands behind his back and suspected that he was quietly clicking his fingers to encourage the little dog to follow.

It was still running round between their feet when they reached the market stalls. Alon scooped it up in his arms, and squirmed with pleasure when a soft pink tongue licked his face. Bron smiled and the battle was as good as won.

"But you must ask the captain's permission to take the puppy on board," she told him.

Veneta decided that she would take the babies back to the ship and Declan said he would go with her. For once, Asandra was more interested in shopping than in following him.

Bron noticed Sythia and one of her twins and went across to speak to them. They were at a stall that sold leather goods made from skins of camels. The stallholder told them that the strange creatures had two lumps on their backs and lived in the mysterious deserts south of the Mare Nostrum. Sythia didn't take much persuasion to buy a bag with a long strap, which she slung across her shoulder and ample bosom.

Asandra meanwhile was inspecting copper jewellery enticingly displayed on black cloth on the counter of a small booth. She called Bron over and both were admiring the delicate spiral work until she noticed a thicker and heavier pendant. It was the shape of a raindrop with a large dark blue stone in the centre and five pale-blue stones hanging from short, gold coloured chains.

Asandra asked the swarthy man hovering behind the display to clasp it round her neck, which he seemed very willing to do. He picked up a polished copper mirror so that she could see the effect.

His admiration was evident, and Bron agreed that it could have been made for the girl, hanging as it did just above the deep cleft between her breasts.

Asandra also asked the price of the mirror, and fumbled in her camel-skin purse just purchased. Bron wondered where she got all her money from, which seemed not to decrease, no matter how long they remained at sea. Then she chided herself for being so naïve and felt sympathy for young, worshipping Koch, who was hovering not far away. Bron wondered whether she should speak to the captain about shipping him home as soon as possible.

It was then that Alon put Cronus down, and her thoughts were interrupted as the puppy made a dash for adventure, generally causing mayhem and outrage wherever he planted his four tiny black and white paws.

It was when he knocked little Lucilla over, bringing to the ground a stack of wickerwork baskets that bounced in confusion all around her, that Bron noticed Sythia's son behaving very strangely.

Tiegan – or was it Joas? She never could tell them apart – had left his mother's side and was sidling up to a stall selling short swords, knives and daggers. The owner of the goods had wandered out into the crowd, to see what all the commotion was about. Nonchalantly, the boy looked about him then deftly laid hold of the handle of a dagger in a decorated scabbard, removed it from the haphazard display and concealed it between the folds of his tunic.

Bron was shocked but stopped herself from crying out to Sythia for fear of the crowd turning on him and administering their own justice. So she kept quiet, deciding that, as they weren't sailing until the following morning, there was plenty of time for Sythia to discipline the boy and return the dagger.

Cronus was finally rounded up and restricted on the end of a rope held by Alon. The party, with Sythia and her son in tow, continued on its way back to the ship, buying snacks as they went. Cronus snuffled about and found plenty to eat on the ground.

Sythia, who had her arms full of parcels and yet more in her new bag, passed a large one to her son before struggling up the gangplank ahead of him. As he climbed aboard, the package shifted in his grasp and he clutched at it awkwardly, but something fell to the deck with a metallic clatter, claiming everyone's attention.

The boy stood still, holding on to the parcel and staring at the expensive dagger at his feet as if he were as surprised as everyone else to see it lying there, then looked up at his mother.

"Tiegan, where in Noden's name did you get that from?" she demanded.

Bron was glad that this twin was not Joas. They were not identical but she could only tell which twin was which when they were standing together. Of the two, Tiegan, the elder, was the more handsome – but in looks only, decided Bron, not in character.

He remained silent, looking down at the dagger. No one would believe he had bought it as the cost, in its ornate scabbard with inlaid enamel, was well beyond the purse of any of the crew or passengers on board the *Juniper*. The explanation was obvious.

Declan came over, bent down and retrieved the weapon, inspecting it admiringly.

"Young man," Sythia addressed him, "I would be obliged if you would take it to the captain. My son and I will be there directly."

She deposited her packages on deck. "Bron, may we use

your cabin? I have something to say to my son." Bron nodded sympathetically, knowing there were few places aboard ship where other passengers could not hear everything that was being said, especially in an argument.

"You, Tiegan, come with me," Sythia commanded, and they retreated into the stern cabin. Everyone else went about their business, but in silence. Shortly afterwards, Declan knocked at the door and mother and son followed him to the captain's makeshift cabin, where confession and decision about punishment were overheard.

The first act of reparation to be made by Tiegan was to go back to the stallholder, in company with Declan, and return the dagger. Sythia asked the captain to suggest further punishment, as she was determined that her son should be taught a lesson that he would remember.

The captain decided that Tiegan should become his cabin boy, at his beck and call, until the ship docked in Malaca, a week away. Sythia considered this for a moment then agreed.

"Like I say, that boy needs a father," she reiterated as a reluctant Tiegan, accompanied by the young sailor, descended the gangway to the quayside.

The crowd on deck dispersed now that all was settled.

It was unfortunate that Koch decided to collect the eggs at that moment. He opened the wire mesh door to the chicken coop at precisely the same time that Alon, arms aching, put Cronus down on the deck.

The puppy looked across to where the chickens were fussing and clucking and obviously thought he had found new playthings. He made a dash towards the coop, pulling the rope lead from Alon's hand, and again all was chaos.

Koch was able to close the door to prevent most of the terrified birds from escaping, but three had run out and were being chased and harassed by Cronus amid clucks and squawks, augmented by protests from the imprisoned cockerel. Two were rescued and returned to the coop, but the third hen was not so lucky and was in the puppy's mouth, where it died of fright in a storm of pink and silver feathers and spattered blood. The little dog continued to worry and tear at the flesh of the chicken until he was pulled off by the bo'sun, who dangled him by the scruff of his neck.

"Who brought this dog on board?" he roared.

Without waiting for a reply, he strode to the starboard rail and threw the puppy into the waters of the harbour.

There came an agonised cry from Alon and, before anyone could stop him, he ran to the side of the ship, kicking off his sandals and pulling off his tunic as he went, climbed upon the rail, and jumped into the sea after his pet.

"Alon!" Bron cried in alarm as she and everyone else rushed to look over the rail. Alon was nowhere to be seen. She screamed, and then the boy surfaced and there was a sigh of relief from the crowd. He began to swim towards the puppy, which was struggling in the water and managing to keep afloat, but was being taken further away from the ship by the outgoing tide.

Then there was another figure, tunic discarded, tall and muscular, poised on the ship's rail, diving into the water to safely reappear moments later. Beefy arms rose and dipped above a short-cropped, silver head and strong bare legs kicked out purposefully. It took Bron several seconds to realise that she was looking down at the bo'sun in the water.

Alon had reached the puppy by now and was holding it in his arms, treading water, and calling for help. Then he must have taken in a mouthful off the top of a wave because he let go of the struggling and splashing dog and sank below the surface.

"Help him!" screamed Bron. The bo'sun dived.

"If that man drowns because of you and your brat," hissed a voice in her ear, "you'll be the next one over the side!"

Bron turned to find Fabia standing behind her. The venom in the woman's voice surprised her.

"He won't drown," Veneta said. "Look!"

Bron looked and, to her great relief, saw the bo'sun's head breaking surface, one arm holding Alon beneath his armpit, the other arm working hard to bring them both to safety.

Alon was making the task more difficult by struggling and reaching out towards the puppy, which was still paddling about in the water. The man said something to the boy, who then kept quite still and allowed himself to be brought to the ship's side. A rope was lowered, Alon was tied to it by his rescuer, and he was slowly hauled up and on to the deck.

The bo'sun meantime had returned to the still struggling puppy, which was staying afloat but obviously tiring. The man grabbed him by the scruff of his neck and swam back to the ship. Holding him with one hand and the rope with the other, he allowed himself to be raised to the rail, then clambered over to safety.

Bron had Alon in a tight embrace and was rocking him backwards and forwards and kissing his wet hair. Fabia rushed to the bo'sun, threw her arms round his wet body and clung to him, squashing the puppy, but he pushed her away, extremely roughly, Bron thought.

He looked at Alon enviously, then at Bron. "When's my turn?" he asked and laughed at her embarrassment.

Veneta came through the throng and wrapped a towel round Alon. "I'll dry him off," she said. "You had better go and make your peace with the captain."

Bron looked over to where Captain Stokovius stood, legs apart, arms folded across his chest, his stance expressing authority, but his face displaying bewilderment.

"Cronus!" called Alon from inside the towel, looking for his pet.

The bo'sun placed the puppy on the deck, where it shook itself vigorously, then trotted after his young master, who was following Veneta towards the cabin.

The man shrugged. "Dogs will be dogs," he said philosophically.

Someone brought him his tunic and sandals. He stood facing Bron, not at all in a hurry to cover his near-naked body. She was conscious of his size and the raw muscle-power of his chest, covered as it was with thick, silver hair, and his powerful arms and legs.

There was a painting of a voluptuous girl on his stomach and the girl's body moved sinuously as he breathed. Bron's eyes were drawn to it, and as he watched her intently, the movement increased.

She raised her eyes to his. "I cannot thank you enough –" she began as he ran his thick fingers through his hair and shook out the water, as the dog had done.

He laughed. "Give me time and I'm sure I'll think of a way," he said.

Bron blushed furiously and made her escape by walking across to the captain.

"I'm so sorry," she told him. "We were on our way to ask your permission to bring the puppy on board."

The captain looked defeated. "Do you ever get the feeling that everything is out of control?" he asked her. When she did not reply, he exclaimed with exasperation, "Women and children! Women and children!" and turned to walk away.

"The puppy?" ventured Bron.

"If it misbehaves again, it will go over the side and stay there!" he replied over his shoulder.

But that was not the end of his worries that day. While everyone was engaged on the starboard side of the ship, no one except Asandra had noticed the return of Declan and Tiegan from on shore.

She drew Bron's attention to the boy, who was standing quite still, looking down at the chicken carcase where Cronus had left it, now in a much worse mess as several people had trodden on it and flattened it in their rush to the rail.

"Come away, Tiegan," Asandra urged him, but he stood like a statue until others noticed him, and nudged each other, and passed the word around that the boy was once again gazing at the entrails of a mutilated chicken.

Sythia came over to ask Declan if the stallholder had been amenable once his dagger had been returned.

"Hush!" Tiegan interrupted his mother and held up his hand for silence. Those watching obeyed. Declan left the crowd to fetch the captain again, who had by now wearily returned to his cabin.

"What do you see?" asked someone.

"Another fight?" sneered Fabia. "Murder even?" and she glared across at Bron.

"Tiegan, son –" began Sythia, who sounded as if she had lost her sense of humour.

"Hush!" ordered the boy again. This time, everyone fell silent, even his mother. He hesitated. Bron had the feeling that he didn't know what to say next.

"Well?" It was Joas who asked the question.

Bron thought that he too was looking unconvinced by his brother's sudden discovery of this gift of divination.

"I see –" began Tiegan and looked at his twin, then took a deep breath. "A storm," he continued, "a storm at sea."

No one spoke for a moment then a sailor laughed. His mates joined in the ridicule.

Tiegan looked disconcerted. "It'll be a big one," he said in vindication, "and put the ship in danger."

The knot of onlookers parted to make way for the captain.

"How soon and how much danger?" he demanded.

"He was right about the women fighting," said one of the legionaries.

"If he's right about this, I'm jumping ship!" muttered a passenger.

"Think about what you're saying, boy," warned the captain.

"He told us about the fight," said the legionary again.

"Yes, but they were always squabbling in and out of our hammocks – it wasn't the first time," volunteered another.

"But the boy couldn't have known that."

Tiegan seemed to retreat into himself and mumbled, "I'm not sure."

"You've not told us anything we don't know already," said the captain. "There are always storms at sea and every storm puts ships in danger, but my ship and my crew are a match for anything the Mare Nostrum can throw at us."

The crew were agreeing with their captain and the faces of people around Bron relaxed.

"It occurs to me," the captain continued, "that you are trying to take our minds off your theft and the punishment your mother and I have agreed to carry out. If that is the case, you're unlucky. Come to my cabin, boy, and I will instruct you on the duties you will perform for me until we reach Malaca."

"His name's Tiegan," insisted his mother.

The captain turned towards his cabin, followed by Sythia and her son.

"But he *was* right about the fight," insisted the legionary.

CHAPTER 15

The passengers who crowded against the ship's rails gazed in wonder at the two-miles-long, sheer, pale grey limestone cliff of Mount Calpe as the *Juniper* sailed through the narrow entrance, twelve miles wide only, and entered the Mare Nostrum.

"We're nearly home – this is Our Sea," Declan told the children.

"Whose sea?" asked Alon.

"Rome's. It's completely surrounded by the empire."

The port of Malaca came and went and Tiegan was released from his duties. Bron knew that they had not been onerous and her respect and affection for Captain Stokovius increased.

Still hugging the coast, the *Juniper* reprovisioned at Carthago Nova then set a north-easterly course for a group of islands. At Balearis Major, the largest, most of the passengers and crew disembarked, congregating on the white sandy foreshore.

Cronus was now accepted as a member of the passenger list by all but the ship's cat and her kitten, and Alon spent a lot of time teaching the puppy to behave, which he did, most of the time. His occasional uninvited excursions into the galley were kept secret through the goodwill of the cook.

Bron watched the dog now, her thoughts elsewhere. He was excitedly running in and out of the waves, chasing the children or trying to catch the large dark brown and white fish-hawks as they plunged into the sea then headed inland with squirming fish clutched in their talons.

"Sythia," Bron asked, as they spread a cloth on the sand, "what do *you* think about Tiegan's prophecy of a storm?"

Sythia considered a moment. "I'm not sure, lovely," she said.

"As people keep telling me, 'e *was* right about the fight between Fabia and that other girl."

"But they also say anyone could have seen it coming."

"That's the bo'sun's fault," Asandra told them. "It's just his game, playing one off against the other. He's very practised at it." Then she added, in a lower voice, "Though–"

Veneta was unwrapping knives and spoons borrowed from the cook.

"Though what?" she asked.

"Can't explain – evil, maybe."

Veneta looked at her sharply before resuming her task. "A belief in good and evil? I thought that was the prerogative of us Christians. Didn't know you believed in evil, Asandra."

"Now you're making fun of me, Veneta. I believe in evil all right. You can't do what I do and not meet it sometimes. I don't just mean doing things *you* wouldn't dream of doing, Veneta. I mean deep, dark places where even I wouldn't want to go – no other word for it – evil."

She gazed towards the horizon. The water was calm and had been since the *Juniper* had sailed into this inner sea, the sun was shining and the temperature was pleasantly warm. The natural peace and beauty lightened everyone's mood.

"Can't imagine a storm on a day like this," Asandra said.

Declan arrived then, struggling up the beach with a wooden crate that he had brought over in the rowing boat. "What do you think, Declan?"

"Can happen, though," he said as he deposited the crate on the sand. "I've seen storms blow up in this sea from nowhere. Can happen."

"But not today, not here, it's too perfect," purred Asandra. "Coming down to the water, Declan? I'm going for a paddle." She hitched her tunic up so that he could not avoid seeing her shapely, sun-burnished legs. Even so, he hesitated.

"I'll come," Koch offered.

"Oh, I knew *you* would!" retorted Asandra, dropping her tunic. "Come on, then."

"I'll race you there!"

"If you must." Asandra sighed and set off half-heartedly, her heavy pendant bumping up and down on her chest.

"Sythia, did you know that Joas has rowed a long way out in that little boat?" Veneta asked, shading her eyes against the sun.

"No, I didn't." Sythia was unpacking food from the crate but now stood and looked to where Veneta was pointing.

"Will he be all right, do you think? I know there's very little tide, but if he loses an oar or falls overboard —"

"I'll swim out and bring him in," Declan offered and sprinted down to the water's edge, discarding sandals and tunic. He waded out until he was in deep water, then struck out towards the boat, which was drawing further and further away from the shore.

Bron and Veneta linked their arms through Sythia's as they stood squinting against the sun. Most of the people at the shoreline, and the few who were swimming around, had stopped whatever they were doing and were also watching the intended rescue. Only the children were unaware of any anxiety.

Asandra had already tired of the company of Koch, who had won their race easily, and was walking back up the beach, gathering Declan's discarded clothing as she came. She buried her face in his tunic.

"That smells good," she said. "All male — fresh air, salt, sea and sweat. A pity he's not inside it at this minute."

Sythia made a sound that was something like a snort. "You're too hot for your own good, my girl!" she admonished her. Asandra looked unabashed.

They continued to gaze out to sea, where Declan was slowly gaining on the boat, his head now just an appearing and disappearing black blob near the horizon.

Bron resumed the subject that had been bothering her. "About Tiegan's prophecy, Sythia —"

"The captain said the ship can withstand any storm," Veneta interrupted, "and I trust him."

"There were other things Tiegan told me," Sythia replied, now sounding troubled herself.

"What things?" asked Asandra with interest.

"I'd rather not say."

"You mean you won't say while I'm listening," Asandra guessed. "All right, I'll go. I think it's a lot of nonsense, anyway." She turned and walked towards the watchers at the edge of the waves. It was just possible to see Declan climbing into the boat.

"Do you want to tell us?" asked Veneta.

"I'll be glad to tell someone," Sythia replied. "I've been bottling it up for days." She paused, then her words came in a rush.

"Tiegan wasn't sleeping well when he was in the men's quarters, away from me, as part of his punishment. I know it was bad, what he did, but he's still only a little boy. He was having nightmares, but the men just threw things at him and told him to be quiet. He's still having them, although he's back with me at night – very vivid he says they are."

"What's in his nightmares?" asked Bron.

"One of them concerns you," Sythia continued, "although they're all mixed up. First there's the storm, and it's a very bad one. Tiegan says that the ship is being smashed to pieces and there are bodies in the water, but they're not anyone he knows, all strange men, except for the bo'sun – he's there, laughing and drowning. There are fires on board –" Sythia paused.

"If anyone hears this," interrupted Veneta, "they'll all be jumping ship, then none of us will reach Ostia."

"I want to know," insisted Bron.

"Best not to know, Bron," counselled Veneta. "It will give you nightmares as well. Sythia can tell us when we get to Ostia."

"*If* we get to Ostia," mumbled Sythia.

"In his nightmares, am I and the children drowned?" asked Bron hesitantly.

"No, dear, you're not in the sea."

Veneta changed the subject. "Look, the boat's back."

As they watched, Declan replaced the oars in the rowlocks and jumped into the lazy waves. He waded to shore, pulling the little boat behind him, with Joas still sitting on the thwart. When it grounded on sand and Joas had clambered out, he dragged it up the slope and overturned it.

Sythia hurried to meet her son. Bron and Veneta left Darius and Gift playing beneath a makeshift shelter and followed her. Tiegan gave his brother a welcome thump on the back.

"Are you all right, son?" Sythia asked him. "You shouldn't have gone out that far."

"It was fun," he said, beaming. "I don't know why everyone was so worried."

"He was in no danger," Declan reassured her. "In fact, he can handle the boat very well for a young'un. Still, Joas, you shouldn't go out so far and worry your mother like that."

"I knew he'd be all right," said Tiegan.

The crowd split up, and Asandra helped Declan back into his tunic then attempted to tidy his hair but Bron saw that he was paying more attention to Cronus than he was to the girl.

After their meal, the children wanted to explore inland. Sythia said she was too old to go exploring and would pack up the remains of the food then return to the ship.

"Stack it up here and I'll collect it when we come back from our walk," Declan told her. "Joas and I will row it back in the boat."

Leaving her busily cleaning the crockery and cutlery in the sand, the rest of the party set off into the grassland behind the shore.

The children raced ahead with the puppy, playing hide-and-seek, splashing in and out among the tall grasses of the marshland and occasionally bringing Bron a bouquet of feathery fronds or wild gladioli the colour of the Mare Nostrum sunsets.

She tried to keep up with them but was carrying little Lucilla and found the pace difficult, so sent Koch ahead to make sure they were taking care.

Veneta, with Darius and Gift, was even slower. When Declan noticed that she was falling behind, he excused himself, and went back to her, Asandra trailing behind him.

Bron followed the children a little further, but there were no paths through the marshes and when her clothes started to cling because of the hot, damp air and she was having to dodge the toads that had made the area their home, she called to Koch and the children and they all retraced their steps to the foreshore. Leaving Declan and Joas loading up the boat, they continued on towards the ship.

Bron was surprised when Tiegan came to walk beside her. For a while he said nothing and eventually she broke the silence.

"Are you feeling well, Tiegan? You're unusually quiet."

The boy hesitated. "Mother says I shouldn't tell you," he said at last.

"Then you had better not."

"It's about my dreams."

Bron was very curious but was reluctant to disobey Sythia's wishes. She said nothing.

"Mother didn't actually say that I shouldn't, but it was better if I kept quiet about it. That's quite different, isn't it?"

"I suppose so."

"Bron, do you believe I see things that are going to happen?"

"Do you believe you do?"

"It started as a joke, you know, the fight – but sometimes I do seem to know things."

"Then this latest warning wasn't a joke, to take everyone's attention off what you did?"

"It started out like that, but then it changed. I really have had some bad nightmares."

"Your mother said one was about me."

"Yes, but nothing to do with the storm."

"What then?"

"Bron, be careful. There's someone wants to hurt you."

"Do you know who it is?"

"It's just a shadow, a big shadow. I hear you screaming."

In spite of the warm sun, Bron's back felt cold and clammy.

"Is there anything else, Tiegan?"

"Yes, but I don't understand it – ropes and carved granite faces and the rowing boat, all jumbled up – but I do understand the big shadow and you screaming."

"Thank you for telling me. You should let your mother know that you have."

Tiegan nodded. "She says you shouldn't go about on your own."

As they boarded ship, the bo'sun was disembarking. He waited at the top of the gangway as the party ascended, but when Bron set foot on the bottom step, he chose to descend. There was room for him to pass Veneta, Asandra and the children, and even Koch when he turned sideways, but as he reached Bron, he purposefully turned to face her and his broad frame precluded any chance of her climbing past him. She stood looking up uncertainly, hoping he would make way for her, but obviously that was not his intention.

In response to his insolent study of her, she pulled the neckline of her tunic higher, to cover her bare chest and neck, and was mortified when she realised he had noticed her unconscious reaction and was amused by it. She flushed, then decided she would not be discomfited in this way and stared at him defiantly. He laughed.

"Ah, goddess, it's not many days since you almost threw yourself into my arms for rescuing your son. Has your gratitude wilted so soon?"

"Of course not, and as I said at the time, there is no way I can –"

"I was coming to that. You'll be pleased to know that I *have* thought of a way – I said I would. In fact, it didn't take long."

When she didn't reply, he said, "Aren't you going to ask me what you can do for me in return?" When she still remained silent, desperate to extricate herself from this embarrassing confrontation but not willing to squeeze past him, he spoke to her again, his voice low, his words full of innuendo.

"Of course, the ship is not the best place for what I have in mind, but if you will walk with me a way, I'm sure we could find somewhere along the shore, somewhere secluded, where no one will ever know…"

He moved down towards her and she stepped backwards, almost losing her balance, so that he grasped an arm to steady her. Bron felt the power of this man who towered above her, not just his physical strength but his blatant masculinity. As his hand moved up her arm to her shoulder then neck, involuntarily she closed her eyes and inclined her head until her ear touched his hand.

He came down another step. "Goddess, come with me. I'll make you forget your Roman officer."

At the mention of Aurelius, Bron came to her senses and opened her eyes wide and regarded him with horror.

Suddenly, there was a roar from above and they both looked up to see the captain leaning over the ship's rail, staring down at them. Bron wondered how long he had been standing there.

"Bo'sun! Let the young lady pass! Where are your manners, man?"

The bo'sun turned back to Bron. "Oh, dear," he said, amused, "I seem to be poaching." Then, turning back, he called, "Yes, Cap'n, sorry Cap'n!" and moved aside to let Bron pass, giving her only just enough room. As she did so, he brought the hand hidden from view from above round to her buttocks and pressed firmly, holding her body hard against his.

"Goddess," he whispered in her ear, "I can wait – but don't leave it too long."

Flustered, she ran up the remaining steps and almost into the arms of the captain, who had moved across to the top of the gangway.

"Thank you, Captain," she said breathlessly, and hurried towards her cabin.

Stokovius's eyes followed her, then he looked back to the dockside where he could hear voices, the bo'sun's and a woman's, raised in argument. He was just in time to see her, one of his passengers, slap the bo'sun's face. He was not surprised when the bo'sun returned the slap – not too hard, or he would have knocked the woman unconscious.

She came on board, crying, one hand over the mark that was gradually reddening her cheek. He tried to remember what the other women called her – Fabia, he thought.

The sooner we get to Ostia and get rid of these women, the better! he decided, but this thought was overshadowed by another that he had not been acknowledging even to himself. There was one on board to whom he would be very reluctant to bid farewell, one he needed to talk to very seriously before she travelled on to Rome and he returned home to Avala.

CHAPTER 16

"Who wants me?" Bron asked the sailor.

The children and puppy had been in bed an hour when one of the crew came looking for Bron. She was sitting on deck with Veneta and Sythia and some of the other women, talking over the day's happenings.

There was intense speculation about how Fabia had come by the large red weal on her cheek. No one had seen who had hit her, and she was not about to tell, but for a couple of hours she had been screeching and throwing anything she could lay hands on around the women's quarters, which now looked like a battlefield. Veneta had tried to calm her but had received a mouthful of invective and was pushed to the floor for her trouble. Finally, Fabia had curled up in a ball on someone's mattress and sobbed herself to sleep, where she had remained.

"A young lad," the sailor replied to Bron's query. "He says he has a message for you. A Roman officer off the *Eagle* paid him to deliver it to the ship."

Bron jumped up excitedly.

"Where is he?" asked Veneta.

"On the dockside. He says he won't leave till he gives his message to the young lady known as Bron."

"I'll come with you," Veneta offered.

"No need," replied Bron gaily, "I'll be back directly," and left them.

She saw the lad waiting at the bottom of the gangway and light-heartedly ran down to speak to him.

"I'm Bron," she told him breathlessly. "I believe you have a message for me."

He nodded but made no comment, looking past her, over her shoulder.

Too late came the realisation that all was not well. She turned and was dismayed to see the bo'sun. His face was flushed, the rims of his eyes were red and there was a wild look in them that frightened her. She turned to mount the gangplank again, but her right arm was forced up behind her back and a large hand placed over her mouth.

"Don't struggle and I won't hurt you," he hissed in her ear, but when he relinquished his grip on her arm and took hold of the leather pouch round her neck, she began to struggle violently, trying to protect the pouch and its contents. Her assailant prised her hands off it and wrenched at the leather thong, then used both hands to pull at it until it snapped, the friction grazing her neck.

Bron didn't know if he was aware that the pouch contained only earth from her son's grave. He threw it at the boy.

"There's your pay!" he said. "And I don't want to see you around 'ere any more!" Frightened, the boy scampered off.

Bron was about to scream, but the bo'sun's hand was over her mouth again.

"Sorry, goddess," he apologised and must have hit her then because she seemed to fly backwards down a long tunnel, the light at the far end gradually receding, and remembered no more.

Asandra joined the group on deck a quarter of an hour later. Veneta wondered out loud what Bron could be doing, as she hadn't returned.

"Chatting, I expect," guessed Sythia.

Time passed. Veneta checked their cabin then led Sythia and Asandra to the top of the gangplank to look over the rail, but Bron was nowhere in sight.

Veneta felt uneasy. "Let's go ashore," she suggested, "and make some enquiries. We'll split up and meet back here shortly. I'm probably being over-protective but I'm not taking any chances."

When they gathered again on the quayside, and there was still no sign of Bron, they discussed the possibilities.

"She's gone off with whoever brought the message," suggested Asandra.

"She wouldn't do that without telling us," Veneta said.

"I don't like it, lovely," worried Sythia. "After what Tiegan warned, I'm thinking the worst."

"Where's the bo'sun?" Veneta asked suddenly.

"He came ashore hours ago," Asandra told her. "Remember, he was leaving the ship as we got back."

"Has anyone seen him since?"

"It was him who hit Fabia, you know," volunteered Asandra, "and that was *before* he got roaring drunk – one of the girls said she'd seen him on the quay much later, staggering about."

They stood aside to make way for some of the returning legionaries. The men had collected their pay at the port authority office and probably had already spent most of it in the local wine shops and brothels and were now very unsteady on their feet. One of them accidentally kicked something and bent to pick it up, swaying as he did so.

"My luck's in," he announced. He fumbled at the leather thong, turned the pouch upside down and began to shake the contents into the palm of his hand, then snorted.

His friends laughed. "Not so lucky," said one. "A handful of earth won't buy what you want," and they climbed the gangplank, still laughing. The legionary threw the pouch down in disgust and followed them.

Veneta bent to retrieve it.

"It's Bron's," she said. "She wears it round her neck. The thong's broken."

"Noden! It took a strong pair of 'ands to do that!" commented Sythia.

"I'm going to see the captain," Veneta declared, and hurried up the gangplank, the others following.

Captain Stokovius listened to her anxiously then organised several search parties from among the men, who hurriedly disembarked, leaving only a skeleton crew on board.

When Bron opened her eyes, she was in semi-darkness and lying on something soft. Her head was pounding, her jaw was painful and the muscles at the top of her right arm and shoulder ached, but she seemed unharmed otherwise. She moved her arms and legs gently and discovered there were no ropes holding her down.

Turning only her head, she looked about her. An oil lamp burning on a shelf in one corner gave sufficient light for her to see that she was in a very small room with wooden walls. The bo'sun was sitting in a chair, slumped over a table. He was moaning quietly.

Bron had no doubt why she had been brought here, wherever it was, and he was probably just waiting for her to wake up. She cursed herself for being a fool. He had known that he only had to bait a trap with the name of Aurelius and she would come running right into it.

But she would be missed on board. She didn't know how long she had been lying here or how far away from the ship they were, but people would be looking for her, and she knew the ship wouldn't sail without her. She could trust the captain for that.

Quietly, she rolled on to her side and sat up, swinging her legs to the floor. Her sandals had been removed and her bare feet touched wood. Unfortunately, the iron frame of the bed on which she had been lying squeaked and the bo'sun raised his head from his arms. Quickly, she dropped back on the mattress and lay quite still.

He picked up the lamp and came over and stood above her.

"Awake, goddess?" he asked her and his voice was thick with alcohol and his words were slurred. "I didn't want to hit you, you know, but you started screaming."

She tried to ask, "Where are we?" but no sound came, so she tried a second time, with no better result.

"What we both need is a drink," he said, and returning to the table, unsteadily poured what she hoped was water into a glass and brought it to her. She raised her head to drink. When she found it was neat alcohol, she sipped only enough to lubricate her lips and throat. He tried to pour more into her mouth but she closed it tightly and the liquid ran over her chin and down her neck. He returned to the table and drank deeply from the bottle.

If I can keep him drinking, she thought, laying back on the bed, *I may be able to get away.*

As if reading her thoughts, he warned, "Don't think of escaping.

You don't know where we are but the sea is out there and the long foreshore, and you could walk all night and never find your way back to the ship. Of course, our revered captain will be looking for you, and he might find you in the morning with luck, but that gives us the rest of the night – time enough. I doubt though that I will have had my fill of you by morning, and if I haven't, I'll take you with me. It goes without saying that I can't return to the ship."

Bron said nothing but now horror overcame her. She was remembering another night, another bed, ten years ago. The man had been Vortin, the High Priest. But she had been a child then with a child's innocence. Now she was a woman, and stronger, though her strength was nothing compared to this man's. However, he was drunk and getting drunker. Perhaps he would pass out.

He came over to her again and knelt beside her. In the flickering light, he stroked her hair and caressed her face and neck, then licked the alcohol off her chest. She turned her head away. But he put his arms round her and pulled her up to him, almost squeezing the breath from her. She was surprised at his lack of haste, his gentleness almost. She struggled and put her head down against his chest and her hands on his biceps and tried to push him away, but before she tried it she knew the attempt would be futile.

"How long?" he was asking her. "How long have you wanted me to hold you like this, my beautiful goddess?"

"I haven't," she protested, and struggled against him again, but he seemed to enjoy it and laughed, so she stopped.

"But I've seen you looking at me when you thought I wasn't noticing. I've seen your lips parted and those two beautiful breasts heaving at the thoughts inside your head."

"I haven't, I-I-I haven't!" Bron stammered, her words almost incoherent between gasps for breath. A cloud of alcoholic fumes was enveloping her and, without meaning to or even wanting to, suddenly she knelt up, her arms went round his neck, and she was responding hungrily and passionately to his kisses.

He paused and she wondered why, till she felt her tunic, then her undershift, fall from her shoulders. Then his hands and lips and teeth were all over her, and she was letting him move from breasts to mouth then back again, then lower, his tongue and lips searching ever lower. And she was helping him, and seemed to be watching herself from the ceiling, and was appalled, but there was nothing she could do about it.

He laid her down and now his large, groping hands were caressing her stomach and hips. She placed her hands over his, guiding them when they fumbled and searched, her mouth all the while reaching for his kisses. She was giving him permission he had not sought or expected and he chuckled hoarsely.

"This was to have been a rape," he slurred, "but you have made it so easy for me, goddess – easier than I ever imagined." He was panting heavily now. "But you won't be a goddess much longer because I'm going to spoil you for everyone else – for the captain and your Roman officer. You'll pay for all those haughty looks and sneers you sent in my direction." He stretched himself out on top of her, and at last was frenzied, tugging at his clothes and hers.

Then something inside Bron cracked. He was Vortin again and her terror returned. She heard Vortin whispering, as he had all those years ago, "Just you and me, Bron, night after night. Just you and me, Bron."

She brought her knee up to her waist then and kicked the bo'sun right where she knew it would hurt him most. He yelled with pain and fell off the bed, giving her the chance to gather up her tunic and stumble round him. She didn't know where the door was but blew out the lamp and in panic began feeling her way round the walls. She didn't realise it, but she was screaming now for the help that she had little hope of attracting.

Suddenly, though, the door burst open amid a confusion of shouts and flaring torches and someone threw a cloak round her. There followed a roaring in her head as she registered the captain's fury, then a bellow of pain, before everything went quiet. As she slipped in and out of consciousness, she was aware of being carried a long distance, safe now in strong arms.

CHAPTER 17

She finally awoke, crying.

"Hush, hush," someone was whispering, and a wet cloth was gently wiping her face and neck.

"Veneta?"

"Yes, my darling. Hush, now. You're safely back on board."

"Where's the bo'sun?" she asked in panic.

"The captain's dealing with him. Don't think about him, Bron dear. Are you hurting anywhere?"

"My head feels twice its size, and I think he hit me on the jaw, and my right arm and shoulder hurt."

"Bron, he didn't...?"

"No, he didn't," Bron whispered, and thought, *but it wasn't for want of encouragement – dear Shubinata, goddess of the Atrebates, what have I done? What possessed me that I would have welcomed him into me? I'm so ashamed. And he knows. He knows! I will deny it but he knows, and so do I and so do you!* And she began to cry again.

Veneta misjudged the reason for her grief. "It's all right, you're safe now. Hush, Bron dear, you're safe now."

But Bron knew she wasn't safe from herself, though how could she tell Veneta all this? How could she tell anyone?

"Where are the children?"

"I took them down to Sythia for the night. The babies are here in the cabin, fast asleep."

"How did the captain find me?"

"When you didn't return," Veneta told her, "he organised several search parties. Someone was told that the bo'sun had been hanging around the fishermen that afternoon, asking to rent one of their huts along the foreshore. It was just a matter of time till they found out which one."

"I need to sleep now," said Bron.

"Is there anything I can bring you?"

"Perhaps the cook has a sleeping draught?"

Veneta returned with a concoction mixed by the cook and Bron drank it gratefully. Veneta left her to sleep, but she couldn't and stayed awake a long time, running through her aching head every detail of the evening's events. As appalled as she was by her behaviour with the bo'sun, whom she wanted to loathe, she could still feel primitive urges inside her, to the point when she almost wished she had not been rescued quite so soon.

Dear Shubinata – help me, she prayed. It was as if the man had cast a spell on her. She was reflecting that she and Fabia had more in common than that woman would ever know, when she fell into a deep sleep.

Next morning, when she awoke, she knew by the movement of the ship and the creaking of timbers that they were at sea. Veneta brought their breakfasts to the cabin when she refused to put in an appearance on deck.

"What has happened to the bo'sun?" she eventually asked.

"He's been tied to the masthead since being brought back on board," Veneta told her. "They've been throwing buckets of cold water over him all night. They need him sober so that –" Veneta hesitated.

"So that what?" asked Bron.

"So that he feels every whiplash."

"What?!"

"The captain has ordered him to be whipped later this morning."

Bron was horrified. "How many?"

"As many as he can withstand."

"But that's barbaric," Bron protested.

Veneta looked at her keenly. "What he did to you, or intended, was also barbaric, Bron. He was drunk and he's powerful and he could have killed you. It's quite possible he would have done, afterwards. Have you thought about that?"

Bron hadn't and said so.

"It seems the captain is taking the whole affair more seriously than you are."

"But, Veneta, don't you think it's barbaric?"

"Until now, I've only been thinking about you, dear. Perhaps the captain won't go as far as that, when it comes to it."

"Have you ever seen a man whipped?" Bron asked her. Veneta shook her head. "No, nor have I, but Aurelius has told me about whipping as punishment in the Roman Army, and even he wouldn't go into details."

Veneta was silent for a moment. "The captain is a good man," she said at last. Bron knew that was true but wondered whether he was also a revengeful man.

The punishment was timed for mid-morning.

There was a knock on the door and Veneta opened it. Declan was standing there.

"The captain wants to know whether you wish to be present," he told Bron.

"No, and he can't make me!"

Declan seemed taken aback by her vehemence. "There's no question of making you, he was just asking."

"Issuing invitations? Well, I'm declining this one!"

"Are all the children below decks?" Veneta asked anxiously.

"Yes, we've seen to that. Most of the women are staying below with them, though some are coming to watch. Fabia says she wants a front seat!"

Veneta settled the matter. "Would you tell the captain that we're staying here."

"I will," Declan said. "I'm glad; it's not something women should see."

As soon as he had shut the cabin door, Bron threw herself on to her mattress and pulled the covers over her head and buried herself in them. She felt Veneta lie beside her, waiting.

A bell rang and suddenly there was a lot of movement on deck.

"What are you thinking, Veneta?" Her voice was muffled under the bedclothes.

"That it's too beautiful a day for this to be happening," Veneta replied.

"It's all my fault," wailed Bron, turning on to her side and bringing her knees up to her chin, a position she found comforting. Veneta's head lay heavy on Bron's hip as her friend tried to soothe her.

"Of course it isn't. You couldn't help what was in that man's head. He's been leering at you since the day we came on board."

Bron peered over the covers. She was sure that all the guilt she was feeling was showing in her face. "Veneta, have you ever seen me leering at him?"

"Good God, Bron, of course not. Whatever put that thought in your head?"

"He did. He said I wanted him as much as he wanted me. Did I, Veneta, did I? Did I inflame him so much that what he did yesterday really was my fault?"

"Bron, stop this! Of course you didn't want it to happen!"

"Because if it was, I should be out there, sharing his punishment!"

"Don't be so ridiculous!" exclaimed Veneta. "This has all been too much for you, it's fevered your brain!"

They heard the captain's command ring out, and waited, breath held. After a few seconds came the swish of the first whiplash. It was followed by another, and another. There was no cry of pain, no sound other than the gasps of those watching and the hiss of the lash through the air and then the thwack! as it found its target and bit into flesh. After the third lashing, the crowd fell silent.

Bron put her fingers in her ears and retreated under the covers again.

Eventually she reappeared and looked at Veneta's pinched, white face. There was another hiss and thwack.

"How many?" she asked, tonelessly.

"I've lost count."

"It's enough!" screamed Bron, and pulling the covers round her, she stumbled forward.

"Bron, don't go out there!" pleaded Veneta.

"I have to!" she cried and flung open the door. Veneta followed.

The sight that greeted them stopped them in their tracks. Some eyes turned towards them, but the lashing continued. The sailor administering the punishment at that moment was tiring and, on a nod from the captain, his place was taken by another.

Captain Stokovius stood to one side of the mast, legs apart, arms folded, his face a mask. Bron looked for some sign of compassion, some twitch of the mouth, a narrowing of the eyes, a movement of the hand to stop the merciless punishment, but there was none.

She looked then at the figure tied to the mast. The bo'sun's tunic had been removed and he wore nothing more than his linen undergarment, which Bron was only too aware she had felt against her skin the evening before. Now it was in shreds where the whip has missed its intended target.

Collapsed, his face pressed against the mast, he was hanging only from his wrists by ropes that cut into his flesh, sending rivulets of blood running down his bare arms and into the matted silver hair under his armpits. The skin on his biceps, shoulders and back was unrecognisable, it was so criss-crossed with cuts and welts and deep wounds, with flesh flapping and blood running free, some congealing in the hot sun.

She saw that quite a few of the men present, as well as most of the women, were studying the wooden planks of the deck, or their shuffling feet, or looking out to sea. One or two at the back of the crowd were creeping away.

Then from the bo'sun came a low moan. It was the first sound he had made.

The captain looked across to the sailor who now held the whip and who was hesitating.

"What are you waiting for?" he bellowed.

"No!" shrieked Bron.

The bo'sun was no longer the centre of attention as she stood there shaking, the bedclothes wrapped round her. The sailor still hesitated.

"Do as I ordered!" bellowed the captain again.

"No, Captain, please!" she begged. "He's had enough. Can't you see you're killing him?"

"It will take much more than this to kill him!"

The captain looked at her, and she knew she was not beautiful today, but white faced and red-eyed, her hair dishevelled, her hands white-knuckled as she clutched at the bed covers.

"If I had my way, he'd never stand up again!"

Bron stumbled over to him and went down on her knees, clasping him round the waist. The covers fell to the deck over her legs and feet, leaving her shivering in her nightshift, in spite of the heat.

"Please, Captain," she begged again. "He didn't hurt me. You got there too soon for that. Please, Captain, he's had enough!"

"Not yet he hasn't!" yelled a voice and Bron turned her head to see Fabia shaking her fists at the man she was said to love. The woman darted forward, snatched the whip from the grasp of the surprised sailor and had to be forcibly restrained. She was shaking from head to foot as she tried to struggle free.

"Get her away from here! Take her below!" ordered Stokovius. "Tie her up if you have to!"

As Fabia was dragged away, cursing and screaming, Bron thought how fragile the line between love, lust and hate. She felt confused and clung tighter to the captain, who was making no attempt to remove her arms from around his waist.

Whether it was her pleading or the sight of Fabia demented with hatred and displaying a desire for revenge as strong as his, or perhaps a little of both, Bron could not be sure, but she felt the captain's body relax slightly.

"Continue!" he commanded, a little less surely, and the whip hissed again. It found the target that the sailor, though not the captain, intended and this time cracked against the wooden planking of the deck.

"All right, enough!" said the captain, at last taking Bron's arms away, and leaving her in a sobbing heap among her bed covers as he strode over to the mast.

"Untie him," he ordered "and throw a bucket of sea water over him. Then take him below and clean up this mess."

The crew were quick to obey, silently scurrying about, sending the onlookers away and carrying out their orders.

It took four men to lift the bo'sun upright. They put his arms round their shoulders so that his legs dangled grotesquely, like a rag doll's. As they turned him away from the mast, he raised his head momentarily and looked at Bron with eyes that were glazed with pain and near unconsciousness. Her eyes met his and his mouth twitched at one corner. Deeply ashamed, she looked away.

"What, mate?" asked a young sailor, bending forward to put his ear against the bo'sun's mouth as they hauled him along, his legs dragging. Then the sailor chortled. "Noden!" he swore. "The idiot says it was almost worth it!"

Only Bron knew what the "almost" meant.

"That's not what he'll say tomorrow," muttered a legionary who had been delegated by the captain to doctor the bo'sun's wounds, as he followed the little procession below.

Veneta went across to Bron and gently guided her back to the cabin, where she lay with a feverish temperature for several days.

When she slept, the bo'sun haunted her nightmares. When she woke, all she could remember of them was his looming shadow and her screams.

Sythia came to keep her company and help Veneta with the children.

"My Tiegan was right again," she whispered to Veneta when she thought Bron was asleep, "but there's still more to come. It 'asn't all 'appened yet – what about the fire and the bodies in the water?"

"Sssh!" warned Veneta. "We've had as much as we can take at the moment."

"Are you praying to your God?"

"Of course, but I hardly know what to pray for. There are forces at work here that I don't understand."

"It's very busy at Noden's shrine in the prow – there's always someone there these days, whispering about last voyages. And people keep cornering Tiegan and demanding more prophecies. It's very upsetting for the boy."

There was certainly a strange atmosphere around the ship that Bron sensed, even without Veneta mentioning it to her. Passengers and crew were quieter. Lessons had been suspended, leaving the children to their own devices, but even they were better behaved and less quarrelsome than usual. Everyone seemed to be waiting for something to happen, for Tiegan's predictions to be fulfilled.

The captain called at the cabin door every day, but apart from sending a message of gratitude through Veneta, Bron declined to see him.

"Bron, take pity on the poor man," Veneta pleaded. "He looks half demented with confusion and guilt. Declan says the crew are muttering about his inability to captain the ship. With the bo'sun out of commission, if he doesn't pull himself together, there'll likely be a mutiny and they'll put someone else at the helm."

But Bron still refused to see him.

CHAPTER 18

Five days out from Balearis Major, thick fog descended.

The ship had been making good time on a north-easterly course towards Corsica and Sardinia. Declan said that the race ran high through the eight-mile channel between the islands, affording fast transit, and once through the gap, it would be only a matter of days to Ostia and the conclusion of their voyage.

But now the *Juniper* lay in a flat calm. An eerie hush enveloped her. There was no sound from the usually restless sea nor from the oars, which had been shipped. Full sails were set, to catch any passing breeze, but there was none and they hung slack and lifeless.

The captain was keeping the crew and oarsmen busy hosing down the decks, sanding paintwork, adding fresh layers, and generally tidying up.

"Everyone's saying it's a waste of time," Veneta told Bron, "when she's going to be broken up in Ostia."

The passengers grew hot, bored and listless, the children irritable and whining, and even Cronus stopped chasing the cat and her kitten and slept on his bed for most of the day. Everyone crept about, shadowy figures as they passed each other in and out of the fog, not seeing clearly from one end of the ship to the other.

"Bron, it's time you took a walk on deck," Veneta decided on the second morning of the fog. "I don't know what you're afraid of. No one blames you for what happened. In fact, they admire you for saving the bo'sun's life, in spite of what he did to you."

When Bron didn't stir from her mattress, Veneta asked Declan to come and talk some sense into her.

"How is he?" Bron asked the young man as he sat beside her.

"The captain?"

"No, I meant the bo'sun."

"His wounds are healing. I think the captain would have killed him if it hadn't been for you."

"Has he said anything about – about what happened?"

Declan looked at her quizzically. "Some, but no one is believing him. He's just boasting and trying to goad Fabia. She's nursing him. I don't know how she puts up with him – that's love for you – but she hates you, Bron. She can't hear your name mentioned without cursing you in the name of all the gods. He just laughs at her."

It was uncomfortably hot and humid in the cabin and Veneta brought them both a drink of water.

"If we're becalmed much longer, the water will be running out," he said gloomily. "The men on the oars are not drinking as much as usual, because they're not working, but even so, it should be rationed, but the captain seems out of his wits. He's bewitched, Bron, and we all know why. Women are bad news on a ship. Always were and always will be. And what with that boy of Sythia's with his crazy gut gazing…"

"He's been right up till now," Bron reminded him.

"Some of it, not all," argued Declan.

"Not yet," said Bron.

When he had gone, Veneta asked, "What *is* the bo'sun saying, do you think?"

"How should I know? You'll have to ask Fabia!" Bron's retort was sharper than she intended. "Sorry, Veneta, but I don't know what he's saying." *Though I can guess*, she thought and cringed inwardly.

"Bron dear, is there something you need to tell me? Something about that night?"

"Do you want me to go into details? Draw you a picture?" Bron's voice was sharp again. "I've had enough of this interrogation! I'm going out on deck, as you suggest. I'll go and find my children, it's time they came back to the cabin," and she swung her legs to the floor and left the cabin, banging the door.

She went to the rail and peered over the side. Only the surface of the water directly below was visible, everything else being hidden in the fog. The water was flat and dark grey, like the sacred pool at home on a dull wintry day. Tears filled her eyes. If she were at home now, standing on the edge of the pool, she would drop an offering into the water for the goddess and her nymphs. But she had nothing she could drop in today, except herself. If she slipped in quietly over the side, she wondered, would the salty water make her feel clean again? Probably not, it looked too murky for that.

She thought that she might have been tempted to take that way out if she had not stopped the bo'sun when she did. At least she had salvaged some respect for herself, but it brought little comfort. Frustration was gnawing away at her precisely because she had done as honour dictated and had stopped him.

When she thought back over the experience, all she could remember was the wild abandonment his lovemaking had excited in her – and it *was* lovemaking, it wasn't rape, and though ashamed, she was feeling deprived and hungry.

To deny herself his body might bring her peace of mind but it certainly brought no other peace. It was all so confusing and she needed to talk to someone maturer and wiser than herself. If only Aurelius were here, he would explain it to her. He would make it all right again.

Veneta was the obvious confidante but she was sure her friend never had an errant thought in her head. Veneta always knew exactly what she should be feeling and felt it, exactly what she should be doing and did it. So Bron was unable to look her straight in the eye any more and shrank from the thought of touching her children, because of the imagined grime that was still on her skin wherever his and her hands had been.

As she walked quietly round the deck, the few passengers she met all expressed sympathy. She nodded her thanks and was encouraged to go below among the women and children. A group moved aside and made room for her to sit with them. Layla brought Lucilla over and Alon ran to hug her and ask if she was feeling better.

"Yes, I'm a lot better, especially now I've seen you three again," said Bron, tickling Lucilla behind the ears, and suddenly realised it was true, and she was experiencing the beginning of healing.

However, while walking back to the cabin, deep in thought, she heard herself addressed by the name that only one man used.

"Goddess!"

She stopped as if struck by a blow then turned to see an indistinct figure leaning back on one elbow against the ship's rail. She looked around to escape, anywhere, but he stopped her again, this time using her name.

"Bron, I want to talk to you. I must. Then you can run if you want."

She was confused by this politeness, this unexpected gentleness, in place of his usual predatory insolence.

He turned his back on her and peered out into the fog, perhaps so that she would not be intimidated, leaving the choice to her. Towards the stern, safety lay in her cabin, but she looked at his back and imagined the criss-cross of bright red wounds and weals beneath his tunic. She wondered later whether that was the reason he had turned his back on her. If so, it had the desired result because she came and stood beside him.

"I'm here," she stated flatly.

"I've been waiting for you," he said.

"I can't imagine what you have to say that would be of the slightest interest to me, except to ask forgiveness, which I am not about to give."

"Forgiveness can wait. Before anything else, I must thank you for saving my life, as insignificant as it is to you – he would have killed me, if it hadn't been for your arms round his waist. Everyone knows that. And everyone knows why he wanted to."

"I couldn't let the whipping go on any longer," Bron said quietly.

"Then, yes, I do ask your forgiveness, but not for what I did – it was the only way I could force you into understanding how you really felt about me –"

Bron opened her mouth to protest but he placed a finger over her parted lips.

"I was desperate for you, Bron, you knew that, but I had to get very drunk before I had the courage to do anything about it."

He removed his hand and when she hung her head and did not

reply he continued, "I need your forgiveness for being so rough and treating you like a common tart. It's not the way I saw your officer treat you and obviously I have a lot to learn about women of your sort –"

He broke off again and his grave expression lightened and his voice took on its usual bantering tone. "Added to which," he continued, "it was all completely unnecessary, wasn't it? When it came to it, your needs were just as urgent as mine, and if I hadn't been a fool and mentioned that Roman – well, instead of attacking the equipment, you would have had it doing what it was designed to do inside –"

At that she drew back her hand a distance and slapped him on his cheek so hard that he stumbled under the blow, fell back against the rail and cried out in pain as the unrelenting oak came into contact with his unhealed cuts and slashes.

She turned and ran for refuge to the cabin then and, finding it unoccupied, threw herself on the mattress, crying face down upon her pillow and punching into it with both fists just as hard as she wished to punch into him, until she was exhausted.

Why am I crying so? she at last asked herself, but knew the answer. What he had said of her was all true.

He had called her "a woman of your sort" as if she were something special, but she wasn't. She was beginning to understand that her rape by Vortin when she was only twelve had dammed up any natural desires she might have felt as she matured. An underground reservoir of instinctive emotions had been filling but had found no release during her arranged marriage to Soranus, the young boy she loved dearly as a friend but seldom as a lover.

Aurelius Catus had cracked that dam wide open, because she loved him, and both had been consumed by the released surge of her loving. However, not even Aurelius had plumbed the depths of these animalistic desires that had been stored away in caverns so deep that she had been quite unaware of their existence. Only the bo'sun had recognised what lay in those black depths. It worried her that she was no better than Fabia and the other girls who lived mostly in the men's quarters, then wondered whether she was being too hard on herself.

She knew, however, that this was not the end of the matter and if the bo'sun found another opportunity, this time most likely she would succumb. Her only hope was Aurelius, and she yearned for him now. Their reunion in Ostia was not many days distant, except that this ship, which should have been bringing them closer by the moment, was now becalmed in a thick grey blanket and was going nowhere.

The *Juniper* sat in the fog for three more days and hardly changed position. The captain had dispensed with the usual two men at the helm but had maintained lookouts atop the mast and in prow and stern.

"We're on one of the busiest shipping routes and there's always the risk of collision in the fog, though little chance of it while everyone is becalmed," Declan explained to Veneta as he strained his eyes, trying to pierce the woolly blanket.

Alon said the captain had told him that coins lay hidden beneath the mast, to make Noden happy, and there would be no collision.

"Veneta and I don't need Noden when we've got our God, Jesus," retorted Layla scornfully.

"Don't be silly, Layla. They didn't put any coins there for Jesus, only for Noden," her brother replied, just as scornfully. "*He* won't be keeping you safe because he hasn't been paid to."

Layla didn't answer and retired to a corner to think about this problem.

"Why are the sails unfurled when there's no wind?" Alon wanted to know.

"If there's any breeze about at all, they will pick it up and show us the direction," explained Declan. "Then the crew will set the sails to suit the conditions."

Veneta wondered out loud whether it was time to organise the school again. "I've been very indolent about it, just like the weather. Will you help me, Bron?"

Bron said she wasn't sure she could, not now. All she wanted was some peace in her life.

Next morning, there was good news to shout down from the crow's nest.

"Tell the captain the fog's lifting!" called the sailor on watch. "I can see the sun from up here!"

There was a cheer from those on deck and suddenly energy seemed to fill the ship as passengers and crew emerged from below.

The air gained warmth as the sun rose higher, burning off the fog, and by mid-morning hardly a wraith remained. At the same time, the main sail began to stir and Bron heard a sound that reminded her of the breeze sighing through branches of trees in Byden wood.

"Set the sails! Take up the wind!" came the order from the captain.

"Praise be to Noden," muttered Declan. "He sounds like his old self."

CHAPTER 19

"Ship five miles astern to larboard! Running parallel!"

Captain Stokovius strode to the ship's rail, where Declan was already positioned.

"Your eyes are younger than mine, Declan. What do you make of her?"

"I don't know, Cap'n, she's too far away to see any markings."

Stokovius shouted up to the crow's nest. "Report to me if she changes course!"

The wind was strengthening by the moment and soon the *Juniper* was skimming over the waves, its distended sails as full blown as a pregnant matron. There was no need for the support of oarsmen.

For some time, Bron had been standing with Veneta and the children at the rail, listening to their chatter and marvelling at Veneta's patience in answering all their questions. She turned her face to the sun and wind, her dark hair rippling behind her, and felt exhilarated and cleansed.

"That ship's gaining on us," Veneta said.

"Is it a pirate ship?" asked Alon apprehensively.

"Don't be silly, of course not," said Bron. "There's nothing on board worth stealing."

"But pirates don't know that," Layla sensibly replied.

There *was* something worth stealing, of course. Her bundle of jewellery was hidden in the cabin, and there might be other valuables on board, such as gifts the captain was taking home.

"Of course it's not a pirate ship," she reiterated, looking anxiously across to Veneta. "Declan's been filling your heads with foolish stories."

"Your mother's right." Bron hadn't noticed the captain approaching but he stood next to her now, and tousled the boy's hair.

"Captain –?" Bron sought confirmation.

"It's a smaller ship than the *Juniper,* and faster – probably a merchant galley. We're keeping an eye out – several eyes, in fact. Off you go now, children. The cook's prepared something special for your midday meal, to celebrate the lifting of the fog."

Veneta looked from him to Bron then gathered up the children and ushered them off to the cabin. In the ensuing silence, Bron did not look at the man standing stiffly at her side but turned seawards, unconsciously gripping the rail.

"Bron –"

"Yes, Captain?"

"I haven't been able to speak to you since – since what happened. You've denied me every opportunity."

"I – I haven't been well," she replied, unconvincingly.

"Are you better now?"

"Quite better, thank you."

"That's good." He paused then continued awkwardly, "I told Aurelius Catus that I would look after you. I said that I and my crew were not barbarians and you would come to no harm."

Bron nodded and agreed softly, guessing what was coming, "Yes, you did promise him that."

"I have failed miserably. I allowed that man – that animal – to touch you, to maul you – he could have killed you – and I could have killed him!" He thumped the rail with his fist. "I wanted to – only Noden knows how much I wanted to."

Bron looked at him and saw misery written all over his face and was consumed with guilt. Her impulse was to tell him that the incident hadn't been as much of an ordeal as everyone imagined, but there was no place for the truth.

She rested her hand on his. "It wasn't your fault, Captain. There was nothing you could have done to prevent it, and I wasn't harmed, not really – you found me too soon for that. Please don't blame yourself. I should have been more wary and taken more care."

"I have never in my life been so out of control," he confessed.

Neither have I, thought Bron, *and Noden knows that too – Noden and one other.*

He laid his other hand over hers. "I've had no peace of mind since." He looked at her earnestly and beseechingly. "And will have none unless you give it to me."

"How, Captain?" Bron asked, wanting to relieve his anxiety but not sure what he expected of her.

"It was only because of your pleading and your tears that I stopped the whipping when I did," he said. "You were so insistent. Tell me that you were prompted by compassion only – and nothing else."

Bron started as if she had been slapped and, to cover her confusion, withdrew her hand from his grasp. She had to say something, he was regarding her so keenly, but the acceptable words were not on her tongue. She made an attempt to recover her composure, and stammered that she didn't know what he meant. He turned back to face the sea.

"Oh, I think you do."

"Captain, I don't know what you think you know, but just remember that you are taking us to Ostia, where Aurelius is waiting for me. Then we will be out of your way and out of your life, and you can go home to your family, and never be inconvenienced by us again. I love him, you know, Aurelius. Little else matters."

"If only life was that simple, Bron. You have a lot to learn, my dear."

By the time the passengers were ready for their evening meal, the unknown ship had drawn parallel with the *Juniper* but remained on the horizon in the deepening dusk.

By the time they were ready for bed, she had forged ahead, still on her parallel course, her presence revealed only by lamps on board, which were unusually numerous to Bron's way of thinking.

During the night, hot and unable to sleep, Bron came out on deck and looked towards the horizon. The black night sky was brilliant with stars. The ship's lights had disappeared altogether.

CHAPTER 20

She was awoken at first light by commotion on deck – shouted commands, running feet and women screaming. She tumbled off her mattress and reached across to shake Veneta, but her friend was already awake and sitting up.

Bron pulled a cover round her. "I'll find out what's going on."

She was back in no time.

"That ship we saw yesterday has changed course in the dark and is heading straight for us! The crew say it *is* a pirate ship! Everyone has to get up on deck."

She scrambled over to the children and began hauling them up off their mattresses, the sharp edge to her voice silencing their sleepy protests, while Veneta bundled the two babies into her arms. On deck, they joined passengers and crew at the ship's seaward rail.

The smaller vessel was under full sail with two single banks of oars employed, skimming through the waves at speed and bearing down on them at an angle that would bring her into sharp collision with the waist of the *Juniper* unless a miracle occurred. Even at that distance, they could distinguish the large black eyes painted on each side of her prow, as menacing as the ram jutting out like a shining, blunted nose just below the water line.

"Dear Jesus," exclaimed Veneta, "if that rams home, it will tear the hold apart!"

The women already on deck were in panic, running in all directions, seeking safety for their frightened children where none was to be found. Others were emerging sleepily from the holds, unaware of the danger that threatened.

Then the ship reverberated as the deep boom! boom! of the rowing drum echoed beneath their feet and she lurched forward, propelled by powerful strokes as sixty oarsmen bent to their task.

Veneta passed the babies to Bron. "Take the children over to the starboard side. I'm going below for the women."

"No, Veneta! You'll die down there."

"We've a few minutes before colliding. I won't stay longer than I have to. And pray!"

With the babies in her arms, Bron hustled Layla, Alon and little Lucilla through the gathering crowd to the far side of the deck aft. She noticed one of the veteran legionaries she knew by sight throwing a wooden crate overboard before clambering up on to the rail.

"What are you doing?" she called out to him in amazement.

"I'll take my chances in the sea!" he shouted back.

"But we need you on board!"

Her plea went unheard among the clamour around them, or perhaps unheeded. He jumped off the rail, clear of the oars, and the last she saw of him was his head bobbing among the waves in their wake, one arm clinging round the floating crate.

Above all the noise and confusion, the captain's orders were being relayed along the length of the ship by the crew, who were quietly and in a disciplined manner moving to their stations. Other men, fit and otherwise, were joining them all along the larboard rail, each holding any weapon they could muster – a variety of army-issue swords, daggers and shields, a javelin, belaying pins, pieces of splintered wood, and one young sailor was clutching a fistful of iron nails. The cook was handing out lethal-looking kitchen knives to those who had been preparing to fight with nothing but their bare hands.

A young soldier called out, "Hey, carpenter, if you give me that saw you're carrying, by Noden! I'll make sure their own mothers won't recognise 'em by the time I've finished with 'em!"

The carpenter shook his head. "There'll be repairs afterwards – and amputations."

The women and children were being herded to the starboard rail, furthest away from the point of impact. Bron saw Sythia and her twins struggling towards them and with a flash of memory that ran an icy finger down her spine, remembered Tiegan's prophecy of fire and bodies of strange men in the water.

"Bron, my dear!" Sythia called as she came over. "Veneta said you'd be 'ere. We brought up everyone we could but some of the oldies won't come, stubborn old things. They said they'd rather drown down there than get cut to pieces on deck."

"I saw one of the men jump overboard."

"So did I. One of them dragged his woman with him. She was trying to fight him off and they both fell down between the oars. I didn't stop to look at what happened to them after that."

Sythia took a deep breath, her ample chest expanding. Her watery blue eyes were bright and there was a determined tightness round her mouth. "If it comes to a fight, no one's boarding without he hears the cut of my tongue and feels the cut of this piece of wood about his head!"

She brandished a broken plank in the air, looking like an ungainly Boadicea, and Bron laughed in spite of her fear.

"Surely they won't hurt women and children."

Sythia was about to make a spirited retort, but looked down at her twins and Bron's children and replied quietly, "Perhaps not. Let's hope not. Anyway, they've got to get on board first."

"We're gathering speed," Bron commented hopefully.

"Captain Stokovius knows what he's doing, my lovely," Sythia assured her.

Veneta joined them at that moment, with Asandra close behind her, followed by Koch.

"The captain has sent Koch to look after us," she informed Bron.

"I want to join the fighting!" he complained.

"Don't fret, lad, there'll be plenty of that!" Sythia told him. "If they board, you'll have all the fighting you can handle!"

His bright blue eyes gleamed with excitement. "I'll protect you!" he told Asandra.

"Thanks," she said without seeming to listen to him. Her eyes were searching the deck and Bron guessed she was looking for Declan, but he wasn't visible in the crowd.

The pirate ship was very close now, approaching at a narrow angle. The *Juniper* seemed to have changed course and Bron noticed that the helmsman had the tiller hard over to starboard, reducing the angle even further.

"If they're going to ram us, why don't they come at us head on?" she asked Koch.

"Declan said they don't want to risk ramming their ship so far into ours that they can't get off again and we stay locked together, which could mean we both go down."

There was nothing more to say or do then but wait for the impact. A hush descended on deck. All that could be heard was the rhythmical boom! boom! of the rowing drum, faster now than before.

Veneta was mouthing a prayer as they clung to each other and to the rail and its stanchions, anticipating the moment of collision.

It took longer than expected. As they watched, the high, curved stem post of the attacking ship loomed larger and larger, its plumed carving towering above the decks of both ships. Suddenly, there was crash after crash and the sounds of splintering wood as two sets of oars converged and interlocked and were woven together or sheared off and riven into thousands of lethally pointed stakes and spars.

The plight of the men on the other end of those oars was only too obvious from the high-pitched screams from below both decks.

The *Juniper* shuddered as the pirate ship continued to advance and then the hulls collided, the forward momentum carrying the locked ships a further length before both came to rest. At least, by the slight alteration of course, the ram had not pierced their hull as intended.

The children were thrown to the deck on impact, Bron and the babies on top of them. They scrambled to their feet, too terrified to cry now. Amid all the commotion, the warning rang around the ship, "Prepare to be boarded!"

There was just as much noise from the pirate ship as her crew whooped and catcalled while crowding at her rail or swarming up the rigging of her foremast, brandishing weapons in one or both hands or with knives and daggers clenched in their teeth as they clung to precarious perches.

Their features and skin colouring betrayed men from every province in the empire and beyond and Bron shrank back at the sight of this near-naked baying, howling enemy.

"Don't be afraid, we far outnumber them!"

She was surprised and not a little comforted to find the bo'sun standing in front of them. She saw that his eyes were alight and his face flushed with excitement in anticipation of the fight ahead. He held a gladius, which he offered to Koch.

"Take it, boy, and don't hesitate to use it! We'll make a man of you today!" Koch obeyed and balanced the weight of the short sword on his palm.

The bo'sun turned to Veneta. "Take some of the younger women down into the galley and bring up all the pots and pans you can, to hurl at them as they come aboard. You could knock a man into the next world with one of those iron cauldrons!"

Veneta nodded and beckoned to Fabia, who was hovering in the background, and the girls who were with her.

"Layla and Alon, you can both help and you'll be safer down there," said their mother. "Go with Veneta."

"We'll go too," offered Sythia. "Come along, boys."

Bron turned to Asandra. "Please take Lucilla and the babies and stay well behind the cabin. Koch will go with you. I'll be of more use hurling missiles."

They went and for once Asandra looked pleased to have the boy with her.

Bron turned to the bo'sun as an idea struck her.

"We could send over flaming torches!" she suggested, looking towards the galley. "The cook's sure to have a fire burning down there."

She was taken quite unawares when the bo'sun's arms came round her shoulders and hips and she was pulled close enough for him to kiss her hard on the mouth.

"So have I, goddess!" he whispered hoarsely. "Take care, and I'll come back for you when it's all over."

She watched him, her body tingling, as he strode away.

Now, the sea and wind were contriving to push the two hulls

together and the rasping and grinding of their planks could be heard above the din of battle.

The pirates were paying out ropes to lower long boarding planks across the gap between the ships' rails. The planks were pushed away by the *Juniper's* crew and Bron closed her eyes against the agonised shrieks of men tipped off and broken in the confusion of smashed oars below or pulped between the grating hulls.

At other places, grappling ropes were flying on board, their iron hooks biting deep into wood wherever they could drag then grip. The crew hacked at the lines and the men clambering up them, but here and there a bare leg was thrust over the rail to be followed by another and a man would scramble aboard, to be met by determined and bloody opposition.

Bron stumbled towards the galley but her flight was suddenly impeded by a huge man bare to the waist, with charred brown skin, and an ugly face that was almost hidden behind thick, black hair. His lips were parted in a wide grin, revealing a mouth of black and broken teeth.

She was confused because he wore Roman Army-issue woollen breeches, but when he started shouting at her in an unfamiliar lingo, she realised with terror that the dirty uniform had probably been looted from a dead Roman.

His arm shot out across her chest and grabbed her right wrist, and when she struggled to free her hand, he spun her around so that she was facing away from him with his body tight against her back. His hand released hers and slid round the front of her waist, pulling her closer, pressing himself against her, his legs separating hers, trapping her right leg in a vice. She kicked back with her left foot, and when that had no effect, bent forward and bit his arm, holding the tough skin between her teeth and not letting go.

He yelled and for a moment released his grip but, before she could escape, his hold on her tightened again, her head was pulled backwards by her hair, and she felt a sharp metal edge against her throat. His mouth was against her ear and she was overwhelmed with odours of alcohol, rotting teeth and sweat.

"You come or I kill! You come! You come!"

There was no mistaking his hesitant Latin or his intentions. She dare not struggle in case the knife slipped, and when he began to drag her crablike across the deck, she could do nothing about it. Men were fighting all round them and there was no one to help her, even if her screams could have been heard above the commotion or her predicament noticed.

They had reached one of the upturned boats and in one swift movement the man had taken the knife away from her throat and pushed her so that she fell forward on to her stomach, straddling the keel, his legs up against hers.

She struggled up and turned, but was off balance and this time, when he knocked her down, she toppled backwards, sure that her back would break over the keel as her attacker fell on top of her.

She tried to push him off but he was too heavy. However, the closeness of their bodies meant that he was having difficulty in pulling up her tunic, and when he lifted himself off her for an instant, she slipped off the keel and down on to the deck.

Then she tried scrambling away on hands and knees but he was behind her again and pushed her down, so that she collapsed on to her stomach with him above her on all fours, his knees on the back of hers, his hands pinning her arms to the deck on each side of her head.

She lay helpless and he nearly crushed the life out of her when he dropped like a sack of grain. She waited for his groping hands and closed her eyes against the humiliation and pain she knew was coming. Still she waited. Then he rolled off her and she was hauled to her feet and turned around.

"Bo'sun!"

The dagger he was wiping on his tunic left a bright red stain.

"Only just in time, goddess."

She looked down at the unseeing eyes of her assailant staring up at her, a surprised expression on his hairy face.

"He forgot the golden rule – never turn your back on the enemy."

"Thank you," she whispered.

"Anyway, he was poaching! Can't allow that."

"Thank you," she whispered again, looking down at the blood trickling from beneath the body.

"Now get back to the galley and keep out of the way. The fighting's not over and I may not be around next time."

Bron needed no second telling.

Veneta had organised a chain. Layla, Alon and the twins were picking up every cooking utensil that could be useful. Soon pots, pans, cauldrons, trivets, crockery and cutlery were being passed to Sythia in the doorway and out to the women on deck, who were handing them to the line of men at the rail or hurling them wherever they had most effect.

Some of the pirates were now taking hold of lengths of rope secured to the yard on their main mast and were swinging themselves through the intervening gap to land on board. Most vulnerable while in the swing, they were being met by a volley of the cook's treasured equipment.

Once the galley had been stripped, Veneta and Bron, who was still unsteady after the attack on her, started passing out lighted faggots of wood from a stack in the corner, then reconsidered and quickly showed the children how to wrap oil-soaked cloth round the sticks, which Bron then dipped into the flames in the tiled firebox.

As soon as the wind on deck flared the flames, the women began hurling them across to the other ship. The first few fell short of their target and were doused in the sea, but the aim was soon corrected so that the torches landed where they could cause most damage, in the sails and on the deck.

When there were no more torn strips from shawls and scarves, Veneta asked the women to take off their undershifts and any other clothing that could be spared, and they finally dragged covers off Bron's and Veneta's beds.

Coughing and choking in the fumes, those in the galley had to come up to breathe fresh air, and Sythia quickly ushered the children into the stern cabin.

Fighting on board continued fierce and bloody, backwards and forwards along the length of the deck. Those who were too old to fight were clearing the area by throwing enemy bodies, both dead and injured, overboard.

Bron saw that the hull of the pirate ship had been pushed away from the *Juniper,* which was again under sail and moving further ahead. She realised that there was no chance of the pirates on board returning to their ship, now well on fire.

A huddle of exhausted women stood round the door to the galley, watching the yellow and orange flames, fanned by the wind, running along the deck of the attacking ship and snaking up the three masts to the sails above. It was not long before the vessel was ablaze from prow to stern.

The noise of battle was quietening as superior numbers on board the *Juniper* gradually fought the boarders to a standstill. Finally, there was no noise at all except for waves and wind, the roaring of flames and crackling of burning timber.

Then the cry went up and echoed around the ship, "No prisoners!" Bron and Veneta were horrified at the cold-blooded slaughter taking place and took refuge in the cabin. Bron gathered Alon and Layla to her and sat with them, their heads buried in the folds of her tunic, while she told Veneta about her rescue from the pirate by the bo'sun.

When the order had been carried out and there were no prisoners, all became unnaturally quiet. Bron hurried across the deck to look for Asandra and her children. She found them where she had left them, the babies and Lucilla safe between Koch and Asandra. The girl was sobbing softly against his shoulder. Nearby were the bodies of two men, one with a broad gash across his throat from which blood was still oozing and the other with the bone handgrip of the sword the bo'sun had given Koch protruding from his bare chest.

Bron was astounded. "Koch, did you –?"

"He did," answered Asandra. "Oh, Bron, he was so brave! That one" – she indicated the man with the gladius buried in his chest – "went after my pendant."

Bron looked down at the body. Hardly a man – a little older than Koch, in fact, with yellow hair and a yellow fuzz on his chin and chest.

Koch was flushed with excitement at his prowess in front of

Asandra, and was luxuriating in her praise, but when he also looked down at the corpse, his eyes were troubled.

"You did what you had to," Bron reassured him, "and I can never thank you enough."

She kissed him on the cheek and retrieved Lucilla from between their feet.

"Come back with me to the cabin," she said to Asandra, "and try not to look about you too much on the way. It will upset you even more. And Koch, will you find the captain and thank him for sending you as our bodyguard, and tell him what you did, and that we are all unhurt."

Koch nodded and left them, his eyes still shining.

"He's not a boy any longer," commented Bron.

"I know," Asandra replied shyly.

As they picked their way across the deck, bodies were being dragged across to the side of the ship, some women and children among them, and there was splash after splash as corpses were thrown unceremoniously into the sea.

"I hope someone's checking they're actually dead," Bron said anxiously.

"Looking at them," replied Asandra, who was trying not to, "I should say there's not much doubt."

In spite of her own advice, Bron felt compelled to walk over to the larboard rail to look down at the floating debris of wood and corpses, then back at the blazing pirate ship.

Veneta joined her and both women surveyed the carnage around them, heard the cries and moans of helpless men, blocked their noses against the smell of spilled blood and guts that left a taste of iron and viscera in their mouths, and knew that they had compassionate work to do.

"So," Bron said wearily, "Tiegan's prophecy has come true yet again."

But wasn't there more? Hadn't he also talked of a storm? And other things?

CHAPTER 21

The *Juniper* was now drifting helplessly – off course and heading north before a light wind. Repairs to the ship were under way and the deck had been cleared and scrubbed then hosed down, everyone having worked all night. The captain did not spare himself, his crew nor his passengers in his efforts to keep the ship seaworthy and afloat.

Below decks, the oarsmen who had survived the collision had jettisoned the oars that were past repair and were strengthening those slightly damaged, under the direction of the ship's overworked carpenter.

High in the rigging, the bo'sun was supervising his gang, patching sails and repairing lines. Bron saw him as she passed backwards and forwards to the makeshift sickroom, which had been the men's quarters.

It was sweltering down there, almost unbearable, as perspiration drenched the faces and bodies of the women at work.

"I can't take any more of this! I can't! I can't!" Bron screamed silently but saw lowered eyes and tight lips and knew that each volunteer was struggling not to be the card that collapsed and brought the rest down with it.

Then they stopped trying to shield themselves from the stench of injury and death and after a very short while ceased gagging at it.

However, it was impossible to ignore the agony of their patients, some of whom were being held down by the distraught carpenter's assistants while limbs were severed.

Happily, some crew members were only slightly injured and were sent back to work after treatment. Declan was alive, though with deep gashes across his head and right cheek. He allowed Asandra to sit by his side, holding his hand while Veneta cleaned the wounds with salt water then deftly stitched the edges of skin together with fishing line.

He grinned with pleasure at all the attention and thanked her by putting his arms round her and kissing her on the cheek, then kissed Bron and Asandra, and was not allowed back on deck until he had walked along the line of women, kissing them all. It was a little light relief for patients and nurses among the darkness of the day's work.

"He's popular, that one," smiled Veneta, pleased with a job well done.

"I would've died if 'e 'ad," whispered Asandra, gazing after him.

"You know, Bron," Veneta said as she bandaged a crew member's hand and Bron rolled up strips of cloth, "I used to think it was you who Declan was wooing, but now I think it was Asandra all the time."

"Do you think so? Do you really think so?" purred Asandra.

"No doubt about it," Veneta answered, intent on her work.

Asandra smiled her pleasure, and Bron changed the subject and asked a question about an elderly equestrian officer who was lying unconscious. *Sometimes*, she thought, *Veneta can be very obtuse.*

Work continued into the second night, broken only by a few brief visits to the deck to breathe fresh air or snatch something to eat or drink. The women not helping in the sick bay were entrusted with looking after the children. Bedtimes came and went without their mothers below being aware of the passing hours until Sythia came to report that all Bron's children were asleep.

"And the captain's found Cronus," she added. "The puppy was hiding among the bedclothes in his own cabin, would you believe? It's cuddled up with Alon now. But there's still no sign of the cat and her kitten."

During the night, the captain came down to visit the injured. He moved from patient to patient with a word of comfort or encouragement, and when he came to two bodies with faces covered, moved aside the cloths to check identities.

"The old lady's all right," he reassured everyone. "She's patched and limping, but she's staying afloat without trouble."

"Where are we now, Cap'n?" a sailor with bandages over his eyes asked.

"Still heading north, running before the wind. Don't you worry about it, son – she'll get us all to Ostia eventually, just as soon as this wind drops and we can steer her south."

Bron was busy cleaning a wound, replacing the pus-bloated maggots sealed in it earlier in the day. She saw the captain sniff and knew why. Gangrene was adding its stench to the already putrid air.

"Bron, are you well?" he asked anxiously. "The bo'sun told me what happened to you."

"I'm very tired," she replied honestly, "but apart from that, I'm all right."

"You must rest," he told her.

"I can't while the others are still working."

He cleared his throat. "Ladies, on behalf of myself and my crew and passengers, may I –" His voice faltered. "No, words cannot express what we owe you. Rome seldom honours her women but, if I had my way, there would be medals struck for all of you."

CHAPTER 22

A little later, Bron decided to take his advice.

"I'm going up top for a few minutes," she told Veneta, "to get some fresh air. I won't be long."

There were no clouds to cloak the very new moon, which was just a sliver of yellow among thousands, perhaps millions, of stars – many more than lit the skies above the green hills at home. Bron wondered yet again which god had time to light them every night.

Holding the rail tightly with both hands, she leaned backwards to ease her aching muscles and lifted her face to the wind blowing from the stern. Its fingers ruffled her hair and blew cool breath around her neck and she filled her lungs with its salty freshness.

Her tunic, bought in the market in Gades, once a pristine pale green, was grimy and spattered with blood. She was very conscious that she must smell like a slaughterhouse and longed for the civilised delights of a Roman bath. All she could do now was ease the top of her tunic away from her perspiring neck.

"You should let me do that."

The bo'sun's voice was soft in her ear and his fingers began to massage her neck and shoulders. He had taken her by surprise but involuntarily she arched her back and rotated her shoulders then relaxed her muscles beneath his hands.

"I've been waiting up here since I came off duty," he told her, the massage changing to a caress. "I thought you would have to come up eventually. There, is that better?"

She admitted that it was, much better. He bent his head and gently kissed her neck then turned her round to face him.

"Have you finished squandering yourself on your patients?" he asked her.

"While Veneta works, I work," she said.

"But you can't work all through the night again," he objected.

"You wouldn't say that if you were one of the injured."

He put his hands on her shoulders and looked down at her.

"I have needs too, as you well know. There are plenty of dark, quiet corners on deck. Let's go and find one and you can make *me* feel better, then I'll send you back to your patients."

"No!"

"They won't miss you for half an hour, goddess, and you do owe me a favour – remember?"

"I owe you my life."

His arms came round her and in his embrace she could hardly move. When he tried to kiss her, she struggled against him.

"Let me go! I want to go!"

"No you don't, not really." His lips were almost on hers.

"Yes, I do! I'm not playing your games!"

"A pity," he observed. "But what about *your* games?"

Again she tried to free herself. "Let go of me or I'll yell and wake everyone up!"

Uncertain at last, he released his hold on her, but his hands gripped the tops of her arms and his fingers dug into her muscles so hard that she knew he had bruised them.

"You don't know as much about me as you think you do!" she spat out at him.

"I know more about you than you know yourself!" His voice was ugly as he brought his face close to hers again. "I know *what* you are!"

Humiliated and sobbing and breathless now, she raised her right hand to hit him again, but he was ready for her this time and grabbed her wrist. He forced her hand down between his legs but she curled her fingers into a fist and wouldn't touch him.

"All right, if you won't, I'll find someone who will!" he hissed and threw her from him.

She stumbled across the deck and scrambled down the companionway, almost knocking Asandra over in the dim light of the hold.

"Bron, whatever's the matter?" she asked in alarm.

Veneta came over and took hold of her friend's agitated hands and sat her down, putting an arm round her shoulders.

"What is it, Bron?"

Patiently, she listened to the whispered, disjointed telling of her encounter.

"You must report it to the captain at once," Veneta told her.

"No!"

"Then I will. It's time that man was stopped from following you about like a randy dog. I'm sorry to be so crude, but that's how it is."

"No, I don't want you to go to the captain."

"But why ever not?"

"This time, he would probably keel haul him, and I couldn't be responsible for that."

"But," Veneta protested, "you're not to blame – are you?"

"No, of course not! I fight him at every turn! But don't forget, he did save my life!"

"Where is he now?"

"Probably gone to wake up Fabia," guessed Asandra.

Veneta didn't report the incident to the captain. Bron persuaded her not to and she was too busy to argue.

CHAPTER 23

At first light, it was noticeable that the height of the dark blue, almost black, waves was increasing alarmingly as the wind gained strength. The ship, running before it, sometimes sailed dangerously close to the rocky outcrops of small, uninhabited islands.

Declan was sent forward to plumb the starboard depths. Bron took Alon forward and they sheltered beneath the curved stem post, watching the young man swing the lead weight in a circle above his head then hurl it forward, pulling it up as the ship passed over it.

"No bottom with this line!" he shouted back to the captain.

"How long is the line?" Bron asked him.

"A safe twenty-five fathoms, but I need to watch out for sand banks."

During the next two days, the wind reached gale force. The sea was whipped into a frenzy and the *Juniper* wallowed helplessly. Twice they heard the shout "Man overboard!", but there was no possibility of picking him up, even if they could have found him in those seas.

On the morning of the second day, it began to drizzle before the clouds burst open and the rain fell as though the sky had been saving it up for weeks.

Life was intolerable for everyone, especially those below decks. Shortage of drinking water added a serious problem to uncooked food, an inability to sleep, and seasickness among crew and passengers. Unusually, Veneta succumbed to sickness herself and stayed in the cabin with the children, all of them in a miserable state.

"Bron," Captain Stokovius shouted at her during an unsteady trip to take him oranges, which he bit into, eating peel and flesh together, "you and Veneta must stay up on deck, near me, with your children."

"But our patients need us," Bron remonstrated.

"I order you," he shouted above the howling of the wind and incessant beating of rain on wood, "not to go down there again, until the storm's over!"

Struggling across to the rail to be sick, Bron saw Declan in the prow, again swinging the plumb line and chanting the depths.

"By the deep, twenty two!" then later, "By the deep, twenty, and the sea colour's lightened!"

The captain strode to the starboard rail and looked for himself.

Bron was still there, soaked to the skin, salt spray washing her face as she spewed over the side.

"What is it, Captain?" she asked him, gripping the rail with one hand and wiping the other across her mouth.

"Bron, listen to me. Go back to your cabin and dress yourself and the children in the warmest clothes you have, then stay there until I send for you."

Before she could answer, a bright flash of blue light streaked from the black shroud of the sky, striking the sea on the horizon. It was followed by a deafening clap of thunder seemingly right above the ship.

"But Captain –"

"Just do as I say."

"What's wrong?"

"We may hit that sand bar. If we do, not everyone will get off the ship but some will and I want you to be among them."

"Get off to what?" she shouted.

"There's a lagoon and an island behind the bar."

Before she could question him further, another flash, sheet lightning this time, lit the sky from one end to the other. Another thunderous clap was sent rolling round their enclosed sphere, loud enough to be announcing the end of the world.

That second of light had shown Bron what the captain had already seen – white water to starboard, the sea breaking on a sand bar, and behind the bar calm water and a shoreline.

"By the deep, eighteen!"

"Tiller harder to larboard!"

"Aye, aye, Cap'n!"

"Get her over, sailor!"

"She's not answering, Cap'n," complained the helmsman on the starboard tiller. Immediately, Stokovius was at his side and together they tried to force the ship to veer seawards, away from the danger.

The other helmsman had abandoned any attempt to control his oar, which was now swinging wildly in the thrall of the sea, but he was managing to cling on with his arms wrapped round it and his legs trailing across the deck.

There was an ear-splitting *crack*! and Bron saw the captain and his helmsman flung to the deck as if thrown there by a giant hand. She realised that the steering oar had snapped.

The ship shuddered violently then lurched and heaved, sending the two men rolling helplessly backwards and forwards across the deck. A wave broke over the larboard rail and collapsed at Bron's feet, then gathered up everything in its path, including both men, as it drained back into the sea.

Captain Stokovius had the presence of mind to grab the other helmsman's legs as he was swept past the man, but the starboard oarsman was not so lucky and was dragged overboard with the wave. His cries faded in the thunder of surf on sand bar. With him into the sea went the rats that, for the last couple of hours, had been scurrying around people's feet in panic.

The ship paused, as if mustering all her strength for the ordeal that lay ahead. It gave a chance for the captain and his crewman to scramble to their feet and for Bron to flee back to the cabin.

Together, she and Veneta threw as much clothing as they could find on to the children. Bron dragged on three tunics over the one she already wore, which was dripping wet. Leaving Veneta with instructions to hide her jewellery in the wrappings round one of the babies, she staggered back on deck, ignoring the captain's orders to stay in the cabin. The tunics weighed her down as the wind drove rain through them.

Helplessly, she watched as the ship floundered nearer and nearer the clash of sea and sand bar, which seemed to grow longer as they approached, running the length of the dark island behind it.

"Goddess, come with me!"

Bron turned to find the bo'sun at her side.

"Where?" she asked, feeling stupid for asking, as there was nowhere to go.

"We've got the boats," he shouted at her. "The ship's going to sink and you with it if you don't come!"

"You're deserting the ship?" she yelled in disbelief. "The captain needs you!"

"Damn the captain to the fury of the storm!" he rasped back at her. "Why should I care what happens to him? Are you coming or not?"

"I can't leave the children!"

"You'll drown!" he told her.

"Then we'll drown together," she said.

"Don't waste time on her!" Fabia was beside him, tugging at his arm. "We must go!"

"Last chance, goddess!" he pleaded.

"No!"

"Then damn your eyes to the fishes!"

As he turned from her, Bron felt a heavy blow to the side of her head, which sent her sprawling against the wall of the galley.

"You shouldn't have done that!" she heard the bo'sun shout, followed by Fabia's satisfied reply, "You're wrong – I should have done it weeks ago!"

By the time Bron struggled to her feet, they had gone.

"Boats away!" someone cried above the crescendo of the storm, and those who heard the cry rushed to the rail and watched in disbelief as both craft, overfilled with passengers and oarsmen, struggled to draw away from the ship.

The distance between them slowly increased as the boats lifted high on each oncoming wave, seemingly suspended by invisible ropes, then tipped over the white, curling crest, to be lost from view, only to reappear as they climbed the following wave.

The watchers quietened when only one boat surfaced into the next wave. It climbed again, but this time did not surmount the shoulder of the crest and was toppled over backwards, jettisoning all inside it.

Bron cried out as she saw heads bobbing and people struggling, some beginning to swim, but one by one they disappeared beneath the surge of water. Of the second boat there was no sign.

"By the deep, fifteen!"

The call had hardly begun its relay along the ship when there was a deafening crash as the *Juniper* hit the sand bar broadside. She slipped back sideways into the sea, but a moment later was lifted higher and crashed again against the bar. For a second time she retreated in the undertow, then for a third and last time was dashed on to the sand bar, and came to rest with a fearful sound of splitting and splintering of old wood.

CHAPTER 24

Relief rippled round the deck, as people realised that escape was a possibility, but Bron looked at the mountainous waves now crashing over the ship and was not so sure.

The vessel settled further in the water, listing heavily to starboard. Women and men rushed to the starboard rail and began clambering over it, jumping and dropping and falling into the water at the base of the sandbank. They all disappeared under the ship.

Several patients were struggling up from below, soaking wet, disoriented, fearfully injured, covered in blood, and screaming. Bron took a step towards them, but a hand was laid on her arm.

"No, Bron. Go back to the cabin and bring Veneta and your children on deck. And don't panic. Panic kills. Make your way to the mast and wait for me there."

When she arrived at the cabin door, Declan was already inside, helping Veneta. They gathered up the two babies and ushered Layla, Alon and Lucilla across the sloping deck.

"Put Cronus down. Dogs can swim," Bron told Alon.

"I don't think Cronus can," he argued. "I didn't teach him."

Under instruction from the captain, two of the crew began chopping at the base of the mast, their axes rising and falling in and out of the waves crashing over them. When one man slipped and fell, he brought down three sailors tied to him, all secured by rope to a stanchion, but they scrambled up and hauled him to his feet. His axe had been swept overboard and someone passed him another.

Meantime, Declan had tied a rope to the rail and was fastening it around his waist. Bron and Veneta watched, water above their ankles, their arms round the children, all clinging tightly to the flukes of an anchor. Around them swirled all manner of debris and drowned rats that had been flushed out of the holds. No one had come up from below for some time.

"Stand by!"

In the lull as the axes were lowered, there was a pitiful mewing above their heads. Eyes turned upwards saw two pairs of yellow lights peering down at them from the rigging.

Declan was nearest, and with presence of mind, grabbed hold of a leather bucket that was rolling about the deck. He held it up above his head and the ship's cat and her kitten, bedraggled and shivering, leapt into it.

At that moment, the mast tipped towards the starboard rail and slowly fell, smashing the rail and landing on the sandbank, the rigging with it. There was a rush towards it, people pushing and jostling to stand on the pole. Twenty or more fell, slipped or were pushed off.

Declan, with the rope round his waist, clambered out on to the mast and let himself down into the sea, swinging himself along the pole, arm over arm, taking the rope with him. Several times he disappeared from view, and when he finally reached the sandbank, a loud cheer went up.

The captain sent three more men across, now using the stretched rope as well as the mast as support.

"Women first," ordered Stokovius, "then the children, and a man with each one!"

The four men on the bank clung to the rope while woman after woman, each with her escort, timidly lowered herself into the sea to attempt the crossing. Not all made it.

Koch took Asandra over. Veneta crossed with her escort, and when she waved her safe arrival, a young legionary came up to Bron. His head had been shaved, revealing a large red gash. Bron remembered helping to clean the wound and sew the skin over it.

"Can you swim?" he asked her.

"A little, but not in this sea."

"You'll be fine," he assured her. "You saved my life, and now I'm going to save yours."

The legionary lowered himself on to the mast and took hold of the rope, then helped Bron down. She sat astride the wooden pole, her arms straight in front of her, her splayed fingers gripping its sides.

"Try to work your way along the mast."

She propelled herself forward a few inches, gaining confidence, when a wave caught her a stinging blow and toppled her into the water.

The legionary grabbed her as she fell and lifted her in his arms.

"Put your left arm over the pole," he shouted, "and keep hold of the rope with the other hand."

Together they scrambled almost the length of the mast then swam the last few feet to reach the safety of the sandbank. Bron collapsed on the sand, and by the time she had recovered a little and sat up, he had already returned to the ship to bring over the children.

The last woman across was Sythia. Because of her bulk, she needed two of the crew to help her, and though the situation was serious, Bron and Veneta had to restrain themselves from laughing as she submerged twice, pulling her rescuers with her, then bobbed up spluttering, legs and arms flailing, entangling herself and them in yards of billowing tunic.

"Thank the gods you made it," Bron called to her when finally their friend staggered breathlessly towards them.

Exhausted, Sythia fell to her knees, burying her face gratefully in the sand and emerging with a gargoyle mask that Bron wiped and kissed affectionately. Veneta hauled her back on to her feet.

"Nearly was a gonner that time, my dears," she panted, dripping water all over them.

Then the children started coming across, most of them terrified, but not one was lost to the waves. The older, stronger boys treated it as a great adventure. Sythia was reunited with her twins, and Bron and Veneta with their five children.

"Where's Cronus?" shouted Alon as soon as he set foot on the sand, before his mother could throw her arms round him. "The captain made me leave him behind. He said he'd put him on the pole to take his chances."

"You must make up your mind that you won't see Cronus again," Bron warned him. "I'm sure he's a brave little dog, but he'll never survive in this sea."

"But you said all dogs could swim!" he remonstrated. "I shouldn't have let the horrible old captain take him away from me!"

"He did right. You couldn't put your life in danger for a dog."

"But he was my friend!"

Gradually, the sea was pounding the *Juniper* to pieces. From where Bron stood among the crowd of survivors, it appeared that the whole of the larboard rail had gone, as well as what had been their cabin, and the galley superstructure. Anxiously, she looked for the captain but couldn't see him.

"Alon, look! On the mast!"

They turned to peer in the direction that Veneta was pointing. Alternately padding along the pole then pausing to cling on as a wave broke over him, the puppy was gradually making his way to safety, but as they watched anxiously, a surge gathered him up and washed him into the sea. He was submerged beneath the weight of the water but surprisingly reappeared, paddling for all he was worth. Alon rushed to where the waves lost energy as they ran up the bar, calling and calling to his pet, and the puppy struggled towards the boy's voice.

"He *can* swim!" he cried delightedly.

It was not long, however, before the puppy was visibly tiring and his vigorous efforts were not bringing him any nearer to land. Again he disappeared.

"Cronus!"

Koch heard the boy's cry and turned, saw the puppy struggling pitifully, and without hesitation, dived back into the sea, surfacing near where Cronus had been, though now there was no sign of the little dog. He immediately dived again and was out of sight for what seemed an eternity to those watching from the sand bar. Then a cheer went up as he reappeared with Cronus held high above his head.

When they came ashore, he placed the puppy in Alon's arms and smiled with pleasure to see the dog lick the salt off Alon's tearful face. The little boy tried to thank him, Bron hugged him, and even

Asandra looked impressed at this second display of bravery.

"Now," said Koch, "we have to go."

"Go where?" asked Asandra.

"Across to the island. The cap'n said I was to take all the survivors over there."

They turned to look across the calm lagoon. It was difficult to comprehend the peace of the still, pale green water on the other side of the sand bar. All they could see beyond it was a sandy foreshore sprinkled with trees, then a rocky outcrop that increased in height as it ran further inland.

"I'm going over first," said Koch, "to test how deep the water is. I want two of you to hold on to the end of this rope. I will coil the rest in a loop round my shoulder. I probably won't need it, but I may."

He stumbled and slid down the other side of the sand bar and waded out into the calm water. For a few feet, his ankles were covered. Then the level rose to his knees and finally to his chest as he pushed onward, his arms held above his head and swinging in opposition to his stride. Then the water began to recede down to his waist, to his knees and ankles, and he waded ashore on the island.

He beckoned and the women began entering the water, their children held in their arms or clinging to their backs, little arms clasped round their mothers' necks in strangling holds. Some of the men carried others across on their shoulders. In a very little time, all were on the sandy foreshore, very thankful to be alive.

With Darius in her arms, Bron approached Koch.

"What about the captain?" she asked fearfully.

"He'll be last off," Koch told her. "He may not make it. In all probability, he won't."

They watched, as all did, the drama still unfolding on the other side of the sand bar and barely noticed that the rain was easing off a little.

Suddenly, a cry went up from the ship.

"What is it?" Bron asked Koch. "What are they shouting?"

"It's every man for himself!" Koch answered her.

Those still on board spread out all over the ship, now with its superstructure washed away and its deck clear of all obstruction. Most of them jumped and tried to swim, floundering in the sea. Some clung to the horizontal mast.

Five or more were hanging from the rope under the mast. Declan, as anchorman, and the three crew holding on to the rope in front of him, were struggling to stand firm, digging out impressions in the wet sand with their heels, trying to get a grip, but were gradually being dragged forward down the bank towards the sea. The men standing on top of the bank rushed to their aid, also hauling on the rope, and they gained some ground backwards up the slope.

Koch ran to tie his rope round the trunk of one of the trees on the island then waded back across the lagoon to the sandbank and knotted the other end to the rope Declan was gripping. He then extricated the young sailor from the coil wound round his waist. It brought relief to the men on the bank as the distant tree trunk took the strain.

Declan collapsed on the sand, and when he had recovered sufficiently, waded across to Veneta, dragging his hands through the salt water of the lagoon, and asked her to bandage them. He was exhausted and subdued and Veneta spoke to him softly as she bandaged the deep cuts and friction burns across his palms, using strips of wet linen torn from Sythia's saturated tunic. She wanted him to rest among the sand dunes, but he declined and waded back to the sand bar, but not before thanking her and kissing her gently on the cheek. Bron smiled to see Veneta's confusion.

They continued to watch the attempted rescues. Finally, the hull of the *Juniper* split in two, and the sea surged through the gap with a noise like thunder. Those on the bank retreated higher up as the waves came crashing and foaming towards them. The two halves of the hull rolled on to their sides and no one was left on deck.

Veneta broke the silence that followed.

"Goodness, Bron, you've got a hefty bruise on the side of your head."

Bron gingerly felt above her ear where Fabia's punch had landed. She reflected that the girl's body was probably sloshing about somewhere in the sea and that was the last punch she would deliver, ever again.

"And look, Bron," said Veneta, "it's stopped raining."
It was early afternoon and the sky was beginning to clear.
Bron had only one thought now – *But where is the captain?*

Section III

THE ISLAND

CHAPTER 25

Bron and Veneta stood huddled with the families, watching the last survivors as they started coming ashore, staggering through the calm shallows of the lagoon and on to the beach. Some fell at the water's edge, needing to be dragged or carried across the sand. Others were stumbling towards the subdued groups gathering under the line of trees.

Bron gazed around her in disbelief at their plight. Everyone appeared to be in shock and no one seemed capable of saying anything except to enquire among themselves about those missing and the welfare of the most injured. Gradually, one after another sank helplessly on to the sand. Many began to sob quietly.

After many moments of utter despair, Veneta rose to her knees and began to pray aloud.

"Jesus, Lord," she began, "thank you for saving us from the sea."

"Thank you, Noden," said another, a male voice.

"Thank you, Jupiter," said another; and another, "Thank you, Fortuna," and soon there was a low murmur of voices as one after another thanked the god or goddess of choice.

This common activity seemed to enervate them and Bron began to look around, searching for a likely leader now that the captain was no longer with them. By common consensus, but unspoken, everyone turned to Declan, even though he was one of the youngest of the group.

"First of all, we need warmth and shelter before night falls," he said, a little uncertainly. "Everyone must dry their clothes as best they can."

"Can I help?" It was the young legionary who had brought Bron across.

"Thanks. What's your name?"

"Petrus. I'm with the British Army."

Declan nodded approval. Bron knew that these men, of British nationality, had a reputation for courage and reliability among the legions. Aurelius had often spoken of their integrity.

"We'll divide the men who've recovered into parties of three," decided Declan. "I want two groups to go off in different directions and bring back wood to build a fire, enough to last all night, at least. Two more groups should bring back anything they can find to eat – send one group over to the sand bar, there's plenty being washed up – and two groups should look for fresh water."

The legionary nodded and walked away to organise the men.

Koch was standing near and offered to lead a group but Declan gave him other work to do.

"Round up some men, Koch, and take a look at the people being washed ashore on the sandbar. Most of them will be dead but perhaps not all. Carry the corpses into the trees over there – we'll have to build a funeral pyre later, but not now. Make absolutely sure they're dead, though. Any who are still breathing, bring them up here for attention."

"It wasn't what I had in mind," complained Koch to Bron.

"None of us had it in mind when we woke up this morning," she said.

"Just get on with it!" Declan retorted sharply. "Take as many men as you need. I want the bar and this foreshore kept free of bodies."

Veneta explained soothingly, "It's not good for morale to see them lying about, and as they rot, there is the added danger of disease, as well as the smell."

"It's a very necessary job," commented Asandra and kissed Koch on his ear. Mollified, he left to do Declan's bidding.

"What can I do?" asked Bron.

"If you and Veneta could organise the women, that would be a real help," Declan said. "You must get the children out of their wet tunics and the women must dry their own clothes as soon as we get a fire going. Then there are plenty of us who need medical attention."

"He's a born leader, that one," commented Asandra dotingly as Declan walked away.

As Bron busied herself with the children, her thoughts flew in all directions.

They were safe – even Cronus had recovered sufficiently from his ordeal to be snuffling about, his inquisitive nose exploring their new surroundings. All safe, that is, except their captain. Could he yet be alive and have come ashore somewhere further along the coast? Was that a possibility? She hoped so, oh, she did hope so! But if he had, was he in need of medical attention? How would they find him? Who would go to look for him? He could die alone on some beach, might even now be breathing his last. She would have to speak to Declan about organising a search party as soon as possible.

And the bo'sun? It was practically certain that he had drowned, as Tiegan had foreseen. She wasn't sure how she felt about it.

Her fortune, her jewellery, was intact, hidden in the folds of cloth wrapped around Gift – she had just checked. Even the pouch of earth, its leather thong still broken, was safely there, though saturated and heavy.

The sun was shining now and the wind, less severe, was driving the storm clouds towards the north. The sea was still boiling but the waves were no longer lashing over the top of the *Juniper's* split hull.

Bron looked about her. The sandy bay that they were speedily making their temporary home was wide and long and curved at each end towards tall grey and pink granite cliffs. The northerly arm of the granite jutted into the sea, far beyond the line of the sand bar.

She watched seagulls as they swooped and circled above the cliff and thought how lucky they were that the *Juniper* had gone aground on that bank and hadn't been hurled against the unforgiving rocks. But was it luck or the captain's skill that had engineered it so?

At their backs, the belt of trees – cork oak, Bron learned later from Declan – was being harassed by the wind, and behind the trees, the rocky ground rose gradually to meet the lower slopes of distant mountains. The whole area was covered in a dense growth of bushes in shades of dark green.

If they had to be shipwrecked, this was a good place to have it happen, and she was sure they could make themselves comfortable, once they had shelter and a fire. She knew they had been blown off course, but surely it would not be too long before a passing ship noticed the wreck.

She spread clothes out on the dark red sand to dry.

"Run about and keep warm," she told the children.

Both Darius and Gift were now at the crawling stage. She worried that they were eating the sand, but Veneta assured her that it would take more than a mouthful of sand, whatever it contained, to make them ill.

Two hours later, the foreshore, lagoon and sand bar were as busy as any Roman forum.

Tired men were wading in and out of the lagoon and bringing up to the tree line all manner of eatables – fruit and vegetables, joints of meat now doubly salted, soggy loaves, even drowned chickens. Bron, Veneta and the women were wiping dry these offerings from the sea, then heaping them in piles laid out on grass and leaves.

The beach was littered with debris being washed up or brought ashore. Bron sympathised with Koch and his party as they passed backwards and forwards, silently engaged on their gruesome task. Further along, wet wood was being stacked to dry out. In the other direction, the injured were resting in the shade of the trees.

Veneta had also been watching all the activity. "That young man is just everywhere," she commented, looking over to where Declan was trying to drag a wooden chest up the beach. "I should have another look at his hands and put on clean dressings, if I can find anything clean."

"Veneta," Bron began hesitantly, "there's been no sign of the captain."

"We all realise it," replied her friend, "but no one's mentioned it. I think we must face the obvious."

Bron could not disguise the break in her voice. "He saved our lives, all our lives. I wasn't able to thank him. I would like to have thanked him."

"Perhaps you will have the opportunity, one day," Veneta replied.

Bron smiled through her tears. "In your Christian afterlife? Still, you may be right. I hope you're right."

"I'm going over to the injured now. Do me a favour, Bron, and ask Asandra, Sythia and some of the other women to join me, to see what we can do. If you wouldn't mind keeping an eye on their children as well as ours…"

"Of course."

Bron set off along the beach on her errand.

"Hey, Bron, look what I've found!" Koch was calling her. He was carrying a leather bucket. "It was floating just off the sandbank."

Curious, Bron went over to look. He had no need to explain further. Before she reached him, she could hear piteous mewing.

Laughing, but on the verge of tears again, Bron carefully put her hand inside the makeshift lifesaver and stroked the wet heads and ears her fingers encountered.

"I'm taking them to Layla to look after," he said and continued up the slope.

Bron rounded up a willing group of women, and sent them across to Veneta, then returned to the children. There was no need to spend effort amusing them as they were happily engaged playing with Cronus and the cats or filling the bucket with wet sand to make forts and ramparts. Bron was surprised how quickly they had recovered from their ordeal.

She gazed thoughtfully at Sythia's twins. She was aware that all Tiegan's predictions had come true and wondered whether he was blessed, or perhaps plagued, with foreknowledge or had just made some lucky guesses.

The groups of men that Declan sent out returned throughout the afternoon. A fire was started with dry wood and they began to rig up shelters, using intertwined branches and greenery, and bark stripped easily from the cork trees.

Cries of delight greeted those who returned with a slaughtered wild sow and her piglet. The men said they had come across a small herd and managed to capture two of the creatures. Before returning, they had dug out a pit, using their bare hands, and had covered it with brush, hoping that by next day they would find another boar or other wildlife trapped there.

The smell of roasting pig brought everyone to watch the grey and black-patched carcases being turned slowly on a branch over the fire. There followed a welcome, unexpected meal, although the portions were small. However, when added to vegetables and fruit that had floated in from the ship, everyone ate well.

The only anxiety was that no one had found fresh water. When Bron spoke to Declan about sending out a party to look for the captain, he said that finding a spring or stream must take priority, and tomorrow the men would have to widen their search and go further into the interior, towards the mountains, which would leave little time for anything else.

Bron was glad that she had not completely weaned the babies on to solid food, for they at least did not go to bed thirsty. She found a tin mug among piled-up utensils that had come ashore, and expressed some breast milk. Lucilla drank thirstily, but Layla and Alon would have none of it.

Sleep that night came easily to everyone, under their makeshift shelters. The fire was to be kept burning all night, to attract the attention of any passing ship, and was the responsibility of those posted on watch throughout the hours of darkness.

Declan and Petrus offered to take first watch, with two of the crew. No one had seen any signs of habitation on the island during their forays but everyone felt safer to have three men posted at a distance while one stayed by the fire, and the men decided to take turn and turn about.

Declan opted to spend the first part of his watch by the fire, and Bron saw him staggering backwards and forwards, bringing logs over to throw on the blaze or to stack at the side.

He then sat so that he could scan the sea's horizon but also had to turn his head only slightly to watch, in the firelight, the patch of grass where Veneta and Bron lay with the children.

Bron was glad of his concern for the family, but knew full well, though she still kept this knowledge to herself, that she was not and never had been the object of his preoccupation.

Asandra had to rest content with a view of his back.

CHAPTER 26

"I had another dream last night."

Bron felt uneasy. Her first thought was of the remains of the chickens they had eaten for their mid-day meal, but she had deliberately thrown their entrails into the fire.

She and Veneta had wandered down to the sea to cool their bare feet and splash water in their faces when they had come upon Tiegan at the water's edge, half-heartedly skimming pebbles into the waves.

"What about?" she asked, still not sure whether his dreams were genuine or whether this was a game he played.

He looked up, shading his eyes against the sun. "It was the same as before. A shadow, and you were there, Bron, and the shadow came up behind you, but this time it moved into the light."

"Who was it?" asked Veneta with interest, sitting beside Bron.

"It – it was a man," hedged Tiegan.

Veneta pressed him further. "Did you recognise him?"

"I recognised him," Tiegan replied, looking at Bron.

"Well?" asked Veneta. "Who was it?"

"I don't think we need to know," Bron cut in, scrambling up. "After all, it *was* only a dream."

"Don't be afraid, Bron. A dream can't hurt you. Who was it, Tiegan?"

Bron knew the name that was hovering on the boy's lips before he said it.

"It was the bo'sun."

"But the bo'sun drowned," insisted Veneta. "You must be mistaken."

"I'm not. It was the bo'sun all right."

Bron's heart began to thump so loudly she was embarrassed that Veneta might hear it. *Of course he was dead. They had as good as seen him drown. She was glad he was dead, it was better so.* All the same, a pain stirred in the pit of her stomach that she tried to ignore.

"Have you told your mother?" Veneta asked.

"Yes, and she said I shouldn't say anything to Bron or anyone."

He cast one last pebble into the waves, and walked back up the beach.

Veneta turned to Bron, who was looking at her anxiously. "Don't let it worry you, Bron. It can't be true. I'm still not sure about that boy."

"He has a good track record."

"I can't dispute that."

"I think I'll take a walk," Bron decided, "just to the end of the beach. I won't be long," and she set off in the direction of the northerly cliff.

Dawdling at the edge of the waves, stepping over debris as she went, her thoughts were of Tiegan's dream. Of course, it was ridiculous, he was being mischievous, he must know the anxiety it would cause her, even if he didn't fully understand the implications – and she was not so convinced of that, either. He was certainly much more complicated than his brother, Joas.

She was so wrapt in her thoughts that she covered the distance to the cliff without noticing anything of her surroundings. Now she looked at the granite towering above her and wondered whose powerful hands had fashioned it. Certainly not the god and goddess she had left behind in Byden. They would not even know this cliff existed. Who, then? Noden, who had saved them from the sea god because he had been paid with coins hidden beneath *Juniper's* mast? Or the Christian god, who had presumably saved Veneta even without being paid? Or some other? It was all a great mystery.

She intended to walk back the way she had come but her attention was caught by a tiny crab that was running across the rocks at the foot of the cliff and slithering in and out of the small, shallow pools left behind by the storm. She wondered what was on the other side of the cliff and decided, if she removed her sandals and was careful, she should be able to walk over the wet rocks and round the headland to satisfy her curiosity. If the cliff continued at the same great height and the sea ran right up to it, she would retrace her steps.

With her sandals in one hand and both arms outstretched to keep her balance, she ventured on to the rocks, their pink and grey hues more definite and more beautiful where wet.

When she rounded the headland, she was surprised to find another beach similar in size to the one she had left, but backed by a sheer cliff face. She jumped down on to the sand and replaced her sandals.

There were several fissures in the granite, some of which led deeper into the cliff, but there were two, slightly wider, sheltering steep sandy paths that led upwards, presumably to the cliff top.

Debris from the ship was being washed up on this beach also, and she thought she must tell Declan, as there was much here worth scavenging.

She wandered along for some time, still dwelling on Tiegan's latest prophecy and shivering because of it, when she noticed, several feet ahead, a heap of something on the sand, irregularly shaped – perhaps part of the sail that had been ripped away?

She approached, mystified. Then she heard a sound, an unexpected sound. If she had not known better, she would have said it was a groan. There it was again, and this time there was no mistaking, it *was* a groan!

She darted across the remaining distance between herself and whoever was lying there. It was a man, his tunic covered in sand and unrecognisable, but though lying on his side, his form was familiar. Was it – could it be – the bo'sun? Had he too escaped the clutches of the sea god? Of all his companions in the boat, had he remained alive, rising from his watery grave to torment her again? Of course, she need tell no one and just let him lie here and die. But then she remembered he *had* given her the chance to live by offering her a place in the boat.

She crouched and reached across to his shoulder and rolled the figure on to his back.

"Captain!"

For a moment, she stared in amazement, then dropped to her knees. It was obvious he had not heard her. His eyes were closed and the upper part of his face, not protected by his beard, was encrusted with salt and sunburnt red and black in ugly patches. She would be afraid to wash or wipe away the salt in case it brought flakes of skin with it. His arms and legs were covered in gashes and massive, dark bruises, though he did not appear badly injured otherwise.

"Oh, Captain, I'm so glad to find you alive!" she said, but realised that he was only just clinging to life. He must have lain here for over twenty four hours. His breathing was irregular and very shallow. He needed medical attention but, before that, shade and a drink of water. Bron looked around, but there was no shelter from the pitiless sun. As for pure water, there was none of that, either.

Then she looked towards the headland and despaired. She would be unable to drag his dead weight along the beach on her own, and certainly would never get him over the rocks.

She would have to go for help. But if the men hadn't returned, there was no way that the women could drag him across the rocks, either. That would finish him off for sure. But she couldn't leave him here, she would have to go for help.

She stood and looked down at him, conscious that he had saved the lives of herself and her children, and wishing only to save his.

"But I don't know what to do," she agonised, willing him to regain consciousness. "Tell me what to do."

There was one thing she could do. She stood and, unfastening the clasps on each shoulder, let her tunic fall around her feet. Gathering it up, she gently laid it over him, so that it also covered his face. Then it worried her that it gave the impression he was already dead so she knelt again and moved the tunic to one side.

"I'm so sorry to do this," she explained unnecessarily, "but it will keep the sun off you."

She was about to replace it when his mouth opened slightly. She put her fingers in her own mouth, not that she had much spittle, and tried to moisten his cracked lips. He sucked at her fingers and she withdrew them with difficulty.

161

"I'm so sorry," she said again, "but there is no water. I have no water for you."

No, but I have something else! The thought struck her like a blow inside her head and she jumped to her feet, away from him. *I can't do that!* she argued with herself, shocked that she should even think it. She stooped and rearranged the tunic over his face again, as if to hide her blushes from his unseeing eyes.

She would go for help immediately. *But what if he died before she could bring help back?* Even if she did what she had thought about, there was no guarantee that he would not be dead by the time she came back. *But at least it will give him a fighting chance and I would never forgive myself if...*

She turned away from the motionless man and walked further along the beach. *He had saved their lives and this was the least she could do.* Aurelius had told her once how the Army had actually eaten their own dead at a time of near starvation in battle conditions, when supplies had not come through. There had been no order and no one talked about it then or afterwards, but it had happened. Years later, Aurelius met an officer who had been part of the reinforcements, and he had spoken of it in a shamed, low voice.

When Bron expressed her revulsion, Aurelius said that people always fed on other people, on their kindness and generosity, their advice, experience and example, and most of all on their love. He had said that her love kept him energetic and alert and, yes, alive in every sense. Didn't they both feel utterly drained after their lovemaking? That was because they were feeding on each other as they filled each other's needs, taking and giving in equal measure, and it was only after their passion had dissipated and they lay quietly together that they felt replete. Bron had had to admit that it was so.

She turned around now and made her way back to the captain, resolved in what she had to do but still uneasy in her mind. However, she comforted herself that no one but she would know anything about it, as her captain was too deeply unconscious ever to remember what she had done for him. Perhaps he was too unconscious to take advantage of her offering, but then she recalled how he had sucked her fingers, and hoped he would be co-operative.

Kneeling beside him again, she drew back her tunic off his face, then hesitated, making sure he was not coming round. Satisfying herself that this was not so, she gently lifted his head on to her lap, turning his face towards her and herself towards him. She cradled his head in her arm, and with her other hand, pulled down her undershift, bared her right breast, then cupped and guided it towards the captain's mouth.

She closed her eyes as his lips closed round her nipple and he began to suck. He was managing so well that her eyes flew open and she looked down at him with suspicion, but satisfied herself that this was a natural instinct and he was still deeply unconscious.

As she studied the grey head nestled in her arm, she thought for the first time what a handsome man he must have been in his youth, and still was, for that matter. She closed her eyes again, unable to begin to describe the emotions that were flooding through every part of her body, emotions that brought a flush to her cheeks and quickened her breathing.

He had stopped sucking now but lay without moving, his lips still clamped to her nipple. She let him stay there for a while, unwilling to let go the moment she knew would never be repeated, then removed her breast from his mouth and instinctively bent to kiss the top of his head.

When she straightened up, a dark shadow was covering them. She raised her eyes, expecting to see a cloud obscuring the sun. Instead, she found herself looking into the dark grey eyes of the bo'sun! She stared at him, unbelieving, then realised where his gaze had dropped and hurriedly pulled her shift up over her breast.

"Well, now, ain't this a sight for sore eyes?" he asked of the space around them. "My goddess and the captain in a maternal clinch!"

"He's unconscious," Bron told him.

"Didn't look that way to me!" he replied, and laughed.

"How long have you been standing there?"

"Long enough to see all I needed to see. Pretty, too."

Bron laid the captain's head gently on the sand and stood up, with as much dignity as she could muster.

"I've only just found him lying here. He's half dead."

"You're not asking me to pity him, are you, goddess? Seems he got a pretty good deal out of it."

Bron's indignation turned to spite. "I should have known you'd turn up. We all thought you were drowned."

He ignored the animosity in her voice that suggested she wished he had been.

"Nearly was. And we thought all of you had drowned."

"We?"

"Our boatload. A couple of the men were washed overboard but the rest of us threw up a few miles along the coast. Lucky's not the word."

"So were we lucky – those of us who made it. The captain stayed on board. The rats had already deserted."

"Ouch! You hit low, goddess!"

"You deserve it! He grounded the *Juniper* on a sandbank and saved the lives of a lot of us, including me and my children. He was probably last off and must have got washed up here."

"He always was a brave buffoon," said the bo'sun grudgingly.

"So I was just doing for him what he did for us, trying to save his life."

"I'm glad you made it, Bron," the bo'sun said with seemingly genuine warmth. "I quite thought I'd lost you."

He reached out a hand towards her and she backed away.

"Do you still think I would hurt you," he asked reproachfully, "after all we've been to each other? I was only going to feel that bruise."

He came towards her and this time she stood her ground. He reached out again and stroked her cheek.

"That Fabia can certainly pack a punch! She shouldn't have done that, though. I would have slapped her for you but we had other things on our minds."

Not for the first time she wondered at his gentleness and concern towards her, which he usually hid successfully beneath his bantering and insolent exterior.

"Where are you all?" he asked.

"Round that headland." Bron pointed back the way she had come.

"I've been trying to find other survivors," he said, "but you seem to be the only ones."

"How did you find me?"

"I saw you from up there." He pointed to the cliff top. "There's a path down. How many in your camp?"

"Over thirty, men, women and children. Will you be coming to join us now?"

"Oh, I don't think so. We're four men and four women, so we're doing very well as we are, very cosy. I've got all I need for the time being – almost." He looked at her keenly and she lowered her eyes before the intensity in his. "I've even got Fabia as a stopgap – though don't tell her I said that," and he grinned wickedly.

Bron glanced down at the captain. "Our men haven't found any water yet."

"They will. There are plenty of springs and streams. It's just a question of locating them."

"I need to get him to the camp. I can't do it on my own."

"So?"

"You have to help us."

"No, I don't, not after what he did to me. He can stay here and rot for all I care, especially after what I just witnessed."

"Bo'sun – what's your name, by the way?"

"Huh," he shrugged ruefully, "my name didn't bother you before you wanted something from me."

Bron knew he was right, and remained silent.

"'Bo'sun' will do, until we're on more intimate terms."

"Then it will always be 'Bo'sun'!" she retorted sharply.

He laughed, not at all affronted. "I thought you wanted my help."

"I do," Bron relented. "I pleaded with him once to save your life –"

"I can't deny that."

"– and now I'm pleading with *you* to save *his*."

The man hesitated. Bron experienced again a mixture of pain and pleasure as she looked at the stature of him and the strong arms that she tried not to remember had been wound round her not so very long ago. With an effort, she controlled her wayward thoughts.

"If you could just carry him across the rocks and on to the beach, that's all I need."

"Is it? Then that's a pity and you don't know what you're missing."

Without further argument, he bent and lifted the motionless body of the captain, slinging him unceremoniously over his shoulder like a sack of potatoes.

Bron had difficulty in keeping up with them as he strode towards the headland and was quite out of breath, so slowed her pace. He waited for her before attempting to clamber across the rocks.

Steadying himself against the granite with one hand, he stepped carefully from boulder to boulder and finally dumped his burden on the sand on the other side of the headland. He stopped only long enough to take in the activity further along the beach and the disintegrating halves of the *Juniper's* hull.

"Thank you," said Bron gratefully.

"Looks like your men are back, so I'm off," he told her. "Don't none of you come trying to find us. And don't ask any favours of me again where he's concerned." He dug the captain in the ribs with his foot. "I've repaid the debt and that's all there is to it."

"I understand."

"I'll be back, though, goddess, when you least expect me. I'll be back to enjoy some of what you gave the captain so freely." Bron flushed angrily. "And I wouldn't be so sure, if I were you, that he actually was unconscious!"

He was gone then, leaving her alone with the man whose life she hoped she had saved. She looked down at him. *Was it her imagination, or did his eyelids flutter?*

CHAPTER 27

For a while, they had been strung out along the sand, like a line of savages, waving, shouting, wildly gesticulating. But as Bron watched from under the trees, their cavortings gradually ceased, arms dropped, smiles faded and slowly they began to trudge back up the beach towards her and the others, who had not even bothered to exert themselves waving at the ship sailing by on the horizon.

This performance had been repeated at least once a day since the shipwreck, and even the most hopeful among them were becoming despondent.

"Why do we have to be rescued?" asked Alon. "I like it here."

It was a week since Bron had found the captain, in which time he had returned to full health and strength, and had taken charge of the camp.

Streams from the mountains had been located in several places, to everyone's relief. Local wildlife was being trapped in a variety of ways and Bron was glad that it was sometimes skinned before being brought back to camp, so disguising its origins. The marines had fabricated fishing rods, spears and harpoons. It meant that the camp enjoyed nutritious meals concocted by the cook, whom everyone had been glad to find among the survivors.

The fire on the beach was kept burning continuously, and there was another alight on the cliff top, and Bron asked Declan why none of the passing ships had come to their rescue. He said it was because the flames could not be seen so far out during the hours of sunshine, and when dark, captains suspected pirates of trying to lure their ships on to the rocks, and would not take the risk.

"Surely someone will be curious enough to investigate," she suggested optimistically.

"At least Vortin won't find you here," Veneta said. "When you don't show up in Ostia, he may give up and go back to Britannia."

"Let's hope so," Bron replied fervently. "But so may Aurelius give up. I don't know how long he'll be able to wait for me. He'll have to leave when the army moves on."

Veneta squeezed her hand. "We'll find him," she promised reassuringly. "It would be very difficult for a legion to get lost."

They wandered up the beach to where the children were engrossed in creating sand sculptures, encouraged by Koch. For several days he had supervised the making of a stack of moulds from pieces of wood nailed together to form rectangles. Today they would begin filling them with sand.

Layla knew exactly what she wanted to build.

"A fortress," she announced.

Koch consulted the other children gathered round him, about ten of them, boys and girls. They put forward a few other vague ideas but finally Layla's suggestion won the day.

"Watch me first, then you can all try," Koch instructed them.

Soon, he had the beginnings of a round tower with crenellated roof and a staircase leading down the outside walls. He told them that the only restriction to what they could build would be the height, as the sand would collapse if taller than about three feet.

Layla and the twins had joined forces but Tiegan soon lost interest and wandered away.

"Tiegan!" Joas called to his brother. "Aren't you going to help any more?"

"Kids' stuff!" Tiegan called back over his shoulder.

"Oh, come back, Tiegan, please!" Layla pleaded. "We need you!"

"Seems to me you'll do just fine without me!" he replied and ran to join the men swimming in the lagoon.

"Figs to him!" said Joas.

After working together for some time, Layla commented happily that Tiegan had been right, they *were* doing just fine without him.

"He is rather grumpy today," she said.

"Take no notice," Joas advised. "He's cross because you and me are good friends."

"I'm friends with him, too," objected Layla, "though you make me laugh more."

When Tiegan returned, he sat at a distance, a frown on his face, watching the sand sculptures growing.

"I'm glad he's not joining in," Layla whispered to Joas. "That sour face would make our fortress fall down!" She giggled and made Joas laugh, and they both looked across to his brother, which only served to deepen Tiegan's frown.

At the end of the day, the children brought the adults over to admire their handiwork. There was one collapsed heap of sand but, standing in a circle, were four groups of towers of varying designs with staircases winding down them and window shapes carved into the upper portions.

It didn't rain overnight and the children were again at work directly after breakfast. Layla and Joas were not so busy with their hands that their tongues were idle. Suddenly Joas asked, "Layla, do you know what love is?"

Layla hesitated. "I-I think so. Do you?"

"I think it's being all mushy. At least, it is when the grown-ups talk about it."

"I know what you mean."

"Tiegan says he loves you."

"I love him," answered Layla airily, "but you're my best friend." Joas laughed. "And you're mine."

"If I lived in this castle, Joas, you could visit me."

"I couldn't, because there are no doors," he replied practically.

Layla looked up and saw Koch coming towards them.

"I'm not going to live in a castle without anyone coming to see me," she decided. "I'll ask Koch about it."

By the end of the day, the sculptures were finished to their creators' collective satisfaction.

"Joas and me are very pleased with our fortress," Layla told Koch, "and see, we have signed our names side by side on our wall." Koch bent to look at the squiggly writing – "*Joas, Layla*" followed by the date, "*CDVI*".

The adults wandered over to inspect the complex of towers with windows and doors carved into their sides, the walls, staircases and entrance arches, and expressed their admiration.

Their meal that evening started with sardines, anchovies, mackerel, and mussels that had been roasted in their shells in a covered pan in the embers of the fire. This was followed by a meat stew that the cook didn't bother to name but which Layla whispered to Joas was snake.

"Layla, how do you know?" he whispered back.

"I'm just guessing, by the shape of the pieces," she answered.

"Or it could be those brown-and-white-patterned lizards we've been chasing," he suggested. They both giggled, their heads together. They were too hungry, however, to refuse a second helping.

Layla looked across to where Tiegan was toying with his stew, pushing the meat around the bowl with his fingers. When he saw her looking at him, he turned his face away.

Layla felt sorry that Tiegan was unhappy about her friendship with his brother, and resolved to make it up with him later in the evening. However, the opportunity didn't present itself because all the children became argumentative and quarrelsome and were sent to their beds early.

Before following her brother into their brushwood shelter, Layla looked at the clouds clustering low over the mountains in the darkening sky and hoped that it wouldn't rain overnight and ruin their beautiful sand sculptures.

CHAPTER 28

Bron didn't know why but she awoke in the early hours and, after tossing and turning for some time, left her bed to take a walk along the beach. She heard thunder in the distant mountains and saw flashes of lightning illuminating their summits, but above her the sky was clear and the moon gave all the light she needed as she paddled along the edge of the waves. There was no doubt that this was a beautiful island.

"Bron!" She heard her name called and walked towards the man sitting on a log by the fire. The watch had been reduced to one man, whose duty it was to make sure that both fires were kept burning all night.

"Captain!" she exclaimed. "I didn't know that they put you on watch."

"I volunteered," he told her. "I don't believe in asking the men to carry out work that I'm not prepared to share. What are you doing, walking about on your own?"

"I'm not sleepy."

"Then come and join me."

She crossed to the fire and sat beside him on the log, just close enough for them to talk together in low voices.

"Bron, dear, I haven't yet thanked you for saving my life."

She looked at him sharply. It was the first time he had called her "dear".

He continued, "They didn't tell me for several days that it was you who found me, and how the bo'sun had survived against all odds – as I had – and that you persuaded him to carry me round the headland."

"I was very glad it turned out that way," Bron said guardedly.

"He thought it was a life for a life, eh?"

"How did you know that?"

She remembered her negotiation with the bo'sun on the beach on just that issue. Did she detect a slight hesitation before the captain answered?

"Just guessed."

"Yes, that's about the cut of it."

He reached out and took her hand. "I'm very grateful to you. What more can I say?"

She gazed out to sea then withdrew her hand gently, hoping that the firelight would not reveal her confusion and, if it did, he would think that the glow in her cheeks was caused by the heat. All she was remembering was the last time they had been on a beach alone together.

"Anyone would have done the same," she said.

"No, they wouldn't," he replied, so decisively that she had that uncomfortable feeling again. She decided to move to safer ground.

"Do you think we will ever be rescued, Captain?"

"Of course we will – and my name's Theon, you know."

"Yes, I did know."

"Then why not call me by my name and not 'Captain' all the time? – when we're alone, I mean."

"It will be strange."

"I'm sure you'll get used to it."

"Theon." It did indeed sound strange. "How soon – being rescued?"

"I've been giving that some thought. I want to reach Ostia, too. The sooner I'm there and paid off, the sooner I'll be able to go home."

"Home…" echoed Bron.

"Are you still homesick for your grey skies and green hills?"

"I can't go home," she replied after a pause.

"Then come with me to Illyricum, Bron."

She listened as he painted word pictures of the land he loved – the blue-grey mountains behind a craggy coastline, and coves he had explored as a boy, dragonflies darting on black wings above lakes with a hundred waterfalls tumbling into them, and the river delta soil so rich that it produced three crops of tangerines a year.

"Oh, Theon," breathed Bron quietly, "you make it sound so lovely. I do wish I could see all that."

"So do I, with all my heart," and he repeated softly, "with all my heart."

Abruptly, he cleared his throat, and asked gruffly if it wasn't time for her to get some sleep. Bron was surprised at being dismissed so suddenly, but scrambled off the log on which they were seated and said yes, it probably was time, though she still wasn't tired.

It was then he noticed that the fire on the cliff top had gone out.

"What a fine watchman I am," he said, "chatting to you instead of attending to my duties! Any member of my crew would certainly be punished for such neglect! I'll have to relight it." He paused then asked her, almost like a naughty little boy, "I'd appreciate it if you didn't say anything about my lapse, Bron – keep it a secret between us?"

She smiled indulgently. "Of course. Shall I come with you?"

"The path to the top is steep –"

"I've climbed it by daylight."

"Come on, then."

Following him, a lighted branch from the fire held high in his hand, they reached the top of the sandy path and walked along the promontory. There was no doubt that the fire was dead. While Bron held the torch, the captain tried to blow some life into it, but there was no response.

"Strange," he said, "but the embers look wet." He put his hand into them. "They *are* wet. The fire's been doused with wet grass. Now, who would have done that and why? I'll have to start another one."

They gathered dry grass and leaves to build up a platform on which to lay twigs then small logs. From a pouch, the captain produced lumps of dried pine resin and scattered them over the pile. When all was prepared to his satisfaction, he lit the grass with his torch, and soon had the fire blazing again. They waited by it for a while, throwing on larger logs, making sure it would stay alight, then descended the path to the beach.

"Now I am ready to sleep," Bron said.

He hesitated a moment before replying. "Then good night, my dear."

CHAPTER 29

It was daylight when she was awoken by a scream of anger –
Layla's.

Leaping to her feet, Bron threw her cover round her shoulders and
hurried from their shelter. On the beach, a group of children and adults
were crowded round the sand sculptures, or what remained of them.

"Who could've done such a thing?" asked Sythia in disbelief,
looking at the trampled remains. "All their 'ard work for nothing!"

"An animal?" asked Veneta, hopefully.

Declan shook his head. "The boars stay in the undergrowth."

"Cronus then, or the cats? They're always roaming about at
night."

"This wasn't done accidentally," Koch commented. "It looks
deliberate to me."

"Who was on watch last night?" asked Petrus.

"Declan was, for the early watch," volunteered Asandra. "There
weren't any animals about then." When everyone looked at her
enquiringly, she added, "I came out to keep 'im company."

The captain joined the angry group. "It wasn't during my late
watch, either," he said, "except..." He paused, then told them of the
curious incident of the fire on the cliff top being doused deliberately.
He made no mention of Bron being with him.

"Could it be someone from the other camp?" Petrus asked.

"Drawing me away so that they could destroy the children's
sculptures?" asked the captain. "I hardly think so."

Layla was still in tears but Bron noticed her exchange glances
with Joas. He opened his mouth to speak but Layla shook her head
and he closed it again.

"What was all that about?" Bron asked Layla as soon as they and
Veneta were alone.

"It might have been Tiegan, Mummy," Layla replied, and told her mother all that Joas had said. Bron smiled, though secretly she was more than a little worried at the intensity of Tiegan's feelings.

"You're only just eight – it's too soon to be thinking about boys," she admonished her daughter.

"I'm not thinking about boys," Layla protested, "it's Tiegan that's thinking about me."

"Then you'd better keep away from him." She knew it was silly advice that could not be carried out in the situation in which they found themselves.

"Let's not tell Sythia," Veneta suggested. "It will only upset her. Hopefully, the incident will be forgotten in a day or so." Bron and Layla agreed.

That was the morning the captain called a meeting, in the shade of the trees. Looking around, Bron reflected that the average age of the group was very young, those who had perished in the storm being mostly the old and sick. She brought her mind back to what the captain was saying.

"So it's time we took the matter into our own hands and organised our own rescue."

"But how?" asked Koch.

"Some of us must go for help."

"You don't even know where we are, Captain," Sythia reminded him.

"I reckon we were driven north-east of Corsica."

"Captain," said Declan, "I trust you with my life, but swimming to Corsica is impossible!"

"Even for you, Declan?" teased Petrus. Everyone laughed.

"No one will need to swim," continued Stokovius.

"How then?" asked Asandra. "It's not as if we 'ad a boat or anything."

"Oh, but we have or, at least, someone has –"

Everyone stared at him.

"He might have sunk it," suggested Veneta.

The captain shook his head. "He's too shrewd for that. It's his trump card, and his personal means of escape, if he has a mind."

"He won't let you 'ave it!" Asandra guessed.

"I don't suppose that he wants to be rescued," said Bron, who was the only person to have seen and spoken to the bo'sun.

"And I don't suppose that Fabia wants to be rescued, neither – at least, not yet!" Asandra chipped in. "She could do a good job of persuading him against it if his thoughts wandered in that direction."

"We won't know if we don't try," commented Veneta.

"Exactly," agreed the captain. "So we need some volunteers, three or four of you, to find their camp and talk to him. We can't offer any payment now but I can certainly arrange it when we arrive in Ostia, if he will trust me till then."

"We could try walking along the coastline to find the camp," suggested Petrus. "The boat will be beached."

"Highly unlikely," said the captain. "It's my guess that he's taken his group off the beach into the hillside somewhere, and he certainly wouldn't leave such a valuable asset in full view where anyone could steal it."

"Anyway," Declan reminded them, "we know only that there's another beach around the headland. After that, it may be cliffs all the way."

"And," added Bron, "remember that he was walking along the cliff top when he saw me with the captain –" She stopped suddenly in confusion. Stokovius came to her rescue, and not for the first time she wondered how much he was aware of what had taken place between them.

"Bron's right, I think you will have to look for them in the hills. Choose among yourselves who will go. Cook will prepare food to carry with you, as you may be gone for several days, and water, though you should find sufficient on the way."

The men voted that four of them should make the journey – Declan, Petrus, Koch and a thin, wiry legionary, whose appearance belied his strength, according to Petrus, and who volunteered his services.

That decided, the search party rested for the remainder of the day, then set off early next morning.

No one had any idea how long it would be before the men returned. Everyone went about camp life as usual, not conjecturing the possible outcome by day, though speculation was rife around the fire in the evenings.

During the afternoon of the third day, several of the children playing hide-and-seek in the scrub saw the party approaching from a distance, and ran to tell the captain. When the four men walked into camp, everyone was there to greet them.

"We can tell by the look on your faces that you weren't successful," the captain commented.

"Not entirely unsuccessful, though," Declan told him.

The captain was insistent that they be served with the remains of the mid-day meal and water before he allowed them to give their account. Then everyone gathered beneath the trees where they could all hear what was being said.

"The four of us fanned out over a wide area and we found their camp, though it took us the day we left here and all yesterday morning. It's about eight miles along the coast, hidden amongst the undergrowth on the foothills, above a little cove."

"They've got everything there," interrupted the legionary who had gone with them. "They're as comfortable as we are, plus their site is on the bank of a stream."

Declan continued, "I decided that only three of us would go into their camp and so we left Koch hiding among the bushes some way away. They were so unprepared that no one was on watch and they were very surprised to see us. Fortunately, they were all there, all eight of them. The bo'sun had to be called out of his shelter."

"He was in there with Fabia and one of the other girls," Petrus said, with something like envy in his voice. Declan grinned across at him.

"When we asked for the boat he just laughed," continued Declan, "and said there was no question of letting us have it. He wouldn't budge an inch."

"You told him there would be something waiting for him once he got to Ostia?" questioned the captain.

"It didn't make any difference. He just laughed at us again. Then they invited us to stay for a meal – I think to make us feel even more uncomfortable."

"Have to admit it was tasty, though," added Petrus.

"So you stayed a while?" asked Sythia.

"It suited our plan," explained Declan, "because we wanted to give Koch as much time as possible."

"To do what?" someone asked.

"Find the boat."

"And I found it!" exclaimed Koch triumphantly.

"Where?" several of them chorused.

Koch took a deep breath, the centre of attention, and glanced across at Asandra, who was also looking at him expectantly.

"I went to the cliff top but couldn't see a way down except for a narrow slit in the rock, wide enough for one person, very steep. They must have had their work cut out to climb up there, and it would have been impossible to haul the boat up, so I guessed it must still be down at water level."

"Makes sense," agreed one of the men, nodding his head.

"I slithered down and got into the little bay. It's stony, not sandy, like here. There were a lot more fissures in the cliff and short tunnels that led nowhere. There was also a huge rock, sort of stranded at the end of the beach. Behind that I found a small cave, full of shallow water, but with a raised, dry area at the back, and that's where the boat was, drawn up and turned upside down."

His listeners gave a cheer.

"I climbed back up the path," continued Koch, "which was just as well, because minutes later one of the men passed where I was hiding and went down to the beach. By the gear he was carrying, he looked as though he was expecting to stay the night."

"He left camp while we were eating," Petrus confirmed.

Koch voiced what all of them were probably thinking. "It means that they're going to guard that boat night and day from now on."

The captain nodded agreement. "Declan, I sense there is more?"

The young man hesitated. "After the meal, as we were preparing to leave, the bo'sun called me over to speak to me privately."

"And?" asked the captain.

"He said we possessed one card that hadn't been played."

"And what was that?" The captain was puzzled. "If we had another, we would have offered it."

"Not *it*, Captain, *her* – Bron."

Everyone's eyes turned to Bron, who hadn't said a word during the discussion.

"Bron?" repeated Veneta. "How does Bron feature in this?"

"She doesn't!" boomed the captain.

"He said," repeated Declan slowly, "that he would consider the deal if we sent Bron to him to offer it."

"No!" the captain was adamant.

"How can I negotiate a deal?" Bron asked. "I can only offer what he's refused already – a cash payment once we reach port."

Petrus put into words what everyone must have been thinking. "I guess he had in mind something more than a bundle of cash, Bron. He meant that you were the payment for letting us have the boat."

"She can't possibly sell herself to that man!" protested Veneta.

The captain was enraged. "Of course not! It's out of the question!"

"What does Bron say?" asked Asandra. "If it means he will agree to let us have the boat –"

"But there's no guarantee that he will, even if…" Petrus did not finish his sentence.

There were murmurings within the group and Bron sensed that opinions were divided, not all sympathetic towards the captain's misgivings. Some people were more concerned with their rescue than Bron's safety.

Declan turned to the captain. "I've been thinking about this and talking it over on the way back. We've a suggestion to make."

"Well?" asked Stokovius.

"They were drinking water from the stream – we weren't offered any wine. It seems fairly obvious they have none."

"At least that's something we've got that they haven't," chortled Koch.

"Another full amphora was washed up this morning," Asandra told him.

"Exactly," said Declan. "Now, if an amphora happened to float into their cove –"

"A diversion," explained the legionary.

"Knowing Fabia, she would get herself and all the men in the camp drunk in no time at all," Asandra contemplated with glee.

"If, then, Bron turned up and lured the bo'sun away…" suggested Petrus.

"…and we were already in hiding somewhere near, we would need only a very short time to get into the cove and steal the boat," Declan calculated.

"And Bron? What of Bron?" Veneta wanted to know. "No, it's too dangerous."

"And I absolutely forbid it!" insisted the captain again, his voice raised above everyone else's.

"It's for Bron to say," Asandra reminded them.

Bron hesitated. She could see the dangers only too well. Once the bo'sun discovered that he had been fooled so completely, she guessed his revenge would wreak havoc for someone, possibly herself. But if it was the only way of getting possession of the boat, and someone going for help, and being rescued, and reaching Ostia soon, and finding Aurelius…

"I'll risk it," she said.

"No, you won't!" The captain was even more adamant. "This discussion is at an end!"

With that, the party broke up into little groups, all talking over the situation. Bron could hear some of the comments.

"I can't see why he won't let her try it." That remark was made by one of the men.

"Dear Noden, of course she can't!" Sythia was defending her. "Would you let your wife?"

"No, but she's not the captain's wife, and if it's the only way to get at that boat…"

Veneta wandered down to the sea to gaze out over the sandbank to the horizon, where they were being treated to a glorious display of pink and gold wash, as they often were at sunset. It was not long before Declan was at her side, then Asandra and Koch.

Bron decided to join them. Veneta saw her and volunteered to put the children to bed, and left. Declan was about to follow when Bron spoke to him quietly.

"Declan, I need to talk to you." She looked over to Asandra and Koch, but they were deep in discussion and taking no notice of her. "I want to get off this island, whatever it costs, and if the price I have to pay is to lure that man away from his camp – once he's drunk – I'm willing to do that, as long as you think it won't take long to get into that cave and steal the boat."

"Bron, I can't promise anything, but Petrus and I will do our best. We can't guarantee your safety, though, and you'll have to get away on your own."

"I know."

"The captain will try to talk you out of it."

"Then we won't tell him."

"He won't be at all pleased."

"He will, once you deliver the boat. How are you going to get the amphora all that way to the cove, though? Eight miles, is it?"

"Eight miles overland – a bit shorter by sea. Petrus and I are both strong swimmers – we can manage eight miles comfortably, even towing an amphora of wine. We won't fill it to the top."

"But why go to all that effort? Why not just swim over and simply steal the boat?"

"Our bo'sun's not stupid. He'll have a guard or two on that cave, day and night now, and they'll be well armed. We'll be naked, tired and defenceless and wouldn't stand a chance."

"But will you need me as a diversion once they're all drunk?"

"You stand a chance of getting him to leave the camp. Without him there, any guard, hopefully falling-about drunk, will desert his post."

"I just hope you're right."

"Veneta is very concerned that you might agree to do this."

"Then we won't tell her, either."

CHAPTER 30

She was glad when it was time to leave. The novelty of life on the island was beginning to pall and the only issue on everyone's mind was rescue. Feelings were running high against the captain, who was still blocking the plan to steal the boat if it meant Bron's involvement, no matter how willing she was to take a chance.

Last night, Declan and Petrus had waited until everyone had gone to bed and, as an extra precaution, until a cloud wandered across the face of the nearly full moon, before wading out to the sandbank, dragging the amphora behind them. Bron watched them breast the crown of the bank before they were lost to her view. She prayed to Shubinata for their safety during the long swim to the cove, and a successful outcome to their joint venture, then went to bed.

Now it was dawn, the hour appointed for her to leave, and she was waiting for Koch on the outskirts of the camp. He was acting as her guide and, on his return, would have to make peace with the captain as best he could and try to allay Veneta's fears.

Koch came panting to her side. "I overslept," he told her.

"Let's waste no more time," said Bron impatiently.

They made their way quietly through the trees, using this cover until they judged they were far enough away from the camp not to be seen, then began to climb through the tall scrub. It was a fresh, spring day and clouds towered high above the dark mountains, reflecting the white patches of snow that lingered in the curves and crevices where the sun had not yet reached.

Bron gazed up at the granite skyline and took pleasure in watching a red kite gliding backwards and forwards high above their heads, distinctive with its long wingspan and forked tail.

Still climbing, they were making slow progress because of the density of the bush. When they reached the height of the cliffs, the ground levelled out, and they continued by following the coastline.

After about an hour, they came to a torrent rushing down the hillside, gorged by snow melt, and stopped to drink and take breath.

"This is such a beautiful island," commented Bron, stretching her hand into the stream and letting the water tumble through her fingers.

"We must go on," Koch urged her. "Declan and Petrus could be in danger while we're hanging around here."

"Of course." She stood up. "If it wasn't for them waiting near the cove, I would turn back."

"Are you scared?" asked Koch.

"Yes. I don't know what to say to him. He might suspect a trick."

"He won't hurt you, will he?" Koch sounded anxious.

"I don't think so."

"He hurts Fabia, very badly at times, but she always goes back for more."

"Love is very strange, Koch."

He nodded his head and sighed in agreement and they continued on their way, aware of the fragrances they were disturbing as they trod among pale pink heather, delicate mauve asphodel covered in bees, blue rosemary, golden broom and the white bells of the arbutus. Also reaching them on the breeze but from further up the hillside came the clean, fresh smell of the pines.

After about another hour, Koch told Bron that they were nearing their destination.

"I'm going to hide now in the bush, just in case anyone from the camp is prowling around, but I'll stay level with you until you make contact with them. Then it's up to you, Bron."

She nodded.

"Don't take any risks, though. Declan said you must get out at any hint of trouble."

"Don't worry, I will."

"Will you be able to find your way back, do you think?"

She nodded. "I'll just follow my nose."

Impetuously, he hugged her, then branched off the path into the undergrowth, travelled several yards before turning to wave, then just seemed to disappear. Bron was comforted, though, to know that he was near, if out of sight.

It was fortunate that he chose to take cover at that juncture because a few yards further on, where the path curved round a huge rock, two men stepped out of the bushes and barred her path. She recognised them as oarsmen from the *Juniper* and guessed that they had been offered a place in the escaping boat because of their rowing skills. The bo'sun was no fool!

"Well, well, look who we have here," the taller of the two said to his companion. "If it isn't the bo'sun's lady." He leered at her in a very objectionable manner. "Bo'sun said you'd come."

Bron was not sure whether she was imagining it, but he seemed to be having difficulty in formulating his sentences, as if there was a blockage between what he thought of saying and what eventually came out of his mouth.

What she wasn't imagining, though, was her anger that the bo'sun had been so presumptuous as to expect her to come to him. She wished that she hadn't been so foolish, but it was too late to turn back now, and Declan and Petrus were waiting somewhere along the shore, waiting for her diversion.

"Then take me to him," she ordered frostily.

"Not so fast! You wait here, lady. Me mate will stay with you." When Bron objected, he told her, "Them's me orders. Wait here! I'll go tell the bo'sun you've come. I reckon he'll be pleased."

Bron did as she was told as she had no option. The guard who stayed with her didn't speak and she turned her face away from him, but was conscious that he was looking her up and down.

"Bo'sun said you'd come," he said eventually, nodding. His words were also slurred. *Good*, thought Bron, *they've found the amphora.*

"Oh, did he!"

"Need that boat, don't you?"

"Of course. Don't you want to be rescued?"

"In time."

They lapsed into silence again.

185

"Seen you about the ship."

"Oh."

"Are you the bo'sun's woman or the captain's? None of us could tell."

"I'm neither," Bron protested.

"Got 'im whipped good and proper, though, didn't you? Poor devil! Seems to me you made a monkey outta both of 'em."

"I would appreciate it if you kept your thoughts to yourself!" Humiliated, Bron hoped that the cutting edge of her tongue would shut him up, but he had one last sally to make.

"There's no doubt that any man would grab the chance to..." He didn't finish his sentence, then added, "But you're trouble, lady, big trouble!"

He was silent after that until his companion returned.

"You can go back to the camp," he was instructed. "Bo'sun's told me where to take 'er. And don't go mouthing off to Fabia. Not a word, the bo'sun said. Keep 'er topped up so she don't notice 'e's missing."

Her guide told Bron to follow and set off into the scrub with her at his heels.

"Where are you taking me?" she asked apprehensively.

"Don't ask questions, just keep up!" he ordered.

The perfume that again wafted round them as they disturbed the plants and herbs of the undergrowth made Bron feel quite light-headed – at least, she convinced herself that that was the cause, and not her apprehension.

She tried again. "Is it much further, where we're going?"

He didn't reply.

A quarter of a mile later, he stopped and Bron saw that he was standing by a tall granite stone. As she approached, she could see that it was carved with the long face of a man.

"How did that get here?" she asked in surprise.

"No idea," replied her guide, "but there are several more of them – look, one here and another over there, and there, like in a circle."

"Are there other people on the island, then?"

"Haven't seen any."

Bron wandered about the ring of stones, each one different in size and features, almost as if the carver had tried to represent the faces of real men or gods. She was so engrossed that she was unaware of what was happening around her. When she eventually became conscious of a lengthy silence and looked back, she was surprised to discover that her guide had disappeared and his place had been taken by the bo'sun, who was lazily leaning against the tallest stone, studying her minutely. He grinned when she saw him.

"Hello, goddess."

"Hello."

"I knew you'd come."

"I don't see how you could have known when I didn't know myself!" she retorted.

"Surprised he let you, though."

"He hasn't. He doesn't know. In fact, he forbade me to come."

"He fears for your safety?" Bron nodded. "And you don't?"

She hesitated, wondering what sort of danger he was hinting at.

"Ah, I see you're not too sure."

"I've come to ask for the boat."

"Of course, the boat. You've come for the boat."

Bron nodded again. "If we are rescued, the captain won't abandon you and your group."

"Why not? He doesn't owe me anything."

"He knows what you did for him after I found him on the beach."

"You told him, I suppose. Does he know what *you* did for him?"

"No."

"Come and sit down, Bron."

He indicated a horizontal stone that had fallen face downwards. She went over and sat beside him.

So far, so good, she thought. She presumed they were well away from the camp and he looked as though he was in no rush to return. She needed to give Declan and Petrus as much time as possible.

"Now, tell me what you have to negotiate with. What have you brought me in return for letting the captain have the boat?"

"You said I should come, so I came. I've offered you rescue –"

"But we could row the boat to Corsica ourselves if we wanted to."

"Money, then. The captain will arrange for you to be paid well once he gets to Ostia."

"That's more interesting, but Declan offered me money. I could have taken up his offer."

This is it, thought Bron.

"I've brought nothing else," she said.

"You know you have," he replied.

He put an arm round her and with his other hand tilted her face up to his and kissed her with a quiet intensity.

"The boat," she said when he drew breath.

"All right, you can have the damn boat!" he said. "Forget the boat! We both know it's not the reason you came."

When they drew breath again and he had untwined his fingers from the dark strands of her hair, he stood up and, taking her hand, drew her up to him.

"Come, Bron," he invited her softly, and led her by the hand over to where a pile of fallen stones were wedged against each other. They formed a shelter and beneath them a deep cavity had been hollowed out. Bron was surprised to see that the ground had been covered with a soft lining of grass and leaves and flowers.

"You see, I have prepared a love chariot for us."

Bron hesitated. "Is this where you come with Fabia?"

"No. It's where I come to be on my own," he explained, and he didn't laugh at her misgivings. "Fabia is just too much to take at times. I haven't told her it's here. It's my secret, and now it's ours."

For the last time she hesitated as they stood together on the threshold.

"Come, beautiful girl," he coaxed her, and Bron felt ashamed of the madness taking hold of her and that she didn't need much coaxing. "We will escape in our love chariot to a world you never even guessed existed."

CHAPTER 31

Declan and Petrus had quietly grounded the amphora on the edge of the stony beach on the previous night. They had then crawled ashore as far away as possible from the man guarding the cave where the boat was hidden. By moonlight that was almost as bright as day, they could see that he was sitting with his back against the large rock Koch had described, his knees drawn up, arms resting across them, head lolling forward. They could hear his snores from where they stood on the other side of the cove.

Taking no chances, though, they crept along the cliff face, exploring each split in the granite, looking for somewhere to spend the night. Their progress was not without noise as they slipped and slid on the stones, but the reverberating snores never wavered.

They felt themselves lucky to eventually find a deep, dry cave on the northern arm of the cliff. In spite of the oil they had smothered all over their bodies to help keep themselves warm while swimming, during a sleepless night they had to resort to exercising to stop their muscles seizing up in the cold.

When daylight filtered through the cracks and crevices of the rocks above, it revealed a magical underworld of granite, stained brown where an ancient river had flowed, coloured pink and green where lichen spores had responded to the light and warmth; and hanging from ceiling and walls, curiously shaped stalagmites, whose drip! drip! they could hear at infrequent intervals.

The guard, having woken from his night's sleep, soon noticed the amphora and with great delight climbed the path to the camp with the good news. It was not long before everyone except the bo'sun came down with a great deal of excited conversation and laughter, and ropes to haul the amphora to their camp.

One of the men returned not long afterwards, grumbling heartily to himself and invoking all sorts of calamities on the head of the bo'sun for sending him on duty without so much as a small mug of wine.

The two men in hiding had to wait till early afternoon before the guard finally left his post, lured by the sounds of noisy merriment from the camp above.

They waited some time, to make sure he hadn't been ordered to return. When he didn't reappear, Declan guessed that either the bo'sun was too drunk himself to send him back, or Bron had managed to lure away her would-be lover.

"Right," decided Declan, "it's time."

Keeping close to the cliff face, they ran along the curve of the bay and into the cave behind the fallen rock. They had to wade through shallow water but the boat was still there, overturned on the dry beach at the back of the cave, dry because it was slightly above the level of the water line.

"The gradual slope down will make it easier for us to refloat her," said Declan.

With effort, the pair of them turned the boat over then hauled it down to the water's edge. Throwing in the oars, which had been lying by its side, Petrus climbed in while Declan gave it a last push off and jumped in beside him. Together, they paddled with their hands across to the side of the cave then stood and propelled themselves along the wall hand over hand, until they reached the entrance. Both had to bend double to negotiate the low roof height there, but once through, they emerged from behind the large rock and so into the open sea.

Taking up two oars each, they were soon round the headland and, lifting and falling in the swell, were making for their own camp eight miles away.

"I'm ravenous – for food this time," he said as he moved her hair aside and lightly kissed her on the neck.

"So am I, Brunus," admitted Bron. "We haven't eaten all day."

"Then I must do something about that. I'll go back to camp and see what I can scrounge. We roasted a boar yesterday evening and there should be some of that left."

Releasing her, he reached for his clothes. Bron lay and watched him dress, fascinated by his strong, muscular body that for the past few hours she had explored so intimately and which had kept her in thrall. The voluptuous woman painted on his stomach swayed and rippled above his controlled muscles, and he guffawed when Bron laughed to see her move.

"You won't run away back to your captain, will you?" he asked anxiously as he was about to leave.

"No, I'll be here."

When he had gone, Bron lay back on the greenery that was their bed and wondered what was happening to her. It was a madness, a passion that had ousted every other thought from her head. It didn't matter that friends were waiting for her at the camp, that Veneta would be out of her mind with worry, that the captain would be breathing fire and vengeance. She had not even considered her children, and every thought of Aurelius had flown. All her physical desire was for this man, whom she was not sure she even liked. She had cornered him into saying that he loved her, which made her feel better, although she knew it wasn't true – how many other women had heard him say the same thing? Bron decided she didn't want to know. She certainly wasn't going to ask him about them.

She got up and dressed and went out to sit on the flat stone in the sunshine. She thought with pleasure of what had happened to her since that morning. As promised, he had led her into realms she had never suspected existed inside her own body, but… but… Twice she had stopped him, had said "No."

He had shrugged and laughed and said philosophically, "You win some, you lose some. Perhaps next time." She just wondered what depths that she hadn't yet plumbed existed inside his head. There was for her a limit. Where was his limit?

She stretched full length on the stone and dozed in the warm sunshine. When she opened her eyes, he was laying out a meal he described as "fit for a goddess". It was, too – served on a palm leaf, cold roast wild boar with a variety of roots and leaves he assured her were edible and delicious, which she found to be the case.

"Did you see Fabia?" Bron asked, curiosity getting the better of her.

"I saw no one," he told her. "They were all down in the cove, cavorting about in the sea. An amphora of wine came ashore during the night and they've over-indulged. I would have been down there with them if I hadn't been over-indulging up here. I know where I'd rather be."

After they had eaten and rested a while, he asked her, "How about a walk?"

"Where to?" she wondered.

"Up into the mountains. I've been wanting to reach them since we came. We can stay out overnight."

"All right. Sounds fun."

"It will be," he assured her. "Now, if you're thirsty, the stream's not far away."

Leaving the remains of their feast for the small creatures they occasionally glimpsed, they wrapped the bone, still covered with meat, in leaves and dropped it into a sack the bo'sun had brought back with him and which he now swung over his shoulder.

They were guided to the stream by the sound of cascading water as it tumbled over rocks, and found it not far distant. It was only a stream, not deep enough for swimming, but sufficient for bathing.

"Are you coming in?" he asked her, plunging in knee-deep, fully clothed. "It's cold, though."

"I'm used to that in the stream at home," she said, laughing, and joined him.

However, the splashing and embracing and laughing and slipping about on the rocks were not enough to keep Bron warm and it was not long before she climbed out of the water then out of her saturated clothes. The bo'sun removed his too and they draped them over the scrubby bushes to dry in the sun.

"Brunus," Bron said as they lay in each other's arms again, formulating the question she had vowed not to ask him, "have you got a wife?"

"In every port," he answered her lightly.

"I mean, someone special, one above the others."

He raised himself up on one elbow and looked down at her, smiling easily. "No one till now, Bron."

"Do you really love me?" She could have bitten her silly tongue off for asking the question yet again. She knew what his answer would be, and it was.

"There will never be anyone else from now on, I promise."

Bron knew there was no question that he and she could be together, ever, not in the real world, not in her life, nor his, and anyway, it was not what she wanted, and she guessed it was not what he wanted, either.

He began fondling her again and her body immediately responded to his straying hands, but she persisted.

"And what about –?"

He covered her mouth with his. "No more questions, goddess, we haven't time for questions."

Damn the man, she thought, *damn, damn, damn! He had no right at his age to be so… be so…* Then she sighed and was lost again and going with him where he was taking her.

That evening they reached the pine-clad foothills of the mountains. Around them flew little black-crowned coal tits and, hanging upside down on a tree trunk, looking for his evening meal, Bron saw a nuthatch in his slatey-blue coat.

She turned back to look out to sea. The sunset was spectacular, a fiery red that reflected in the ocean and turned the cliffs red, pink and orange among the greys and greens.

Above them towered the range of mountains, darkening as the sun set, grey turning black but some with white heads, a background against which an eagle soared. Bron pointed out a glint of silver high among the peaks.

"Ice and snow melt, I expect," he said, "or it might be an ancient glacier."

They climbed on beneath the light of a full moon. When Bron tired, they stopped and he expertly lit a fire by twirling two sticks together until the friction produced smoke then flames in a clump of grass. They ate the remains of the meat, and as Bron hunted about for twigs and branches to keep the fire alight all night, he scavenged for flexible boughs to form a roof, covered it in brushwood and made a makeshift shelter for them. Bron had to admire his knowledge and expertise in everything he tackled. She made their bed as soft and sweet-smelling as she could, using the greenery to hand.

From where they lay, she watched the silhouettes of bats swooping and diving across the face of the moon, and was lulled to sleep listening to the hoo-hoo-hoo-hooooo of the owls.

CHAPTER 32

Breakfast over, hand-in-hand, they began their descent towards the coast. Their route crossed a large area of shale, and when she slipped on the unstable surface, he swept her up in his arms and carried her. Bron put her arms round his neck and smiled, kissed the side of his mouth, then leant her head against his shoulder, wondering again at the overwhelming influence he had over her physically.

He had set primitive traps along their route and they found sufficient small animals in them to provide a substantial mid-day meal. When he produced a knife from his sack and prepared to skin them, Bron laughed at his forethought.

"What else have you got in there?" she teased him.

"Secrets – you'll see," he replied, in the same light teasing tone.

As they drew nearer and nearer to the stone circle, Bron confessed, "I don't want to go back to the real world, Brunus."

"Then stay hidden here, where I can always find you."

"You know I can't do that."

"What will you tell our revered captain when you get back? The truth?"

"I can't do that, either."

"Pity. I'd relish the look on his face when you made your confession. Drive him crazy knowing where your mouth has been – I've watched him slavering over it often enough!"

Bron recalled the captain's face and could picture nothing ugly, only his look of care and concern for her.

They reached the shelter among the fallen stones. Bron stretched out her fingers and stroked the golden and pink lichen on the roof of their love chariot, as Brunus had named it. He bent double and, taking her hand, led her down into the hollow.

"Bron, before I let you go –"

"I will lie in bed longing for you every night. You will let me see you again, Brunus, won't you? Soon?"

"That depends."

"On what?"

"On you doing a little something to please me. I've been very patient, you must admit."

Bron felt a prickle of apprehension at the back of her neck. She tried to keep her tone light and casual.

"I thought I had been pleasing you since yesterday morning. You've certainly been pleasing me."

"Come here." She came and, pushing back her hair, he whispered in her ear.

"No. I've already said 'No'. Why do you ask me again?"

"Because I'm not used to a woman, any woman, refusing me once I've made up my mind. Come, Bron, I promise I won't hurt you – it's fun!"

"For you, maybe!"

"For sure it is. Look, I've come prepared."

His hands dived into the sack he had let fall and they came out holding a coiled rope made from split saplings.

"It's not what I want," she protested.

"But it's what I want!"

Now she was really concerned, though not yet afraid. What they had shared was nothing to do with love but it had drawn them close, surely closer than merely physically, which must count for something.

"Brunus, don't spoil the memory of what we've been to each other. Let me go now."

He came towards her, twisting the rope in his hands. "Bron, beautiful Bron, don't be difficult. A parting present for me?"

His words were provocative but his grey eyes glittered dark and hard. There was no gentleness in them now when he looked at her.

She remembered another occasion when she had been trussed

up on a bed, but then her tormentor had been Vortin, High Priest of her village.

"No, Brunus, no! How many times do I have to say it?"

"Then you can forget the boat!" he shouted and swore at her. "No co-operation, no boat! The boat is no longer part of the deal. It never was, in fact. You don't think I'd give the captain that pleasure, do you, of rowing out of here to safety and leaving us abandoned without a means of escape? I'm not that obsessed with you!"

She ignored the last hurtful comment, which had nevertheless found its mark.

"Brunus, are you going back on your word and refusing to let us have the boat? But you promised and I – I –" Words failed her. She was aware of what she had yielded to him without shame or limit, until this last request. She reminded herself that her lust had been equally as powerful as his. Now she was in danger from the consequences. What was it Veneta often quoted about "sowing the wind and reaping the whirlwind"? Well, here now was her whirlwind.

"You're too trusting, Bron – and too willing, if I may say so, except in this last business. You didn't really think I was going to let you have the boat, did you? More fool you! Tell a woman you love her and she oozes like oil. By the way, that wasn't true, either."

Bron couldn't believe the change that had come over him. The switch from gentle lover to tormentor in a matter of seconds was bizarre. Well, she could match him! Could turn just as easily!

Disregarding her own safety, she blurted out, "You've no reason to gloat so! While I've been entertaining you away from your camp, we've stolen your precious boat!"

She enjoyed the look of utter disbelief on his face and hoped that Declan and Petrus had been successful in carrying out their plan.

"Yes, stolen, from under your nose! How do you think that amphora of wine came to be washed up on your beach? That was a happy accident, wasn't it? Except that it wasn't the accident you thought it was! Anyway, it did the trick all right. Go and look in the cave if you don't believe me!"

"How do you know about the cave?"

"Koch discovered it the day they came to make a deal with you."

"But Koch wasn't with them!"

"No, because he was down in the cove looking for the boat!"

The bo'sun was speechless. His face turned red, then white, and Bron flinched and wondered what she had ever seen in him to desire. Now all she wanted to do was get away from the cruelty in his eyes.

"I will go and see for myself, and if what you say is true, you're not going anywhere! You're staying here for me!" When she started to argue, he brought his face close to hers. "What's the matter, Bron? Isn't it what you wanted, to stay here with me? A few moments ago you were practically begging me not to send you back!"

He pushed her to the ground and knelt on her chest, then dropped one knee on each side of her. Even as he trussed her up – hands first, cord run down to her ankles, which were tied together in similar fashion – she was conscious of his large erection. Fortunately for her, though, he was too angry to do anything about it and stormed out of the shelter.

"I'll be back!" he called as he left. Then there was silence.

At first she was relieved when he didn't return during the remainder of the day, then at nightfall, and she was able to sleep a little, undisturbed, though she was cold and ached from the way she was forced to lie. Slowly the night dragged on. She did manage to hobble and roll from the hollow into the scrub outside the shelter on a couple of occasions to relieve her bladder.

It was then she decided to try to fray the ropes on the edge of one of the granite stones as soon as the sun was up and it was light enough to see what she was doing, to make sure she cut the rope and not her wrists.

She was on her feet before dawn and out in the stone circle, and spent some time crawling round on elbows and knees, looking for the sharpest edge, one that she could reach. She decided on the edge of the horizontal stone and set to work. By the end of about an hour, she had made some progress, and the cords were beginning to fray, but she realised that it would take her all day to release herself, and the bo'sun would likely have returned by then.

She was suddenly aware of a disturbance in the undergrowth – someone was approaching – and scrambled back to the shelter and threw herself into the hollow, where she lay quite still. She resolved to give as good as she got, and Brunus would not leave without her marks on him. She could bite and scratch and kick even if she couldn't prevent him from carrying out whatever unnatural design he had on her.

Then she remembered that he would enjoy her even more if she resisted, and decided to lay unmoving and still, like a dead fish on a fishmonger's marble slab.

A silhouette appeared in the entrance and blotted out the daylight.

This is it! she thought with resignation, but instead of a man's voice calling to her, she heard a woman's, one she recognised.

"Fabia?"

"Yes."

"Have you come to gloat?"

"No."

"What then?"

"I could kill you, you know. How does that feel?"

Bron started as the cold blade of a knife was pressed hard against her throat. But if this was Fabia's intention, why hadn't she slit her throat already, why was she talking about it?

"It makes me afraid."

"Good, but it's not why I've come."

Through her relief, Bron noticed that Fabia's words were also thick and slurred, and sounded most peculiar. *So she's also been heavily into the wine,* Bron thought, and took comfort.

"What then? Has he sent you?"

"No, he doesn't know I'm here."

Bron was puzzled. "Then how did you find me?"

"It wasn't that difficult – the men were taunting me about it. He brings us women here all the time."

Bron was stunned into silence! As Fabia's words seeped into

her understanding, she couldn't believe that she had been taken in so completely by his lies. She thought of all the tenderness she had showered upon him without stint or inhibition and the contempt she felt was more for herself than for him.

When she didn't reply, Fabia laughed derisively. "I suppose he told you that this was your secret place, your love chariot, and together you would ride to –?" She had no need to complete her sentence. When Bron still didn't reply, she added, "We were all told that, first time."

Fabia couldn't see her victim's face in the darkness but Bron sensed her enjoyment at the abject misery and humiliation her words were producing.

"He got himself drunk last night and he's still sleeping it off. He won't sleep forever, though, so I'd better get a move on."

Bron was immediately on the alert for her own safety. "Doing what?"

"Rescuing you."

"But I thought you hated me."

"I do, but the sooner you're out of his life and out of mine, the better. Can you get yourself outside? I can't see a thing in here."

"Yes, I can."

Fabia moved away and Bron crawled out into the stone circle. She wedged herself up against one of the partially fallen stones.

It was then she saw Fabia's face. It was dark mauve and black, her nose was swollen and her lips split and encrusted with blood. Bron stared. No wonder it was so difficult for the girl to speak.

"Did he do that to you?"

"Yes, we had quite a night of it."

"I'm so sorry," Bron mumbled.

"So you should be. I notice there isn't a mark on you – yet." She shrugged. "It's happened before, though not as bad as this, and I daresay it will happen again."

"Then why in Heaven's name do you stay?"

Fabia looked at her. "Have you never been in love?" she asked. Bron didn't answer. *Yes, she had been in love, she was in love –*

with Aurelius, whom she had betrayed so completely – and she knew that what she was looking at wasn't love.

"Hold out your wrists."

Fabia approached with the knife in her hand, her left hand. Her right arm hung limply by her side.

"Brunus did that to you, as well? Surely he couldn't have done that to you!"

"'Brunus' is it now? You did pick all the locks, didn't you? Yes, that's his handiwork as well." She continued to push the knife backwards and forwards across the cords round Bron's wrists.

"He beat you up instead of me?" Bron asked slowly.

Fabia nodded. "It wasn't only because you refused him. It was the boat as well. The man who should have been on guard is lucky that he's only got two broken legs and isn't floating face down in the bay. Brunus won't be made a fool of."

Staring at the expression on Fabia's disfigured face, Bron realised the extent of the pain the woman was barely controlling.

"Fabia, come with me! Come back to our camp. Veneta will look after you. You should get treatment for your arm."

"No, I'll stay here. He'll see to it for me when he sobers up. He's always sorry afterwards and vows never to do it again –"

The cords flew apart and Bron massaged her wrists over the marks they had left.

"I can manage now, I can do the rest myself. Why don't you go back, Fabia? He'll kill you if he finds you here. I'll throw the knife away, so it will look as though I frayed the ropes on the edge of the stones."

Fabia nodded agreement and turned to go, but at the edge of the stone circle, she paused and faced Bron again.

"He doesn't love you, you know. He may have said he does, but he doesn't."

"I know that."

"I'm the only one he really loves. We belong together, you see, him and me. All the rest are only passions of the moment, like you, and they're soon burnt out."

Bron looked at her standing there, beaten and injured, and felt an overwhelming pity for her. Fabia was deceiving herself just as surely as all his women must deceive themselves, as she had herself.

When Bron didn't speak, Fabia asked, "Why? You could have anybody you wanted. Why try to take him away from me?"

"I don't know why. It was some sort of sickness. You should know about that better than most. I'm cured of it now, though. You won't see me again."

"That's good, because I *will* kill you if there's a next time."

Then she turned and was gone.

Bron freed herself from the rest of the rope then threw the knife as far as she could into the bushes, and fled.

Koch met her when she was a couple of miles away from the safety of the captain's camp. He had just rounded a bend in the path, and as she ran to greet him, she saw the captain and four more men following on his heels.

She flung her arms round Koch then ran to the captain. He held out his arms for her and, once inside them, with his cheek against her hair, she knew she was safe again.

"Theon," she breathed, so softly that no one else heard.

"Bron, my dear," he said, releasing her, "we were coming to find you. We were all so worried when you didn't return. I had a great deal to say to Declan and Petrus when they arrived back in the boat, for leading you into such danger – but all that's over, now that you're safely here. Come, Veneta and the children are waiting for you."

As they walked the remaining distance, Bron gave an untrue account of what had happened to her since she left at dawn two days previously, being careful not to refer to the bo'sun as 'Brunus'. She was able to show everyone the marks of the cords on her wrists and ankles, and her story was accepted, though they wondered at her rescue by Fabia. They also wondered at the accuracy of Tiegan's predictions.

Declan and Petrus had rested after arriving back, but had set out for Corsica on the previous morning in the rowing boat.

Section IV

ITALIA –

OSTIA AND ROME

CHAPTER 33

"Are you being sick?" Asandra asked as she surprised Bron leaning over the ship's rail, her stomach heaving. "I'd 'ave thought you'd spent long enough at sea not to be bothered by it any more."

Bron straightened and wiped her face with a damp cloth, hoping to hide her confusion.

"I'll be all right once we land," she said, relieved when Asandra turned away to get a better look at the approaching harbour.

Just then a sudden swell forced her to grab the rail again, and when Veneta and the children appeared at her side, she was clinging to it miserably, feeling worse than ever.

Oblivious as only a child can be, Layla pointed excitedly. "Look, Mummy, there's the lighthouse!"

Forgetting her nausea for a moment, Bron gazed at the four-tiered brick structure imposingly guarding the entrance to Ostia's ancient port.

With sails furled, their rescue vessel, the merchant trader *Fortuna*, was slowly rowed between the lighthouse and larboard mole of the port. They passed a large marble podium set in the sea on which a statue had once stood, and entered the outer harbour, where the fishing fleet was tied up.

Further in, two jutting fingers of land, covered with warehouses and booths, noisy with bargaining and bustle, reached towards each other, allowing a narrow entrance to the inner harbour.

Bron looked around at the other merchant ships secured to wharves and jetties and watched as the *Fortuna* was expertly manoeuvred into a berth at the dockside, opposite a large warehouse bearing the name of the ship's owner.

She wanted to disembark as soon as possible but there was a delay in lowering the gangplank, and looking round for an explanation, she noticed Captain Stokovius in conversation with the captain of the *Fortuna*. It was not long before he came over.

"The captain won't allow any of you to disembark until he has been paid for our passage from the island to Ostia," he told them, "so I'm going ashore immediately to collect my back pay."

"Do you expect it's still there?" asked Declan. "The *Juniper's* owners must think she foundered in the storm."

"We'll soon know," Stokovius replied and signalled to the captain, who ordered the gangplank lowered so that he could leave the ship.

After Bron's escape from the bo'sun and the theft of the rowing boat, they had waited on the island another five weeks before being rescued, all that time not knowing whether Declan and Petrus had reached help or had drowned on the way.

There was such waving, shouting and hallooing from the sand bar when the *Fortuna* appeared on the horizon, and much rejoicing when she dropped anchor at a safe distance and sent boats to take the survivors off the island.

Standing at the ship's rail now, deep in the misery of her thoughts, Bron took no part in the excited chatter about her. In spite of her reassurance to Asandra, she knew she would not be all right once they disembarked. After her return to the captain's camp, she had hoped, with time, to obliterate all memory of her brief and now humiliating liaison with the bo'sun, but nature was making sure she would remember it, one way or another, for the rest of her life.

As yet, no one suspected her pregnancy, and she would be hard put to explain how it had come about, as she had maintained adamantly that she had parried all the bo'sun's advances.

Abortion was out of the question. That had been tried with her first born, High Priest Vortin's son, and had been humiliatingly unsuccessful. But she couldn't keep this child, conceived in dark passion. Somehow, she would have to make an excuse to leave Ostia before the birth, then give it away to someone, anyone, before returning. And Aurelius must never find out!

Her thoughts returned to the present and she realised that her friends had just agreed to stay in Ostia until their debts to the captain were settled, and were discussing finding work.

Sythia was confident that she would be able to rent a couple of rooms. "Then I'll take in washing," she declared. "Either that, or I'll get work in the baths, repairing clothes – I've done it before. Don't no one go worrying about me and my boys."

"Bron," Veneta whispered, "Asandra and the girls are saying that they'll be able to pay off their debt in no time at all. You know what that means. I loathe what they do to earn a living! They run such risks every time they let a stranger into their beds."

How do they avoid all those unwanted pregnancies? Bron wondered, but said aloud, "Veneta, it's what they do. They know no other way. Would you rather they did it for nothing?" *As I have,* her conscience added.

Bron had already discussed with Veneta about selling a piece of her jewellery to pay what they owed. She was glad that the repayment arrangements would keep the captain in Ostia for a little longer. She felt safe when he was around though she fervently hoped he would have gone home by the time her need drove her away.

He was back with the money within the hour, having found it waiting for him at the *Juniper's* shipping office, together with the payment Aurelius had left for him, and he paid off the *Fortuna's* captain. The party was then allowed to disembark.

Bron stood, back aching, with Veneta and the children on the quayside, looking round at the friends with whom they had shared so much over the preceding months. Everyone seemed unsure what to do next. No one had any contacts in the city. Eventually, they hugged and kissed all round, wished each other god speed, then went their separate ways, needing to find accommodation before nightfall.

Petrus and Koch said they would accompany Asandra and the other young women, to make sure they found rooms.

"Must be in the port area, near the ships – best for business," insisted Asandra. Bron felt very sorry for Koch when she saw the look of anguish on his young face.

"Are you coming with us, Declan?" Asandra asked and pouted when he elected to go with Veneta and Bron and the children, to help them find something better in the city centre.

"I'll find you tomorrow, to make sure you're comfortable," the captain promised.

Carrying Darius and Gift between them, Bron and Veneta set off after Declan, who was giving Lucilla a ride on his shoulders, with Layla and Alon and the puppy running and jumping along by their sides. Bron wished she didn't feel so nauseous, but there was nothing she could say or do about it. It was her own fault and she would have to bear the inconvenience and keep quiet.

They walked along the road that led to the Marine Gate, passing through the heavily built-up area that had spilled outside the city wall. When they continued on, through the gateway between two flanking towers, ancient Ostia lay before them.

Stretching straight ahead, the Decumanus Maximus, bordered by open-fronted shops with balconies and apartments above, was wide enough to allow the ebb and flow of two-way traffic.

"Where do we begin?" asked Bron, at a loss.

"Along the side roads," decided Declan, and turned to his left and left again. His instinct proved fruitful because they found themselves in an area of apartment blocks. He was directed to a prestigious, monumental entrance on their right, flanked by brick pillars. On the other side of the entrance were two multi-storey blocks of apartments set in spacious, well-cared-for gardens with trees, bedding plants and fountains.

The caretaker's office was unoccupied so Declan left them sitting on stone benches around a fountain and went off to look for him. He returned with a talkative little man he had found weeding the flowerbeds, who showed them a four-roomed apartment on the third floor of the eastern block, which they agreed to rent, initially for a month.

"Now you should leave and find somewhere for yourself and Koch," Veneta told Declan with concern.

When he had left, Bron collapsed into a basket-weave chair in the triclinium and closed her eyes. She wished she didn't feel so exhausted all the time. How was she going to continue to hide her pregnancy from Veneta? Her friend had lived with the temple prostitutes when she was a priestess in Byden, and possessed a sixth sense about such matters.

"Mummy, come and explore!" called Alon. Reluctantly, Bron prised herself from the chair and followed the children in and out of the comfortably furnished rooms, all light and airy, with far-reaching views both towards the sea and inland.

The room where she had been sitting was furnished with the usual three-sided table backed by benches covered in cushions, where diners could lie and eat in Roman fashion. There was also a small couch, a cupboard whose top was badly stained and which obviously had been used as a side serving table, and a couple of basket chairs with box footstools on which lay leather cushions.

The walls were colourful with painted panels of seascapes and ships in sunshine and storm, and the floor was covered with a black-and-white mosaic divided by twisted rope borders into rectangles containing symbols of the sea.

The two bedrooms were less ornate, painted the colour of pale honey, the wooden floors covered in rush mats. The children had already claimed one of the rooms by bouncing all over the mattresses.

Finally, Veneta led her into the kitchen. A large cauldron hung by iron chains from a tripod, and on a tiled hearth with raised edges stood a gridiron. There were several three-legged stools, a bucket turned upside down in one corner and an amphora with a little oil in the bottom.

In shelves and cupboards the children were finding all manner of equipment and utensils – sufficient for their temporary needs.

"I think this will suit us very well," commented Veneta. "The latrine's on the ground floor."

"I'm hungry," complained Alon, "and so is Cronus."

"There is work to do before you eat," Bron told him and sent him and Layla out with the wooden bucket. They soon staggered back with it, half full of sparkling water drawn from a nearby well they had discovered.

Veneta had coaxed the *Fortuna's* cook into giving them some bread, cheese and oranges, and she and Bron now laid these on one of the tables in the kitchen for their midday meal. After that, Veneta put the three youngest down on the mattresses to sleep while Bron took Alon and Layla with her to find a craftsman willing to buy her jewellery. When Alon moaned at the prospect of being dragged round the shops with his mother and sister, she told him flatly, "No money, no food!" and he stopped complaining.

Back on the Decumanus Maximus, Bron smiled to see her children's eyes wide with wonder, but she too was impressed by the strangeness and beauty of the buildings in the first mainland Roman city they had visited. They stroked and fingered ornamental marble, stone and brickwork as they passed.

"I can smell fried fish!" exclaimed Layla.

Bron pointed to stalls where fishmongers at marble counters were selling their wriggling stock, caught in nets from tanks then killed and cooked as requested.

They crossed the road, mindful of the chaos of carts and carriages and draught animals, and wove their way between shoppers towards one of the counters. Layla drew her mother's attention to a section of floor mosaic, picturing a dolphin biting an octopus.

For their meal, Bron chose half a large fish that was already frying in the pan.

"Take away or eat here?" asked the fishmonger.

"Eat here!" answered Alon, monopolising a place on a bench at one of the tables.

They were each given a wooden platter on which a portion of fish had been served and sprinkled with squeezed lemon juice. Layla, her mouth crammed full of the white flesh, pronounced it delicious.

When they had finished their meal, and the fishmonger had wrapped the remainder of the fish for them to take home, Bron enquired the way to the jeweller's. In her purse was the heavy gold betrothal ring decorated with a motif of clasped hands that Vortin had given her eleven years ago. A fair price would pay the rent and keep the family in necessities for many months.

Bron had already made up her mind that, when her pregnancy made it impossible to stay in Ostia any longer, she would leave Veneta with some of Vortin's other gifts – the hooped earrings with their pendants, the pair of brooches and glass phial of incense. She would take with her only her silver bracelet and his gift to their son, the solid gold torque small enough for a baby's neck that ended in hollow finials, each containing a gold nugget.

They safely negotiated the broad, busy junction at the convergence of the Decumanus Maximus and the road leading to the River Tiber. A notice pointed to the public baths somewhere to their right. *Oh, bliss,* Bron thought, then realised that she would have to resist any suggestion from Veneta that they visited the baths together, in case her friend saw the telltale changes in her body.

They found the entrance they were seeking and walked beneath an archway topped by an ornate pediment. Small shops opened off a quadrangular courtyard, with accommodation above. Most of the traders there were jewellers who belonged to the same guild of craftsmen.

The betrothal ring was very saleable, made as it was of gold from Britannia, and Bron went from trader to trader, pitting one valuer against another, until she was satisfied with the price offered, and came away with a bag chinking with coins.

The children wanted to explore further, but by then she had had enough.

"Tomorrow," she promised as they retraced their steps.

They returned to find the younger children amusing themselves.

"I'll stay with them while you go shopping," she told Veneta.

When the door closed, she dropped on to the couch in the triclinium. The children were so quietly occupied that she dozed off and was woken by a knock at the door. She started up, confused, forgetting for the moment where she was. When the knock came again, she slapped her face to wake herself up and put some colour into her cheeks, then went to open the door. The captain stood there, looking slightly apologetic.

"I met Declan," he explained, "and he told me where you were staying."

"Come in, Theon," she said at once.

He followed her into the triclinium, and when she indicated the couch, sat on the edge of it.

"Can I get you something to drink?"

"No, thank you."

She sat in the chair facing him. He looked awkward, as if he didn't quite know why he had come. Bron broke the silence.

"I'm glad you're here." She was sorry to see the pleasure vanish from his face when she added, "because I sold a ring this afternoon, so we can pay what we owe you, straight away."

"Thank you," he said again, "but there's no rush."

She could see that he also had been shopping. He was wearing new sandals, a new light grey, belted tunic and dark blue cloak. His grey hair and beard had been cut and tidily combed. She thought again, as she had when she found him half dead on the beach, what a handsome man he still was.

"Have you enquired about Officer Catus?" he asked her.

"No, I will leave that till tomorrow."

A key turned in the lock of the front door.

"That will be Veneta back," said Bron.

Captain Stokovius stood up.

"I'll go now," he said. "I just wanted to make sure you were all right. You won't be leaving just yet, will you?"

"Not just yet."

After another silence, in which they heard Veneta bustling about in the kitchen, Bron asked, "Had Declan found work when you saw him?"

"Yes, all the young men have. I wanted to put Koch on a ship and return him straight away to his mother, but I recognise that he's not at all the same child who stowed away. He has matured into a young man and isn't about to leave Asandra and go home."

"I could foresee that problem," Bron sympathised.

The captain nodded. "I persuaded him to send her a message via a troop carrier, to let her know he's safe and well, and making his own way in the world. I have written to Regina, endorsing his message, for her peace of mind. Of course, it won't reach her for months."

"How long will you be staying in Ostia?" Bron asked. She didn't welcome the thought that she might never see him again once he left to go back to his village and his family.

"Only until I've been paid back what I am owed, then I will be travelling home. May I come and see you again tomorrow?"

"Yes, of course, Theon. You're always welcome here. After all, none of us would be alive if it wasn't for you."

They heard Veneta coming from the direction of the kitchen.

"Hello, Captain," she greeted him cheerily.

"Just came to see you were settled in," he explained.

"So, have you found somewhere suitable to stay?" Veneta asked. Bron was ashamed that she hadn't thought to ask him.

"It will do well enough," he replied. "After all, there's only me, and it won't be for long."

Bron took him to the kitchen, where the money was hidden, to pay him what they owed, then accompanied him to the door. She held out her right hand, intending to shake hands, but he took it in both of his and raised it to his lips before turning away and descending the stairs.

Bron waited till he had left the building before closing the door.

CHAPTER 34

She had stopped being sick so no longer feared that her secret would be discovered. On the only occasion Veneta had caught her in the act, in the latrine downstairs, she said she had eaten something tainted. She was looking and feeling very well, but her waist was beginning to thicken and her breasts had increased in size. She was sure that her friend would be noticing any time now, so she must get away soon.

The captain came to see the family every day, but whether out walking, at the theatre or relaxing at home, he and Bron were never alone together. There seemed to be an unspoken agreement between them that this should not happen.

There was no message from Aurelius. He must have decided they had all been lost at sea. It grieved her to think of his distress, but there was nothing she could do about it. They enquired at the military office in town and discovered that the Third Victrix legion had been posted to Narona, in Illyria – much too far away for them to join him.

That, at least, worked in her favour. What excuse could she have made to flee from Ostia if he had been here, waiting for her? She could not have borne his expressions of intense love and longing, feelings she had shared – still shared. Waves of guilt flooded through her and once again she felt utterly wretched at her disloyalty and betrayal of the young man to whom she had sworn undying love – and why? Because of a madness that had taken hold of her like devil possession.

Captain Stokovius seemed in no hurry to leave Ostia, though they had all settled their debts with him, so it was strange when one day he did not pay them his usual visit. Bron missed his genial company.

"Where's the captain today?" asked Alon.

"I don't know," she replied. "I hope he's not unwell."

When Declan visited that evening, Bron asked if he knew.

"Asandra saw him earlier, down in the docks," he said. "I think he was trying to arrange his passage home."

"I don't want him to go away," whined Layla.

"We'll certainly miss him," Veneta said, looking at Bron. Bron said nothing.

They were puzzled when there was still no sign of him during the following day. However, he arrived as they were setting out the family's evening meal, apologising for his timing.

"Don't worry, there's plenty," Veneta assured him as she filled their bowls with chicken stew.

The conversation flowed, but he was not his usual relaxed self. Alon and Layla, with little Lucilla in tow, clamoured for him to play with them, so they all went down into the gardens and he obliged by giving them piggyback rides round and round the fountains until he was dizzy.

When they were in bed, he told them wonderful stories of sunken ships and sea monsters.

"They'll be having nightmares," Bron remonstrated.

The children insisted that he should kiss them goodnight and tuck them up.

"They miss their father," she observed.

"Thank you for letting me borrow you," he whispered to Layla and Alon as he shut their bedroom door.

"Borrow them?" Bron asked as they returned to the triclinium and sat together on the couch. Veneta was clearing up in the kitchen.

"I was away when my own were this young," he explained. "I missed it all, all their growing up. I didn't realise till now quite how much I had sacrificed, or what I was putting Avala through, bringing them up on her own. I expect they've all left home by now."

"You chose the sea instead."

"Yes, she's been my mistress all these years. I am questioning whether I chose well," he said. "We never had an ordinary family life, Avala and me – that's why I'm going home."

"When?" asked Bron sharply.

"Tomorrow. I take ship in the morning."

"So soon?"

Veneta had come into the room, wiping her hands on a cloth, and overheard his news.

"We'll all miss you so much," she said.

He looked up at her and smiled, hesitated, then asked in a rush, "Veneta, my dear, may I – that is – would you mind if I took Bron into the garden for five minutes? There are things I need to say to her."

"You don't have to ask my permission, Captain – Bron can decide for herself."

"Of course I'll come," Bron replied with alacrity, glad of the opportunity to say their goodbyes privately, though she wasn't sure quite what he needed to say to her, or her to him, for that matter.

She followed his sturdy figure down the stairs and out into the night air. The stars were bright in a black sky and were dancing and drowning in the water in the fountain basins. It was the beginning of July.

She had thrown a light shawl round her shoulders but it wasn't necessary as the breeze was hot. The gardens were lit at intervals by torches in iron sconces set in concrete along the paths, giving sufficient light to walk, without being intrusive.

She followed the captain to the stone bench circling one of the fountains and sat beside him.

"What a beautiful evening, Bron – does it remind you of anything?"

"Yes." She nodded. "We met accidentally by the nymphaeum at the villa on Vectis, at the beginning of the voyage."

He laughed. "It wasn't so accidental. I was strolling about the grounds when I saw you over there, and I made sure we met."

"Oh, I didn't know. It all seems a long time ago."

He paused a moment then said, "Bron, Avala and I have been

together thirty years, to all intents and purposes man and wife, though we never wed."

He took a deep breath and continued.

"My father sailed for the Romans and died at sea. My mother died in childbirth, I believe, when I was only five years old. I was brought up by a neighbour, a deep-sea fisherman. They were my second family. Avala was one of their daughters.

"When I was twenty-six, I got Avala pregnant. She was only fourteen. No one minded very much – it had always been planned that we would be together eventually. However, I wasn't ready for the responsibility and restriction to my freedom, so I ran away and joined the Roman fleet. I never went home again, not for long periods, though however short the time, I always managed to impregnate her again. We have five children, four boys and a girl. Thorsten, the eldest, is twenty-eight now. There is also Iesa, Avala's daughter, who I accepted as my own. It was my fault that she was born, as I was away so long, and Avala was a full-blooded young woman."

He paused and Bron waited for him to go on, wondering where his revelations were leading.

He continued, "I must admit that I haven't been celibate all these years away from home. You've seen that there are plenty of temptations and opportunities on board ship and in the ports. I daresay I have a few children I know nothing about."

When she still remained silent, he appealed to her. "Say something, Bron."

She was at a loss. "I don't know what to say, Theon. I didn't know you expected me to say anything. I've just been listening."

"And you, my dear." He took hold of her hands between his strong brown fingers and her shawl fell from her shoulders. "You once let slip that you have a husband at home in Britannia, you have your adorable little family, and you have a Roman officer who loves you and I know you love him."

"Yes," she breathed, beginning to see some reason for his recital.

"Do you know what I am saying to you, Bron?"

"I – I think so," she replied hesitantly.

"At first, I treated you like a daughter, being the same age as Iesa, but things changed. My feelings changed. Oh, Bron, help me out here – say something!"

"You're explaining to me why –"

"Why I have never swept you up in my arms and taken you to bed. There, it's said. As Officer Catus told me when you all boarded, you and Veneta are not camp followers, you are respectable, honourable women. If it had not been for that, I would have given way to my desire for you a long time ago."

"Oh, Theon, I'm not – I'm not –" She wanted to tell him that she wasn't the respectable young woman everyone thought she was, that she was no better than the camp followers he had alluded to so disparagingly.

It was at that moment that she experienced a faint flutter under her right ribs. Her baby had moved and she had felt it for the first time. She pulled her hands out of his and covered her face and shook with a sob so deep that it seemed to have welled up from where the baby lay.

Immediately, his arms were around her and he pressed her head to his shoulder.

"Don't, Bron, don't," he pleaded with her. "You're referring to the bo'sun, of course." She held her breath. "It drove me crazy to think of him touching you where I couldn't. So I flogged him. Then tying you up as he did on the island! I wish I'd whipped him to death on board! I hope they never rescue him!"

Bron put her fingers over his lips. "Don't say such things, Theon. Don't let him make you as vicious as he is. Though it wasn't all his fault, it wasn't!"

"Maybe so." She looked up at him. "You grow more radiant by the day, Bron. I can't blame any man… Close your eyes."

"Why?"

"Just do as I say, for once." Bron did so and he kissed her lids.

"What was that for?"

"Because I don't want the stars in your eyes to escape until we meet again."

Bron looked away from him. "We'll never see each other again,

Theon, but I'll never forget you and how brave you were in the storm, and saving all our lives."

"But you paid me back and saved mine."

"That was the bo'sun's doing, carrying you around the headland."

Stokovius stood and pulled her up to face him. Holding her shoulders, he looked down into her eyes again.

"No, Bron, I mean you – what *you* did for me."

She took a deep breath and held on to it.

"He was right for once, the bo'sun. He said he thought I wasn't as unconscious as I appeared."

Bron let the breath go and felt the heat rising in her cheeks. "You mean you knew what was happening, what I did, what you did?"

Now it was his turn to close his eyes. He smiled. "Yes, I knew, and I shall take the memory with me to the grave."

He kissed her then, a gentle, lingering, loving kiss, and she felt the increasing hardness of his desire for her against her stomach.

"Come," he said abruptly, "I'll take you back to Veneta, where you're safe."

He drew her arm through his, patted her hand, and they turned and walked back to the apartment.

Next day, the family went down to the harbour to see their captain leave. They waved to him until the ship was out of sight.

"I didn't want him to go," lamented Alon.

"We'll never see him again," wailed Layla.

"No, I don't suppose we will," Veneta said, blowing her nose.

Bron was silent, holding back her own tears. She thought, now that he had gone, there was nothing to stop her leaving. Again and again she had asked herself if she could abandon her children. Her heart had cried out, "No! Never! Never!" but her head told her that she must, as soon as possible.

But go where? Who knows? She certainly didn't. Rome was the obvious answer – she could get lost there, in the back streets and alleyways. Yes, Rome seemed the right place to make for. So, Rome it must be.

CHAPTER 35

Bron hardly slept that night, knowing she must leave early, before anyone else was up and about.

Unsuspecting, Veneta was fast asleep and breathing quietly on the mattress beside her. Fearful of disturbing her, Bron crept from the room and closed the door quietly.

She had a quick wash in the kitchen and dressed in the clothes she had laundered the day before and left folded on the table.

Then it was time to write the note. She had already decided to use the wax tablet kept ready for their shopping list. Scraping the surface smooth with the flat end of the metal stylus lying beside it, she composed a few lines that said everything yet said nothing, and laid it on the table.

The moment of parting from her children had come and she knew she must get it over quickly. She looked down at them, their well-loved little faces in innocent oblivion, hair tumbled on pillows, and her decision to leave faltered. But she hardened her heart, kept her tears in check, and left the room without a backward glance.

She was bequeathing her children's welfare and happiness to her friend without asking permission, but knew Veneta would not let her down. Hadn't the priestess loved and protected her all the time she was growing up in Byden temple? Bron felt sure that the same love and protection would be extended to her children once she had left, however bewildered and distressed Veneta felt.

She let herself out, closing the front door quietly behind her. Secreted in the garden was a sack containing a change of clothing and sandals, her jewellery and toiletries. Retrieving this, she left the apartment blocks behind and made her way along silent streets, through the Marine Gate and down to the port.

There were few people about so early. Those who were, paid

scant attention, allowing her to go about her business in the same way they hoped she would allow them to go about theirs.

Making her way to the apartments behind the sanctuary of Bona Dea, inappropriately the goddess who protects women, she climbed dark stairs to the top floor. Listening with her ear against the peeling paint of a brown door, she knocked discreetly, and when there was no reply, returned to the stairs and descended to the hallway at street level.

A shaft of candlelight stretched across the floor as a door opened and a man emerged and came along the passage towards her. Bron pressed herself against the wall and he didn't see her but accidentally knocked against her as he passed.

"Sorry, sweetheart, maybe another night," he apologised and went on his way.

Bron crossed to the same door and tapped lightly. It was opened immediately by a young girl.

"Come in," she was invited.

"I don't need your services," Bron told her, "except to ask you to give Asandra a message when you see her."

"Asandra?"

"Yes – number twenty-three, top floor."

Bron took a few coins from her leather purse and gave them to the girl.

"What's the message?"

"Just say 'Veneta needs her'."

"That all?"

"Tell her the message is from Bron."

"Asandra – Bron says Veneta needs you."

"That's it. Thanks."

Retracing her steps, Bron passed through the Marine Gate again and hurried along the Decumanus Maximus. She kept her head down, not looking to right and certainly not to left at the wealthy apartment buildings, behind which she was only too conscious lay the gardens and insulae in which her children were sleeping. Tears blinded her vision and she didn't know on which part of the road she was walking, until she stumbled on a large cobblestone. Stopping to wipe her eyes with her knuckles, she looked about her.

She was standing outside the colonnaded forecourt of the enormous Round Temple. The forum lay ahead. Holding her head up now, she hurried on through the forum, covering her nose with the scarf to avoid breathing in the stench of the nearby communal latrines, which was particularly strong on this windless morning. She passed the warehouses and the theatre that fronted Guild Square, where the children loved to play, and past the great portico leading to the Baths of Neptune complex.

A little further and she had reached the baths used by the cart drivers, and so into their large square, already bustling with commercial carts and wagons arriving from Rome. There she dodged warily between turning wheels and stamping hoofs as drivers and animals, thirsty after all-night journeys, impatiently waited their turn to drink from fountains and water troughs.

Her route lay between the two sturdy square towers of the Porta Romana. Three vaulted passageways connected the towers, through which she could see tall umbrella pines bordering the road that led directly to Rome, the road she intended to follow.

Once through the gateway, she could not help but look back into Ostia, and her gaze was directed skywards to the two protecting statues of Minerva towering above her. Their tidily furled wings brushed their feet and reached up above their helmets, victory shields in place at their sides. *Not for them the destructive weakness of human desire*, Bron reflected.

Setting out at a steady pace, she was glad to leave behind the family tombs that clustered along the road, and the morbid columbaria, like extensive dove cotes but containing cinerary urns of ashes instead of plump, white birds.

Now it was fully daylight and carts and wagons were trundling past her in both directions, bringing in fruit, vegetables and flowers from outlying districts and taking out fresh and salted fish, or stacked high with merchandise off the ships.

She had not walked far when a four-wheeled carruca pulled up a few yards ahead, the bells round the necks of the lumbering oxen clanging hollowly as the woman driver brought them, with great difficulty, to a halt.

"Want a ride, dearie?"

Bron nodded gratefully and was invited on to the wooden seat beside her. She was a sturdy, middle-aged person with a friendly face browned and wrinkled by the sun, her wind-blown hair a mixture of grey and black.

"Glad of the company," said the woman. "He had a skinful last night and I don't expect to get much conversation out of him before we get to Rome." She jerked her head backwards and Bron noticed a man lying across bales of cloth in the back of the wagon. "You going to Rome?"

Bron nodded. "How long will it take?"

"We'll be there early tomorrow morning. If we're not, we'll have to wait outside the wall till nightfall because vehicles aren't allowed in during the day. The whole city is pedestrianised. By the way, my name's Isabeta."

Bron smiled. "Mine's Br–" She hesitated. "Mine's Brena."

"It'll do," said Isabeta. "Not your real name, though, is it? Never mind – none of my business."

The first part of the journey passed pleasantly, their conversation interrupted only by snuffling and an occasional deep-throated snore from the comatose passenger in the rear.

They stopped at the many watering places along the road or to buy food, and Bron enjoyed their shared meals of eggs, cheese, ham and salads.

"When's your baby due?" Isabeta asked suddenly. Bron must have registered surprise because her companion added, "It doesn't show yet, but you can't have as many babies as I've had and not recognise the symptoms. Running away, are you?"

Bron looked down, shamefaced. "It's due in December."

"None of my business, of course. I never judge other people."

"Perhaps you can help me," Bron said hopefully. "I need somewhere to disappear until it's all over – somewhere discreet and safe."

"Only one area you can do that," Isabeta said. "One of the red light districts. There's nowhere more discreet, and it's safe, unless you take unnecessary risks. Would you mind that?"

Bron shook her head. "I'd be grateful if you could direct me."

"Do better'n that. Can take you there. The market where we sell our goods is one place the girls pick up their clients."

They drove on through the green countryside. The driver's husband slept till evening, when he had to make a dash for the bushes at the side of the road. The oxen plodded on.

"He'll catch us up," said his wife, which he did. She made the introductions then left him to take over the driving while she and Bron clambered back into the wagon for a rest. Bron had not realised how tired she was, and slept soundly throughout the dark hours.

Isabeta woke her just before dawn so that she wouldn't miss the sight of the sun rising behind Rome's seven steep-sided, wooded hills. Bron sat up immediately then sucked in her breath as she gazed at the towers, columns, domes and archways lit by the pink and golden early morning light.

They trundled in through the two-towered, crenellated Porta Ostiense, set in the city wall, then bumped and jolted along a street cobbled with large stones. Isabeta's husband cursed and swore whenever other vehicles or pedestrians strayed into his path, or he and his passengers were flung first to one side then the other as the cart tilted over a particularly large stone.

"Ouch!" Bron rubbed her elbow where it had come into contact with hard wood.

"It's more comfortable in winter," Isabeta observed. "The mud washes in between the stones and makes for a smoother ride." Then she added, apologetically, "He's not the most patient carter in the world." Bron would have agreed fervently, but politely held her tongue.

She craned her neck upwards as they passed into the shadow of a high, pointed structure that Isabeta called a pyramid. She said it housed the mummified body of a famous Roman magistrate.

Turning right, they slowly made their way along a side road, then turned several times to left and right, until Bron would have lost all sense of direction in the maze of mean streets had it not been for the position of the rising sun.

The tired oxen were walking even slower, if that were possible, in anticipation of the end of their journey, rest and fodder. They had not long to wait. Bron was surprised when the street they were dawdling along opened out into a large area full of confusion and bustle as traders set up their wares on tables, on the sidewalk, in the roadway, in doorways, on the plinths of statues, or anywhere else they could find level space. While her husband led the oxen away, Isabeta prepared to sell from the cart.

Bron offered to pay for her ride from Ostia, but Isabeta wouldn't hear of it.

"Like I told you, glad of the company," she said. "He always sleeps on the journey. He's as wet as the fish our neighbour's selling. Wouldn't last a day without me around."

Bron gazed about her, one hand shielding her eyes against the bright sunlight, as she tried to decide which direction to take. Every narrow passageway looked as uninviting as the next.

"Any of these streets," Isabeta said helpfully. "Look, there's one of the girls – that one with a gold chain round her ankle. You could follow her."

Bron looked over to the bread and pastry stall where a slim, swarthy-skinned young girl with black hair down to her waist was filling a basket with crusty round loaves and cakes.

"I will. Thanks."

Isabeta nodded and smiled. "Good luck."

CHAPTER 36

Veneta stood with the wax writing tablet in her hand, reading Bron's message over and over again, unable to believe what it was telling her. Her mind in turmoil, she sat down heavily on the stool.

Rays from the early morning sun were just beginning to find their way through the kitchen window and Veneta registered vaguely that it was going to be another hot day. She could hear the children beginning to stir.

Reaching towards the bundle that lay on the table, and opening it, she saw the earrings, brooches and incense. Now she had to believe that Bron had gone.

There was a knock at the door.

She's back! thought Veneta and hurried to open it, but it was Asandra standing there, a puzzled expression on her face.

"Oh, Asandra, thank goodness you're here."

"What is it? Bron's message sounded urgent."

"Bron left you a message?"

"Yes, she called at the apartments and asked one of the girls to tell me, when I came home from work, that you wanted to see me."

"You'd better come inside."

Veneta led the way to the kitchen and indicated the wax tablet in its wooden frame. "Read that," she said.

Asandra looked embarrassed. "Veneta, you know my reading ain't so good."

"Sorry, Asandra, I was so upset I forgot. It's from Bron. I found it lying on the table this morning with her jewellery."

"Why is she *writing* to you?"

"Because she's gone."

"Gone?" Asandra was incredulous. "Gone where?"

"She says," replied Veneta, "'*Darling Veneta, I am leaving for a little while. I hope to find Aurelius, but if not, I will make a life for us somewhere then send for you all. Tell my babies I love them. Ask Asandra to come and live with you to help with the children, then she can stop doing what she is doing, which will please you. Please don't think ill of me, dear Veneta. It won't be for long. I love you all. Bron.*'"

Asandra gaped. "She's left you with all the children?"

"What do you make of it?" Veneta asked her.

"Has she gone mad?" Asandra wondered.

"I don't know what's behind it, but there's something, something she hasn't been telling me. All I know is, I've got to tell the children."

"Perhaps she'll be back."

Veneta shook her head.

"About coming to live here," Asandra said hesitantly, "I wouldn't mind. In fact, I wouldn't mind at all. The sailors are like madmen when they come off the ships" – she wrinkled her nose – "and they smell so awful!"

"Would you? Would you really, Asandra? It will be difficult for me to cope with all five children – and the dog – on my own. I could pay you, of course."

"Then that's settled. I'll move in, just till you hear from Bron that she's coming back or is sending for you."

There was no easy way that Veneta could break the news to Layla and Alon. Both children were devastated at the disappearance of their mother without warning or reason.

Sythia came to lend her support, bringing the twins to play, and Declan and Koch came round that evening to help in any way they could. They brought Petrus with them, who was calling to say goodbye as he was on his way to Rome.

Veneta and Asandra spent all day and all night trying to calm the children, reassuring them that they would see their mother again and she still loved them.

No one could offer any explanation for Bron's sudden disappearance.

CHAPTER 37

Bron turned to follow the girl at a distance. They left the market place and entered a narrow street with doors on both sides; some shut, others open, revealing erotic pictures and seductive notices with arrows pointing up dark stairways.

The girl paused at one entrance and looked back the way she had come, over Bron's head. Bron also looked back and saw a man following them. The girl disappeared up the staircase. Bron, embarrassed, walked past the doorway. When she turned again, the man had also disappeared.

She retraced her steps and climbed the stairs. On a landing on the first level were four doors.

Which? thought Bron. The answer came when one opened and the man and girl appeared, crossed the landing and went inside another of the rooms. Bron heard the key turn in the lock.

She quickly slipped through the door they had left half open. Facing her was a green couch covered in cushions. At the end of the room to her right was a small desk, behind which sat a plump woman, probably in her late fifties but dressed to look much younger, her hair dyed a flaming red. Her face was made up with thickly applied rouge to lips and cheeks, blue eyelids and blackened lashes and eyebrows. Bron guessed she had been very pretty in earlier years.

"It's extra for women," Bron was told.

"I'm not a client," she said quickly.

"What then? It's no good asking whether your man's here because I wouldn't tell you, either way."

"I'm looking for a room," explained Bron, "somewhere I can stay out of sight for six months. I'd be willing to work – cleaning and such – in payment."

"You in the family way?"

"Yes."

"Sorry, dear, I don't need any complications here, no babies, and certainly no irate husbands looking for runaway wives."

"There'd be no one looking for me," said Bron.

"Then why hide?"

The woman looked her up and down appreciatively.

"Would you go on the game?"

"No, not that."

"Pity, I reckon you'd make me a lot of money. In that case, sorry, can't help."

Bron thanked her and went down the stairs.

Further along the street, she saw footsteps painted on the paving stones and followed them to another doorway, and another rejection.

A narrow alleyway led off to the right and Bron tried several brothels along there, with the same result. No one wanted the complication of a pregnant girl unless she was willing to work with the other girls. She was adamant about that. When she pointed out her unsuitability, because of her pregnancy, to one of the brothel keepers, he thrust out his lips and sent a noisy kiss in her direction.

"Turns some of us on," he grinned.

She decided to go back to the market, hoping to find Isabeta and ask her advice, but got lost and found herself going round in circles. Then she tripped on the edge of a kerbstone and went flying, scattering her possessions around her, grazing her arm on a wall as she put out a hand to steady herself, and cutting her knees when she landed on them. Desperate and tired, she knelt on the hard stones where she had fallen and began to cry. Silently, she cursed the bo'sun, cursed herself even more for her weakness in succumbing to his animal sexuality, and shocked herself by cursing their baby, poor little mite, the innocent victim of her now incomprehensible desires.

"Here, let me help you." The voice was genuinely sympathetic. "That was quite a tumble you took."

Bron looked up into the face of an elderly woman. Two strong arms helped her to her feet and guided her over to a doorstep.

"Sit there a moment," the woman said and went inside the hallway to the bottom of the staircase. She called to someone on the landing above then returned and inspected Bron's injuries.

"Nasty graze on your arm – got grit in it," she said, "and there's blood running over your sandals." She raised Bron's skirts and revealed the blood-soaked, torn woollen stockings sticking to the gashes in her knees.

A girl appeared with a basin of warm water, cloth and towel. While the woman set to work, dabbing at Bron's arm and mopping up the blood, the girl collected up comb and mirror and other objects that had fallen into the road, and returned them to Bron's sack.

"Thank you so much," Bron said, trying to recover her composure.

"You sit there for a while," said the woman, "there's no hurry to leave."

She tipped the water into the road. "I'll take the basin upstairs then come back to make sure you're all right."

Bron nodded and rested her head against the doorpost, closing her eyes. The fall had sapped all her energy. She opened them when a man's voice addressed her.

"Hello, you're new here. One of Nella's girls?"

Bron shook her head. "Is Nella the owner?"

"Yeah, she runs this joy palace."

"Now, Felix, leave her alone." The woman was back. "She's just a friend. The twins are waiting for you upstairs."

"If you give her a job, let me know," the man said, winking at Bron. "I'll be first in the queue."

"Don't mind him," said the woman, sitting down beside her. "It's what we do here. Not me so much these days, except for some of our old clients. Most men want them younger, of course. You all right, dear?"

"The fall shook me up."

"What's your name?"

"Brena. It's not my real name, but I'm using it while I'm here."

"People know me as Nella," said the woman. "That's not my real name, either, but I've used it for so long that I hardly remember answering to anything else. You got somewhere to stay?"

Bron shook her head. "I only arrived today. I've been trying to find a room."

"I wouldn't have thought this was the right area for you, unless – you're not one of us, are you?"

"No, but this is where I need to be."

"Why's that, now?"

Bron was glad to unload her burden.

"I've run away from my family. I'm pregnant and need somewhere to stay till the birth, and someone to give my baby to, who'll look after it. Then I'll go back home."

"Would you like to stay the night?"

"Oh, may I? I'd be so grateful – I can pay you."

"Come upstairs, then. Hold on to the banister rail. Here, give me your sack."

She led Bron to the top of the staircase, three floors up, and into a small room containing a bed and various other pieces of furniture, with rag rugs on the floor and one small window.

"I hope you have everything you need," said Nella. "There's a public latrine fairly near but there's a pot under the bed so you don't need to go out during the night. I'll ask one of the girls who's not busy to bring you up some water to wash. If you want something to eat, give her the money and she'll go to the market for you."

"This is so kind of you," said Bron, sinking on to the bed.

"Have a rest now," said Nella. "Don't be nervous of asking for anything you need. We can talk later."

When she had left the room, Bron took off her sandals, climbed on to the bed and lay back against the pillows. When one of the girls came in and left a bowl of water and towels, she was already fast asleep.

CHAPTER 38

"You obviously needed that." Nella was standing in the doorway. "I thought I should let you know that it's mid-afternoon. I've sent out for some food for you. Hope you don't mind."

With an effort, Bron sat up and rubbed her eyes. "No, I'm ravenous."

"Good. Take your time, there's no rush. Freshen up and have something to eat, then we can have a chat."

When her benefactor returned about an hour later, Bron had enjoyed a snack of scrambled eggs and bread. Now, naked, she was enjoying a cool wash. It was a relief not to have to dive for a towel and cover herself up to conceal her pregnancy. Nella sat on the bed and waited patiently for her to finish and dress in her change of clothing.

"I do so appreciate your kindness." Bron came over to the bed and sat beside her. "But I don't expect something for nothing. I'm willing to earn my bed and board. I don't mind what I do, provided it doesn't endanger the baby. I'll clean and cook and shop and mend – I can, you know."

"There's no need, really there isn't."

She must have looked puzzled because Nella continued, "You could become one of my girls. I'd be glad to have you. You'd make me – us – good pickings."

"Oh, no, I couldn't do that."

"Why not?"

"I just couldn't. I've had too much love in my life to cheapen it in that way."

If the older woman thought that she had already cheapened it by a pregnancy that needed to be hidden, she didn't say so.

"Then I have another idea. How about becoming our maid?"

"What would I have to do?"

"All the things you said, plus receptionist. Some of the men are so nervous, poor things – first-timers and the youngest ones especially. They need a warm smile and a word of encouragement. Others are quite the reverse and need handling differently – but I'll train you."

"Yes, I can cope with all that."

"You'll also have to keep the men from seeing one another – make sure they don't pass each other in the waiting room. Could be a father and son, you see, wanting the same girl, or a father and his daughter's husband. Goes without saying that it's all completely confidential – no gossiping about our clients in the market place, no matter how entertaining they are – and some of them are, I can tell you."

She chuckled. Bron interrupted her with the thought uppermost in her mind.

"I intend giving my baby away. What will happen to it?"

"Give it away?" repeated Nella incredulously. "My dear, I don't do that."

"You mean I will have to make enquiries elsewhere?"

"You misunderstand me. Babies are money. I *sell* them. Of course, I'd be doing you a favour by getting rid of it, but I expect I could give you a cut." She sounded as if she expected to be thanked for her offer.

"But I couldn't *sell* my baby!"

"That's your choice, of course. But if you want *me* to dispose of it for you, I'll sell it, no matter what your scruples dictate."

Bron stood and walked over to the window. She looked out at the blocks of apartments, the maze of dark streets and passageways, at the people going about their business or, having none, lounging about in dirty doorways. She knew that she could be out there alone if it wasn't for Nella, even if the reason for the woman's hospitality was to make money out of her and her baby.

"Brena, if you're so restrained by these fine principles, how come you got yourself into this situation in the first place?"

For a while, Bron was silent, then she turned away from the window.

"Where do the babies go?"

"I simply take them from women who don't want them and sell them to women who do, and make a bit of profit along the way. What's wrong with that? It's better than them ending up in the Tiber or some hole in the ground or down a latrine."

Bron was horrified. It would have been bad enough if someone else's baby was being discussed, but it was intolerable when it was *her* baby.

She must have looked miserable because Nella continued, "I would never take a baby away from a mother who wanted to keep it. If she changes her mind, even at the very last minute – and there have been a few such – I don't go through with the transaction."

Bron was glad about that, but of course it wouldn't affect her situation, as she was not a mother who wanted to keep her baby. However, now that they were actually discussing it, she was being made to think about the consequences.

"Who do the babies go to?"

"High-born women, mostly."

Those who can afford to pay a good price, Bron thought.

Nella read her mind. "No point in selling to women who can't afford to pay for them, and pay well – there's no sense in that, no comfortable living to be had from that. I'm well known among those who need to know, mothers and would-be mothers."

"Who are they, these girls who give their babies away?" asked Bron, as if she was distancing herself from the whole trade and was not one of them.

"Girls like yourself – and women, some of them not so young. All clean – I have them examined, the babies, too. Can't afford to take disease into the homes of magistrates, army officers, politicians and such. Diseased and defective babies wouldn't do my business any good." She continued, proudly, "There are even some barren wives in the ruling families who are my clients. Some of them take more than one baby."

"Don't their menfolk object?"

"Believe me, if a man can't function as he should, he's often only too glad for his wife to go into the country for several months and return with a baby he can pass off as his own."

"And afterwards?"

"The natural mothers just start the rest of their lives without the encumbrance of their unwanted children. Some hang about for a while, but they all go, eventually."

"No further contact, not ever?"

"Wouldn't do. Unbreakable rule. Neither woman knows the identity of the other. Wouldn't do at all." She paused. "Are you going to be a mother that hangs around?"

"Oh no," said Bron, biting into her bottom lip until it hurt, making herself concentrate on the identity of her baby's father and not on the baby itself. "I will have to get home."

"And where's 'home'?"

"Ostia – at least, for the time being."

"You got other children?"

"Yes," Bron admitted.

"Thought so. I've seen you naked. I could see you've suckled babies before. That and your wish to go home as soon as possible."

Bron's eyes filled with tears.

"Cheer up, it's not so bad. At least you've got a home and family to go back to. Most of my girls would do anything to have that. Most of them are working here so that one day they won't need to work here, if you see what I mean. And that brings me back to your job. How would your high principles cope with additional duties as our decoy?"

"What does that involve?"

"Just hanging around and bringing the men in."

"I don't wish to be ungrateful, but I've no wish to entice a man away from…"

"There you go again!" said Nella with some exasperation. "You won't be bringing in any man who doesn't want to come. They get as far as the market. You must have some idea of how many brothels there are about here. I just want to make sure they come to this one and not to that red-headed cow's abattoir along the road, or to any of the others."

When Bron still hesitated, Nella said, "I saw the effect you had on Felix this morning. He was still asking about you when he left. The men would follow you."

"How would they know to do that?"

"They'll know. Besides, you'll wear the trademark – a gold chain round your ankle."

Bron remembered the girl she herself had followed that morning.

"All right, I'll give it a try, but may I wear my own anklet rather than yours?"

"You can wear what you like as long as you bring 'em in. Now, you rest for the remainder of the afternoon, and we'll send you out this evening and see how you get on."

Bron sent out for her evening meal and enjoyed a bowl of vegetable soup with crusty bread and salad, then tidied her hair, cleaned her teeth with salt, and went downstairs. Nella was in her bedroom, on her knees, rummaging about in a large carved and polished wooden chest.

"Here," she said, throwing a tunic across the room for Bron to catch, "try that on."

"White?"

"Virginal."

"Hardly that." Amused, Bron took off her own tunic and put the white one on, over her blue undershift. It fell in soft folds from her shoulder, a little too big, but that was an advantage as it satisfactorily concealed her slight but telltale bulge. She turned to Nella.

"I'm ready," she announced.

Her new employer looked at her approvingly. "What's that you're wearing round your ankle?" She was inspecting Bron's right foot.

Bron had had a brainwave. Rather than wear a cheap gold chain, she had decided to experiment with the torque that Vortin, High Priest of Byden, had given her for their baby's neck, the son she had smothered. It fitted her ankle as if it had been made to measure.

The torque was of solid gold in a twisted-strand design, of a deep, rich shade that glowed rather than shone. Unusually, the two finials at each end were hollow and each contained, Bron had been told by Vortin, a gold nugget. As she walked, the nuggets clattered lightly like nuts in tiny shells.

Nella smiled. "Music to my ears!" she exclaimed. "If they don't see you, they'll hear you. Off you go now, and start earning me some money!"

CHAPTER 39

Bron left the house and turned in the direction of the market, her footsteps accompanied by the rattle. She enjoyed watching the puzzled expressions of people she passed as they turned to look at her, trying to decide where the sound came from.

When she reached the market, she went to look for Isabeta. Once immersed in the noisy bustle, however, it was no longer possible to hear the sounds the nuggets were making in their tiny, golden prisons.

Isabeta and her husband must have sold out because there was an empty space where their carruca had stood. Bron guessed that they were probably on their way back to Ostia to collect more merchandise, and regretted not being able to say goodbye. How glad she was to know she could return to Nella's at any time.

Thoughts of Nella made her consider the reason she was in the market. How should she behave? She ought to have asked. She could not bring herself to ogle all the men who passed by. After all, they might be about their legitimate business or just out enjoying themselves for the evening, with no intention of ending up at places like her employer's or "that red-headed cow's", as Nella described the plump woman Bron had met earlier in the day. But neither could she walk about with her eyes fixed permanently on the ground.

She determined to act naturally, to wander around the stalls, seeing what they had to offer, and just go back to base every half-hour or so. "Land your catch," Nella had said. "We'll do the rest."

After about half an hour, Bron decided it was time to "land her catch", and left the market. She was unaware whether there were any fish in her trawl, but when she glanced over her shoulder just before turning a corner, she noticed three men in tow.

Surprised, she nearly missed her next turning and started giggling to herself, partly through nervous reaction and partly because she was flattered that she had, indeed, attracted three men. Mostly, though, she giggled because she had a mental picture of all four of them getting lost in the maze of little streets, and trailing round and round till dawn, accompanied by the rattle at her ankle, until the would-be paramours were too exhausted for anything else and went home.

She was pleased, therefore, when she reached the familiar doorway without further confusion. She tore up the stairs and into the reception room, where Nella sat at the desk and several of the girls lounged about in various stages of undress.

"There's three of them!" she announced breathlessly.

"I knew you could do it!" Nella was exultant. "Behind the curtain now and through the communicating door, and get yourself something to drink before you go out again. And well done!"

Bron did as she was told, and as she slipped through the communicating door into Nella's bedroom, she heard the first of the men enter the room she had just left. She listened with interest while the first two, one at a time, selected the girl he wanted and was taken through a communicating door in the other direction.

The third man argued that he wanted the girl he had followed, but Nella told him that she was not available. He grumbled somewhat but dark little Adama, she of the oval face and almond eyes, told him that her name meant "earth creature", and she could fulfil his deepest desires, and she got him out of the room and upstairs.

When the hallway was clear, Bron went along to the kitchen, drank a beaker of white wine, then went back to the market.

She was already tiring of the clattering at her ankle, but Nella liked the idea, so she left the torque in place.

She made four more trips that evening, netting thirteen men in all, most of them new clients, she was told. One of them admitted that he was on his way to the redhead's establishment when he saw and followed Bron. Nella was delighted. Added to the clients who found their own way to her brothel, the girls were occupied all night.

"Not ten minutes to call their own!" Nella gloated.

The girls were not so pleased. "Hardly time to get a drink or a wash or a pee!" they grumbled in Bron's hearing.

"You've had it too easy," Nella told them. "If you can't stand the pace, I'll find girls who can!"

Their grumbles lessened over the months that followed when their personal money, hidden all over the house, began to accumulate.

Some girls left when they decided that they had made enough to "go straight"; others went because they thought they could get a better job in a better-class district, or set themselves up in their own apartment. No matter how many left, there were always others willing to take their places.

What pleased Nella more than anything was when girls who were being put out on the streets because of lack of work at the other brothels, came to her to beg for jobs. Her delight was complete when two turned up one morning after being thrown out of the redhead's premises because their employer could not pay her rent. One of them was the dark-skinned girl Bron had followed from the market on the day she arrived.

Bron, too, began to prosper. During the day, she cooked and cleaned and mended their clothes, as she said she would, and her trips to the market were combined with shopping for whatever was required in the brothel. She was so busy that she never had time to act as receptionist.

"You stay with me," Nella said to her one day, "and we'll go far. How do you fancy an apartment on Palatine Hill?" The other girls laughed. "I mean it," said Nella.

"What's special about Palatine Hill?" asked Bron.

"What's special about Palatine Hill?" repeated one of the twins, incredulous that Bron had never heard of the area.

"It's only where all the noble families have their palaces and villas!" Adama enlightened her.

"Then that's obviously where I should be!" exclaimed Bron, and everyone enjoyed the joke and laughed with her.

CHAPTER 40

As the days passed, life for the family in Ostia gradually began to settle down into some semblance of normality. Veneta had started to give Layla and Alon lessons again and it was not long before Sythia asked to bring Joas and Tiegan on a daily basis.

It was after one of these sessions that Tiegan furtively beckoned Veneta to one side.

"What is it?" she asked him. "Why the secrecy?"

"I need to warn you," Tiegan whispered.

"Warn me?"

"I had a sort of daydream while you were talking to us."

"What about?"

"Flowing water. You mustn't go near the river."

"The Tiber? Why ever not?"

"It's not good, what I feel. In fact, it's very bad. I only seem to know about bad things. Please stay away from the river."

"But for how long?" Veneta's question was lighthearted, almost dismissive, until she saw the serious expression clouding his young face. "All right, if you say so, Tiegan, though I don't understand why."

"I just know that danger's waiting there for you."

A couple of months after Bron had left, when Veneta was in the apartment alone with Darius and Gift, there was a knock at the door. She was singing to herself as she went to open it, but when she saw who was standing there, the notes stuck in her throat.

"Bo'sun!"

"Veneta!" he beamed. "Are you pleased to see me?"

"So you *were* rescued!"

"Obviously," he agreed amiably. "We arrived in Ostia three days ago. Where's Bron?"

"Bron?"

"Yes, your friend and mine. Bron – you remember."

She ignored his sarcasm. "She isn't here."

"I already know that. The girls down in the port told me. They said she'd run away. I want to know where she went."

"I don't know, no one does."

He peered past her. Veneta turned to see Gift toddling towards them. She bent and picked her up.

"I heard that she'd left without her children."

"Yes."

"But why?"

"I don't know that, either. Of what interest is it to you?"

"We have some unfinished business."

"That's not what Bron said. She said she never wanted to see you again."

"Is that what she said? What else did she say?"

"That you tied her up." It was on the tip of her tongue to add, "and Fabia rescued her", but she remembered the description Bron had given of Fabia's injuries and remained silent.

"Anything else?"

"What else is there? You were livid at the theft of the boat and tied her up, but she escaped. You're an evil man and are not welcome here. Please go."

She tried to shut the door but he put his foot in the opening.

"Didn't she tell you how well we got on for the couple of days she was with me?"

"Please take your foot away so I can close the door."

"How good we were together, how many times we… anywhere we could – in our little nest, in the stream, up in the mountains. She couldn't get enough of me, nor I of her. It seems that you don't know your protégée very well."

"I don't believe you!"

"That's up to you, but what do you think we were doing for three days, playing knuckle bones?"

When Veneta didn't answer, he asked, "So Bron's gone and the captain's gone. They didn't go together?"

Veneta shook her head.

"How long ago did she leave?"

"A couple of months."

"Hmmm," he said, a frown wrinkling his forehead, "that would have been about three months, and now it's five. I wonder…"

"Please go."

"I'm going. Did she say anything about Rome? That would be the obvious place for her to hide."

"Who said she was hiding?"

"I did. She hasn't gone to him, has she, her Roman officer?"

"No, he's in Narona, Illyria."

"So far away! That *is* fortunate. The girls also told me that Asandra is living here now. Tell her that Fabia has got work in a hovel down in the docks. Poor cow, she'll need a shoulder to cry on when I've left to go after Bron. Tell Asandra."

"I'll tell her."

He took his foot away from the door.

"She was good, your Bron, good as gold. None better. I've missed her, nights. Fabia's no substitute."

He nodded his head in farewell and left.

CHAPTER 41

Veneta shut the door quickly and leant back against it, Gift still in her arms. After a few minutes, she took her back to the bedroom then went to the triclinium and curled up on the couch, clutching a cushion tightly to her chest.

She tried to make head or tail of what the bo'sun had hinted at – hardly hints, though, his remarks. There could be no mistaking what he was insinuating. Suddenly she remembered catching Bron one morning some months ago being sick in the latrine downstairs. She said she'd eaten something that didn't agree with her and Veneta had believed her. How could she have been so blind? Had Bron been too ashamed to tell her the truth – that he had forced himself on her?

But that wasn't the picture the bo'sun had painted so lasciviously, enjoying Veneta's discomfort. Bron and him? It required some swallowing. It didn't make sense. Bron and him? Together in that way? No, it couldn't be! Bron had always disliked him, been afraid of him – although there had been times when she had seemed to waver, unsure, when she had started to tell Veneta something then had stopped.

Five months, he had said. Veneta counted backwards to check. That would more than explain Bron's completely unexpected flight two months ago, before her pregnancy became visible – if she was pregnant, and Veneta had little doubt about that now.

Where was she? In Rome? On her own, with four months to go? Veneta's instinct was to send someone to search for her. But there was no way of finding her if she didn't want to be found. She decided that she could best help by looking after her children and maintaining a happy home until their mother was ready to return. Veneta was sure she would return, eventually.

In the meantime, she resolved to say nothing other than that the bo'sun had come looking for Bron and was travelling on to Rome. And she mustn't forget his message to Asandra.

"I'll go and find her at once," Asandra said with concern when Veneta told her about Fabia.

"May I come with you?"

"'Course, but why?"

"She rescued Bron, and I just want to make sure that she has what she needs. In spite of everything, I feel sorry for the girl."

Next morning, they left Sythia in charge of the children and walked to the port's red light area. Asandra led the way through the narrow streets and alleys, enquiring of the girls and men they met on the road. She laughed at Veneta, who was holding the end of her scarf over her nose and mouth.

"No one's going to tell us anything if you look so disapproving," she scolded. Veneta let the scarf drop.

Eventually, they were directed to an apartment building right on the waterfront. In an inner hallway they found, seated in a basket chair before a table, a wizened little man who was absorbed in picking his nose.

"Fabia? You friends of 'ers? You'll 'ave to come back, she's busy right now."

Veneta and Asandra wandered along the dockside, exchanging pleasantries with the women working variously around the boats, Asandra flirting with the fishermen and sailors, until they judged it was time to return to the dark hallway.

"You can go up, 'e's gone," the man told them. "Fourth floor, second door on the left. Don't keep 'er long. She's got work to do. Time's money."

Asandra started up the stairs, Veneta following closely, not wanting to get separated for a moment.

A pale, thin but handsome boy of about fourteen appeared in one doorway and lounged against the door jamb, watching them pass on their way to the next flight of stairs.

"This way, ladies," he cajoled. "There's nothing up there that you can't get in my bed – and more."

"Thanks, sonny, but no thanks," Asandra retorted. "I'll be back later to change your nappy."

The boy swore at her and disappeared inside, banging the door behind him.

"But he's so young," Veneta said.

"Oh, Veneta, you don't know the half!" replied Asandra, but did not enlighten her further.

They found the second left-hand door on the fourth floor landing and Asandra tapped on it lightly. They could hear the sound of sandals scuffed on bare floorboards before the door opened a couple of inches.

"Yes?"

"Fabia?"

"Yes. Who –?"

"Fabia, it's us, Asandra and Veneta!"

The door opened a little further. "What are you doing here?"

"We've come to find you, to make sure you're all right," Veneta replied. "May we come in?"

The door opened yet further, enough to reveal Fabia's suspicious face.

"You don't need to come in. I'm all right. How did you find me?"

"We asked around," Asandra told her.

"The bo'sun came to see us," Veneta explained. "He said you were here in the port."

"Asking about Bron, was he?" Fabia's voice was bitter.

"Bron's gone, probably to Rome," Veneta said.

"I know. He told me. He's going after her."

"Please let us in," Asandra pleaded and Fabia opened the door wide enough for them to enter. She was wearing only a faded and grubby, unbelted tunic that had once been red. Above it, her face was sallow and lined, her yellow hair matted.

Veneta tried to ignore the dishevelled bed, the full night pot under it, the smell of sweat, urine, fish and odours of Fabia's profession.

The one chair in the room was hidden beneath a pile of discarded clothing, leaving only the bed to sit on. Veneta wished she could have sat on it, as a sign of acceptance of Fabia's way of life, but couldn't bring herself to do so.

So the three women stood in the centre of the small room, looking awkwardly at each other.

"What will you do after the bo'sun's left?" Asandra asked her.

"Dunno. Same as I'm doing now, I suppose."

"You were kind to Bron..." began Veneta.

"Wasn't no kindness to Bron," interrupted Fabia. "I just wanted rid of her, so he couldn't get his hands and whatever else on her, so he'd come back to me – but it made no difference."

"But the way he treats you..." remonstrated Veneta.

Fabia's voice pitched higher. "That's our business, nobody else's!"

"But how do you put up with it?"

"I still love him."

It was a statement of fact and there was no answer to it.

"Now you'd better go," Fabia told them. "There'll be a client waiting for me downstairs and you're costing me and my pimp money."

"Fabia –" Veneta ventured.

"Just go."

Veneta took a tentative step towards the still open door, then turned back.

"Asandra, give her our address. We won't bother you again, Fabia, but we're there if you need us."

"Gone over to the other side, Asandra? Respectable now, are we? It won't do you any good, you know. You're one of us and always will be!"

Veneta stood and watched as Asandra took Fabia by the hand, repeated their address, twice, and kissed her cheek.

Moments later they were outside, in the relatively fresh air of the port.

"I hate leaving her here," Veneta said.

"She really is letting herself go down 'ill."

"And doesn't seem to care one way or the other."

"We've done all we can, Veneta," Asandra comforted her as they made their way home. "Don't worry about it no more."

CHAPTER 42

Over the next few months, Veneta watched Asandra's feelings for Declan mature from infatuation to a deepening love.

"You don't have to tie yourself to us all the time, Asandra," she said on more than one occasion, "You know you are free to walk out with him any evening."

Asandra smiled. "I know that," she said, "but he never asks. I think he's too shy." Veneta had never noticed that Declan was shy with anyone. "Still," continued Asandra, "it's a change from the men I'm used to meeting, who can't wait. I like to see that in him and I *can* wait. I just hope I don't have to wait too long, that's all."

"And Koch?" asked Veneta.

Asandra grinned. "Koch never stops asking me," she said.

"He adores you, as if you didn't know, and his parents have that large estate on Vectis. Declan has nothing to his name."

"Then it's a pity I'm in love with the wrong man."

"Sometimes life deals out all the wrong cards," mused Veneta.

"And you, Veneta? Never thought of marrying again?"

"Not for an instant. It's not yet a year since my husband was killed during the fighting in Byden. I'm still in love with him. I don't think there will ever be anyone else for me."

"Don't you want children?"

"I would love them, but not with just anybody."

"But time's running out. How old are you now?"

"Forty-six."

"That old? Then it's too late already."

One evening, when the children were in bed, Declan and Koch were lolling at the table, having enjoyed a platter of seafood, followed by dates and figs. Veneta and Asandra were clearing the table and bringing in more wine.

"Asandra," Koch said hesitantly, "do you fancy a walk round the gardens?"

"I need to help Veneta clear up in the kitchen," Asandra said.

"Don't worry about that," Veneta assured her, "it won't take me long."

Asandra seemed about to make some other excuse when Declan interrupted. "I can help Veneta," he offered. "Why don't you go?"

Asandra looked a little annoyed and tossed her head. "All right, I will!" she said and marched out with Koch following her.

"Take your shawl with you!" Veneta called after them.

"Those two!" Declan laughed. "It's a pity they don't come to some understanding."

"That's unlikely," commented Veneta, "when she's in love with you. Oh! Perhaps I shouldn't have said that, though you must realise it. She reckons you're too shy."

Declan frowned. He walked backwards and forwards to the kitchen, helping to clear the table, the frown still on his face.

"Have you ever thought there might be another reason?" he asked eventually.

"No, what other reason?"

Declan sounded frustrated. "Had it not occurred to you that I might not be in love with Asandra?"

"The thought had crossed my mind, but not seriously. She's a lovely girl, and now she's stopped doing what she was doing –"

To her surprise, he thumped the table hard, twice.

"Declan! Whatever's the matter?"

"Hell, Veneta, stop treating me like a little boy. Don't you know I'm in love with *you*?"

Veneta stared at him. "With me?"

"Yes, hook, line and sinker in love! Come here!"

He crossed to her and swept her up in his arms and kissed her soundly. Amazed, she dropped the plates she was carrying and all four smashed to smithereens on the mosaic floor, but she was so nonplussed that she didn't utter a sound, which would have been difficult, anyway, with his lips firmly pressed against hers.

When he let her go, she looked at him aghast. "Declan?"

"Yes?"

"How – how long?"

"All my life, it seems." She looked at him, puzzled, and he added, "It just crept up on me when we were on the *Juniper*."

"As long ago as that? And all that time I thought you were being so kind to us because you were falling in love with Bron."

"Nonsense! Bron's a beautiful girl, but not my type. No, it's been you all along, Veneta."

"How old are you, Declan?"

"Twenty-six."

"I'm old enough to be your mother."

"I know that, and I can't help it. It doesn't make any difference." He grinned. "Except that all your curves are plumper."

He came towards her again but she stopped him by taking his hand and drawing him over to the couch. His usually twinkling eyes were now very serious.

"You know I was married," she said.

"Yes."

"I've been widowed for only a year."

"I realise that."

"It's too soon. I'm not ready to love again."

"I'll wait."

"I can't ask you to do that, when I don't know for how long, if ever –"

"I'll chance it, if you'll just let me hang around."

"What about Asandra?"

"Damn Asandra! I love you, not her."

"Oh, dear," said Veneta, anticipating all sorts of difficulties ahead.

He grinned. "Let's hope she falls for Koch."

Putting his arm round her shoulder, he kissed her again, gently. She was surprised that she didn't try to prevent this second kiss.

He looked down at her. "If you give me an outright refusal, I'll run away to sea."

Veneta smiled at his threat, said half in jest.

"I *am* giving you an outright refusal, Declan – it just wouldn't do. But I don't want you to go signing on board ship again on account of me."

His eyes brightened with a hope she hadn't intended to convey. "Then I'll stick around," he said.

They heard the key in the lock and both jumped guiltily to their feet. Asandra and Koch came into the room.

"You weren't gone long," Veneta commented.

"Asandra said she was cold," said Koch, frustration and disappointment in his voice.

"Didn't you take your shawl?" asked Veneta, still feeling confused.

"What's all this?" demanded Asandra, looking at the pieces of smashed pottery all over the floor.

"I had an accident," explained Veneta. "I was just about to sweep it up."

"I'll do it," offered Declan.

"You didn't get much clearing up done," commented Asandra, looking at the table.

"We were talking instead," said Veneta sheepishly. "Anyway, you weren't gone long enough."

"Believe me, with Koch it *was* long enough!" Asandra hissed in her ear.

"Give him a chance, Asandra," Veneta whispered back. She didn't want to see Asandra hurt, and everything was transpiring to make sure she was going to get hurt, however one looked at the triangles.

Turning the matter over in her mind in bed that night, listening to Asandra's quiet breathing on the mattress next to hers and feeling very guilty, Veneta was surprised at herself for not being more dismissive of Declan's boyish declaration of love. Perhaps it was because there had been nothing boyish about that first kiss. He was a very lovable young man and she was astonished and bemused by his feelings for her. Perhaps, just perhaps, if she wasn't so in love with Selvid still…

Mentally, she shook herself. A twenty-year age gap was too much, and any relationship could ruin both their lives. It wasn't so bad, perhaps, at twenty-six and forty-six, but that would eventually become fifty and seventy – if she and the marriage lasted that long. He would be in his prime and she an old woman. She would have lost long ago whatever it was he found desirable in her. In truth, he would probably have left her years before for a woman of his own age, or younger. Then she would not only be old but old *and* lonely. What *was* she thinking about even to be considering the possibility? But if she refused him, she would be old and lonely, anyway. Then she reminded herself that Declan had not mentioned marriage.

It took a long time for her to get to sleep.

CHAPTER 43

It was November now and Bron's time was drawing close. Her bulge was very large, all out at the front, and very obvious. She had long ago abandoned Nella's white tunic, as she seemed able to attract men whatever she wore and whatever shape she was.

"There's no woman ash beautiful ash a pregnant woman," slurred one of their clients, coming too close and breathing cheap wine vapour all over her.

Bron found this sentiment incomprehensible. Whenever she inspected her figure in the girls' polished silver mirrors, she thought she looked like one of the whales they had seen from the deck of the *Juniper*.

"It's their primordial caveman fantasies," Nella declared, laughing. "Makes them feel strong and protective."

By now, Bron was finding the rattle at her ankle thoroughly annoying, but was being discouraged from removing the torque.

"Haven't you heard what they call you?" Nella asked when, yet again, Bron wanted to take it off. "'The girl with the golden ankle'."

So it became her trademark, news of her spread, and men often came from some distance to look for her.

"I'll be dining out on this story for months to come," one very young nobleman told her. "My friends won't believe that I actually found my way over here and followed your rattle, and – I hope you'll allow me this little lie – may I tell them that you rattle in bed?" Bron returned his mischievous grin and gave her permission.

At first she was flattered that she was obviously attractive to the men she trawled in night after night. Nella said she was only bringing in those who were coming anyway, but Bron was not so sure. There had been many a man who had seemed to be simply a customer at a stall, or just out for an innocently good time with his friends, who finished up in Nella's reception room.

Whatever the truth of it, she needed Nella. So, once again, she set out for the market, making for Isabeta's pitch. She had found Isabeta on many occasions since that first journey to Rome, and always enjoyed her company.

Bron preferred the market in winter. It was a safe little world on its own, seemingly isolated from the rest of Rome, its boundaries the oil lamps and torches on the stalls or fixed to poles around the site, hanging from ropes slung between them, or high on the buildings enclosing the square. There were pools of deep shadow between the lights from which the market's customers emerged, or into which they disappeared, dark and mysterious in their enveloping cloaks and hoods, worn to keep out the winter cold.

On this particular evening, wearing such a black cloak and hood, she was chatting animatedly to Isabeta, when she had the uneasy feeling that she was being watched. Nothing new in that, but her instincts told her that this time it was different. She pulled her hood closer round her face and glanced about her, but saw nothing out of the ordinary. Stallholders were crying their wares and buyers were haggling over prices, all as usual.

Then, half in and half out of the shadows, she saw a figure, a tall young man in legionary uniform with tousled light-brown hair. Deeply shocked, she realised it was Petrus, Declan's friend! He was staring at her, a puzzled expression on his handsome face. Bron pulled her hood even closer.

Should she run? All she could manage these days was an undignified waddle. She could slip away into the shadows, except that she knew that damned rattle would betray her whereabouts, as well as the two men who were standing close by, ready to follow when she left. There was nothing for it, she would have to return to Nella's, and hope he wouldn't follow. The chances were that he hadn't recognised her, especially in her condition, but he was still in Ostia when she left so must know she had run away. He might put two and two together and make four.

"Isabeta, I'm going now and won't be back tonight," she whispered to her friend. "If anyone comes asking about me, please say you don't know who I am. I'll explain later."

"Of course, dearie. See you tomorrow. Take care."

Bron passed into the shadows behind Isabeta's carruca, and as she guessed, the two men she had enticed followed her. When she couldn't be seen, they followed the rattle.

She hurried as quickly as she could through the narrow streets, now so familiar, turning to look behind whenever the shadows closed round her, hoping the lamps would reveal whether Petrus was following. At first, she was relieved to see only two men, but on turning round a few yards from her destination, was alarmed to find Petrus hurrying to catch up.

She clambered up the stairs and burst through the door of the reception room, almost out of breath.

Nella and the girls looked at her, startled. "Brena, dear, I didn't expect you quite yet."

"Nella, there's someone following me who I know and don't want to see. He's not a threat, just an old friend…"

"Leave it to us. Out of sight with you."

Bron escaped behind the curtain and through the door and listened from Nella's bedroom, as she often did. She heard her employer accommodate the first two men then open the door to the landing and welcome Petrus.

"Come in," she said warmly. "I don't think we've met before. I'm Nella. I own this establishment. I have girls to suit every taste and I'm sure you can find just what you're looking for. What *are* you looking for?"

"That girl," said Petrus, "the one they call 'the girl with the golden ankle', where is she? Who is she?"

"I regret you've picked the one young lady who's not available. She's just our maid. But I am sure there is another one here to take your fancy –"

"What's her name?" Petrus interrupted her.

"Nella, same as me – she's my daughter – and you may have

noticed that she's also heavily pregnant. Her husband's with the army, fighting the Vandals up north. Now, sir, would you like to know our prices?"

"Nella, you say?"

"Yes, she's named after me."

"I'm sorry, I must have been mistaken. In the half-light, I thought it was someone else – must have been mistaken. Sorry to have troubled you. No, not tonight, some other time, maybe."

Bron heard him close the door and his footsteps recede along the landing, down the stairs and fade away.

She wanted to rush after him and call out, "Petrus, it *is* me, it's Bron! How are my children? Petrus, I want to go home!" but the opportunity had passed and it was probably just as well.

She emerged from Nella's bedroom. "Thanks," she said.

The girls clamoured to know who the handsome young legionary was – was he the father of her baby?

Bron shook her head. "Just a friend," she said.

She thought that the twinge in her lower abdomen was a reaction to her distress at seeing Petrus, who had brought a reminder of all she had abandoned five months earlier.

With all her experience, she should have known better.

CHAPTER 44

"The whole world is going to Rome!" bewailed Veneta when Sythia told her the news.

"I've made enquiries, and that's where 'is cohort's gone, and if 'e's there, that's where we should be."

"And if they've moved out?"

"We'll follow 'em. I can take in washing and mending wherever I find myself, just as easily as 'ere. It's time my boys felt their father's 'and again."

"The children will miss them, and I will miss you, Sythia."

"You're staying in Ostia then, my lovely?"

"Until Bron comes back, certainly. If you bump into her, Sythia, you will tell her that we want her home, won't you? We love her, no matter what made her run away. The children miss her so much."

"I'll tell her, of course."

It was now six months since Bron had left. If she *was* expecting a baby, it would be due about now. Not for the first time, Veneta wished she could be with her, to lend support in whatever she was going through, but her own place was here, with the children, and they would all just have to wait for their mother's return. Veneta hoped she had someone kindly to be with her throughout the ordeal of birthing the bo'sun's child.

"How soon before you leave?" she asked Sythia.

"A few days only. Time for us to get together once more so the boys can say their goodbyes to Alon and Layla."

Layla was distraught when she heard the news, and Alon not much better.

"Don't forget me, Joas," she pleaded as they strolled hand-in-hand towards Guild Square, which lay behind the open-air theatre. It was the families' final outing together.

"Of course I won't."

"But you will make other friends in Rome."

"I suppose so." He must have seen her mouth quiver because he added, "But you'll always be my very *best* friend."

Veneta and Sythia, walking leisurely behind the children, heard this exchange. Veneta longed to comfort Layla, who must be feeling that her whole world was falling apart. First, she had left her father behind in Britannia, then her mother had vanished without explanation, and now her dearest friend was going away and she might never see him again. Veneta knew that these experiences were all part of growing up, but she could not expect an eight-year-old to appreciate that.

As the fortunes of Rome had declined, so had Ostia's, and Guild Square was dilapidated now. For the children, it was an intriguing playground, but the women were content to wander beneath the roofed colonnade that ran round three sides of the huge rectangle, from where they were able to keep a watchful eye on their charges.

Chased by Cronus, they were happily running from mosaic to mosaic that had once advertised the trades of those who had worked in the adjoining booths, now boarded up. Their favourite was a black-and-white picture of an elephant, symbol of the ivory trade. Veneta and Sythia smiled at the repeated, noisy, critical comments about its long nose and curling teeth.

After that, they scrambled happily on and off podiums that had long ago displayed statues of prominent citizens, or ran up and down the steps leading to the abandoned temple of Ceres – ironically, the goddess of plenty.

When they tired, Veneta unpacked the food she had brought in a wickerwork basket and soon all were sharing their last meal together.

Sythia, replete, lay back on the grass, appreciating the warm sunshine.

"I will remember this day," she sighed contentedly, "when we are in the grime of Rome."

Mention of Rome seemed to blight everyone's enjoyment, and they began to pack the remains of the meal back into the basket in gloomy silence.

The three youngest had wandered off and Veneta and Sythia had to walk over to the other side of the square to collect them. The four older children were left to finish the task of clearing up.

"Are you looking forward to seeing your father again?" Layla asked Joas as she folded the linen cloth.

"Of course," he replied. "We've got such a lot to tell him, haven't we, Tiegan? About the pirates and being shipwrecked –"

"And me being able to tell what's going to happen in the future," added his brother.

"You haven't done that lately," commented Alon.

"I haven't *said* anything but I still get my dreams sometimes. I know where your mother is."

"Mummy?" interrupted Layla, excitedly. "Where?"

"In Rome."

"We guessed that." Alon was dismissive.

"It's not a guess, I *know.*"

"If you know so much," said Layla, challenging him, "perhaps you can tell us whether Joas and me will meet again."

"Oh yes, you'll meet again." He paused, then added, "But I'm the one you're going to marry."

"Marry?" repeated Layla in amazement. "I'm not going to marry you, Tiegan, not even when I'm grown up."

"Of course you're not!" Joas butted in.

"Then we will have to wait and see, won't we?" sneered Tiegan.

"I can't think why anyone would want to marry my sister!" Alon contributed, genuinely mystified.

The argument was cut short when Veneta and Sythia returned with the younger children.

"What time do you leave tomorrow?" Veneta asked.

"We pick up our transport at the forum mid-morning."

"We'll come to see you off," promised Veneta.

When they arrived next morning, Sythia and the twins were already waiting for them. The wagon that was to take them to Rome was drawn up on the Decumanus Maximus.

This road dissected the forum, which contained the town's legal, public and civic offices and today was thronged with the town's business people.

Sythia had persuaded a fishmonger to allow them to travel with him all the way to Rome. He was transporting fish, preserved in salt dug from pans on the River Tiber.

"I dread to think what we'll smell like when we get there," Sythia said as she and Veneta kissed each other goodbye. "At least it's being pulled by mules, which will be faster than oxen. I just 'ope it don't rain on the way."

Joas and Tiegan piled up some empty wooden boxes to form steps and they and the fishmonger, who was only too glad to pick up the fare, helped Sythia clamber into the wagon. The boys followed, then arranged the boxes as seats.

Veneta stood with her arm around Layla, who was in tears.

"If you come to Rome, my dear, look us up," Sythia said, her eyes also glistening. "Thank you for your friendship."

"God bless you," Veneta said as the wagon moved off.

Tiegan turned towards her. "Veneta, remember what I told you – don't go near the river!"

"What?"

"The Tiber – don't go there!"

"Goodbye!" yelled Layla and Alon. The twins and Sythia waved back.

"Layla, Layla! I meant what I said!" shouted Tiegan as the distance between them increased.

"Joas, don't forget me!" was her only reply.

As they turned to make their way home through the crowds, Veneta asked her, "So what did Tiegan say?"

"That he was going to marry her!" Alon answered.

"And he knew that Mummy was in Rome," added Layla, sniffling. Veneta handed her a handkerchief, murmuring, "He's a strange boy."

Layla blew her nose. "He frightens me sometimes," she said.

CHAPTER 45

"Curse the bo'sun! Curse him!" Bron screeched as she felt another wave of pain gathering strength. "I'm never going to let a man near me again, ever!"

Nella smiled grimly. "I've heard that before!"

The baby arrived at about breakfast time. Bron let out one last, long scream, and it was all over. Nella gently wrapped the slippery, little blood-covered body in clean cloths and smiled her approval.

"It's a boy," she said, "a perfect baby boy. He's a big one, although he's come early. Well done!"

"Congratulations, Brena," echoed Adama.

"I'm taking the baby away to wash him," Nella told them. "Adama, clean her up, then get her a drink of water, and anything else she needs."

"I just want to sleep," murmured Bron.

"You must drink or you won't be able to feed him," Nella said.

"I'm not going to feed him! I don't even want to see him."

"Don't be so foolish, Brena," Nella reprimanded her. "Who else do you think is going to feed him? Of course you must."

"I can't feed him then give him away."

"Well, you've got to, you've no choice. Adama – water, if you please. Take no notice of what madam wants or doesn't want."

"Yes, Nella." Adama brought the water and Bron drank it. Then the girl gave her a very welcome bed bath.

In twos and threes the girls came up to see her.

"We're having a party downstairs," the twins told her. "We've all had quite a night of it. It was strange how it affected everybody, one way or another, even the men."

They let her sleep then, until they had all had their midday meal.

When she awoke, she wondered what baby was crying. The crying became louder, then Nella walked into the room with a bundle and Bron remembered where she was.

"He's a beautiful baby," Nella said. "What are you going to call him?"

"I'm not giving him a name," Bron replied. "Once I name him, it will be as if he belongs to me, and he doesn't. I don't want to see him."

"You'll have to see him if you're feeding him," Nella said. "And if you won't name him, then I will." She thought for a moment. "How about Honorius, after the emperor? Should be lucky."

"If you like. It's a name. It'll do."

"Yes, I think it'll do very well," said Nella with satisfaction.

She came across to the bed.

"He's hungry," she said and put the baby into Bron's arms before she could object. "I'll come back in about half an hour with something for you to eat." With that, she left the room.

Bron lay back against the pillow, not looking at the baby in her arms, who was still crying.

"Oh, do stop that noise, you!" she scolded him. "Come on, then, if you must."

She bared her right breast and brought the baby close, letting him nuzzle against her for a few moments, then guided his mouth to her nipple. He began to suck at once. Looking down at him, her eyes lingering on his screwed-up little face; she had to agree with Nella – he certainly was a fine-looking baby.

She thought then of the bo'sun and looked for a likeness between father and son. Thankfully, she saw none, except perhaps in the sturdiness of body and limbs and the square-tipped fingers. Over his head was a fine dusting of light brown hair. Bron wondered what colour the bo'sun's hair had been before it turned silver.

"You've a good appetite, I'll say that for you," she said. By now he had fallen asleep so she drew him off her nipple. It was no good trying, and she had known all along it would be no good trying. She could not distance herself from her baby, no matter what his parentage.

"Hello, Honorius," she whispered to him. "I'm your mother, but

I think you know that already. I shall call you Rius. We're going to get along together just fine – although it will only be for a very short time."

Then it was her turn to cry.

When Nella returned with a tray of chicken broth, newly baked bread and frost-sweetened grapes, she found mother and baby fast asleep.

The baby thrived and Bron along with him. In the absence of his grandparents, Nella became a caring replacement, and the girls became doting "aunts". Several times Nella had to remind them that this was a brothel and not a nursery, their duties lay elsewhere and not with the youngest and most endearing of their male companions. She grumbled good-naturedly as she sprinkled perfume about the reception room to mask the smell of breast milk and nappies.

The days passed into weeks and the weeks into months. Bron knew that approaches were being made to the list of desperate women seeking babies, and lately had caught Nella looking at her and Rius contemplatively. She always looked away hurriedly when she realised that Bron was watching her, but both knew that the time for giving up Rius was fast approaching.

Bron tried to prepare for that day but had no hope of being ready and told herself that she would think about it tomorrow. In the meantime, she was blissfully happy with her son.

By now, it was early spring in the year AD 408, nine months since she had left Ostia. She had once or twice put the torque round her ankle again and gone out into the marketplace, but was increasingly resistant, and Nella accepted that. Instead, she became receptionist and continued to carry out all the household chores, so was always busy.

She was nervous about telling Nella of her new and wild idea of taking Rius back to Ostia with her. She believed that the family would forgive her – but what if the bo'sun had been rescued from the island and was living there and learned of his son's existence and took him from her? Who knew what woman would be entrusted with his care while his father was at sea, and Bron would never know where he was from one week to the next. That would be worse than what Nella had in mind. At least, Nella's client would be respectable, perhaps even affluent.

Even so, taking Rius back to Ostia was an attractive possibility. She was also missing her other children more and more.

So she determined to ask Isabeta to act as go-between. Isabeta could find the family and explain Bron's predicament, the reason for her flight, and plead with Veneta to take her back. Bron was sure her friend would welcome her with open arms, like the father of the prodigal son in the Christian scriptures. She had no doubt that the children would, too.

Accordingly, she sought out Isabeta on one of her shopping trips to the market. Her friend agreed to do all she could to plead Bron's cause.

"Isabeta, you've always been such a good friend to me. Tell them how beautiful Rius is, especially Layla – she loves babies. Oh, and by the way, my real name is Bron, not Brena."

"Glad to help, dearie," the older woman said. "We leave for Ostia this evening and should be back in four days' time, perhaps five. My husband will grumble at the delay, but I'll deal with him. He's been talking of replacing the oxen with mules and the delay will give him a chance to purchase them in Ostia. They'll be faster and will make up any lost time. Leave it to me. I'll do all I can."

Bron thanked her again and went back to tell Nella what she was proposing. Disconcerted by the news, Nella said she was in the midst of negotiations with two women – both of high station – and didn't know if she could procrastinate for five days.

"However, I meant what I said when I promised not to take a baby away from a mother who wanted to keep it."

"Then you'll put everything on hold until I've finally made up my mind?"

Nella sighed. "Yes, as long as you don't take forever."

CHAPTER 46

Bron returned to the market on the fourth day, then the fifth, but there was no sign of Isabeta and her husband and their pitch remained vacant. She went back on the sixth day, then the seventh, and was surprised to find a stall selling leather goods and shoes where their carruca should have stood.

Apprehensively, she sought out the market manager. He listened to her query, then asked sympathetically, "You haven't heard then?"

"Heard what?" asked Bron with foreboding.

"Sit down, young lady."

Bron sat on a low wall with Rius on her lap. He was fast asleep.

"I thought everyone knew. I'm sorry to be the one who has to tell you, but Isabeta and her husband are dead."

Bron couldn't believe it. "Dead? How?"

"Aren't you the girl with the golden ankle?"

Bron nodded. "I was. Tell me what happened."

"They were killed on their overnight journey to Ostia."

"But how?"

"He was trying out some new mules."

"But they drove oxen."

Her informant shook his head. "They bought some mules before they left. He'd been drinking heavily to celebrate the deal and other carters said he was driving like a maniac, almost as if he were trying out stallions for the circus. They collided with a caravan of carts coming in the other direction and Isabeta was thrown out of the carruca and trampled by the horses."

Bron was horrified.

"She didn't know much about it," the man said kindly. "She was dead before they could get to her. The horses broke her neck."

"And her husband?" Bron asked.

"He walked away from it with hardly a scratch, but his body was fished out of the Tiber two days later."

"Isabeta always said that he couldn't manage without her."

"Friends of yours, were they?"

"Good friends," Bron replied, deeply saddened by the news. "I'm sorry."

After he had left, she suddenly realised that Isabeta had not been able to get to Ostia to deliver her message to Veneta – and Nella was waiting for a decision. She held Rius close to her, so tightly that he began to cry.

"What are we going to do, Rius?" she asked him in desperation. "I could take you away, but we can't keep running for the rest of your life, and we have a family waiting for us in Ostia."

She was still sitting on the wall when Adama found her an hour later.

"Brena, whatever's wrong?"

When Bron didn't answer, she said, "You can't sit here all day. Come back and tell Nella. She's got to know sooner or later, whatever it is. Shall I carry Rius for you?"

Bron refused and cuddled him close to her again.

"Oh, Brena," Adama said, her voice husky with sympathy, "we love Rius, too. We don't want to lose him."

When they arrived back, Nella took one look at Bron's face and sat her on the couch. The establishment was quiet, the girls without clients and resting in their rooms.

"Red wine, Adama, please," Nella said then turned to Bron. "Tell me."

While she sipped the smooth, comforting liquid, Bron explained what had happened to her friends, her hoped-for messengers.

"So what have you decided to do?" Nella asked her bluntly.

In that instant, Bron made up her mind.

"I'm taking Rius back to Ostia. I don't know why I ever ran away.

It was stupid of me. I should have trusted everyone, no matter who his father was, and told them I'd been lying. It isn't fair to make Rius suffer for what I did!"

"Was he a married man? You never told us."

"No, just the sort of man I shouldn't have let... I shouldn't have given... I can't even make the excuse that he forced me or even seduced me. I was as eager as he was. I was such a fool, Nella. I don't know how it all happened, but it did."

"And now you have Rius. It's not all bad, is it? When will you leave?"

"As soon as possible, now that I've made up my mind – tomorrow, or the next day."

"Brena, have you considered that your family may have come to Rome looking for you?"

"But they don't know where I went."

"They probably guessed. Anyway, I want you to sleep on it. I told you that I have two mothers ready to buy Rius if you give your permission. Both of them are high-born ladies – the highest, in fact. I want you to think over what you are denying him if you refuse them."

Bron opened her mouth to scream her protest but Nella forestalled her. "I know, Brena, money isn't everything. I know that. You must give me your final answer in the morning, and I will go along with whatever you decide. Whatever it is, I will have to go to them tomorrow, they've waited long enough."

"I'll give you my final decision in the morning," Bron promised.

"Good. Now take the rest of the afternoon off and try to relax. After you've put Rius to bed, perhaps you'll relieve me at my desk for the evening."

Having made her decision, Bron found she was able to relax a little and occupied herself with laundry and mending in preparation for their journey. After his evening feed and her meal, and their usual playtime together, she laid him in her bed. When she saw he was fast asleep, she plumped up pillows all round him, and went downstairs.

Nella looked up from her books as she came into the reception room, and smiled.

"You're looking much better," she observed. "Quite radiant, in fact."

Bron returned her smile. "Are we busy?"

"Every room occupied and I've asked two clients to come back shortly. The men haven't forgotten you, Brena. They still ask what happened to the girl with the golden ankle."

Bron laughed. "She gave birth, that's what happened to her."

"One of them's in here tonight. He's paid double for the twins. Most upset, he was, when I couldn't produce you, but I told him you'd be here by the time he was ready to leave – though I reminded him that you were our maid, and nothing more. Is Rius asleep?"

"Fast asleep. You can go now and put your feet up."

"Thanks, I will. I'll be next door if you need me."

Bron made herself comfortable in the chair Nella had vacated and drew the appointments book towards her. She checked which girls were in which rooms and how long they had been there, then counted the coins in the cash tin.

Engrossed in these tasks, she was only dimly aware of footsteps in the hallway outside and the reception door opening then closing. She was conscious of the twins whispering together, then a voice that she had hoped never to hear again spoke softly to her.

"Hello, goddess, I've found you at last!"

Her head shot up as if jerked by a puppet string, and she found herself looking into the mocking deep grey eyes of the bo'sun.

CHAPTER 47

"Brunus!" she gasped.

"Goddess, I've been scouring Rome for you. It's taken a long time – eight months, in fact. How are you?"

"I'm well."

"You certainly look very well."

She continued to stare at him, and as she looked, she saw a changed expression brighten his eyes. She recognised that look of consuming lust and was horrified to feel pain quickening low in her body, a response that she had deluded herself into thinking would never contaminate her again.

Then she thought of Rius, and panicked. Did Brunus know about their son? What exactly did he know? She had to find out.

"How did you find me?" she asked as coldly as she could manage.

"I bumped into Petrus. I wanted to knock him flat for stealing the boat, but I was too interested in what he had to say." He looked over his shoulder to where the twins were standing, listening intently to this conversation. "It's very public here, can't we go somewhere more private?"

"No, we can't!" Bron sounded almost hysterical. "No," she repeated more quietly.

"Why not? Aren't you the girl with the golden ankle? The men talk about you. I'll pay, if that's the problem."

"How dare you suggest that I get paid for my services – those services!"

"All right, all right! I, of all people, should know that payment isn't necessary." Bron jumped to her feet, mortified. "Calm down. I didn't think for one moment that you were charging now – though you could, you know. You'd make a fortune. So why can't we go somewhere more private?"

"Because I'm working." She didn't say she was terrified that she would succumb to him again. She tried to think only of his cruelty, his lies. Then thoughts of Rius made her concentrate.

"So what did Petrus tell you?"

"He thought he'd made a mistake. He said he came out of curiosity, looking for the girl who rattled, and found someone who looked very much like you. He couldn't be sure because she was wearing a hooded cloak, but he followed her, anyway. When he came up here he was given some story that she was the owner's married daughter. He believed it because the girl he followed was heavily pregnant. What do you think of that? Silly, eh? He said it couldn't have been you because we all knew – didn't we? – that you hadn't been near a man while you were on the island, though he did concede it could possibly have been the captain's dregs. He said you were very upset when the captain sailed."

"We all were."

"Mmm. But we know, don't we, goddess, that you had been with at least one man – maybe the captain as well?"

"Theon and I never once –"

"Slow off the mark, was he? More fool him. So it *is* mine."

"What is?"

"The baby. You were pregnant then and you're not now. Where's our baby? My son should be allowed to see his own father. Or perhaps I have a daughter?"

"You're talking nonsense. There is no baby. Nella tells the men I'm her pregnant daughter to keep them away. I'm an assistant here, nothing else – oh, I acted as decoy at one time, but no longer."

He leant across the desk, breathing deeply, and brought his face so close that his lips brushed hers. "If there's no baby, why did you run?" he asked quietly.

Bron pulled away from him. She was floundering and was glad when there was a knock at the door. She motioned the twins to the couch and went across to open it. Breaking the rules, she allowed the new client in, and the two men stood regarding each other.

"Adama, as usual?" Bron asked the man, and when he nodded, said that she would be available at any moment, and would he care to sit and wait.

He was a long-standing, valued client, in his sixties, who was besotted with little Adama. For some time, he had been trying to persuade her to let him set her up in her own rooms in the wealthier part of Rome, but so far she had hesitated to take that step. Bron knew that he would allow no disturbance in the establishment that might endanger the girls' safety, and his self-confident and authoritative bearing implied that.

The bo'sun glared at her. "I'll be back tomorrow!" he threatened, and strode out.

Bron panicked. "I've got to speak to Nella! Twins, would you take over here."

"Are you all right?" one of them asked.

"He's the father of Rius, isn't he?" the other whispered.

Bron didn't reply and stumbled through the door to her employer's bedroom. Nella was lying on the bed with her eyes closed but sat up, confused, when Bron blundered in.

"Whatever's the matter? Am I not allowed even a few moments' shuteye?"

"We've got to get away – tonight!" Bron almost shrieked at her.

"We?" asked Nella.

"Rius and me! Oh, Nella, he's here!"

"Who is?" she queried, so obtusely that Bron was irritated.

"His father. He'll take him away! I just know he will!"

"Brena, calm down."

"He found me! He's the man who booked the twins. That's just like him! One wasn't enough!"

Nella swung her legs to the floor and motioned Bron to sit beside her on the bed.

"You'd better tell me everything, from the beginning," she said, "– if you want to, of course."

Bron did want to. It was such a relief to give up all the lying and evasion and tell her story.

"First of all, my name's Bron and not Brena," she confessed, then began with her first meeting with the bo'sun at the ship's rail, ending with the three days she spent with him on the island and her humiliation at being tied up for his pleasure, an ordeal that Fabia had thwarted.

"That was the last time I saw him," she said. "When we were rescued, we left him and his party on the island."

"You've been a very silly girl," Nella commented when the story was told.

"I know. The worst thing is that when he looked at me in that certain way he has, I would gladly have gone with him into any of our rooms and got lost in his body again for as long as his energy held out. Worse than that, I think he knew it."

"Then you're more of a fool than I thought you were! Pull yourself together, girl! What you lack is self-discipline. However, *you* don't come into the picture any more. It's Rius you must think about now. Do you want him to go to such a father?" Bron shook her head. "Of course you don't! I presume you can't return to Ostia now?"

Bron shook her head again miserably. "He'd soon find us there."

"Bron, do you trust me?"

"I have no option. I have no one else to turn to."

"Then will you leave this to me? I'll make a couple of visits in the morning and bring you back a solution, one way or another, by midday. If this man returns before then, the girls will say you're out. Now, go up to Rius and get a good night's sleep. It'll be a busy day tomorrow."

"I can't – I just can't part with him!"

"Girl, you will do what you have to do and no nonsense. Go and get some sleep."

CHAPTER 48

Next morning, Bron came downstairs, the baby in her arms, after a sleepless night. She was told by the girls that Nella had hired a carriage and had left an hour before, intimating she wouldn't be back till midday.

Not being able to concentrate on anything, Bron padded about the rooms like a dispossessed body with a mind elsewhere. On the couple of occasions that there was a knock at the door, she fled into Nella's room and left the girls to deal with whoever was standing outside – first a fishmonger who offered part of his catch as payment, and was soon sent on his way, then a girl seeking work, who was told to come back later.

Bron asked the twins to surreptitiously patrol the streets outside and report back if they saw the bo'sun anywhere near. They returned very quickly, shaking their heads, having picked up a client each, so she gave up that idea.

She became more and more distressed and more nervous as the day wore on. When midday came and went, she dragged herself, with Rius in her arms, up the stairs to her own room and lay on the bed exhausted, her forehead and hair damp with perspiration.

Nella found them curled up asleep together when she returned in the early afternoon.

"Bron," she whispered, gently touching her arm. Bron was awake in an instant, and sat up, waking Rius as she did so.

"Nella! You've come to take him away!" She began to cry.

"Hush, Bron, listen, I have good news. I visited both my ladies this morning – you know, who were waiting to buy Rius. Both still want him." Bron grabbed hold of her son and turned away, shielding him from the threat.

"No, Nella, I can't! I can't!"

"Hear me out. I asked them both the same question. One refused and the other gave me the answer I was hoping for. That's where we will take Rius. Bron, dear, she is willing to take you as well, as nursemaid. So you can stay with him – for a while, at least."

Bron stopped sobbing and stared at her, open-mouthed. "I can go, too?"

"Yes, she'll employ you, as well as taking him."

"Oh, but I'll do it for nothing, of course I will!" cried Bron, beginning to laugh, though tears still streamed down her face. "But Nella, you once told me that it would never do for the two mothers to meet, ever."

"That has been my rule all these years, and I know I'm crazy for changing it now, and I'll probably regret it, and so will my client, and you certainly will –"

"No, Nella, I won't, I won't, not ever!"

"So it's on one condition, Bron – that you never let Rius or anyone else know that you are his real mother. Fausta Loricata insists on that. I have to extract that promise from you. If you cannot give your word, I take Rius and leave you here."

Bron was ready to promise the moon if it meant she could stay in safety with her baby.

"Of course I promise. Of course I do."

"Then say it, Bron. 'I promise…'" Nella coaxed her.

"I promise never to let Rius or anyone else know that I am his mother," Bron said easily, with no thought for the future. Nella nodded approval and Bron chose to ignore the troubled expression in her eyes.

"Old age must be softening my brain," Nella muttered.

"But why is she giving me this wonderful opportunity?" Bron asked. "I can't believe it's for my sake."

"Rius will be the third baby this lady has bought. The other two died very soon after she took them home, having had a procession of unsuitable nannies. She thinks that he will stand a much better chance of survival if he has your maternal love and attention and, more importantly, your milk rather than the white water some wet nurse produces."

"Then I will be allowed to feed him?"

"Yes. And, Bron, accept the wages. You'll need a nest egg for the future, whatever it holds."

Bron burst into tears again.

"There's no time for that if you want to get away before his father returns. A carriage is waiting for us."

Bron obediently stopped crying. "I told you that my ladies are high born," said Nella. "Only the best is good enough for our little Rius."

She looked down at him. "We'll all miss him," she said quietly, then shrugged, remembering she was a business woman, "but there'll be more babies. They'll never stop coming while there are girls as silly as you. I've got a good price for him as you're not dirty, like us – her words."

Bron reacted strongly, objecting to hearing her friend described so disparagingly, but Nella asked, "Who cares what she says, as long as she pays well?"

"Has she paid you for me?" asked Bron.

"Of course. I will receive a procurement fee, then a generous ten per cent of your wages for the first six months, repayable if you abscond, so you'd better stay put and we will all benefit from the arrangement. If you run away, you can be sure it won't only be the bo'sun who's out looking for you! Come now, gather your things together – as quick as you can! I'll send a couple of the girls up to help."

"I have so many questions," Bron told her.

"They can wait. We'll have time on the journey," Nella replied.

CHAPTER 49

The days, weeks and months passed and still there was no word of Bron. The children didn't ask after her quite so often now. They knew Veneta would tell them if she had any news.

It was winter and the weather became colder, though still considered mild by those who had sailed from Britannia. Local people were worshipping at the fires of their mid-winter religious festivals, kept very low-key in these days of Christianity's official status. Veneta suggested that they should join the strong local Christian contingent and commemorate the birth of Jesus.

Declan grinned. "Is this the Christian equivalent of 'If you can't beat 'em, join 'em'?" he asked.

Veneta returned his smile. "We all need a festival to lighten the dark days of winter."

The church was not far from their apartment, squeezed on to a site where other buildings had been knocked down to make room for it. It was of red brick with a dome above, not as prestigious and ornate as the pagan temples.

"There's no marble and no statues," Asandra complained. "In fact, it's very plain, except for the berries and foliage in the vases."

A central aisle led to the altar below the dome, where it met two transverse aisles. They sat in the central section among the worshippers already there.

"What does that mean?" asked Asandra, looking at the wooden cross on the altar.

"It's to remind us that Jesus was crucified," explained Veneta in a whisper.

"The Romans did it to him," said Layla.

"And his own people," added Veneta.

Asandra was mystified. "So Christians worship a dead man and not a god? And which baby is the priest talking about?"

"That's Jesus, too."

When they were outside again, Declan shook his head. "You just never know how children will turn out," he said. "What did he do, Veneta?"

"Nothing wrong," insisted Layla.

"God had come to earth as a man, to show us how we could live, and was being punished for everyone else's wrong doing," Veneta explained, "so that we need not be."

Declan frowned and swivelled one of the rings in his ear. "That's a difficult one."

"Then what?" Asandra wanted to know.

"He came to life again," contributed Layla.

"Come off it, people don't come back from death!"

"He did," Layla answered her. "You can't kill God."

Asandra commented that it all needed some thinking about. "How do you know all this, Layla?"

"Veneta told me, of course."

Gradually, winter was overcome by the first spring flowering, the days grew longer and the air warmer.

Late one afternoon, exhausted after a specially trying day with the children, a day in which nothing had happened as planned, Veneta asked Asandra if she would mind coping with them for an hour or so.

Overhearing this conversation, Layla took Veneta's hand, worry wrinkling her young forehead.

"Veneta, you're not going to leave us as well, are you? Because we've been naughty all day?"

"Oh, my darling, of course not. I won't leave you. I'd just like to take a walk along the river bank, to get some fresh air and calm down."

Layla seemed reassured, then suddenly anxious again. "But have you forgotten what Tiegan said? He warned you about going near water."

Veneta smiled. "I can't live my life not going near rivers, dear," she said. "Don't worry, I'll be careful not to fall in. Thanks, Asandra. I won't be long."

Leaving the apartment blocks behind her, she turned right along a track and so to the road that followed the line of the town wall and led directly to the river, past the Maritime Baths. The channel here was not as wide as further inland and a brick bridge, with centre arch wide and high enough to allow boats to pass through, connected the opposite bank. Veneta decided to cross over.

Here the path was lined by trees and bushes, more picturesque than the stone quayside, wharves and jetties of the town bank opposite.

Further along, the river flowed round two sharp bends and unexpectedly turned north, its course having been diverted overnight during an ancient, violent storm.

Veneta was enjoying the peace and calm of the rural path when she noticed a rowdy group of five men, obviously tipsy, coming towards her. As they drew closer, she could see that four of them were marines and the other a legionary. She hoped to pass them without incident, but was discomforted and not a little anxious when they began catcalling, shouting greetings and making personal comments while still a distance away.

She left the path, hoping to skirt round them, but as she moved aside, one or other of them blocked her way, and when she stepped across in the opposite direction, the same happened. She tried again, with a similar result.

"Please let me pass," she said, trying not to sound too alarmed.

"Please let me pass," they mimicked, copying her tone and accent.

They formed a circle round her and, with great hilarity, began pinching her bottom and poking her breasts, but they were erratic in their movements and a gap opened up between them. Veneta saw her chance and dived through it.

They let her go without trying to follow and continued on their way, laughing and commenting on lost opportunities and frigid women. She ran a short distance, frightened and irritated at having her quiet walk ruined, but eventually calmed down and slowed to a more leisurely pace.

A little later, she was surprised to hear her name called, and looking across to the river, saw Koch and Declan waving frantically from the deck of a trading vessel under sail on its way to Rome.

Many of the merchant ships that arrived in Ostia with commodities such as grain destined for Rome had too deep a draught to negotiate the Tiber and their cargoes had to be transhipped into smaller vessels. Declan and Koch were often engaged in this work and, if it was at the end of their day, would sometimes inveigle the captain of the river craft into letting them sail with him to the bend in the river. Then they would jump ship and swim ashore, their tunics drying as they ran together to the garden apartment for a family meal. Veneta presumed that that was what they were doing this evening.

She waved back as they passed her, sailing in the same direction, and continued her walk, watching the comings and goings of the ships in the river and the activity on the town bank.

Suddenly she was aware of movement in the bushes at the side of the path, followed by inebriate giggling. Before she could turn, she had her arms pinned to her sides by someone who breathed alcoholic fumes all over her. The men she hoped to have escaped had retraced their steps and caught up with her by surreptitiously using the trees and bushes as cover.

Once again they surrounded her, then began pushing her off balance from one to the other, which they found very amusing, all the more so when she demanded that they stop. Finally they did so, leaving her standing in the centre of the circle as they moved round her, making sure they left no escape gaps this time, pretending every now and then to pounce, all the while making lewd suggestions and offering invitations to go with them into the bushes.

When she made no response, the legionary threw his cloak around her and pulled her to him, trying to fondle her but getting tangled up in its folds.

"Why don't you come with us to the baths?" he hiccupped.

"I need – where are the public latrines?" one of the sailors asked breathlessly. "Don't bother – can't wait," and he pulled his tunic up and his undergarment aside, exposing himself to Veneta and demonstrating graphically why he needed the latrine so urgently.

The other men guffawed, and while their attention was diverted, Veneta saw her chance and scrambled out from beneath the cloak and made off towards the river.

They gave noisy chase and there was no escape for her except to wade out into the cold flow until she was up to her neck, where she stood shivering, hoping that they would not think it worthwhile to follow. However, the sailor who had urinated in front of her had already begun pushing his way through the water. He was still holding his flabby penis in his hand, and despite her discomfort, Veneta thought that she would be very ashamed of it if she were a man. She closed her eyes in resignation.

Suddenly, there was an explosion of noise and, eyes wide open now, she was amazed to see on the bank a mêlée of flying fists and flailing arms; knees were buckling and bodies crashed heavily to the ground. In fact, there were only two newcomers, Declan and Koch, who apparently had seen what was happening from the deck of the trader.

The drunken bullies were no match for two sober, strong and fit young men in a rage and were soon overwhelmed. When those on the bank had been dealt with, Declan waded into the river and dragged the shivering sailor on to the grass. Veneta heard knuckles cracking and an exploding gasp from her would-be assailant, who must have thought that a battering ram was being driven into his guts.

Two of the group made an erratic run for it, the sailor scrambled away on all fours, spitting blood, and the remaining two, who had been left lying flat on their backs, were hauled to their feet and had their backsides kicked until their legs came to life and sped them away along the path, but in the wrong direction.

"What's the count?" asked Koch.

"I broke at least two of their fingers," Declan answered, "and I saw a tooth being spat out –"

"– and I reckon even their own mothers won't recognise them once the bruises surface!" Koch chortled at the prospect.

"Hey, I'm still here!" Veneta called weakly as she began to wade towards them.

Declan was contrite. "Oh, Veneta, I'm so sorry," and he went out to meet her, throwing his arm about her and helping her on to the bank.

Even with the warmth of his body against hers, she was shivering violently and her teeth were chattering.

"Th-th-thank you both," she managed to say, suddenly very tearful.

Declan looked down at her with concern. "Hold on to her, Koch, I won't be a moment."

He set off at a run towards the bridge, in the wake of the legionary, and was soon back, the young man's cloak over his arm. "Courtesy of the military," he said, wrapping the fine, blue woollen cloth round Veneta. "He didn't want to part with it, as it's obviously stolen – there'll be some centurion on the warpath and a flogging in the offing – but I managed to persuade him."

He looked at Veneta again. "You're still freezing and you can't walk through the town as wet as that. Koch, would you run to the apartment and ask Asandra for some dry clothes."

"I'm on my way!" Koch set off at a good pace.

"You shouldn't stay so wet till he comes back. You'd better get out of those sodden things."

Veneta nodded and stumbled to the cover of the bushes, where she undressed and left her discarded clothes in a heap. When she returned to Declan, the cloak wrapped tightly about her, he considerately had his back to her and was watching the activity on the river, but he turned towards her when she thanked him again.

"I feel a little warmer now," she said.

Gently, he put his arm round her and drew her towards him. "Are you quite recovered?" he asked.

"Almost."

All the while, she kept her body taut beneath the cloak, trying to maintain a neutral space between them, realising the compromising situation they were placing themselves in and not wishing to make it more difficult for him. She didn't want to play the temptress.

Because she was holding on to the cloak so tightly to prevent it slipping from her shoulders, she was unable to stop him from nuzzling his face into her neck.

"Oh, God, Veneta, I can't take much more of this, always being so close to you and never allowed to touch!"

Her teeth began chattering again, more from nervous reaction than from the cold.

"Let's walk up and down for a while, until Koch returns," she suggested, and with an effort that showed in his face, he let her go, but then his frustration exploded in a diatribe against the men who had attacked her.

"They're animals!" he raged. "No, worse! I don't know of any animal that behaves as they did! I'll have them hauled up before their commanding officers and I'll make sure they're brought before the military and marine courts, or the civil magistrates, or all three!"

"But we don't know who they are," Veneta said.

"They won't take much finding, the state they're in," he said grimly.

"Perhaps you could ask some of the girls – Fabia might know them."

"Fabia? Did nobody tell you? She's been long gone. She left for Rome weeks ago, chasing after the bo'sun."

They discussed inconsequential matters, anything that Veneta could think to talk about, until she had exhausted her subjects and her energy. The distress she had suffered was beginning to affect her emotionally and this time she did not demur when Declan once again put his arms round her.

Strands of still-wet hair were straggling against her face and neck. He reached one hand behind her head and pulled out the restricting hairpins. Her thick brown hair tumbled in waves about her shoulders.

"You'll never know how often I've wanted to do that," he whispered hoarsely, and before she knew what was happening, his hands were beneath the cloak, caressing her body.

"Declan, don't!" she pleaded with him. "Please don't!"

There was an anguished, strangulated cry behind them that sounded like a trapped animal in pain. They turned to find Asandra staring at them open-mouthed, grey eyes wide, Veneta's change of clothing clutched in her arms.

"Veneta! Declan! How could you?" she cried. "Been at it a long time, 'ave you? Behind my back? It's obscene! Oh, how could you, when I loved you both so much!"

Veneta pulled herself away from the young man. "It's not what it looks like!" She started towards Asandra, but the girl was in no state of mind to listen to explanations. She dropped Veneta's clothes and fled.

CHAPTER 50

Frantically, Veneta dressed in the clothes Asandra had brought, then she and Declan half walked, half ran back to the apartment, quite forgetting to take with them her pile of wet clothing. They found, not surprisingly, that Asandra had gone.

"What's up?" asked Koch. "Asandra flew in here like a mad woman, threw some things into a sack, and ran out. She wouldn't tell me what had happened. 'Ask them!' was all I got out of her. What did happen?"

The children were equally disturbed, clamouring to know where Asandra had gone and asking if she was leaving them forever.

"It was a terrible misunderstanding," Veneta said.

"What sort of misunderstanding?"

"Koch, come with me." Declan led him into the bedroom that Veneta and Asandra had shared. Veneta busied herself telling the children something of what had occurred, reassuring them as best she could, keeping herself occupied by preparing the evening meal, and hearing the low voices from the bedroom meanwhile.

When they came into the kitchen, Declan said, "I've explained everything."

Koch looked surprisingly cheerful. "With Declan out of favour," he said, "Asandra might look at me more kindly."

Veneta wanted to say that love didn't work like that, but kept her peace, not wishing to burst his bubble.

"You must find her and sort out this mess," she told them.

Declan said he didn't think it could be sorted. "Anyway, why should I try? What she saw is the truth. Why should I conceal it from everybody any longer?" Koch agreed with him wholeheartedly.

"I want her here, or somewhere else safe," Veneta insisted. "I don't want her going back to her old ways. Oh, how I wish I'd listened to Tiegan's warning!"

They searched for her in the port and asked after her for days but she was nowhere to be found. None of the girls knew of her whereabouts or, if they did, they weren't prepared to say. The days turned into weeks and Veneta and Declan gave up, though Koch kept hoping to find her.

Veneta confided her anxiety to Declan. "He's got so thin," she said, "in spite of the double helpings of everything I give him."

Declan was spending more and more time at the garden apartment, conscious that Veneta was now playing mother, father and teacher, while coping with all the work entailed in running a household with five young children.

They asked again why Asandra had left, as suddenly as their mother, they said.

"Is it something that we do wrong?" Layla questioned with great concern.

"No, no, it's nothing to do with you," Veneta hastened to reassure them.

"Nobody really loves us except you, Veneta," Alon commented.

She wanted to say "Jesus does" but lacked the energy to contradict him, as all the evidence, as far as the children were concerned, pointed to the truth of what he said.

They had now lived in Ostia for just over a year. Late one evening, there was an unexpected knock at the door. When Veneta opened it, she saw waiting there a young girl who could not have been more than fifteen years old but was made up to look older. Her tunic was short and her neckline low, and there was no doubting the profession she followed.

"Is Koch here?" she asked without any preliminaries.

"Who are you?"

"I've got a message for him."

Veneta returned to the triclinium to tell Koch that there was a young lady at the door asking for him.

"What's the message?" he asked, eyeing her suspiciously.

"You're wanted down in the port," she said.

"What for?"

"Asandra needs you. You're to come with me."

There was no hesitation after that.

"Asandra has sent for me," he told Veneta and Declan as they relaxed in the triclinium. "I'll be back as soon as I've found out where she is and what she wants."

But he didn't come back, not that evening nor the next.

"He hasn't turned up for work, either," said Declan. "He'll lose his job if he's not careful."

Koch finally put in an appearance at the apartment three days later. His job had already been lost, but he didn't seem to care unduly.

"I've come to let you know what's happened," he said when Veneta let him in. "It's Asandra – some maniac beat her up. She wouldn't tell me who it was or I'd kill him!"

"Is she badly hurt?" asked Veneta, concerned and blaming herself for the girl being in this predicament.

"She's bandaged down to her waist, so I don't know what injuries she has there, and she won't say what he did to her. She had to have stitches where he – where he –"

Declan brought him a glass of red wine.

"Her nose is broken, and there's an injury to her head. They say she'll mend, in time – her body, anyway. I'm staying with her till she does. It will take weeks. They're letting me stay there."

"Koch, if you need any money –"

"Thanks, Veneta, but no. She wouldn't take it from you, anyway. When she's a bit better and will let me leave her, I'll get another job and support us."

Veneta felt wretched. "That beautiful girl –"

Koch interrupted her. "She's not beautiful any longer. Even when she's healed, she won't look the same."

Declan laid a hand on his shoulder. "I'm so sorry."

"At least she may look at *me* now, in the way she's always looked at you," Koch said. "I'll let you know how it goes."

When he had left, Veneta covered her face with her hands. "I'm so ashamed," she admitted. "We're responsible for this."

"Not you, darling – me. Never you. And you can't take the troubles of the whole world on your shoulders." He kept his distance from her, knowing his lack of control if he touched her. "But she's also to blame for prostituting her body again."

When she took her hands away from her face, Veneta noticed Layla standing in the doorway.

"I got woken up by the loud voices."

"Back to bed, young lady!" said Veneta. "I'll come with you." She ushered her along the hallway.

"Veneta," Layla whispered as she was being tucked up in bed, anxious not to wake her brothers and sisters, "you told me that Jesus took all our troubles on his shoulders."

"That's right, he does," replied Veneta, smiling down at her, then kissing her lightly on the forehead.

"Then why did Declan think you had them all on your shoulders?"

Out of the mouths of babes... mused Veneta. "You're right, darling, I'm doing it all wrong."

With Koch gone, Declan practically lived in the garden apartment, except for going back to his own rooms every night. Veneta knew that he would rather stay, but never gave him the opportunity of discussing it.

On one occasion, when he said he was feeling as dull as an old married man, though without the advantages, she said to him, "You should go out for an evening, Declan, to the theatre or the forum, and meet some girls your own age."

Veneta said what she knew she should say, but the thought of the apartment without him there filled her with alarm. She reprimanded herself for being the proverbial dog in a manger.

When he replied that he didn't want any girls his own age, she pre-empted his next remark by answering it, "No, my dear, it won't do, it would never do."

"'Obscene' – wasn't that what Asandra called it? How could she call what I feel for you 'obscene'?" he asked miserably.

"She did, but she was shocked and hurting, and a woman in love will say all manner of things she doesn't mean. It wasn't obscene, it was – it was –" If she was honest, she would have said, "It was beautiful, shocking and very exciting and if Asandra hadn't come along, I don't know quite what would have happened", but she held her tongue in check and finished lamely, "It's just not possible."

One morning, three months later, a public holiday in Ostia to thank all the gods who regularly surrendered the sea's bounty to feed the local population (the authorities were taking no chances of offending any of the deities), Veneta found at the door the same young girl who had brought Koch the message previously.

"Hello," the girl said brightly, with confidence, "I've brought you another message, but from Koch this time. He wants you all to meet him in Guild Square as soon as you can after your midday meal."

"Why can't he come here and have the meal with us?"

"In Guild Square," she repeated and left.

"Can you think why he wants to see us all there and not here?" Veneta asked Declan.

"No idea," Declan replied, "though I've given up trying to understand what that young man thinks or does. I sometimes bump into him around the port. Nothing about him makes sense any more. Got to hand it to him, though, whatever Asandra looks like now – and people have told me that she's no longer pretty – he's as faithful as ever, perhaps even more so."

After they had eaten, Veneta made sure that the children were dressed in their best tunics to walk through the town to the square. When they passed under the ornate entrance, they could see two figures at the far end, holding hands.

As they drew nearer, Veneta realised that it was Koch with Asandra, but not the lively, laughing, bubbling-over-with-fun Asandra they had once known. This version was quiet, subdued and thinner and she deferred all the time to Koch, who spoke for them both. Her oval face, once so pretty, was wan and still showing signs of scars not fully healed and her grey eyes looked a shade darker.

That her nose had been broken was obvious. Veneta was also shocked to see that where her brown hair had been cut away to stitch a gash in her head, it was growing back silvery grey. The only brightness about her was her presumably new, pale blue tunic and a bunch of summer flowers she carried.

"We're glad you could come," Koch said in greeting.

Today, the children had no thought for the elephant mosaic. They were staring at Asandra, seeming not to recognise her, unsure, wanting to go towards her but hanging back. Only Cronus seemed not to notice any difference and was running round her feet, barking for attention. She smiled and bent to stroke him.

"Hello, Cronus, at least you 'aven't forgotten me."

At the sound of the familiar voice, all five children ran over to kiss and hug her. They catapulted their questions at her.

"We've missed you so much!"

"Where have you been?"

"Why did you leave us?"

"What's wrong with your face?"

"It's a long story," she said, stroking their heads and cheeks as they clung to her legs or round her waist. "You must ask Veneta to tell it to you sometime."

Veneta flinched, but Asandra wasn't looking at her. Her eyes had slid across to Declan, who stood awkwardly, changing his weight from foot to foot and fiddling with an ear ring.

"Do you still love us?" Alon asked anxiously.

Asandra brought her gaze back to the little boy who was looking up at her so earnestly. "Always and always," she answered, with something like her old enthusiasm. "Never doubt it."

"We wanted to tell you our news before you heard it from someone else," Koch said, when he could get a word in.

Veneta and Declan waited, mystified.

Koch continued, "Can't you guess? Asandra at last said 'Yes' and we were married this morning. We're very happy, aren't we, sweetheart?" She smiled at him and he kissed her on top of her head, avoiding the scar.

"Married?" repeated Declan.

Veneta was astounded. "Where?"

"In the sanctuary to the Good Goddess, on the foreshore. And that's not all," Koch continued, "I'm taking her home with me, to Vectis. We sail tomorrow."

Veneta's mouth was still open. She remembered Bron's description of his gracious mother, Regina Marcella, and wondered whether she would be able to accept her new daughter-in-law. Whatever happened, Veneta guessed that it would be an uphill struggle for everyone concerned.

Suddenly, Veneta and Declan remembered their manners and mechanically moved across to the couple to congratulate them and wish them god speed. As Declan kissed Asandra on the cheek then left her quickly to shake Koch by the hand, Veneta saw her eyes follow him, and into them came the familiar soft look of love and longing which was now unbearable to watch. Veneta guessed that, if Declan turned and held out his arms to her, she would forsake her promises, her new marriage vows, and would follow him to the ends of the earth and back again, if that was what he asked of her.

"God bless you both," Veneta said earnestly, and was sad when Asandra stiffened and drew away from her embrace and kiss. "Asandra, I'm so sorry that things have turned out as they have, but I wish you both every happiness." She lowered her voice. "And, my dear, dear friend, be kind to Koch – he loves you so much."

Veneta knew that she had no right to plead so and was not surprised when Asandra said nothing in response.

Going over to Koch, she gave him a big bear hug. "Koch, dear, I'm so happy for you and wish you every blessing. I'm sure we shall meet again, as I intend to go home myself one day, Bron or no Bron, and will call in at Vectis on the way."

They exchanged pleasantries for a few minutes more, but the strong ties between them all had been snapped. They would never again be as happy together as they were on the island and more recently in the apartment. Veneta was glad to escape as soon as she could, and was sure that Declan felt the same, but the children had to be dragged away. They had known nothing but loss since arriving in Ostia.

"Was that really Asandra?" asked Layla on the way home.

"Was it, Veneta, was it?" asked Alon.

"Of course it was."

"But," he observed, "Asandra never had a bent nose."

Their homecoming was very subdued. The children played quietly, without squabbling, which was most unusual for them, and Veneta and Declan had little to say to each other, except to discuss the marriage and future prospects for the young couple. Neither of them expected it to last for long.

"Because she's still in love with you," said Veneta.

"I know it," he was honest enough to reply.

Veneta was glad when it was time for the children to go to bed.

"Declan, will you stay the night with us?" she asked. She saw his eyes brighten, and to avoid any misunderstanding, added quickly, "I hope you won't mind sharing with the boys. I'll have the girls in with me."

The light in his eyes faded with his hopes and he shrugged. "Of course, Veneta. Glad to."

She lay awake a long time, with Layla, Lucilla and Gift asleep on the other mattress, aware of Declan in the next room, and comforted by his close presence. She guessed that he was also awake, conscious of her lying so near to him.

Turning the day's surprising events over in her mind, she decided that there was nothing to keep them in Ostia any longer and that it was time to travel on to Rome to look for Bron. She would speak to Declan in the morning and ask if he would go with them. She was certain he would not refuse.

CHAPTER 51

Tears, hugs and kisses swamped Bron and Rius as she took her leave of the girls, promising to bring him back to see them soon.

"Of course you won't," Nella commented brusquely as they clambered into the carriage. "You'll never be allowed to come back here."

"But –"

"No 'buts'. It's a new life you'll be leading with Fausta Loricata and you must forget everything and everybody that went before. You'll no longer be able to come and go just as it pleases you. She'll lay down the ground rules and you'll play it by her book, or you'll be out of there a lot faster than you went in, and without Rius."

Bron lapsed into silence while they were bumped and jolted on iron-rimmed wooden wheels, their journey made a little less uncomfortable by the bed on which they sat, clinging to the ropes that kept the canopy secured to the wooden base.

Their view forward was restricted by the broad back of the driver, who resolutely drove his two horses with scant attention to the pedestrians thronging the roads. His attitude seemed to be that it was up to them to scatter and not for him to drive round them.

Bron tried to glimpse, through a small slash in the side of the canopy, the houses and buildings they were passing but had to concentrate on sitting upright on the bed so that she should not squash Rius between herself and Nella.

"Is this the lady's carriage?" she asked eventually.

"No," replied Nella. "Hers is a much finer affair altogether. This is on hire – though it's her money paying for it."

"I thought vehicles weren't allowed on the streets during the day."

"They're not, but like everything else in life, there's one rule for the poor and quite another for the rich."

"So where are we going?"

"To an inn. I was there this morning and booked a room for the day."

"I don't understand," said Bron, mystified.

"I am simply following instructions. Fausta Loricata gave me clothes for both of you, fine clothes – you really are a very lucky young woman. I took them to the inn this morning, with some simple jewellery for you to wear, as befits her son's wet nurse –"

"*Her* son!" Bron interrupted, holding Rius tightly to her.

"Yes, he's her son now – and don't go forgetting it! She's paid me well and he's hers. Play along with that and you won't have any trouble."

"I don't know whether I will be able to –"

"If you give her any cause to complain, just once, she will have you out of her house quicker than you can spit! Cheer up! He'll be with you much more than he'll be with her. Society women see very little of their children. Most youngsters think their nannies are their mothers, anyway, at least in the early years."

Bron was mollified. "What happens once we've changed?"

"Then her own carriage will take you home."

"But how will she account for the sudden appearance of a five-month-old son?"

"Her husband has only recently been admitted to the Senate, so they haven't been in Rome long," Nella explained. "She has told everyone that their nanny will be bringing the baby to the house just as soon as it's decorated and furnished. She has a nursery ready for him and an adjoining room for you – or whoever she employed. He's a very lucky boy to be taken into such a family, and you will also benefit if you don't cause her any problems."

"And where do they live?"

"Where they all live, those who *are* anybody – on Palatine Hill."

"Strange," mused Bron, "that's where I once said I should be."

Nella nodded slowly. "Your stars must be in a lucky configuration, at least for this phase of your life."

The carriage turned a corner and the horses were pulled to a halt. The driver jumped down and came round to the back of the canopy, untying ropes and helping Nella through the opening, then Bron with the baby.

They were standing outside an inn in a busy side street with citizens hurrying about their business and women gossiping in front of the nearby wine shop.

Nella led the way through the entrance door. She spoke to a man behind a desk then signalled Bron to follow her up the stairs and into a room on the first landing.

Bron laid Rius on the large bed before removing her cloak and laying it over the back of a chair.

Nella indicated a sack on the floor. "Put it in there," she said, "with all your other clothes. You won't be needing them any more."

"But it's new," Bron objected.

"You won't mind leaving it when you see what Fausta Loricata has sent for you."

She took down a protective linen cover that had been hanging from a hook in the wall and drew from it a pale yellow undershift with long sleeves and a brighter yellow mantle, both of cotton, with a pair of chained bronze brooches to keep the mantle fastened on her shoulders.

Bron flushed with pleasure. "What lovely colours!"

"And here are your undergarments, pure white silk, and brown leather sandals. Rius will look just as splendid."

Bron inspected the clothes chosen for him – like hers but in two shades of blue, a white cotton napkin and a beautiful woven and embroidered woollen shawl.

There was a tap at the door and a servant entered with a jug of hot water, sponges, olive oil and towels. She poured the water into a pottery bowl held in an iron tripod.

"You are both to wash before getting dressed," Nella said. "The woman will help you then a girl will be coming to dress your hair and make up your face. I'll look after Rius," and she added sadly, "for the last time."

"I think I'm going to like this job," said Bron, beginning to strip off and dropping all her clothes into the sack.

To maintain secrecy, there was no more serious conversation

between them while the servant and then the beautician were in the room. When they were alone again, Nella handed Bron a mirror.

She stared at her reflection and saw that she looked even better than she felt. Her long, dark hair had been drawn back away from her face and left to fall in curls over the nape of her neck, and her make-up had been so skilfully applied that it enhanced her natural bloom and colouring without overpowering either. She fingered the necklace of green and yellow glass beads that rested at the base of her neck. There was a bracelet to match but she was unable to wear the pendant earrings because her ears had never been pierced.

Nella shook her head regretfully. "We could have made a fortune, you and I, if you'd agreed to work for me. However, that's all in the past. You've a new life ahead of you both now. I hope you make the most of it and don't do anything silly to spoil it all. You seem to be rather good at that."

Bron pulled a face, acknowledging agreement.

"Your carriage will be here soon but this is as far as I'm allowed to go, so concentrate on what I'm saying. The driver will take you to the Loricatus house, to the front door, of course. You are to knock and request the doorman to let his mistress know that her son and his nanny have arrived. Don't mention his or your name."

"Is she going to give us different names?"

"Probably. You must be prepared for that."

"He'll always be Rius to me."

"His name will be whatever his mother decides it'll be!" Nella retorted sharply, and Bron fell silent.

They waited without speaking further, listening to the gurgling noises Rius was making. Bron had fed him before they washed and he was well content.

A tap at the door let them know that the carriage had arrived. Bron stood.

"Nella, I haven't the words –"

"I know, girl," the older woman replied gruffly. "Leave it at that."

They hugged each other then Nella picked up the baby from

the bed and put him into his mother's arms. She had to push Bron away from her.

"Go!" she said. "Shut the door behind you and don't look back."

Obediently, Bron did as she was told.

The enclosed carriage waiting for them was very fine, as Nella had said it would be. Pulled by four black horses, it was also black, with an insignia, presumably the family crest, painted in gold leaf on the side doors. A black blind was pulled down over the opening on each side.

Having secured the reins, the driver descended from his perch, bringing with him a small set of steps, and helped Bron with Rius in her arms into the carriage, then closed the door. The vehicle rocked as he resumed his seat, she heard him speak to the horses, and they began to move forward.

Resisting the temptation to pull aside the blind to see if Nella was at the door of the inn, waving goodbye, but knowing she wouldn't be, she lay back against the soft cushions and closed her eyes.

"Make way! Make way!" the coachman shouted at intervals. The cries that followed the cracking whip were human, not equine.

A picture of Aurelius came into her head and she was ashamed that she hadn't thought of him for a while. He would never find her on Palatine Hill, but nor would the bo'sun, not for some time, anyway, unless he was very clever, or his bribes magnanimous – the reason Nella had not told the girls where Bron was headed.

The horses slowed and she sensed they were climbing a hill. There were other vehicles around them. Another rule for the rich, as Nella had said. Curious, she pulled the blind away a little and peered round it.

All that she saw filled her with delight and her heart raced. The single-storey homes they were passing stood in the centre of large plots, protected by walls with ornate iron gates set in them. The higher up the hill they travelled, the larger became the plots. The houses were painted red ochre and white, blue and white, sea green and white and hibiscus yellow and white. They were colonnaded, porticoed, balconied and turreted, their windows shuttered against the afternoon sun, their regulated, terraced gardens planted with colourful flowers and bushes and the gravel paths swept clean.

But it was outside a house sparkling all white that the horses stopped. The driver opened the door of the carriage. Clutching Rius tightly, Bron stepped down on to the steps placed ready for her. Moving across to the gate, he opened it and saluted smartly as she passed through. Then it clanged shut behind her, separating her from all that had been familiar in her life up till now.

Self-consciously, she began to walk towards the house, the gravel crunching beneath her feet. Reaching the wide, shallow stone steps leading up to the front door, she mounted them, took a deep breath and grasped the iron ring held in the mouth of an ornamental lion's head.

"Here we go, Rius, you and me. Whatever the future holds, we'll face it together! I love you, darling."

Then she rapped the knocker sharply, twice.

Inside there was a shuffling of feet and slowly the door opened.

To be continued in Part IV...

Reminder List of Characters

Bron's family:

Soranus	Husband, left behind in Byden
Layla	Daughter, aged seven years when she boards ship
Alon	Son, six years
Darius	Son, six months
Gift	Girl aged six months, adopted from a brothel
Lucilla	Niece, her brother's daughter, one year old
Veneta	Friend, one-time pagan priestess, now a Christian
Aurelius Catus	Lover, a junior officer in the Third Victrix Legion

On board *The Juniper*:

Theon Stokovius	Captain
Brunus	Bo'sun
Declan	A young sailor
Sythia	Following her legionary husband to Rome
Tiegan & Joas	Sythia's twin sons, eight years old
Asandra	A young camp follower
Fabia	Camp follower, a little older
Leeza	A sick child
Zohira	Her mother
Petrus	A young legionary

During the voyage:
On the island of *Vectis*:

Reginus Marcellus	Farmer
Regina	His wife
Briard	Their elder son
Koch	Their younger son

At *Felicitas Julia*:

Palladius	A young legionary, injured

In *Italia*:
***Ostia*:**

Isabeta	With her husband, a carrier between Ostia and Rome

***Rome*:**

Nella	A brothel keeper
Adama	One of her girls
Honorius (Rius)	A baby
Fausta Loricata	A senator's wife

The family of Captain Theon Stokovius:

Avala	His woman
Thorsten	His eldest son
Iesa	His wife's daughter

BRON'S FAMILY TREE

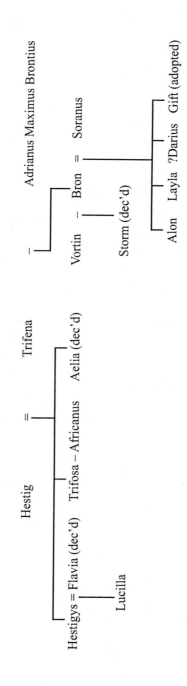

= marriage   – liaison

1	*From Pollus harbour	Poole, Dorset
	Vectis	Isle of Wight
2	Bay of Burdigala	Bay of Bordeaux (present-day Biscay)
	Gallia	France
3	Magnus Portus	La Coruña
4	Calle	Porto on the River Durius
5	Felicitas Julia	Lisbon
6	Sacrum Point	Cape St. Vincent
	Lusitania	Portugal
7	Portus Hannibalis	Faro
8	Hispalis	Sevilla
9	Gades	Cadiz
10	Mount Calpe	Gibraltar
11	Malaca	Malaga
12	Carthago Nova	Cartagena
13	Balearis Major	Mallorca
14	Sardinia	Name unchanged
15	Corsica	Name unchanged
16	Uninhabited island	North of Corsica
17	Ostia	Sea port for Rome
Seas:	Ibericum Mare	Mediterranean Sea
	Mare Nostrum, 'Our Sea'	Mediterranean

Other places mentioned:

Illyricum	The home of Captain Stokovius
Mucurum	Makarska, Croatia
Narona	Vid, near Metkovic, Croatia
Adriaticum Mare	Adriatic Sea

* Author's note:

Poole, Dorset: Timber pilings from a deep layer of silt on the sea bed have been radio-carbon dated to BC 250, the oldest port structures by several centuries anywhere on the British coast. They are thought to have been part of an Iron Age trading complex with massive stone and timber jetties providing berths for ships; two have been traced, 80 metres long. They were built from an estimated 10,000 tonnes of rock and rubble, reinforced with hundreds of oak tree trunks, sharpened at one end so that they could be rammed into the sea. The name Pollus is my own invention as I have not discovered evidence of a Roman name.

Glossary of Terms

Amphora	Two-handled vase/container
Carruca	Four-wheeled cart
Decurion	In charge of a turma of cavalry (32 men)
Gladius	Short, double-edged stabbing sword, about two inches in width
Heads	Promontories
Insulae	Blocks of apartment buildings
Mansio	Hotel
Moles	Stone structures serving as piers or breakwaters
Portico	Entrance hall
Samian ware	Expensive, glazed red pottery
Signifer	Standard bearer
Torque	Necklace or collar, usually of twisted metal
Triclinium	Main room of villa, for lounging and eating. Its name derived from the three-sided table at which diners lay on couches, each propped up on one elbow, eating food with the other hand
Turma of Cavalry	32 horsemen
Vectis ware	Black pottery made on the island of Vectis (now Isle of Wight)

On board ship:

Aphlaston	Stylised bird's neck and head at the stern of a ship, facing towards the prow
Belaying pin	Wooden pin round which to belay (coil) running rope to secure it
Haruspice	A 'gut-gazer', one who foretells the future from entrails
Keel hauling	Tying a man up and dragging him under the ship from one side to the other, hauling him under the keel
Larboard	Left side of a ship, now referred to as 'port'
Starboard	Right side of a ship
Oculus	A large eye painted on the prow of a ship to protect the crew and frighten the enemy
Pularius	Man in charge of chickens

About the Author

Born in Clapham, London, before the war, at the age of five Iris Lloyd moved out to a new estate in Queensbury, Middlesex, with her parents and her brother. They were caught at her grandmother's in Clapham on the first night of the Blitz, and soon were all evacuated by her father's employers to Chesham, Buckinghamshire, returning to Queensbury when she was fourteen years old. Her sister was born during the post-war baby boom.

When seventeen, she joined a superb church youth club, and wrote eight annual pantomimes for them to perform (usually directing and choreographing as well, as she has been dancing since the age of three), then nine more scripts co-written with a friend for his drama group. Three have been published by Cambridge Publishing Services Ltd and are performed regularly by amateur companies.

In the 1950s, Iris also wrote the script of a romantic musical set in 1730, which was performed by a church group. Recently, she entered two full-length plays for competitions at her local professional theatre, the Watermill, in Newbury.

Two years (1959-61) were enjoyed as secretary to the editor of children's books at Macmillan's publishers in London, where she met author Ray Bethers, and later she line edited for him five of his short children's books.

In recent years, she wrote and performed, one Sunday morning on Radio Oxford/Berkshire, a dramatic monologue and (with a friend) a two-hander between Barabbas and the mother of the thief on the Cross. She has written sketches and plays for stage, church and parties. Three of her poems have been published in anthologies.

A correspondent for many years for the Newbury Weekly News, her local independent newspaper, she had several half-page and full-page articles on various topics published. And in her last parish, she was chief editor of the church magazine and of a prestigious village book, which was produced for the millennium. Having moved to

Hungerford, Berkshire, three years ago, she has now taken on sole editorship of the monthly parish magazine.

Iris was married to Denis, who for twenty-seven years was self-employed in the construction industry, and was widowed twenty years ago. She is the proud mother of two daughters and grandmother to three lively grandchildren.

For exercise, she still teaches tap dancing to adults.

Author's contact: iris.lloyd@virgin.net
www.irislloyd.co.uk